FALLEN

Karin Slaughter

WINDSOR
PARAGON

First published 2011
by Century
This Large Print edition published 2012
by AudioGO Ltd
by arrangement with
The Random House Group Ltd

Hardcover   ISBN: 978 1 445 82578 6
Softcover   ISBN: 978 1 445 82579 3

British Library Cataloguing in Publication Data available

Printed and bound in Great Britain by
MPG Books Group Limited

*To all the librarians in the world
on behalf of all the kids y'all helped
grow up to be writers*

SATURDAY

SATURDAY

CHAPTER ONE

Faith Mitchell dumped the contents of her purse onto the passenger seat of her Mini, trying to find something to eat. Except for a furry piece of gum and a peanut of dubious origin, there was nothing remotely edible. She thought about the box of nutrition bars in her kitchen pantry, and her stomach made a noise that sounded like a rusty hinge groaning open.

The computer seminar she'd attended this morning was supposed to last three hours, but that had stretched into four and a half thanks to the jackass in the front row who kept asking pointless questions. The Georgia Bureau of Investigation trained its agents more often than any other agency in the region. Statistics and data on criminal activities were constantly being drummed into their heads. They had to be up to date on all of the latest technology. They had to qualify at the range twice a year. They ran mock raids and active shooter simulations that were so intense that for weeks after, Faith couldn't go to the bathroom in the middle of the night without checking shadows in doorways. Usually, she appreciated the agency's thoroughness. Today, all she could think about was her four-month-old baby, and the promise Faith had made to her mother that she would be back no later than noon.

The clock on the dash read ten after one o'clock when she started the car. Faith mumbled a curse as she pulled out of the parking lot in front of the Panthersville Road headquarters. She used

3

Bluetooth to dial her mother's number. The car speakers gave back a static-y silence. Faith hung up and dialed again. This time, she got a busy signal.

Faith tapped her finger on the steering wheel as she listened to the bleating. Her mother had voicemail. *Everybody* had voicemail. Faith couldn't remember the last time she'd heard a busy signal on the telephone. She had almost forgotten the sound. There was probably a crossed wire somewhere at the phone company. She hung up and tried the number a third time.

Still busy.

Faith steered with one hand as she checked her BlackBerry for an email from her mother. Before Evelyn Mitchell retired, she had been a cop for just shy of four decades. You could say a lot about the Atlanta force, but you couldn't claim they were behind the times. Evelyn had carried a cell phone back when they were more like purses you strapped around your shoulder. She'd learned how to use email before her daughter had. She'd carried a BlackBerry for almost fifteen years.

But she hadn't sent a message today.

Faith checked her cell phone voicemail. She had a saved message from her dentist's office about making an appointment to get her teeth cleaned, but there was nothing new. She tried her phone at home, thinking maybe her mother had gone there to pick up something for the baby. Faith's house was just down the road from Evelyn's. Maybe Emma had run out of diapers. Maybe she'd needed another bottle. Faith listened to the phone ring at her house, then heard her own voice answer, telling callers to leave a message.

She ended the call. Without thinking, she

4

glanced into the back seat. Emma's empty car seat was there. She could see the pink liner sticking out over the top of the plastic.

'Idiot,' Faith whispered to herself. She dialed her mother's cell phone number. She held her breath as she counted through three rings. Evelyn's voicemail picked up.

Faith had to clear her throat before she could speak. She was aware of a tremor in her tone. 'Mom, I'm on my way home. I guess you took Em for a walk . . .' Faith looked up at the sky as she merged onto the interstate. She was about twenty minutes outside of Atlanta and could see fluffy white clouds draped like scarves around the skinny necks of skyscrapers. 'Just call me,' Faith said, worry needling the edge of her brain.

Grocery store. Gas station. Pharmacy. Her mother had a car seat identical to the one in the back of Faith's Mini. She was probably out running errands. Faith was over an hour late. Evelyn would've taken the baby and . . . Left Faith a message that she was going to be out. The woman had been on call for the majority of her adult life. She didn't go to the toilet without letting someone know. Faith and her older brother, Zeke, had joked about it when they were kids. They always knew where their mother was, even when they didn't want to. Especially when they didn't want to.

Faith stared at the phone in her hand as if it could tell her what was going on. She was aware that she might be letting herself get worked up over nothing. The landline could be out. Her mother wouldn't know this unless she tried to make a call. Her cell phone could be switched off, or charging, or both. Her BlackBerry could be in

5

her car or her purse or somewhere she couldn't hear the telltale vibration. Faith glanced back and forth between the road and her BlackBerry as she typed an email to her mother. She spoke the words aloud as she typed—

'On-my-way. Sorry-I'm-late. Call-me.'

She sent the email, then tossed the phone onto the seat along with the spilled items from her purse. After a moment's hesitation, Faith popped the gum into her mouth. She chewed as she drove, ignoring the purse lint clinging to her tongue. She turned on the radio, then snapped it back off. The traffic thinned as she got closer to the city. The clouds moved apart, sending down bright rays of sunshine. The inside of the car began to bake.

Ten minutes out, Faith's nerves were still on edge, and she was sweating from the heat in the car. She cracked the sunroof to let in some air. This was probably a simple case of separation anxiety. She'd been back at work for a little over two months, but still, every morning when Faith left Emma at her mother's, she felt something akin to a seizure take hold. Her vision blurred. Her heart shook in her chest. Her head buzzed as if a million bees had flown into her ears. She was more irritable than usual at work, especially with her partner, Will Trent, who either had the patience of Job or was setting up a believable alibi for when he finally snapped and strangled her.

Faith couldn't recall if she had felt this same anxiety with Jeremy, her son, who was now a freshman in college. Faith had been eighteen when she entered the police academy. Jeremy was three years old by then. She had grabbed onto the idea of joining the force as if it was the only life

6

preserver left on the *Titanic*. Thanks to two minutes of poor judgment in the back of a movie theater and what foreshadowed a lifetime of breathtakingly bad taste in men, Faith had gone straight from puberty to motherhood without any of the usual stops in between. At eighteen, she had relished the idea of earning a steady paycheck so that she could move out of her parents' house and raise Jeremy the way that she wanted. Going to work every day had been a step toward independence. Leaving him in day care had seemed like a small price to pay.

Now that Faith was thirty-four, with a mortgage, a car payment, and another baby to raise on her own, she wanted nothing more than to move back into her mother's house so that Evelyn could take care of everything. She wanted to open the refrigerator and see food that she didn't have to buy. She wanted to turn on the air conditioner in the summer without worrying about having to pay the bill. She wanted to sleep until noon, then watch TV all day. Hell, while she was at it, she might as well resurrect her father, who'd died eleven years ago, so that he could make her pancakes at breakfast and tell her how pretty she was.

No chance of that now. Evelyn seemed happy to play the role of nanny in her retirement, but Faith was under no illusion that her life was going to get any easier. Her own retirement was almost twenty years away. The Mini had another three years of payments and would be out of warranty well before that. Emma would expect food and clothing for at least the next eighteen years, if not more. And it wasn't like when Jeremy was a baby and Faith could dress him in mismatched socks and yard sale

7

hand-me-downs. Babies today had to coordinate. They needed BPA-free bottles and certified organic applesauce from kindly Amish farmers. If Jeremy got into the architectural program at Georgia Tech, Faith was looking at six more years of buying books and doing his laundry. Most worryingly, her son had found a serious girlfriend. An older girlfriend with curvy hips and a ticking biological clock. Faith could be a grandmother before she turned thirty-five.

An unwelcome heat rushed through her body as she tried to push this last thought from her mind. She checked the contents of her purse again as she drove. The gum hadn't made a dent. Her stomach was still growling. She reached over and felt around inside the glovebox. Nothing. She should stop at a fast-food place and at least get a Coke, but she was wearing her regs—tan khakis and a blue shirt with the letters *GBI* emblazoned in bright yellow on the back. This wasn't the best part of town to be in if you were law enforcement. People tended to run, and then you had to chase them, which wasn't conducive to getting home at a reasonable hour. Besides, something was telling her—urging her—to see her mother.

Faith picked up her phone and dialed Evelyn's numbers again. Home, cell, even her BlackBerry, which she only used for email. All three brought the same negative response. Faith could feel her stomach flip as the worst scenarios ran through her mind. As a beat cop, she'd been called out onto a lot of scenes where a crying child had alerted the neighbors to a serious problem. Mothers had slipped in the tub. Fathers had accidentally injured themselves or gone into coronary arrest. The

8

babies had lain there, wailing helplessly, until someone had figured out that something was wrong. There was nothing more heart wrenching than a crying baby who could not be soothed.

Faith chided herself for bringing these horrible images to mind. She had always been good at assuming the worst, even before she became a cop. Evelyn was probably fine. Emma's naptime was at one-thirty. Her mother had probably turned off the phone so the ringing wouldn't wake the baby. Maybe she'd run into a neighbor while checking the mailbox, or gone next door to help old Mrs. Levy take out the trash.

Still, Faith's hands slipped on the wheel as she exited onto Boulevard. She was sweating despite the mild March weather. This couldn't just be about the baby or her mother or even Jeremy's unconscionably fertile girlfriend. Faith had been diagnosed with diabetes less than a year ago. She was religious about measuring her blood sugar, eating the right things, making sure she had snacks on hand. Except for today. That probably explained why her thinking had gone sideways. She just needed to eat something. Preferably in view of her mother and child.

Faith checked the glovebox again to make sure it was really empty. She had a distant memory of giving Will her last nutrition bar yesterday while they were waiting outside the courthouse. It was that or watch him inhale a sticky bun from the vending machine. He had complained about the taste but eaten the whole bar anyway. And now she was paying for it.

She blew through a yellow light, speeding as much as she dared down a semi-residential street.

The road narrowed at Ponce de Leon. Faith passed a row of fast-food restaurants and an organic grocery store. She edged up the speedometer, accelerating into the twists and turns bordering Piedmont Park. The flash of a traffic camera bounced off her rearview mirror as she sailed through another yellow light. She tapped on the brakes for a straggling jaywalker. Two more grocery stores blurred by, then came the final red light, which was mercifully green.

Evelyn still lived in the same house Faith and her older brother had grown up in. The single-story ranch was located in an area of Atlanta called Sherwood Forest, which was nestled between Ansley Park, one of the wealthiest neighborhoods in the city, and Interstate 85, which offered the constant roar of traffic, depending on which way the wind was blowing. The wind was blowing just fine today, and when Faith rolled down her window to let in more fresh air, she heard the familiar drone that had marked most every day of her childhood.

As a lifelong resident of Sherwood Forest, Faith had a deep-seated hatred for the men who had planned the neighborhood. The subdivision had been developed after World War II, the brick ranch houses filled by returning soldiers who took advantage of low VA loans. The street planners had unabashedly embraced the Sherwood concept. After taking a hard left onto Lionel, Faith crossed Friar Tuck, took a right on Robin Hood Road, coasted through the fork at Lady Marian Lane, and checked the driveway of her own house on the corner of Doncaster and Barnesdale before finally pulling into her mother's driveway off Little John

10

Trail.

Evelyn's beige Chevy Malibu was backed into the carport. That, at least, was normal. Faith had never seen her mother pull nose-first into a parking space. It came from her days in uniform. You always made sure your car was ready to leave as soon as a call came in.

Faith didn't have time to reflect on her mother's routines. She rolled into the driveway and parked the Mini nose-to-nose with the Malibu. Her legs ached as she stood; every muscle in her body had been tensed for the last twenty minutes. She could hear loud music blaring from the house. Heavy metal, not her mother's usual Beatles. Faith put her hand on the hood of the Malibu as she walked toward the kitchen door. The engine was cold. Maybe Evelyn had been in the shower when Faith called. Maybe she hadn't checked her email or cell phone. Maybe she had cut herself. There was a bloody handprint on the door.

Faith felt herself do a double take.

The bloody print showed a left hand. It was about eighteen inches above the knob. The door had been pulled closed but hadn't latched. A streak of sunlight cut through the jamb, probably from the window over the kitchen sink.

Faith still couldn't process what she was seeing. She held up her own hand to the print, a child pressing her fingers to her mother's. Evelyn's hand was smaller. Slender fingers. The tip of her ring finger hadn't touched the door. There was a clot of blood where it should have been.

Suddenly, the music stopped mid-thump. In the silence, Faith heard a familiar gurgling noise, a revving up that announced the coming of a full-on wail. The sound echoed in the carport, so that for a moment, Faith thought it was coming from her own mouth. Then it came again, and she turned around, knowing that it was Emma.

Almost every other house in Sherwood Forest had been razed or remodeled, but the Mitchell home was much the same as when it had first been built. The layout was simple: three bedrooms, a family room, a dining room, and a kitchen with a door leading to the open carport. Bill Mitchell, Faith's father, had built a toolshed on the opposite side of the carport. It was a sturdy building—her father had never done anything halfway—with a metal door that bolted shut and safety glass in its one window. Faith was ten before she realized that the building was too fortified for something as simple as tool storage. With the tenderness that only an older brother can muster, Zeke had filled her in on the shed's true purpose. 'It's where Mom keeps her gun, you dumbass.'

Faith ran past the car and tried to open the shed door. It was locked. She looked through the window. The metal wires in the safety glass formed a spider web in front of her eyes. She could see the potting table and bags of soil stacked neatly underneath. Tools hung on their proper hooks. Lawn equipment was stowed neatly in place. A black metal safe with a combination lock was bolted to the floor under the table. The door was open. Evelyn's cherry-handled Smith and Wesson revolver was missing. So was the carton of ammunition that was usually beside it.

The gurgling noise came again, louder this time. A pile of blankets on the floor pulsed up and down like a heartbeat. Evelyn used them to cover her

12

plants during unexpected freezes. They were usually folded on the top shelf but now were wadded up in the corner beside the safe. Faith saw a tuft of pink sticking up behind the gray blankets, then the bend of a plastic headrest that could only be Emma's car seat. The blanket moved again. A tiny foot kicked out; a soft yellow cotton sock with white lace trim around the ankle. Then a little pink fist punched through. Then she saw Emma's face.

Emma smiled at Faith, her top lip forming a soft triangle. She gurgled again, this time with delight.

'Oh, God.' Faith uselessly pulled at the locked door. Her hands shook as she felt around the top edge of the jamb, trying to find the key. Dust rained down. The sharp point of a splinter dug into her finger. Faith looked in the window again. Emma clapped her hands together, soothed by the sight of her mother, despite the fact that Faith was as close to a full-on panic as she had ever been in her life. The shed was hot. It was too warm outside. Emma could overheat. She could become dehydrated. She could die.

Terrified, Faith got down on her hands and knees, thinking the key had fallen, possibly slid back under the door. She saw that the bottom of Emma's car seat was bent where it had been wedged between the safe and the wall. Hidden behind the blankets. Blocked by the safe.

Protected by the safe.

Faith stopped. Her lungs tightened mid-breath. Her jaw tensed as if it had been wired shut. Slowly, she sat up. There were drops of blood on the concrete in front of her. Her eyes followed the trail going to the kitchen door. To the bloody handprint.

13

Emma was locked in the shed. Evelyn's gun was missing. There was a blood trail to the house.

Faith stood, facing the unlatched kitchen door. There was no sound but her own labored breath.

Who had turned off the music?

Faith jogged back to her car. She took her Glock from under the driver's seat. She checked the magazine and clipped the holster to her side. Her phone was still on the front seat. Faith grabbed it before popping open the trunk. She had been a detective with the Atlanta homicide squad before becoming a special agent with the state. Her fingers dialed the unlisted emergency line from memory. She didn't give the dispatcher time to speak. She rattled off her old badge number, her unit, and her mother's street address.

Faith paused before saying, 'Code thirty.' The words nearly choked her. Code 30. She had never used the phrase in her life. It meant that an officer needed emergency assistance. It meant that a fellow cop was in serious danger, possibly dead. 'My child is locked in the shed outside. There's blood on the concrete and a bloody handprint on the kitchen door. I think my mother is inside the house. I heard music, but it was turned off. She's retired Blue. I think she's—' Faith's throat tightened like a fist. 'Help. Please. Send help.'

'Acknowledge code thirty,' the dispatcher answered, her tone sharp and tense. 'Stay outside and wait for backup. Do not—repeat—do not go into the house.'

'Acknowledged.' Faith ended the call and tossed the phone into the back seat. She twisted her key into the lock that kept her shotgun bolted to the trunk of her car.

14

The GBI issued every agent at least two weapons. The Glock model 23 was a .40-caliber semiautomatic that held thirteen rounds in the magazine and one in the chamber. The Remington 870 held four rounds of double-ought buckshot in the tube. Faith's shotgun carried six extra rounds in the side-saddle attached in front of the stock. Each round contained eight pellets. Each pellet was about the size of a .38-caliber bullet.

Every pull of the trigger on the Glock shot one bullet. Every pull on the Remington shot eight.

Agency policy dictated that all agents keep a round chambered in their Glocks, giving them fourteen rounds total. There was no conventional external safety on the weapon. Agents were authorized by law to use deadly force if they felt their lives or the lives of others were in danger. You only pulled back on the trigger when you meant to shoot, and you only shot when you meant to kill.

The shotgun was a different story with the same ending. The safety was to the rear of the trigger guard, a cross-bolt slide that took lithe muscle to move. You didn't keep a round in the chamber. You wanted everybody around you to hear that round racking, setting up to blast. Faith had seen grown men drop to their knees at the sound.

She looked back at the house as she disengaged the safety. The curtain on the front window twitched. A shadow ran down the hallway.

Faith pumped the shotgun with one hand as she walked toward the carport. The action made a satisfying *tha-thunk* that echoed against the concrete. In a single fluid motion, the stock was against her shoulder, the barrel straight in front of her. She kicked open the door, holding the weapon steady as she yelled 'Police!'

The word boomed through the house like a clash of thunder. It came from a deep, dark place in Faith's gut that she ignored most of the time for fear of switching something on that could never be shut off.

'Come out with your hands in the air!'

No one came out. She heard a noise from somewhere in the back of the house. Her vision sharpened as she entered the kitchen. Blood on the counter. A bread knife. More blood on the floor. Drawers and cabinets gaping open. The phone on the wall hung like a twisted noose. Evelyn's BlackBerry and cell phone were smashed to pieces on the floor. Faith kept the shotgun in front of her, finger resting just to the side of the trigger so that she didn't make any mistakes.

She should've been thinking about her mother, or Emma, but there was only one phrase that kept going through her mind: *people and doorways*. When you cleared a house, these were the biggest threats to your safety. You had to know where the people were—whether they were good guys or not—and you had to know what was coming at you from every door.

Faith pivoted to the side, pointing the shotgun into the laundry room. She saw a man lying face-down on the floor. Black hair. Skin a yellow wax. His arms wrapped around his body like a child playing a spinning game. No gun on or near him. The back of his head was a bloody pulp. Brain matter speckled the washing machine. She could see the hole the bullet dug into the wall when it exited his skull.

16

Faith pivoted back to the kitchen. There was a pass-through to the dining room. She crouched and swung around.

Empty.

The layout of the house came to her like a diagram in her head. Family room on her left. Large, open foyer on the right. Hall straight ahead. Bathroom at the end. Two bedrooms on the right. One bedroom on the left—her mother's room. Inside was a tiny bathroom, a door that led to the back patio. Evelyn's bedroom door was the only one in the hall that was closed.

Faith started to go toward the closed door, but stopped.

People and doorways.

Her mind saw the words engraved in stone: *Do not proceed toward your downward threat until you are sure everything behind you is clear.*

Faith crouched as she turned left, entering the family room. She scanned along the walls, checked the sliding glass door that led into the backyard. The glass was shattered. A breeze rustled the curtains. The room had been ransacked. Someone was looking for something. Drawers were broken. Cushions gutted. From her vantage point, Faith could see behind the couch, that the wingback chair was clear of extra feet. She kept her head swiveling back and forth between the room and the hall until she was sure she could move on.

The first door was to her old bedroom. Someone had searched here, too. The drawers in Faith's old bureau stuck out like tongues. The mattress was ripped open. Emma's crib had been busted to pieces. Her blanket was ripped in two. The mobile that had hung above her head every month of her

17

life had been ground into the carpet like a pile of dirt. Faith swallowed the burning rage this ignited inside of her. She forced herself to keep moving.

Quickly, she cleared the closets, under the bed. She did the same in Zeke's room, which had been turned into her mother's office. Papers were scattered on the floor. The desk drawers had been thrown against the wall. She glanced into the bathroom. The shower curtain was pulled back. The linen closet gaped open. Towels and sheets spilled onto the floor.

Faith was standing to the left of her mother's bedroom door when she heard the first siren. It was distant, but clear. She should wait for it, wait for backup.

Faith kicked open the door and swung around in a crouch. Her finger went to the trigger. Two men were at the foot of the bed. One was on his knees. He was Hispanic, dressed only in a pair of jeans. The skin across his chest was shredded as if he'd been whipped with barbed wire. Sweat glistened on every part of his body. Black and red bruises punched along his ribs. He had tattoos all over his arms and torso, the largest of which was on his chest: a green and red Texas star with a rattlesnake wrapped around it. He was a member of Los Texicanos, a Mexican gang that had controlled the Atlanta drug trade for twenty years.

The second man was Asian. No tattoos. Bright red Hawaiian shirt and tan chinos. He stood with the Texicano in front of him, holding a gun to the man's head. A cherry-handled Smith and Wesson five-shot. Her mother's revolver.

Faith kept the shotgun trained on the Asian's chest. The cold, hard metal felt like an extension of

18

her body. Adrenaline had pumped her heart into a frenzy. Every muscle inside of her wanted to pull the trigger.

Her words were clipped. 'Where's my mother?'

He spoke in a twangy southern drawl. 'You shoot me, you're gonna hit him.'

He was right. Faith was standing in the hallway, less than six feet away. The men were too close together. Even a headshot carried the risk that a pellet would stray, hitting—possibly killing—the hostage. Still, she kept her finger on the trigger, the shotgun steady. 'Tell me where she is.'

He pressed the muzzle harder against the man's head. 'Drop the gun.'

The sirens were getting louder. They were coming from Zone 5, on the Peachtree side of the neighborhood. Faith said, 'You hear that sound?' She mapped their path down Nottingham, calculating the cruisers would be here in less than a minute. 'Tell me where my mother is or I swear to God I'll kill you before they hit the door.'

He smiled again, his hand tightening around the gun. 'You know what we're here for. Hand it over and we'll let her go.'

Faith didn't know what the hell he was talking about. Her mother was a sixty-three-year-old widow. The most valuable thing in the house was the land they were standing on.

He took her silence for equivocation. 'You really wanna lose your mommy over Chico here?'

Faith pretended to understand. 'It's that simple? You'll trade?'

He shrugged. 'Only way we'll both walk outta here.'

'Bullshit.'

'No bullshit. Even trade.' The sirens got louder. Tires screeched in the street. 'Come on, bitch. Tick-tock. Deal or no deal?'

He was lying. He'd already killed one person. He was threatening another. As soon as he figured out Faith was bluffing, the only thing he'd give her was a bullet in the chest.

'Deal,' she agreed, using her left hand to toss the shotgun out in front of her.

The firearms instructor at the shooting range carried a stopwatch that counted every tenth of a second, which was why Faith knew that it took her right hand exactly eight-tenths of a second to draw her Glock from her side holster. While the Asian was distracted by her shotgun dropping at his feet, she did just this, pulling the Glock, snaking her finger around the trigger, and shooting the man in the head.

His arms flew up. The gun dropped. He was dead before he hit the floor.

The front door splintered open. Faith turned toward the foyer as an entry team in full raid gear flooded into the house. And then she turned back toward the bedroom and realized the Mexican was gone.

The patio door was open. Faith ran outside as the Mexican vaulted over the chain link fence. The S&W was in his hand. Mrs. Johnson's grandchildren were playing in her backyard. They screamed when they saw the armed man heading toward them. He was twenty feet away. Fifteen. He raised the gun toward the girls and fired a shot over their heads. Brick siding sprayed onto the ground. They were too scared to scream anymore, to move, to save themselves. Faith stopped at the

20

fence, lined up her Glock, and squeezed the trigger.

The man jerked as if a string had been pulled through his chest. He stayed up for at least a full second, then his knees buckled and he fell backward onto the ground. Faith jumped over the fence and sprinted toward him. She slammed her heel into his wrist until he let go of her mother's gun. The girls started screaming again. Mrs. Johnson came out onto the porch and scooped them up like baby ducklings. She glanced back at Faith as she shut the door. The look in her eyes was shocked, horrified. She used to chase Zeke and Faith with the garden hose when they were little. She used to feel safe here.

Faith holstered her Glock and tucked Evelyn's revolver into the back of her pants. She grabbed the Mexican by the shoulders. 'Where's my mother?' she demanded. 'What did they do to her?'

He opened his mouth, blood oozing beneath the silver caps in his teeth. He was smiling. The asshole was smiling.

'Where is she?' Faith pressed her hand to his battered chest, feeling his broken ribs move beneath her fingers. He screamed in pain, and she pushed harder, grinding the bones together. 'Where is she?'

'Agent!' A young cop steadied himself with one hand as he jumped over the fence. He drew down on her, his gun angled toward the ground. 'Back away from the prisoner.'

Faith got closer to the Mexican. She could feel the heat radiating from his skin. 'Tell me where she is.'

21

His throat worked. He wasn't feeling the pain anymore. His pupils were the size of dimes. His eyelids fluttered. The corner of his lip twitched.

'Tell me where she is.' Her voice got more desperate with each word. 'Oh, God, just—please—tell me where she is!'

His breath had a sticky sound, as if his lungs were taped together. His lips moved. He whispered something she couldn't make out.

'What?' Faith put her ear so close to his lips that she could feel spit coming out of his mouth. 'Tell me,' she whispered. 'Please tell me.'

Almeja.

'What?' Faith repeated. 'What did you say?' His mouth opened. Instead of words, blood pooled out. 'What did you say?' she screamed. 'Tell me what you said!'

'Agent!' the cop yelled again.

'No!' She pressed her palms into the Mexican's chest, trying to force his heart to pump again. Faith made a fist and slammed it down as hard as she could, beating the man, willing him to come back to life. 'Tell me!' she yelled. 'Just tell me!'

'Agent!' She felt hands around her waist. The cop practically lifted her into the air.

'Let me go!' Faith jammed her elbow back so hard that he dropped her like a stone. She scrambled across the grass, crawling to the witness. The hostage. The murderer. The only person left who could tell her what the hell had happened to her mother.

She put her hands to the Mexican's face, stared into his lifeless eyes. 'Please tell me,' she pleaded, even though she knew it was too late. 'Please.'

'Faith?' Detective Leo Donnelly, her old partner

on the Atlanta force, stood on the other side of the fence. He was out of breath. His hands gripped the top of the chain link. The wind whipped open the jacket of his cheap brown suit. 'Emma's fine. We got a locksmith on the way.' His words came thick and slow, like molasses poured through a sieve. 'Come on, kid. Emma needs her mom.'

Faith looked behind him. Cops were everywhere. Dark blue uniforms blurred as they swept the house, checked the yard. Through the windows, she followed Tactical's progress from room to room, guns raised, voices calling 'Clear' as they found nothing. Competing sirens filled the air. Police cruisers. Ambulances. A fire truck.

The call had gone out. Code 30. Officer needs emergency assistance.

Three men shot to death. Her baby locked in a shed. Her mother missing.

Faith sat back on her heels. She put her head in her shaking hands and willed herself not to cry.

CHAPTER TWO

'So, he tells me he was changing the oil in his car, and it was hot in the garage, so he took off his pants . . .'

'Uh-huh,' Sara Linton managed, trying to feign interest as she picked at her salad.

'And I say, "Lookit, bud, I'm a doctor. I'm not here to judge. You can be honest about . . ."'

Sara watched Dale Dugan's mouth move, his voice mercifully blending in with the lunchtime noise of the pizza parlor. Soft music playing.

23

People laughing. Plates sliding around the kitchen. His story was not particularly riveting, or even new. Sara was a pediatric attending doctor in the emergency department at Atlanta's Grady Hospital. She'd had her own practice for twelve years before that, all the while working part-time as the county coroner for a small but active college town. There was not an implement, tool, household product, or glass figurine she had not at some point or another seen lodged inside a human body.

Still, Dale continued, 'Then the nurse comes in with the X-ray.'

'Uh-oh,' she said, trying to inject some curiosity into her tone.

Dale smiled at her. There was some cheese lodged between his central and lateral incisors. Sara tried not to judge. Dale Dugan was a nice man. He wasn't handsome, but he was okay-looking, with the sort of features many women found attractive once they learned he'd graduated from medical school. Sara was not as easily swayed. And she was starving, because she'd been told by the friend who'd set her up on this ridiculous blind date that she should order a salad instead of a pizza because it looked better.

'So, I hold up the X-ray and what do I see . . .'

Socket wrench, she thought, just before he finally reached the punch line.

'A socket wrench! Can you believe it?'

'No!' She forced a laugh that sounded like the sort of thing that came out of a windup toy.

'And he still kept saying he slipped.'

She tsked her tongue. 'Quite a fall.'

'I know, right?' He smiled at her again before

24

taking a healthy bite of pizza.

Sara chewed some lettuce. The digital clock over Dale's head showed 2:12 and a handful of seconds. The red LED numbers were a painful reminder that she could be at home right now watching basketball and folding the mountain of laundry on her couch. Sara had made a game of not looking at the clock, seeing how long she could go before her self-control crumbled and she watched the blurring seconds tick by. Three minutes twenty-two seconds was her record. She took another bite of salad, vowing to beat it.

'So,' Dale said. 'You went to Emory.'

She nodded. 'You were at Duke?'

Predictably, he began what turned into a lengthy description of his academic achievements, including published journal articles and keynote speeches at various conferences. Again, Sara feigned attention, willing herself not to look at the clock, chewing lettuce as slowly as a cow in a pasture so that Dale would not feel compelled to ask her a question.

This was not Sara's first blind date, nor, unfortunately, was it her least tedious. The problem today had started within the first six minutes, which Sara had marked by the clock. They had rushed through the preliminaries before their order had been called. Dale was divorced, no children, on good terms with his ex-wife, and played pickup basketball games at the hospital in his free time. Sara was from a small town in south Georgia. She had two greyhounds, and a cat who chose to live with her parents. Her husband had been killed four and a half years ago.

Usually, this last bit was a conversation stopper,

25

but Dale had breezed over it as a minor detail. At first, Sara had given him points for not asking for details, and then she had decided that he was too self-absorbed to ask, and then she had chided herself for being so hard on the man.

'What did your husband do?'

He'd caught her with a mouthful of lettuce. She chewed, swallowed, then told him, 'He was a police officer. The chief of police for the county.'

'That's unusual.' Her expression must have been off, because he said, 'I mean, unusual because he's not a doctor. Wasn't a doctor. Not white collar, I guess.'

'White collar?' She heard the accusatory tone in her voice but couldn't stop herself. 'My father's a plumber. My sister and I worked with him for—'

'Whoa, whoa.' He held up his hands in surrender. 'That came out wrong. I mean, there's something noble about working with your hands, right?'

Sara didn't know what kind of medicine Dr. Dale was practicing, but she tended to use her hands every day.

Oblivious, his voice took on a solemn tone. 'I have a lot of respect for cops. And servicepeople. Soldiers, I mean.' He nervously wiped his mouth with his napkin. 'Dangerous job. Is that how he died?'

She nodded, glancing at the clock. Three minutes nineteen seconds. She'd just missed her record.

He took his phone out of his pocket and looked at the display. 'Sorry. I'm on call. I wanted to make sure there's service.'

At least he hadn't pretended the phone was on

26

silent ring, though Sara was sure that was coming. 'I'm sorry for being so defensive. It's difficult to talk about.'

'I'm sorry for your loss.' His tone had a practiced cadence Sara recognized from the ER. 'I'm sure it was hard.'

She bit at the tip of her tongue. Sara couldn't think of a polite way to respond, and by the time she thought to change the subject to the weather, so much time had passed that the conversation felt even more awkward. Finally, she said, 'Well, anyway. Why don't we—'

'Excuse me,' he interrupted. 'I need to go to the bathroom.'

He got up so quickly that his chair nearly fell over. Sara watched him scamper toward the back. Maybe it was her imagination, but she thought he hesitated in front of the fire exit.

'Idiot.' She dropped her fork onto her salad plate.

She checked the clock again for the time. It was two-fifteen. She could wrap this up by two-thirty if Dale ever came back from the toilet. Sara had walked here from her apartment, so there wouldn't be that protracted, awful silence as Dale drove her home. The bill had been paid when they ordered the food at the cash register. It would take her fifteen minutes to walk home, giving her time to change out of her dress and into her sweat pants before the basketball game started. Sara felt her stomach rumble. Maybe she could pretend to leave, then backtrack and order a pizza.

Another minute ticked by on the clock. Sara scanned the parking lot. Dale's car was still there, assuming the green Lexus with the DRDALE

27

license plate belonged to him. She didn't know if she felt disappointed or relieved.

The clock marked another thirty seconds. The hallway leading to the bathrooms stayed empty for another twenty-three seconds. An older woman with a walker inched her way down the hall. No one was behind her.

Sara dropped her head into her hand. Dale was not a bad man. He was stable, relatively healthy, gainfully employed, had most of his hair, and except for the cheese between his teeth, had the appearance of good hygiene. And yet, all of this wasn't enough. Sara was beginning to think *she* was the problem. She was turning into the Mr. Darcy of Atlanta. Once her good opinion was lost, it was gone forever. Changing the direction of a steamship was easier than changing Sara's mind.

She should try harder at this. She wasn't twenty-five anymore, and forty was breathing heavy down the back of her neck. At five feet eleven inches, her dating pool was already limited. Her auburn red hair and fair skin were not to every man's taste. She worked long hours. She couldn't cook to save her life. She had apparently lost her ability to conduct any small talk whatsoever, and the mere mention of her dead husband could send her into a hissy fit.

Maybe her standards were too high. Her marriage hadn't been perfect, but it was pretty damn good. She had loved her husband more than life itself. Losing him had almost killed her. But Jeffrey had been gone for almost five years now, and if Sara was being honest, she was lonely. She missed a man's company. She missed the way their minds worked and the surprisingly sweet things

28

they could say. She missed the rough feel of their skin. She missed the other things, too. Unfortunately, the last time a man had made her eyes roll back in her head, she'd been fighting boredom, not writhing in ecstasy.

Sara had to face the fact that she was extremely, awfully, horribly bad at dating. There hadn't been much time to practice. From puberty on, Sara had been serially monogamous. Her first boyfriend was a high school crush that had lasted until college, then she'd dated a fellow student all through medical school, then she'd met Jeffrey and never given another man a second thought. Except for a disastrous one-night stand three years ago, there had been no one since. She could only think of one man who had even remotely given her a spark, but he was married. Worse, he was a married cop.

Even worse, he was standing at the cash register less than ten feet away from her.

Will Trent was wearing black running shorts and a long-sleeved black T-shirt that showed his broad shoulders to good advantage. His sandy blond hair was longer than it had been a few months ago, when Sara had last seen him. He'd been working a case that involved one of her old patients at the children's clinic back home. She'd stuck her nose so far into Will's business that he'd had no choice but to let her help with the investigation. They had shared what felt like a flirtation, and then when the case was over, he had gone back home to his wife.

Will was extremely observant. He must have noticed Sara sitting at the table when he walked in. Still, he kept his back to her as he stared at a flyer pinned to the bulletin board on the wall. She didn't need the clock to count off the seconds as she waited for him to acknowledge her.

He turned his attention to another flyer.

Sara pulled out the clip holding up her hair, letting the curls fall past her shoulders. She stood up and walked over to him.

There were a few things she knew about Will Trent. He was tall, at least six-three, with a runner's lean body and the most beautiful legs she had ever seen on a man. His mother had been killed when he was less than a year old. He'd grown up in a children's home and never been adopted. He was a special agent with the GBI. He was one of the smartest men she had ever met, and he was so dyslexic that, as far as she could tell, he read no higher than a second-grade level.

She stood shoulder to shoulder with him, staring at the flyer that had caught his attention. 'That looks interesting.'

He made a very bad show of acting surprised to see her. 'Dr. Linton. I was just . . .' He tore one of the info tags off the flyer. 'I've been thinking about getting a bike.'

She glanced at the ad, which had a detailed drawing of a Harley Davidson underneath a headline asking for members to join. 'I don't think Dykes on Bikes is your kind of ride.'

His smile was crooked. He'd spent a lifetime covering up his disability, and even though Sara had found out, he was still loath to acknowledge there was a problem. 'It's a great way to meet women.'

'Are you looking to meet women?'

Sara was reminded of yet another one of Will's traits, which was that he had an uncanny knack for keeping his mouth shut when he didn't know what to say. This resulted in the sort of awkward moments that made Sara's dating life look downright ebullient.

Thankfully, Will's order was up. Sara stood back as he took the box of pizza from the tattooed and multipierced waitress. The young woman gave Will what could only be called an appreciative glance. He seemed oblivious as he checked his pizza to make sure they'd gotten the order right.

'Well.' He used his thumb to twist the wedding ring on his finger. 'I guess I should go.'

'All right.'

He didn't move. Neither did Sara. A dog started barking outside, the high-pitched yips traveling through the open windows. Sara knew there was a post and water bowl by the front door for people who brought their pets to the restaurant. She also knew that Will's wife had a little dog named Betty, and that the care and feeding fell mostly to him.

The yipping intensified. Will still made no move to leave.

She said, 'That sounds a lot like a Chihuahua.'

He listened intently, then nodded. 'I think you might be right.'

'There you are.' Dale was finally back from the restroom. 'Listen, I got a call from the hospital . . .' He looked up at Will. 'Hi.'

Sara made the introductions. 'Dale Dugan, this is Will Trent.'

Will gave a tight nod. Dale returned it.

The dog kept barking, a piercing, panicked yelp. Sara could tell from Will's expression that he was prepared to die rather than acknowledge ownership.

She found some mercy in her heart. 'Dale, I

31

know you need to get to the hospital. Thanks so much for lunch.'

'Sure.' He leaned in and kissed her squarely on the lips. 'I'll call you.'

'Great,' she managed, resisting the urge to wipe her mouth. She watched the two men exchange another tight nod that made Sara feel like the only fire hydrant at the dog park.

Betty's yips intensified as Dale walked across the parking lot. Will mumbled something under his breath before pushing open the door. He untied the leash and scooped up the dog with one hand, keeping the pizza box steadied in the other. The barking stopped immediately. Betty tucked her head into his chest. Her tongue lolled out.

Sara petted the dog's head. There were fresh sutures crisscrossing her narrow back. 'What happened?'

Will's jaw was still clenched. 'She got into it with a Jack Russell.'

'Really?' Unless the Jack Russell had a pair of scissors for paws, there was no way another dog had made the marks.

He indicated Betty. 'I should get her home.'

Sara had never been to Will's house, but she knew the street that he lived on. 'Aren't you going right?' She clarified, 'This way?'

Will didn't answer. He seemed to be gauging whether or not he could lie to her and get away with it.

She pressed, 'Don't you live off Linwood?'

'You're the opposite direction.'

'I can cut through the park.' She started walking, giving him no choice. They were silent as they headed down Ponce de Leon. The traffic noise was loud enough to fill the void, but even the exhaust from the cars couldn't overshadow the fact that they were in the middle of a brilliant spring day. Couples walked down the street hand in hand. Mothers pushed baby carriages. Runners darted across four lanes of traffic. The cloud cover from this morning had rolled eastward, exposing a sky of denim blue. There was a steady breeze in the air. Sara clasped her hands behind her back and looked down at the broken sidewalk. Tree roots pushed against the concrete like gnarled old toes.

She glanced at Will. The sun picked out the sweat on his brow. There were two scars on his face, though Sara had no idea what had caused them. His upper lip had been split open at some point, then badly stitched together, giving a raffish quality to his mouth. The other scar followed the line of his left jaw and dipped into his collar. When she'd first met him, she'd taken the scars for signs of boyhood mischief, but knowing his history, knowing that he had grown up in state care, Sara now assumed the damage had a darker story.

Will glanced at her and she looked away. He said, 'Dale seems like a nice guy.'

'Yes, he does.'

'Doctor, I guess.'

'That's right.'

'Looked like a good kisser.'

She smiled.

Will shifted Betty in his hand to get a better grip. 'I guess you're dating him.'

'Today was our first date.'

'You seemed friendlier than that.'

Sara stopped walking. 'How's your wife, Will?'

His answer didn't come quickly. His gaze fell

33

somewhere over her shoulder. 'I haven't seen her in four months.'

Sara felt an odd sense of betrayal. His wife was gone and Will had not called her. 'You're separated?'

He stepped aside so that a runner could pass. 'No.'

'Is she missing?'

'Not exactly.'

A MARTA bus lurched up to the curb, its engine filling the air with a protracted grumble. Sara had met Angie Trent almost a year ago. Her Mediterranean looks and curvaceous figure were exactly the sort of things mothers were thinking of when they warned their sons about loose women.

The bus pulled away. Sara asked, 'Where is she?'

Will let out a long breath. 'She leaves me a lot. That's what she does. She leaves, and then she comes back. And then she stays some and then she leaves again.'

'Where does she go?'

'I have no idea.'

'You've never asked her?'

'No.'

Sara didn't pretend to understand. 'Why not?'

He glanced out into the street, watching the traffic zoom by. 'It's complicated.'

She reached out and put her hand on his arm. 'Explain it to me.'

He stared at her, looking ridiculous with the tiny dog in one hand and a pizza box in the other.

Sara narrowed the space between them, moving her hand to his shoulder. She could feel hard muscle beneath his shirt, the heat from his skin. In

34

the bright light of the sun, his eyes looked impossibly blue. He had delicate eyelashes, blond and soft. There was a stubbly spot along his jaw that he'd missed shaving. She was a few inches shorter than him. She stood on her tiptoes to look him straight in the eye.

She said, 'Talk to me.'

He was silent, his eyes tracing back and forth across her face, lingering on her mouth, before meeting her gaze again.

Finally, he said, 'I like your hair down.'

Sara was robbed of a response by a black SUV slamming on its brakes in the middle of the street. It skidded to a halt about twenty yards away, then jerked into reverse. The wheels squealed against the asphalt. The smell of burned rubber filled the air. The SUV stopped directly in front of them. The window rolled down.

Will's boss, Amanda Wagner, yelled, 'Get in!'

They were both too stunned to move. Car horns blared. Fists were waving. Sara felt like she was caught in the middle of an action movie.

'Now!' Amanda ordered.

'Can you—' Will began, but Sara was already taking Betty, the box of pizza. He fished into his sock and handed her a house key. 'She needs to be locked in the spare room so she doesn't—'

'Will!' Amanda's tone didn't leave room for equivocation.

Sara took the key. The metal was warm from his body. 'Go.'

Will didn't have to be told twice. He jumped into the car, his foot skipping along the road as Amanda pulled away from the curve. More horns blared. A four-door sedan fishtailed. Sara could see a teenager in the back seat. The girl's hands pressed against the window. Her mouth gaped open in terror. Another car was coming from behind, speeding, but swerved at the last moment. Sara locked eyes with the young girl, then the sedan straightened and drove away.

Betty was shaking, and Sara wasn't much better off. She tried to soothe the dog as she walked toward Will's street, holding it close, pressing her lips to its head. Both of their hearts were pounding wildly. Sara wasn't sure what was making it worse—thinking about what might have happened between her and Will or the bad accident Amanda Wagner had nearly caused.

She'd have to watch the news when she got home to find out what was going on. Surely, wherever Will was going, the news vans would follow. Amanda was a deputy director with the GBI. She didn't ride around looking for her agents on a whim. Sara imagined Faith, Will's partner, was probably doing her own mad rush to the crime scene right now.

She had forgotten to ask for his house number, but thankfully, Betty's collar had a tag with the details. Even without that, she easily spotted Will's black Porsche parked in a driveway toward the end of the street. The car was an older model that had been fully restored. Will must have washed it today. The tires were gleaming and her reflection bounced off the long nose of the hood as she walked past.

She smiled at his house, which she'd never seen before. He lived in a red brick bungalow with an attached garage. The front door was painted black. The trim was a buttery yellow. The lawn was well tended with sharp edges and sculpted shrubs. A colorful flower bed circled the mimosa tree in the front yard. Sara wondered if Angie Trent had a green thumb. Pansies were hardy plants, but they had to be watered. From the sound of it, Mrs. Trent wasn't the type to stick around for that kind of thing. Sara wasn't sure how she felt about that, or even if she understood it. Still, she heard her mother's nagging voice in the back of her head: *An absent wife is still a wife.*

Betty started to squirm as Sara walked up the front path. She tightened her grip. That was all she needed to make the day worse—lose the dog that belonged to the wife of the man she'd just been longing to kiss in the middle of the street.

Sara shook her head as she climbed the front steps. She had no business thinking about Will this way. She should be glad Amanda Wagner had interrupted them. Early on in their marriage, Jeffrey had cheated on Sara. It had nearly ripped them in two, and putting their relationship back together had taken years of hard work. For better or worse, Will had made his choice. And this wasn't a fly-by-night romance, either. He had grown up with Angie. They had met in the children's home when they were kids. They had almost twenty-five years of history together. Sara didn't belong between them. She wasn't going to make another woman feel the same pain she had, no matter how dismal her other options.

The key easily slid into the front lock. A cool breeze met her as she walked through the doorway. She set Betty on the floor and took off her leash. Freed, the dog made a beeline for the back of the house.

37

Sara couldn't control her curiosity as she looked around the front rooms. Will's taste definitely ran toward the masculine. If his wife had contributed to the decorating, it certainly didn't show. A pinball machine was given pride of place in the center of the dining room, just under a glass chandelier. Will was obviously working on the machine—the electronic guts were neatly laid out by an open toolbox on the floor. The smell of machine oil filled the air.

The couch in the living room was a dark brown ultra-suede with a large matching ottoman. The walls were muted beige. A sleek black recliner was turned toward a fifty-inch plasma television with various electronic boxes stacked neatly underneath. Everything seemed to be in its proper place. There was no dust or clutter, no laundry piled into an Everest-like mountain on the couch. Obviously, Will was a better housekeeper than Sara. But then, most people were.

His desk was in the corner of the main room, just outside the hallway. Chrome and metal. She traced her finger along the arm of his reading glasses. Papers were neatly stacked around a laptop computer and printer. A pack of Magic Markers rested on a pile of colored folders. There were small metal bins with rubber bands and paper clips that were separated by color and size.

Sara had seen this setup before. Will could read, but not easily and certainly not quickly. He used the colored markers and clips as cues to help him find what he was looking for without having to actually scan what was on a page or in a folder. It was a neat trick that he'd probably taught himself early on. Sara had no doubt that he'd been one of those kids who sat in the back of the classroom and memorized everything the teacher said, only to be unable—or unwilling—to write down any of it come test day.

She took the pizza box into the kitchen, which had been remodeled in the same rich browns as the rest of the house. Unlike Sara's kitchen, the granite counters were neat and tidy, a coffeemaker and television the only items on display. Similarly, the fridge was empty but for a carton of milk and a pack of Jell-O pudding cups. Sara slid the box onto the top shelf and walked to the back of the house to check on Betty. She found the spare bedroom first. The overhead lights were off, but Will had left on the floor lamp behind another leather recliner. Beside the chair was a dog bed shaped like a chaise longue. A bowl of water and some kibble were in the corner. There was another television mounted on the wall, with a fold-up treadmill underneath.

The room was dark, the walls painted a rich brown that complemented the living room. She turned on the overhead light. Surprisingly, there were bookcases along the walls. Sara ran her finger down the titles, recognizing classics mixed in with a handful of feminist texts that were usually assigned to earnest young women their first year in college. All of the spines were cracked, well read. It had never occurred to her that Will would have a library in his house. With his dyslexia, reading a thick novel would have been a Sisyphean task. The audiobooks made more sense. Sara knelt down and looked at the CD cases stacked beside an expensive-looking Bose player. Will's tastes were certainly more highbrow than hers—lots of

39

nonfiction and historical works that Sara would normally suggest for insomniacs. She pressed down a peeling sticker and read the words 'Property of the Fulton County Library System.'

The tip-tap of toenails announced Betty in the hallway. Sara blushed, feeling caught. She stood to fetch the dog, but Betty ran off with surprising speed. Sara followed her past the bathroom and into the second room. Will's bedroom.

The bed was made, a dark blue blanket covering matching sheets. There was just one pillow leaning against the wall where the headboard should have been. One bedside table. One lamp.

Unlike the rest of the house, there was a utilitarian feel to the room. Sara didn't want to dwell on why the lack of romantic setting gave her relief. The walls were white. No art hung on the walls. Will's watch and wallet were on top of the chest of drawers beside yet another television. A pair of jeans and a T-shirt were laid out on the bench at the foot of the bed. There was a pair of folded black socks. His boots were under the bench. Sara picked up the shirt. Cotton. Long-sleeved. Black, like the one Will had been wearing.

The dog jumped on the bed, pushed down the pillow and settled like a bird in a nest.

Sara folded the shirt and put it back by the jeans. This was bordering on stalker behavior. At least she hadn't smelled the shirt or rummaged through his drawers. She scooped up Betty, thinking she should shut the dog in the spare room and get out of here. She was doing just that when the phone started to ring. The answering machine picked up. She heard Will's voice back in the bedroom.

'Sara? If you're there, please pick up.'

She went back to his room and picked up the phone. 'I was just about to leave.'

His voice sounded tense. She could hear a baby crying in the background, people shouting. 'I need you to come here right now. To Faith's. Her mother's house. It's important.'

Sara felt a rush of adrenaline sharpen her senses. 'Is she all right?'

'No,' he answered bluntly. 'May I give you the address?'

Without thinking, she opened the bedside drawer, assuming she'd find a piece of paper and pen. Instead, she saw a magazine like her father used to keep in the back of his toolbox in the garage.

'Sara?'

The drawer wouldn't close. 'Let me get something to write on. Hold on.'

Will seemed to be the only person in America who didn't have a cordless phone. Sara left the receiver on the bed, found some pen and paper on his desk, and came back. 'All right.'

Will waited for someone to stop shouting. He kept his voice low as he gave Sara the address. 'It's in Sherwood Forest, on the back side of Ansley. Do you know it?'

Ansley was only five minutes away. 'I can figure it out.'

'Take my car. The keys are on a hook by the back door in the kitchen. Can you drive a stick?'

'Yes.'

'The news people are already here. Find the first cop you see, tell them you're there at my request, and they'll let you back. Don't talk to anyone else.

41

Okay?'

'Okay.' She hung up the phone and pushed the bedside drawer shut with both hands. Betty was back on the pillow. Sara picked her up again. She started to leave, then thought better of it. Will was in shorts the last time she'd seen him. He'd probably want his jeans. She put his watch and wallet in the back pocket. There was no telling where he kept his gun, but Sara wasn't going to go looking through his things any more than she already had.

'Can I help you?'

Sara felt a rush of horror burn through her body. Angie Trent was leaning against the bedroom door, palm resting casually against the jamb. Her dark, curly hair cascaded around her shoulders. Her makeup was perfect. Her nails were perfect. Her tight skirt and revealing top would've easily won her the cover shot on the magazine in Will's drawer.

'I-I—' Sara hadn't stuttered since she was twelve.

'We've met before, right? You work at the hospital.'

'Yes.' Sara stood away from the bed. 'Will got called out on an emergency. He asked me to bring your dog—'

'*My* dog?'

Sara felt the vibrations of a growl building in Betty's chest.

Angie's mouth twisted in distaste. 'What happened to it?'

'She was . . .' Sara felt like a fool just standing there. She tucked Will's jeans under her arm. 'I'll put her in the spare room and go.'

'Sure.' Angie was blocking the door. She took her time letting Sara pass, then followed Sara to the spare room, watched her put Betty on the dog bed and pull the door to.

Sara started to leave out the front door, but then she remembered she needed Will's keys. She fought to keep her voice from shaking. 'He told me to bring his car.'

Angie crossed her arms. Her ring finger was bare, but she had a silver band around her thumb. 'Of course he did.'

Sara went back into the kitchen. Her face was so red she was sweating. There was a duffel bag by the table that hadn't been there before. Will's car keys were hanging on a hook by the back door, just as he'd said. She grabbed them and went back into the den, aware that Angie stood in the hallway watching her every move. Sara walked as quickly as she could toward the front door, her heart in her throat, but Angie Trent wasn't going to make it that easy for her.

'How long have you been fucking him?'

Sara shook her head. This couldn't be happening.

'I asked you how long you've been fucking my husband.'

Sara stared at the back of the door, too ashamed to look at her. 'This is a misunderstanding. I promise you.'

'I found you in *my* house in *my* bedroom that I share with my husband. What's your explanation? I'm dying to hear it.'

'I told you I—'

'You got a thing for cops? Is that it?'

Sara felt her heart stop mid-beat.

43

'Your dead husband was a cop, right? You get some kind of thrill out of that?' Angie gave a derisive laugh. 'He'll never leave me, honey. You'd better find yourself another dick to play with.'

Sara couldn't answer. The situation was too awful for words. She fumbled for the doorknob.

'He cut himself for me. Did he tell you that?'

She willed her hand to steady so she could open the door. 'I have to go now. I'm sorry.'

'I watched him slice the razor blade into his arm.'

Sara's hand wouldn't move. Her mind tried in vain to process what she was hearing.

'I've never seen so much blood in my life.' Angie paused. 'You could at least look at me when I'm talking to you.'

She didn't want to, but Sara made herself turn around.

Angie's tone was passive, but the hatred in her eyes made her hard to look at. 'I held him the whole time. Did he tell you about it? Did he tell you how I held him?'

Sara still could not find her voice.

Angie held up her left arm, showing the bare flesh. With excruciating slowness, she traced her right index finger from her wrist down to her elbow. 'They said the razor cut so deep that he scraped the bone.' She smiled, as if this was a happy memory. 'He did that for *me,* bitch. You think he'd do that for you?'

Now that Sara was looking at her, she couldn't stop. Moments slipped by. She thought of the clock back at the restaurant, the seconds blurring. Finally, she cleared her throat, not sure she could speak. 'It's the other arm.'

44

'What?'

'The scar,' she said, relishing the surprised look on Angie Trent's face. 'It's on his other arm.'

Sara's hands were sweating so badly she could barely turn the doorknob. She cringed as she rushed outside, thinking Angie would come running after her or worse, call her out on the lie.

The truth was that Sara had never seen a scar on Will's arm, because she'd never seen his bare arm. He always wore long-sleeved shirts. He never rolled up the sleeves or unbuttoned the cuffs. She had made an educated guess. Will was left-handed. If he'd tried to kill himself while his hateful wife was cheering him on, he'd sliced open his right arm, not his left.

CHAPTER THREE

Will picked at the collar of his shirt. the mobile command vehicle was scorching hot, filled with so many uniforms and suits that there was hardly room to breathe. The noise was equally unbearable. Phones were ringing. BlackBerries chirped. Computer monitors played live feeds from all three of the local news stations. Adding to the cacophony was Amanda Wagner, who had been yelling at the three zone commanders on scene for the last fifteen minutes. The Atlanta chief of police was on his way. So was the director of the GBI. The jurisdictional pissing contest was only going to intensify.

Meanwhile, no one was really working the case.

Will pushed open the door. Sunlight sliced

45

through the dark interior. Amanda stopped yelling for a few seconds, then revved back up as Will closed the door. He took a deep breath of fresh air, scanning the scene from the top of the metal steps. Instead of the usual rapid activity that followed a shocking crime, everyone was milling around waiting for orders. Detectives sat in their unmarked cars checking their email. Six cruisers blocked each end of the street. Neighbors gawked from their front porches. The Atlanta PD crime scene unit van was here. The GBI crime scene unit van was here. The fire truck was still angled in front of the Mitchell house. The EMTs were smoking on the back bumper of their ambulance. Various uniformed officers leaned against emergency vehicles, shooting the breeze, pretending not to care about what was going on in the command center.

Still, they all managed to glare at Will as he stepped down onto the street. Scowls went around. Arms were crossed. A curse was muttered. Someone spat on the sidewalk.

Will didn't have many friends in the Atlanta Police Department.

The sound of chopping blades filled the air. Will looked up. Two news copters hovered just above the crime scene. They wouldn't be alone for long. Every ten minutes, a black SWAT MD 500 swept by. An infrared camera was mounted on the nose of the mosquito-like helicopter. The camera could see through dense forests and rooftops, picking out warm-blooded bodies, directing searchers to the bad guys. It was an amazing device, but completely useless in the residential area, where at any given moment there were thousands of people milling

46

around not committing crimes. At best, they were probably picking up the glowing red forms of people sitting on their couches watching their televisions, which in turn showed the SWAT copter hovering overhead.

Will checked the crowd for Sara, wishing she would show up. If he'd been thinking at all when Amanda pulled up on the street, he would've told Sara to come with them. He should have anticipated Faith would need help. She was his partner. Will was supposed to take care of her, to have her back. Now, it might be too late.

He wasn't sure how Amanda had heard about the shootings so quickly, but they were on scene within fifteen minutes of the last shot being fired. The locksmith was just opening the shed door when they rolled up. Faith had been pacing back and forth like a caged animal while she waited for her child to be freed, and she kept pacing long after Emma was in her arms. As soon as she saw Will, Faith started babbling, talking about her backyard neighbor, Mrs. Johnson, her brother Zeke, the shed her father had built when she was little, and a million other things that made absolutely no sense the way she was stringing them together.

At first, Will thought that Faith was in shock, but shocked people don't pace around squawking like lunatics. Their blood pressure drops so quickly they generally can't stand. They pant like dogs. They stare blankly at the space in front of them. They talk slowly, not so fast you can barely understand them. Something else was at play, but Will didn't know if it was some kind of mental break or Faith's diabetes or what.

47

Making it worse, by that point, there were twenty cops standing around who knew exactly what a person was supposed to look like when an awful thing happened. Faith didn't fit the profile. She wasn't crying. She wasn't shaking. She wasn't angry. She was just crazy, totally out of her mind. Nothing she said had a bit of reason. She couldn't tell them what had happened. She couldn't walk them through the scene and explain the bloodshed. She was worse than useless, because the answers to all their questions were locked up inside of her head.

And that was when one of the cops had mumbled something about her being under the influence. And then someone else volunteered to get the Breathalyzer out of his car.

Quickly, Amanda had intervened. She dragged Faith across the front lawn, banged on the neighbor's door—not Mrs. Johnson, who had a dead man in her backyard, but an old woman named Mrs. Levy—and practically ordered her to give Faith a place to collect herself.

By then, the mobile command center had pulled up. Amanda had gone straight into the back of the vehicle and started demanding this case be turned over to the GBI immediately. She knew that she wouldn't win the territorial fight with the zone commanders. By law, the GBI could not simply waltz in and take over a case. The local medical examiner, district attorney, or police chief generally asked the state for assistance, and usually that only happened when they'd failed to make a case on their own or didn't want to spend the money or manpower tracking down leads. The only person who could yank this case from Atlanta was the governor, and any politician in the state could tell you that crossing the capital city was a very bad idea. Amanda's screaming tactics were for show. She didn't yell when she was angry. Her voice got low, more like a rumble, and you had to strain your ears to hear the insults flying out of her mouth. She was trying to buy them time. Trying to buy Faith time.

In the eyes of the Atlanta PD brass, Faith wasn't a cop anymore. She was a witness. She was a suspect. She was a person of interest, and they wanted to talk to her about the men she had killed and why her mother had been kidnapped. The Atlanta police weren't a bunch of yokels. They were one of the best forces in the country. But for Amanda yelling at them, they would've had Faith at the station by now, drilling her like they were working a terrorist at Gitmo.

Will couldn't blame them. Sherwood Forest was not the kind of neighborhood where you'd expect to find a shootout in the middle of a beautiful Saturday afternoon. Ansley Park was a stone's throw away. Cast the net a bit farther and you'd encompass about eighty percent of the city's real estate tax revenue—multimillion-dollar homes with tennis courts and au pair suites. Rich people weren't the type of folks who let bad things happen without assigning blame. Someone would have to pay for this. If Amanda couldn't find a way to prevent it, that person would probably end up being Faith. And Will was at a loss as to what to do.

Detective Leo Donnelly walked up, his feet shuffling along the asphalt. He had a cigarette dangling out of his mouth. Smoke twined into his eye. He winked to keep it out. 'I'd hate to hear that bitch in bed.'

He meant Amanda. She was still screaming, though her words were hard to make out through the closed doors.

Leo continued, 'I dunno. Might be worth it. The old ones are tigers when you get 'em in the sack.'

Will suppressed a shudder, not because Amanda was in her mid-sixties, but because Leo was clearly considering the possibilities.

'She knows she's not going to win this, right?'

Will leaned against one of the police cruisers. Leo had been Faith's partner for six years, but she had done most of the heavy lifting. At forty-eight, Leo wasn't an old man by any stretch, but he had aged in cop years. His skin was yellow from an overburdened liver. He'd beaten prostate cancer but the treatment had taken its toll. He was an okay guy but he was lazy, which was perfectly fine if you were a used-car salesman but incredibly dangerous if you were a cop. Faith counted herself lucky that she'd gotten away from the man.

Leo said, 'Haven't seen a clusterfuck like this since the last time I worked a case with you.'

Will took in the scene: the hum of the command center's generator mixing with the metallic whir coming from the television vans. The cops standing around with their hands resting on their belts. The firemen shooting the breeze with each other. The complete and total lack of activity. He decided he should talk to Leo. 'That so?'

'What's your CSU guy's name—Charlie?' Leo nodded to himself. 'He managed to talk his way into the house.'

Special Agent Charlie Reed was head of the GBI's crime scene unit and would do anything to

50

get onto a crime scene. 'He's good at his job.'

'Lots of us are.' Leo leaned against the cruiser a couple of feet down from Will. He made a puffing noise with his mouth. 'Never known Faith to be a drinker.'

'She's not.'

'Pills?'

Will gave him the nastiest look he could muster. 'You know I gotta talk to her.'

Will couldn't keep the derision out of his tone. 'You're in charge of this case?'

'Try not to sound so confident.'

Will didn't waste his breath. Leo's time in the sun would be short-lived. As soon as the Atlanta chief of police came onto the scene, he'd kick Leo to the curb and put together his own team. Leo would be lucky if they let him fetch coffee.

'Seriously,' Leo said. 'Faith doin' all right?'

'She's fine.'

He took a last drag on his cigarette and dropped it to the ground. 'Neighbor's freaked out. Almost watched her granddaughters get shot down.'

Will tried to keep his expression blank. He knew a little bit about what had happened here, but not much. The guys from the tactical team had gotten bored after standing around for five minutes with nothing to break. The details of the crime scene had leaked like a rusty pipe. Two bodies in the house. One in the neighbor's backyard. Two guns on Faith—her Glock and a Smith and Wesson. Her shotgun on the floor of the bedroom. Will had stopped listening when he'd overheard a cop who'd just arrived on scene saying that he'd seen Faith with his own two eyes and she was as high as a kite.

For his part, Will only knew two things to be

51

true: he had no idea what had happened in that house, and Faith had done the right thing.

Leo cleared his throat and spit a chunk of phlegm onto the asphalt. 'So, Granny Johnson said she heard some screaming in the backyard. She looks out the kitchen window and sees the shooter—Mexican guy—aiming down on her grandkids. He squeezes off a shot, takes out some bricks on the house. Faith runs up to the fence and shoots him dead. Saves the little girls.'

Will felt some of the weight lift off his chest. 'Lucky for them Faith was there.'

'Lucky for Faith the neighbor's a good witness.'

Will started to stick his hands in his pockets, too late remembering he was still in his running shorts.

Leo chuckled. 'I like these new uniforms. You supposed to be the cop in the Village People?'

Will crossed his arms over his chest.

'Los Texicanos,' Leo said. 'The guy in the backyard. He's affiliated, got tats all over his chest and arms.'

'What about the other two?'

'Asian. Both of 'em. No idea if they're ganged up. Don't look like it. Don't dress like it. Bodies are clean—no tats.' Leo took his time lighting another cigarette . He blew out a steady stream of smoke before continuing. 'Scott Shepherd over there—' He nodded toward a beefy-looking young man in tactical gear. 'Says he had his team suited up outside the house waiting for backup. They heard a gun go off. It's a possible hostage situation, right? One officer inside, two if you count Evelyn. Imminent danger. So, they breech the door.' Leo took another hit off his cigarette. 'Scott sees Faith standing there in the hall, feet spread, Glock out in front of her. She sees Scott, doesn't say a word, just takes off into the bedroom. They go in after her and find a dead guy laid out on the carpet.' Leo touched his finger to his forehead. 'She nailed him right between the eyes.'

'Must've had a good reason.'

'Wish I knew that reason. He didn't have a gun in his hand.'

'The other guy did. The one who ran into the backyard and shot at the kids.'

'You're right. He did.'

'Fingerprints?'

'We're working on it.'

Will would've bet his house that they would find two sets of prints—one from the Asian and one from the Mexican. 'Where'd you find the third guy?'

'Laundry room. Bullet to the head. Nasty shot, took off half his skull. We dug a thirty-eight out of the wall.'

Faith's Glock was a .40-caliber. 'Does the S&W take a thirty-eight?'

'Yep.' Leo pushed away from the car. 'Nothing on the mother yet. We got teams out looking for her. She ran the drug squad, but I think you already know that, Ratatouille.'

Will forced his jaw not to clench. About the only thing Leo was really good at was pushing buttons. This was the reason for the nasty stares and hostile stances from Will's brothers in blue. Every cop out here knew that Will Trent was the reason Evelyn Mitchell had been forced into retirement. One of the most loathsome jobs he had at the GBI was investigating corrupt cops. Four years ago, he'd made a solid case against Evelyn's narcotics squad.

53

Six detectives had gone to prison for skimming money off drug busts and taking cash to look the other way, but Captain Mitchell had walked away scot-free, her pension and most of her good reputation intact.

Leo said, 'Tell the kid I can give her ten more minutes, tops, but then she's gotta get her shit together and start talking to me.' He leaned in closer. 'I heard the dispatch call. She was told to stay outta the house. She needs to be real clear on why she went in anyway.'

Leo started to leave, but Will asked him, 'How did she sound?'

He turned around.

'The phone call to dispatch. How did she sound?'

Unsurprisingly, Leo hadn't considered the question. He did now, and quickly started nodding his head. 'Maybe a little scared, but clearheaded. Calm. In control.'

Will nodded, too. 'That sounds exactly like Faith.'

Leo flashed a grin, but Will couldn't tell if he was relieved or just playing his usual role of smartass. 'I meant that about the shorts, man.' Leo slapped him on the arm. 'You should try to get those pretty legs of yours on TV.'

Leo waved to the reporters standing at the yellow tape line. They pressed forward as one, thinking he was going to give them a statement. There was a collective groan as he walked away. The cops holding the line pushed them back just because they could. Will knew they couldn't care less about crowd control. Their eyes kept going to the command center like they expected an

54

announcement from on high. The cops were just as eager as the reporters to find out what had happened. Maybe more so.

Captain Evelyn Mitchell had served with the Atlanta force for thirty-nine years. She had come up the hard way, clawing her way out of the secretarial pool, advancing to meter reader, then traffic cop, and finally being given a twenty-two and a badge that wasn't made of plastic. She was part of a group known for being first: first women driving solo, first women detectives. Evelyn was the first female lieutenant on the Atlanta force, then the first female captain. No matter the reasons for her retirement, she had more medals and commendations than all of the cops on scene combined.

Will had learned a long time ago that police officers were blindly loyal. He'd also learned that there was a distinct pecking order to that loyalty. It was like a pyramid, with every cop in the world at the bottom and your partner at the top. Faith had been with the Atlanta Police Department since she joined up, but she'd moved to the GBI two years ago, partnering with Will, who wasn't exactly the most popular guy in class. Leo might still be halfway on Faith's side, but as far as the general members of the APD were concerned, she had lost her spot on their pyramid. Especially since the first cop on scene, an eager young rookie, had been rushed into emergency surgery after Faith elbowed his testicles up into his brain stem.

Will saw a flash of yellow as the tape line was lifted. Sara had put up her hair, pinning it tightly behind her head. The linen dress she was wearing looked worse for wear. She had a folded pair of

55

jeans under her arm. At first Will thought she looked confused, but the closer she got, the more he thought she looked annoyed, maybe even angry. Her eyes were red rimmed. Her cheeks were flushed.

She handed him the jeans. 'Why do you need me here?'

He put his hand at her elbow and led her away from the reporters. 'It's Faith.'

She crossed her arms, keeping some distance between them. 'If she needs medical attention, you should take her to the hospital.'

'We can't do that.' Will tried not to focus on the coldness in her voice. 'She's at the neighbor's house. We don't have much time.'

'I heard what happened on the radio.'

'We think there's a drug connection. Keep that to yourself.' Will stopped walking. He waited for her to look at him. 'Faith's not acting right. She's confused, not making sense. They want to talk to her, but—' He didn't know what to say. Amanda had told Will to make the call to Sara. She knew the woman had been married to a cop, and assumed that her allegiance hadn't died with the man. 'This could be really bad for Faith. She killed two men. Her mother's been kidnapped. They're going to be eyeballing her for a lot of reasons.'

'Did she overreact?'

'There was a hostage situation. The kids next door were in the line of fire.' Will skated over the missing details. 'She shot one guy in the head and one in the back.'

'Are the children okay?'

'Yes, but—'

The back doors of the command center banged

56

opened. Chief Mike Geary, the zone commander for Ansley and Sherwood Forest, jumped down from the steps. He was in full uniform, a scratchy, dark blue polyester that was too tight across the pouch of his stomach. He blinked up at the sun, a deep line creasing his well-tanned forehead. Like most of the old guard, he kept his gray hair clipped in a military-style crew cut. Geary put on his hat and turned back around to hold out his hand to Amanda. Something stopped him just shy of touching her, though, and he dropped his hand before she could take it.

'Trent,' he barked. 'I want to talk to your partner right now. Go get her. We're taking her to the station.'

Will shot Amanda a look as she navigated the rickety stairs in her high heels. She shook her head once. There was nothing more she could do.

To his surprise, it was Sara who saved them. 'I have to examine her first.'

Geary wasn't pleased to be met with resistance. 'Who the hell are you?'

'I'm a trauma doc from the Grady ER.' Sara deftly left out her name. 'I'm here to evaluate Agent Mitchell so that any testimony she gives will be admissible.' She tilted her head to the side. 'I'm sure it's not your policy to take statements under duress.'

Geary snorted. 'She's not under duress.'

Sara raised an eyebrow. 'Is that your official position? Because I would hate to have to testify that you conducted a coercive interrogation against medical advice.'

Confusion clouded in on Geary's anger. Doctors were usually more than willing to help the police, but they had the power to shut down any interview if they thought it would jeopardize their patient. Still, Geary tried. 'What kind of medical treatment does she need?'

Sara didn't back down. 'I can't tell you that until I evaluate her. She could be in shock. She could be injured. She could need hospitalization. Maybe I should just transfer her to the hospital right now and start running tests.' Sara turned around to call to the EMTs.

'Wait.' Geary hissed out a curse, telling Amanda, 'Your bullshit stalling tactics are being noted, Deputy Director.'

Her smile was fake sweetness and light. 'It's always nice to be recognized for something.'

Geary announced, 'I want her blood drawn and taken to an independent lab for a full tox screen. You think you can do that, Doctor?'

Sara nodded. 'Of course.'

Will put his hand back under Sara's arm and led her toward the neighbor's house. As soon as they were out of earshot, he said, 'Thank you.'

Again, she pulled away from him as they walked up the driveway. By the time they reached the front porch, she was several feet ahead, though the distance between them felt more like a chasm. This wasn't the Sara from half an hour ago. Maybe it was the crime scene, though Will had seen her on a crime scene before. Sara had been a coroner at one time. She was far from out of her element. Will didn't know what to do about the change. He had spent a lifetime gauging the moods of other people, but getting a read on this particular woman was beyond his abilities.

The door opened and Mrs. Levy peered at them

58

from behind her thick glasses. She was wearing a yellow housedress that was frayed at the collar. A white apron with baby geese waddling around the hem was wrapped around her thin waist. Her heels hung out of the back of her matching yellow bedroom slippers. She was somewhere north of eighty, but her mind was sharp and she clearly cared for Faith. 'Is this the doctor? I was told to only let a doctor in.'

Sara answered, 'Yes, ma'am. I'm the doctor.'

'Well, aren't you pretty? Come on in. What a crazy day this has been.' Mrs. Levy stepped aside, throwing wide the door so they could come into the foyer. Her breath whistled through her false teeth. 'I've had more visitors this afternoon than I've had all year.'

The living room was sunken a few steps and furnished much as it probably had been when Mrs. Levy first bought the house. Harvest gold wall-to-wall shag carpet was flattened to the floor. The couch was a tightly cushioned, mustard-colored sectional. The only update to the décor was a recliner that looked like the kind that had a mechanical lift to make it easier to get in and out of. The only light in the room came from the flickering console television set. Faith was slumped on the couch with Emma held to her shoulder. All of the talk had drained out of her. Her spirit seemed to have gone with it. This was more what Will had been expecting when he'd heard that Faith was involved in a shooting. She tended to go quiet when she was really upset. But this wasn't quite right, either.

She was too quiet.

'Faith?' he said. 'Dr. Linton is here.'

59

She stared at the muted television, not answering. In some ways, Faith looked worse than she had before. Her lips were as white as her skin. Sweat gave her face a luminescence. Her blonde hair was matted to her head. Her breathing was shallow. Emma made a cooing sound, but Faith didn't seem to notice.

Sara turned on the overhead light before kneeling in front of her. 'Faith? Can you look at me?'

Faith's eyes were still on the set. Will took the moment to slip on his jeans over his shorts. He felt a lump in his back pocket and pulled out his watch and wallet.

'Faith?' Sara's voice became louder, firmer. 'Look at me.'

Slowly, she looked at Sara.

'Why don't you give me Emma?'

Her words slurred. 'Sh'sleeping.'

Sara wrapped her hands around Emma's waist. Gently, she lifted the baby from Faith's shoulder. 'Look at her. She's gotten so big.' Sara did a cursory exam, looking into Emma's eyes, checking her fingers and toes, then her gums. 'I think she's a little dehydrated.'

Mrs. Levy offered, 'I've got a bottle ready, but she wouldn't let me give it to her.'

'Why don't you go get it now?' Sara motioned for Will to come over. He took Emma. She was surprisingly heavy. He put her on his shoulder. Her head fell against his neck like a moist sack of flour.

'Faith?' Sara spoke succinctly, as if she was trying to get an old person's attention. 'How are you feeling?'

'Took her to the doctor.'

'You took Emma?' Sara cupped Faith's face in her hand. 'What did the doctor say?'

'Dunno.'

'Can you look at me?'

Faith's mouth moved like she was chewing gum.

'What's today, sweetie? Can you tell me what day of the week it is?'

She pulled away her head. 'No.'

'That's all right.' Sara pressed open Faith's eyelid. 'When's the last time you had something to eat?'

She didn't answer. Mrs. Levy came back with the bottle. She handed it to Will, and he cradled Emma in his arm so that she could drink.

'Faith? When is the last time you had something to eat?'

Faith tried to push Sara away. When that didn't work, she pushed harder.

Sara kept talking, holding down Faith's hands. 'Was it this morning? Did you eat breakfast this morning?'

'Go 'way.'

Sara turned to Mrs. Levy. 'You're not diabetic, are you?'

'No, dear, but my husband was. Passed away almost twenty years ago, bless his soul.'

Sara told Will, 'She's having an insulin reaction. Where's her purse?'

Mrs. Levy supplied, 'She didn't have it when they brought her here. Maybe she left it in the car.'

Again, Sara directed her words to Will. 'She should have an emergency kit in her purse. It's plastic. It says 'Glucagon' on the side.' She seemed to remember herself. 'It's oblong, about the size of a pen case. Bright red or orange. Get it for me

61

now, please.'

Will took the baby with him, jogging toward the front door and out into the yard. The lots in Sherwood Forest were larger than most, but some of them were long and narrow rather than wide. Will could see directly into Evelyn Mitchell's bathroom from Mrs. Levy's carport. He could see a man standing in the long hallway. Will wondered not for the first time how the old woman hadn't heard the gunfight next door. She wouldn't be the first witness who didn't want to get involved, but Will was surprised by her reticence.

It didn't occur to him until he was a few feet from the Mini that Faith's car was part of the crime scene. There were two cops standing on the other side of the car, four more in the carport. Will scanned the interior. He saw the plastic case Sara had told him about mixed in with various lady items on the passenger's seat.

He told the cops, 'I need to get something out of the car.'

'Tough shit,' one of them shot back.

Will indicated Emma, who was sucking on the bottle like she'd been on a ten-mile hike. 'She needs her teething thing. She's teething.'

The cops stared at him. Will wondered if he'd screwed up. He'd changed his share of diapers at the children's home, but he had no idea when babies got their teeth. Emma was four months old. All her food came from Faith or a bottle. As far as he could tell, she didn't need to chew anything.

'Come on.' Will held up Emma so they could see her little pink face. 'She's just a tiny baby.'

'All right,' one of them relented. He walked around the car and opened the door. 'Where is it?'

62

'It's that red plastic thing. Looks like a pen case.'

The cop didn't appear to find this odd. He picked up the kit and handed it to Will. 'She all right?'

'She was just thirsty.'

'I meant Faith, dipshit.'

Will tried to take the kit, but the man wouldn't let go.

He repeated his question. 'Is Faith going to be okay?'

Will realized there was more going on here. 'Yes. She's going to be fine.'

'Tell her Brad says we're gonna find her mom.' He let go of the kit and slammed the door.

Will didn't give the man time to change his mind. He jogged back to the house, trying not to jostle the baby. Mrs. Levy still stood sentry at the door. She opened it before Will could knock.

The scene inside had changed. Faith was lying on the couch. Sara was cupping the back of her head, making her drink from a can of Coke.

Sara immediately started in on Will. 'You should've called in the medics first thing,' she admonished. 'Her blood sugar is too low. She's stuporous and diaphoretic. Her heart is racing. This isn't something you play around with.' She took the kit from him and popped it open. Inside was a syringe filled with a clear liquid and a vial of white powder that looked a lot like cocaine. Sara cleaned the needle with a cotton ball and some rubbing alcohol that she had obviously gotten from Mrs. Levy. She talked as she pressed the syringe into the vial and squirted in the liquid. 'I'm assuming she hasn't eaten since breakfast. The

63

adrenaline from the confrontation in the house would've giving her an enormous sugar kick, but it made the crash harder, too. Considering what happened, I'm surprised she didn't slip into a coma.'

Will took her words as hard as they were meant to be. No matter what Amanda said, he should've pulled an EMT in here half an hour ago. He had been worried about Faith's career when he should've been worried about her life. 'Is she going to be okay?'

Sara shook the vial, mixing the contents before drawing them back into the syringe. 'We'll know soon enough.' She lifted Faith's shirt and swabbed a patch of skin on her belly. Will watched the needle go in, the rubber stopper sliding down the plastic cylinder as the liquid was injected.

Sara asked, 'Are you worried they'll think she was impaired when she shot those two men?'

He didn't answer.

'Her comedown was probably hard and immediate. She would've been slurring her words. She probably appeared intoxicated.' Sara cleaned up the kit, putting everything back in its place. 'Tell them to look at the facts. She shot one man in the head and one in the back, probably from a distance, with two innocent bystanders downrange. If she'd been impaired, there's no way she would've been able to make those shots.'

Will glanced at Mrs. Levy, who probably didn't need to be hearing this conversation. She waved off his concerns. 'Oh, don't worry about me, dear. I don't remember much of nothin' these days.' She held out her arms for Emma. 'Why don't you let me take care of the little lamb?' Carefully, he

64

transferred the baby to Mrs. Levy. The old woman walked off toward the back of the house. Her bedroom slippers made a slapping sound on her dry heels.

Will asked Sara, 'What about the diabetes? Can they say it was that?'

Her tone was businesslike. 'How was she acting when you got here?'

'She looked . . .' He shook his head, thinking he never wanted to see Faith that bad off again. 'She looked like she'd lost her mind.'

'Do you think a mentally or chemically altered person could've killed two men with a single shot to each?' Sara put her hand on Faith's shoulder. Her tone softened. 'Faith, can you sit up for me, please?'

Slowly, Faith moved to right herself. She looked groggy, as if she had just woken from a long nap, but her color was coming back. She put her hands to her head, wincing.

Sara told her, 'You'll have a headache for a while. Drink as much water as you can tolerate. We need your tester to see where you are.'

'It's in my purse.'

'I'll try to get another one from one of the ambulances.' She took a bottle of water off the coffee table and twisted off the cap. 'Switch to water. No more Coke.'

Sara left without looking at Will. Her back felt like a wall of ice. He didn't know what to do with that, so he ignored it, sitting on the coffee table in front of Faith.

She took a long drink of water before she spoke to him. 'My head is killing me.' The shock of what happened came back to her like a bolt of lightning.

'Where's my mother?' She tried to stand, but Will kept her down. 'Where is she?'

'They're looking for her.'

'The little girls—'

'They're fine. Please, just stay here for a second, okay?'

She looked around, some of her wildness returning. 'Where's Emma?'

'She's with Mrs. Levy. She's asleep. I called Jeremy at the school—'

Her mouth opened. He could see her life coming back to her in spurts. 'How did you tell him?'

'I talked to Victor. He's still the dean of students. I knew you wouldn't want me to send a cop to Jeremy's classroom.'

'Victor.' Faith pressed her lips together. She had dated Victor Martinez for a while, but they had broken up almost a year ago. 'Please tell me you didn't mention Emma.'

Will couldn't remember exactly what he'd told Victor, but he guessed Faith hadn't gotten around to telling the man that he had a daughter. 'I'm sorry.'

'It doesn't matter.' She put down the bottle of water, her shaking hands spilling some onto the carpet. 'What else?'

'We're trying to track down your brother.' Dr. Zeke Mitchell was a surgeon in the Air Force, stationed somewhere in Germany. 'Amanda reached out to a friend at Dobbins Air Reserve. They're cutting through some of the red tape.'

'My phone . . .' She seemed to realize where she'd left it. 'Mama has his number by the phone in the kitchen.'

'I'll get it as soon as we're finished,' Will promised. 'Tell me what happened.'

She took a stuttered breath. He could see her struggle with the knowledge of what she had done. 'I killed two people.'

Will held both her hands. Her skin was still cold and clammy. She had a slight tremor, but he didn't think it was from her blood sugar issues. 'You saved two little girls, Faith.'

'The man in the bedroom—' She stopped. 'I don't understand what happened.'

'Are you confused again? Do you need me to get Dr. Linton?'

'No.' She shook her head for so long he thought maybe he should get Sara anyway. 'She's not bad, Will. My mom is not a dirty cop.'

'We don't need to talk about—'

'Yes, we do,' Faith insisted. 'Even if she was, which she's not, she's been retired for five years. She's not on the job anymore. She doesn't go to the fundraisers or the events. She doesn't talk to anybody from that old life. She plays cards on Fridays with some of the ladies in the neighborhood. She goes to church every Wednesday and Sunday. She watches Emma while I'm at work. Her car is five years old. She just made the last mortgage payment on the house. She's not mixed up in anything. There's no reason for anybody to think...' Her lip started to tremble. Tears threatened to fall.

Will told her the concrete things he could point to. 'There's a mobile command center outside. All the highways are being watched. Evelyn's photo is on all the news stations. Every cruiser policing the metro area has her picture. We're lighting up all the snitches to see if they've heard anything. They've trapped and traced all your phones in case any ransom demands are made. Amanda pitched a fit, but they put one of their detectives in your house to monitor all mail and calls. Jeremy's at your house. They've got a plainclothes assigned to him. You'll get somebody, too.'

Faith had worked kidnapping cases before. 'Do you really think there's going to be a ransom demand?'

'It could happen.'

'They were Texicanos. They were looking for something. That's why they took her.'

Will asked, 'What were they looking for?'

'I don't know. The house was turned upside down. The Asian said he'd trade my mother for whatever they were looking for.'

'The Asian said he'd trade?'

'Yes, he had a gun on the Texicano—the one in the backyard.'

'Hold on.' They were doing this the wrong way. 'Work with me, Faith. Treat your memory like a crime scene. Start from the beginning. You had that in-service this morning, right? Computer training?'

She started to nod. 'I was late getting home by almost two hours.' She laid out every detail from her morning until now, how she had tried to call her mother, how she'd heard music playing in the house when she got out of her car. Faith hadn't realized that something was wrong until well after the music stopped. Will let her run through the story—the torn-up house, the dead man she'd found and the two that she had killed herself.

When she was finished, he played it all back in

his head, seeing Faith standing in the carport by the shed, going back to her car. Despite her recent medical issues, her memory seemed crystal clear now. She had called dispatch, and then she had gotten her gun. Will felt this detail picking at a spot in his brain. Faith knew that Will was home today. They had talked about it yesterday afternoon. She was complaining about having to go do computer training, and he told her he was going to wash his car and take care of the yard. Will lived 2.3 miles away from where they were sitting. He could've gotten here in under five minutes.

But Faith hadn't called him.

'What is it?' she asked. 'Did I miss something?'

He cleared his throat. 'What was the song that was playing when you pulled up?'

'AC/DC,' she said. ' "Back in Black." '

The detail seemed strange. 'Is that what your mom usually listens to?'

She shook her head. She was obviously still in shock, her mind reeling from what had happened.

He wrapped his hands around her arms, trying to get her to concentrate. 'Think this through, all right?' He waited for her to look at him. 'There are two dead men in the house. Both are Asian. The guy in the backyard is Mexican. Los Texicanos.'

She focused herself. 'The Asian in the bedroom—he was wearing this loud Hawaiian shirt. He sounded southside.' She meant his accent. 'He had a gun on the Texicano. He was threatening to kill him.'

'Did he say anything else?'

'I shot him.' Her lip started to tremble again.

Will had never seen Faith cry and he didn't want to now. 'The guy in the shirt had a gun pointed at someone's head,' he reminded her. 'The Texicano was already beaten up, possibly tortured. You feared for his life. That's why you pulled the trigger.'

She nodded, though he could see self-doubt brimming in her eyes.

He said, 'After Hawaiian Shirt went down, the Texicano ran out into the yard, right?'

'Right.'

'And you chased after him, and he raised his gun toward those little girls and fired, so you shot him, too, right?'

'Yes.'

'You were protecting the hostage in the bedroom and you were protecting those two girls in your neighbor's backyard. Right?'

'Yes,' she said, her voice stronger. 'I was.'

She was getting back to her old self. Will allowed himself to feel a little bit of relief. He dropped her hands. 'You remember the directive, Faith. Deadly force is authorized when your life or the lives of others are at stake. You did your job today. You just have to articulate what you were thinking. People were in danger. You shoot to immediately stop the threat. You don't shoot to wound.'

'I know.'

'Why didn't you wait for backup?'

She didn't answer.

'The dispatcher told you to wait outside. You didn't wait outside.'

Faith still didn't answer.

Will sat back on the table, hands between his knees. Maybe she didn't trust him. They had never talked openly about the case he'd built against her

70

mother, but he knew Faith assumed that it was the detectives on the squad, not the captain in charge, who had messed up. As smart as she was, she was still naïve about the politics of the job. Will had noticed in every corruption case he'd worked that the heads that tended to roll in this business were the ones that didn't have gold stars on their collars. Faith was too low on the food chain to have that kind of protection.

He said, 'You must've heard something inside. A yell? A gunshot?'

'No.'

'Did you see something?'

'I saw the curtain move, but that was after—'

'Good, that's good.' He leaned forward again. 'You saw someone inside. You thought your mother might be in there. You sensed an immediate danger to her life and went in to secure the scene.'

'Will—'

'Listen to me, Faith. I've asked a lot of cops these same questions, and I know what the answer is supposed to be. Are you listening to me?'

She nodded.

'You saw someone inside the house. You thought your mother might be in serious danger—'

'I saw blood on the carport. On the door. A bloody handprint on the door.'

'Exactly. That's good. That gives you cause to go in. Someone was badly injured. Their life was at stake. The rest of it happened because you were provoked into a situation where deadly force was justified.'

She shook her head. 'Why are you coaching me? You hate when cops lie for each other.'

71

'I'm not lying for you. I'm trying to make sure you keep your job.'

'I don't give a shit about my job. I just want to get my mother back.'

'Then stick to what we just talked about. You won't do anybody any good sitting in a jail cell.'

He could read the shock in her eyes. As bad as things were right now, it had never occurred to her that they could get worse.

There was a loud knock at the door. Will started to get up, but Mrs. Levy beat him to it. She sashayed down the hall with her arms swinging. He guessed she'd put Emma in one of the beds and hoped she'd thought to stack some pillows around her.

Geary was the first to come in, then Amanda, then a couple of older-looking men, one black, one white. Both had bushy eyebrows, clean-shaven faces, and the kind of brass and ribbons on their chests that came from a glorious career of riding a desk. They were window dressing, here to make Geary look important. If he were a rap star, they would've been called a posse. Because he was a zone commander, they were called support staff.

'Ma'am,' Geary mumbled to Mrs. Levy as he took off his hat. His boys followed suit, tucking their hats under their arms, just like the boss. Geary walked toward Faith, but the old woman stopped him.

'Can I get y'all some tea or perhaps some cookies?'

Geary snapped, 'We're conducting an investigation, not a tea party.'

Mrs. Levy seemed unfazed. 'Well, then. Please, make yourself at home.' She winked at Will before turning on her heel and heading back down the hallway.

Geary said, 'Stand up, Agent Mitchell.'

Will felt his stomach tense as Faith stood. None of her earlier shakiness was on display, though her shirt was untucked and her hair was still a mess. She said, 'I'm ready to make a statement if—'

Amanda interrupted, 'Your lawyer and a union rep are waiting at the station.'

Geary scowled. He obviously didn't care about Faith's legal representation. 'Agent Mitchell, you were told to wait for backup. I don't know how they do it in the GBI, but the men on my force follow orders.'

Faith glanced at Amanda, but told Geary evenly, 'There was blood on the kitchen door. I saw a person inside the house. My mother's S&W was missing. I feared there was an immediate threat to her life, so I went into the house to secure her safety.' She couldn't have said it better if Will had supplied a script.

Geary asked, 'The man in the kitchen?'

'He was dead when I entered the house.'

'The one in the bedroom?'

'He had my mother's revolver pointed at another man's head. I was protecting the life of the hostage.'

'And the man in the yard?'

'The hostage. He took the revolver after I shot the first man. The front door was breached and my attention was diverted. He ran into the backyard with the gun, which he fired at two young girls. I had my shot and I took it to save their lives.'

Geary glanced at his brass window dressing as he decided what to do. The two men seemed

73

unsure themselves, but ready to back up the boss without question. Will felt himself tense, because this was the part where things either went down hard or easy. Perhaps an overriding loyalty to Evelyn Mitchell persuaded the man to take a softer approach. He told Faith, 'One of my officers will drive you to the station. Take a moment to collect yourself if you need to.'

He started to put his hat back on, but Amanda stopped him.

'Mike, I feel the need to remind you of something.' She gave him that same sweet smile as before. 'The GBI has original jurisdiction over all drug cases in the state.'

'Are you telling me you've found evidence that narcotics are a factor in these shootings?'

'I'm not telling you much of anything, am I?'

He glared at her as he put his hat back on. 'Don't think I'm not going to find out why you've been wasting my time.'

'That sounds like a wonderful use of your resources.'

Geary stomped toward the door, his minions scrambling after him. Outside, Sara was coming up the front porch steps. She quickly put her hands behind her back, hiding the blood sugar monitor she had borrowed.

'Dr. Linton.' Geary took off his hat again. His men followed suit. 'I'm sorry I didn't recognize your name earlier.' Will assumed this was because Sara hadn't offered it. Obviously, someone else had filled him in. 'I knew your husband. He was a good cop. A good man.'

Sara kept her hands behind her back, twisting the plastic monitor. Will recognized the look she gave the men—she didn't want to talk. For Geary, she managed a dry 'Thank you.'

'Please let me know if I can ever be of assistance.'

She nodded. Geary put on his hat, and the gesture was mimicked like a wave at a football game.

Faith spoke as soon as the door was closed. 'The Texicano in the yard said something to me before he died.' Her mouth moved as she tried to remember what she'd heard. ' "Alma" or "al-may." '

'*Almeja?*' Amanda asked, giving the word an exotic sound.

Faith nodded. 'That's right. Do you know what it means?'

Sara opened her mouth to speak, but before she could get a word out, Amanda provided, 'It's Spanish slang for "money." It means "clams." Do you think they were looking for cash?'

Faith shook her head and shrugged at the same time. 'I don't know. They never really said. I mean, it makes sense. Los Texicanos means drugs. Drugs mean money. Mom worked in narcotics. Maybe they think she . . .' Faith glanced at Will. He could practically read her mind. After his investigation, a lot of people thought that Evelyn Mitchell was just the kind of cop who had stacks of cash lying around her house.

Sara took advantage of their silence. 'I should go.' She handed Faith the blood sugar monitor. 'You need to follow your schedule religiously. Stress is going to make it harder. Call your doctor and talk about your dosage, whatever adjustments you need to make, what signs you need to look for. Are you still seeing Dr. Wallace?' Faith nodded.

'I'll call her service on my way home and tell her what happened, but you need to be on the phone with her as soon as possible. This is a stressful time, but you have to stay on your routine. Understood?'

'Thank you.' Faith had never been easy with gratitude, but her words were more heartfelt than anything Will had ever heard come from her mouth.

Will asked Sara, 'Are you going to do a tox screen for Geary?'

She directed her words to Amanda. 'Faith works for you, not APD. They need a warrant to draw her blood and I'm guessing you don't want to go to the trouble.'

Amanda asked, 'Hypothetically what would a tox screen find?'

'That she wasn't intoxicated or impaired by any of the substances they test for. Do you want me to do a blood draw?'

'No, Dr. Linton. But I appreciate your help.'

She left without another word, or even a glance Will's way.

Amanda suggested, 'Why don't you go check on the merry widow?'

Will thought she meant Sara, then logic intervened. He walked to the back of the house to find Mrs. Levy, but not before seeing Amanda pull Faith into a tight hug. The gesture was shocking coming from a woman whose maternal instincts were more closely related to those of a dingo.

Will knew that Faith and Amanda shared a past that neither woman ever talked about or even acknowledged. While Evelyn Mitchell was blazing a trail for women in the Atlanta Police

76

Department, Amanda Wagner was doing the same in the GBI. They were contemporaries, about the same age, with the same ball-breaking attitudes. They had also been lifelong friends—Amanda had even dated Evelyn's brother-in-law, Faith's uncle—a detail Amanda had failed to mention to Will when she assigned him to investigate the narcotics squad that was headed by her old friend.

He found Mrs. Levy in the back bedroom, which seemed to have been turned into a catchall for whatever struck the old woman's fancy. There was a scrapbooking station, something Will only recognized because he had worked a shooting in the suburbs where a young mother had been murdered while she was pasting crinkle-cut photographs of a beach vacation onto colored construction paper. There was a pair of roller skates with four wheels. A tennis racket leaned against the corner. Various types of cameras were laid out on the daybed. Some were digital, but most were the old-fashioned kind that used film. He guessed from the red light over the closet door that she developed her own photographs.

Mrs. Levy was sitting in a wooden rocking chair by the window. She had Emma in her lap. Her apron was wrapped around the baby like a blanket. The little geese were reversed across the hem. Emma's eyes were closed as she sucked fiercely on the bottle in her mouth. The noise reminded Will of the baby in *The Simpsons*.

'Why don't you have a seat?' the old woman offered. 'Emma seems to be perking up just fine.'

Will sat on the bed, careful not to jostle the cameras. 'It's a good thing that you just happened to have a bottle for her.'

77

'It is, isn't it?' She smiled down at the baby. 'Poor lamb missed her nap with all this excitement.'

'Do you have a crib for her, too?'

She gave a raspy chuckle. 'I assume you've already looked in my bedroom.'

He hadn't been that bold, but Will took this as an opening. 'How often do you watch her?'

'Usually just a few times a week.'

'But lately?'

She winked at him. 'You're a smart one.'

He was more lucky than smart. It had struck him as odd that Mrs. Levy just happened to have a baby bottle lying around when Emma needed it. He asked, 'What's Evelyn been up to?'

'Do I look rude enough to pry into someone's business?'

'How can I answer that without insulting you?'

She laughed, but relented easily enough. 'Evelyn never said, but I'm assuming she had a gentleman friend.'

'For how long?'

'Three or four months?' She seemed to be asking herself a question. She nodded her answer. 'It was just after Emma was born. They started out slowly, maybe once a week or every two, but I'd say in the last ten days it's been more frequent. I stopped keeping a calendar when I retired, but Ev asked me to watch Emma three mornings in a row last week.'

'It was always in the morning?'

'Usually from around eleven to about two in the afternoon.'

Three hours seemed like a long enough time for an assignation. 'Did Faith know about him?'

78

Mrs. Levy shook her head. 'I'm certain Ev didn't want the kids to find out. They loved their father so much. As did she, mind you, but it's been ten years, at least. That's a long time to go without companionship.'

Will guessed she was speaking from experience. 'You said your husband's been dead for twenty years.'

'Yes, but I didn't like Mr. Levy very much and he didn't care for me at all.' She used her thumb to stroke Emma's cheek. 'Evelyn loved Bill. They had some bumps along the way, but it's different when you love them. They're gone and your life splinters in two. It takes an awful long time to put it back together.'

Will let himself think about Sara for just a second. The truth was that he never stopped thinking about her. She was like the news crawl that ran at the bottom of the television while his life, the main story, played on the screen. 'Do you know the gentleman's name?'

'Oh, no, dear. I never asked. But he drove a very nice Cadillac CTS-V. That's the sedan, not the coupe. Black on black and the stainless steel grill on the front. A very throaty V8. You could hear it blocks away.'

Will was momentarily too surprised to respond. 'Are you a car person?'

'Oh, not at all, but I looked it up on the Internet because I wanted to know how much he paid for it.'

Will waited her out.

'I'm guessing around seventy-five thousand dollars,' the old woman confided. 'Mr. Levy and I bought this house for less than half that.'

'Did Evelyn ever tell you his name?'

'She never acknowledged it. Despite what you men want to think, we ladies don't sit around talking about y'all all the time.'

Will allowed a smile. 'What did he look like?'

'Well, bald,' she said, as if this was to be expected. 'A bit paunchy around the middle. He wore jeans most of the time. His shirts were often wrinkled and he kept the sleeves rolled up, which I found rather perplexing because Evelyn always liked a sharply dressed man.'

'What age do you think he is?'

'Without the hair, it's hard to tell. I'd put him around Evelyn's age.'

'Early sixties.'

'Oh,' she seemed surprised. 'I thought Evelyn was in her forties, but I suppose that doesn't make sense with Faith being in her thirties. And the baby's not a baby anymore, is he?' She lowered her voice as if she was afraid someone would hear. 'I guess it's coming up on twenty years now, but that's not the kind of pregnancy you forget. There was that bit of a scandal when she started to show. Such a pity how folks behaved. We've all had our bit of fun now and then, but as I told Evelyn at the time, a woman can run faster with her skirt up than a man can with his pants down.'

Will hadn't considered Faith's teenage predicament beyond thinking it unusual she had kept the child, but it had probably rocked the neighborhood to have a pregnant fourteen-year-old in their refined midst. It was almost commonplace now, but back then, a girl in Faith's predicament was generally suddenly called away to tend a never-before-mentioned frail aunt or given

80

what was euphemistically called an appendectomy. A handful of less fortunate ones ended up in the children's home with kids like Will.

He asked, 'So, the man in the expensive car is in his early sixties?' She nodded. 'Did you ever see them being affectionate?'

'No, but Evelyn wasn't the showy type. She would get in the car with him and he would drive off.'

'No kiss on the cheek?'

'Not that I ever saw. Mind you, I never even met him. Evelyn would drop Emma off here, then go back to her house and wait.'

Will let that sink in. 'Did he ever go into her house?'

'Not that I could tell. I guess people do things differently now. In my day, a man would knock on your door and escort you to his car. There was none of this pulling up and beeping the horn.'

'Is that what he did—beep the horn?'

'No, son, that was just a figure of speech. I suppose Ev must've been looking out the window, because she always came out as soon as he pulled up.'

'Do you know where they went?'

'No, but like I said, they were usually gone for a couple'a–three hours, so I assumed they were seeing a movie or having lunch.'

That was a lot of movies. 'Did the man show up today?'

'No, and I didn't see anyone in the street, either. No cars, no nothing. The first I heard there was trouble was when the sirens came. Then I heard the gunshots, of course, one and then about a minute later one more. I know what gunfire sounds like. Mr. Levy was a hunter. Back then, all the policemen were. He used to make me go so I could cook for them.' She rolled her eyes. 'What a boring gasbag he was. Rest his soul.'

'Lucky man to have you.'

'Lucky for me he's not around anymore.' She stood with difficulty from the rocker, keeping the baby steady in her arms. The bottle was empty. She put it on the table and offered Emma to Will. 'Take her for a second, will you?'

He put Emma on his shoulder and patted her back. She gave an unusually rewarding burp.

Mrs. Levy narrowed her eyes. 'You've been around babies before.'

Will wasn't about to get into his life story. 'They're easy to talk to.'

She rested her hand on his arm before going to the closet. Will had been right. There was a darkroom set up in the small space. He stood in the doorway, careful not to block her light as she thumbed through a stack of five-by-seven photographs. Her hands had a slight tremor, but she seemed steady on her feet.

She explained, 'Mr. Levy never set much store by my hobbies, but he was called onto a crime scene one day and they asked if anyone knew a photographer. Twenty-five dollars they paid—just for taking pictures! The old bastard wasn't going to say no to that. So he called me and told me to bring my camera. When I didn't faint over the mess—this was a shotgun incident—they said I could do it again.' She nodded toward the bed. 'That Brownie Six-16 helped keep this roof over our heads.'

He knew she meant the box camera. It looked

worn but well loved.

'I moved into surveillance work later on. Mr. Levy had drunk himself off the job by then, and of course I'm a woman, so it took some time for them to understand I wasn't there for flirting and screwing.'

Will felt his face start to redden. 'Was this with the Atlanta Police Department?'

'Fifty-eight years!' She seemed as surprised as Will that she'd lasted that long. 'I may be a bag of bones now, but there was a time Geary and his ass-kissers would've snapped to instead of brushing me off like a speck of lint on their shiny trousers.' She picked through another pile of five-by-sevens. Will saw black-and-white shots of birds and various household pets, all taken from a vantage point that implied they were being spied upon rather than admired. 'This little so-and-so's been digging in my flower bed.' She showed Will a picture of a gray and white cat with dirt on its nose. The lighting was harsh in the black-and-white print. The only thing missing was a board over his chest with his name and inmate number.

'Here.' Finally, she found what she was looking for. 'This is him. Evelyn's gentleman friend.'

Will looked over her hunched shoulder. The photo was grainy, obviously taken from behind the blinds covering the front window. The lens pressed open thin, plastic slats. A tall, older man leaned against a black Cadillac. His palms rested on the hood, forearms twisted out. The car was parked in the street, its front tires turned against the curb. Will parked his car the same way. Atlanta was a city of hills, resting on the piedmont of the Appalachian Mountains. If you drove a car with a

83

manual transmission, you always banked the wheels against the curb to keep the car from rolling.

'What is it?' Faith stood in the doorway. Will passed her the baby, but she seemed more concerned with the photograph. 'Did you see something?'

'I was showing him Snippers.' Mrs. Levy had somehow pulled a sleight of hand. The photo of the man was gone and in its place was the flower-garden-digging cat.

Emma shifted in Faith's arms, obviously picking up on her mother's troubled mood. Faith kissed her on the cheek with several quick smacks and made faces until the baby smiled. Will knew Faith was putting on a show. Tears filled her eyes. She hugged the infant tightly to her chest.

Mrs. Levy spoke. 'Evelyn's a tough old bird. They won't break her.'

Faith swayed back and forth with the baby the way mothers automatically do. 'You didn't hear anything?'

'Oh, darlin', you know if I'd'a heard something, I would've been over there with my hogleg.' Will recognized the slang for a large-caliber handgun. 'Ev's going to come out of this just fine. She always lands on her feet. You can take that to the bank and cash it.'

'I just—' Faith's voice caught. 'If I'd gotten here sooner, or—' She shook her head. 'Why did this happen? You know Mama's not mixed up in anything bad. Why would someone take her?'

'Sometimes there's no rhyme or reason to the stupid things people get up to.' The old woman's shoulders twisted in a slight shrug. 'All I know is that you're gonna eat yourself alive if you keep going down that road asking what if I did this or what if I did that.' She pressed the back of her fingers to Faith's cheek. 'Trust in the Lord to look over her. "Lean not into thine own understanding." '

Faith nodded, solemn, though Will had never known her to be religious. 'Thank you.'

Amanda's heels thudded down the carpeted hallway. 'I can't stall them anymore,' she told Faith. 'There's a cruiser outside waiting to take you to the station. Try to shut up and do what your lawyer says.'

'The least I can do is watch the baby,' Mrs. Levy offered. 'You don't need to take her down to that filthy station, and Jeremy wouldn't know which end the diaper goes on.'

Faith obviously wanted to take her up on the offer, but she hedged, 'I don't know how long I'll be.'

'You know I'm a night owl. It's no bother.'

'Thank you.' Faith reluctantly handed the baby to the old woman. She smoothed down Emma's crop of fine brown hair and kissed the top of her head. Her lips stayed there for a few seconds more, then she left without another word.

As soon as the front door closed, Amanda cut to the chase. 'What?'

Mrs. Levy pulled the photograph from under her apron.

'Evelyn had a frequent visitor,' Will explained. Mrs. Levy had a good memory: The man was bald. His jeans were baggy. His shirt was wrinkled, the sleeves rolled up. She'd failed to mention a more important detail, which was that he was Hispanic.

The tattoo on his arm was blurry, but Will easily recognized the symbol on his forearm that identified him as Los Texicanos.

Amanda folded the picture in half before sticking it into the pocket of her suit jacket. She asked Mrs. Levy, 'Have the uniforms talked to you yet?'

'I'm sure they'll get around to the little old ladies eventually.'

'I assume you'll be as cooperative as usual.'

She smiled. 'I'm not sure what I can tell them, but I'll go ahead and lay out some fresh cookies in case they come calling.'

Amanda chuckled. 'Careful, Roz.' She motioned for Will to follow her as she left the room.

Will reached into his wallet and pulled out one of his cards for Mrs. Levy. 'This has all my numbers. Call me if you remember anything or if you need help with the baby.'

'Thank you, sonny.' Her voice had lost some of its old lady kindness, but she tucked the card into her apron anyway.

Amanda was halfway up the hall by the time Will joined her. She didn't say anything about the photograph, or Faith's condition, or the pissing contest she'd had with Geary. Instead, she started giving him orders. 'I need you to review all of your case files from the investigation.' She didn't have to tell him which investigation she meant. 'Comb through every witness statement, every CI report, every jailhouse snitch's last hurrah. I don't care how small it is. I want to know about it.' Amanda stopped. He knew she was thinking about his reading issues.

He kept his voice steady. 'It's not a problem.'

She wouldn't let him off that easy. 'Pull up your panties, Will. If you need help, speak up now so I can deal with it.'

'Do you want me to start now? The boxes are at my house.'

'No. We've got an errand to run first.' She stood in the foyer, her hands on her hips. She was a trim woman, and Will often forgot how short she was until he saw her straining her neck to look up at him. 'I managed to pry some information loose while Geary was throwing his tantrum. The Texicano in the backyard has helpfully identified himself as Ricardo vis-à-vis the large tattoo on his back. We don't have a full ID on him yet. He's mid-twenties, approximately five-nine, and one hundred seventy pounds. The Asian in the bedroom is around forty years of age, slightly shorter and thinner than his Hispanic friend. I would guess he's not from this part of town. He might've been brought in just for this.'

Will remembered, 'Faith said he had a southern drawl.'

'That should help narrow things down.'

'He was also wearing a loud Hawaiian shirt. That's not very gangsterish.'

'We'll add that to his list of crimes.' She glanced down the hallway, then looked back at Will. 'Now, the Asian in the laundry room is an odd story, too, which we know courtesy of the wallet he carried in his back pocket. Hironobu Kwon, age nineteen. He's a freshman at Georgia State. He's also the son of a local schoolteacher, Miriam Kwon.'

'He's not affiliated?'

'Not that we can find. APD swooped up Mama Kwon before we could get to her. We'll have to find her tomorrow morning to see what she knows.' She pointed her finger at Will. 'Softly, softly. We're still not officially on the case. It's just you and me until I can find a way in.'

He said, 'Faith seems to think the Texicanos were looking for something.' Will tried to gauge Amanda's expression. Usually it hovered somewhere between amused and annoyed, but now it was completely blank. 'Ricardo was beaten to a pulp. He had a gun pointed at his head. He wasn't looking for anything except to save his life. It's the Asians we should be talking to first.'

'That seems entirely logical.'

'It points to a larger problem,' he continued. 'The Texicanos I can understand, but what would the Asians want with Evelyn? What's their play?'

'That's the million-dollar question.'

He put a finer point on it. 'Evelyn headed the drug squad. Los Texicanos control the drug trade in Atlanta. They have for the last twenty years.'

'They certainly have.'

Will felt the familiar sting of his head hitting a brick wall. This was the same runaround Amanda always gave him when she had information that she wasn't going to share. Somehow, this time was worse, because she wasn't just screwing with his head, she was covering for her old friend.

He tried, 'You said that the guy in the Hawaiian shirt was probably brought in for 'this.' What's "this"? Kidnapping? Finding whatever Evelyn had hidden in her house?'

'I don't think anyone is finding what they're looking for today.' She paused to let her meaning sink in. 'Charlie's helping out the locals with the crime scene, but they're not as weak to his charms as I'd like. His access has been very limited and closely supervised. They say they'll share lab results. I'm iffy on their ME.'

The Fulton County medical examiner. 'Has he shown up?'

'He's still combing through that apartment fire in People's Town.' Budget cuts had left the medical examiner's office devastated. If there was more than one serious crime happening within the city limits, that usually meant the detectives were in for a long wait. 'I'd love to get Pete on this.'

She was referring to the GBI's medical examiner. Will asked, 'Can't he make some phone calls?'

'Unlikely,' she admitted. 'Pete's not exactly covered up in friends. You know how strange he is. He makes you look normal. What about Sara?'

'She'll keep her mouth shut.'

'I'm aware of that, Will. I saw your do-si-do in the street. I meant do you think she knows anyone in the ME's office?'

Will shrugged.

'Ask her,' Amanda ordered.

Will doubted Sara would welcome the call, but he nodded his agreement anyway. 'What about Evelyn's credit card statements, phone records?'

'I've ordered them pulled.'

'Does she have GPS in her car? On her phones?'

She didn't really answer him. 'We're going through some backdoor channels. As I said, this isn't exactly aboveboard.'

'But what you told Geary is right. We've got original jurisdiction over drug cases.'

'Just because Evelyn was in charge of the narcotics division doesn't mean this is drug-related. From what I've gathered, they've found no indication of drugs in the house or on any of the dead men.'

'And Ricardo, the dead Texicano, of the drug-related Texicanos?'

'Odd coincidence.'

'How about the living, breathing, drug-related Texicano who drives a black Cadillac that Evelyn Mitchell has no qualms about getting into and going for a ride?'

She feigned surprise. 'You think he's affiliated?'

'I saw the tattoo in the photograph. Evelyn's been seeing a Texicano for at least four months.' Will tried to moderate his tone. 'He's older. He must be higher up in the organization. Mrs. Levy says the visits have stepped up over the last ten days. They've been going somewhere together in his car, usually out by eleven and back by two.'

Again, Amanda ignored his point and made her own. 'You busted six detectives on Evelyn's squad. Two of them were paroled for good behavior last year. Both transferred out of state—one to California, one to Tennessee, which is where they were this afternoon when Evelyn was taken. Two are in medium security at Valdosta State, four years away from release and no good behavior in sight. One is dead—drug overdose, which is what I call the thinking man's karma. The last one is waiting to get his dance card punched at D&C.'

The Georgia Diagnostic and Classification Prison. Death row. Will reluctantly asked, 'Who'd he kill?'

'A guard and an inmate. Strangled a convicted rapist with a towel—no loss there—but then he beat the guard to death with his bare hands.

90

Claimed it was self-defense.'

'Against the guard?'

'You sound like the prosecutor on his case.'

Will tried again. 'And Evelyn?'

'What about her?'

'I investigated her, too.'

'You did.'

'We're not going to talk about the elephant in the room?'

'Elephant? For chrissakes, Will, we've got the entire goddamn *circus* in here.' She opened the front door. The sun cut through the dark house like a knife.

Amanda slipped on her sunglasses as they walked across the lawn toward the crime scene. A pair of uniformed cops were making their way toward Mrs. Levy's house. They each glowered at Will and gave Amanda a curt nod.

She mumbled to Will, 'About time they got going,' as if she hadn't been the cause of the delay.

He waited until the men started banging on the front door. 'I guess you know Mrs. Levy from your days with the APD?'

'GBI. I investigated her for murdering her husband.' Amanda seemed to enjoy Will's horrified expression. 'Never could prove it, but I'm sure she poisoned him.'

'Cookies?' he guessed.

'That was my working theory.' An appreciative smile curved her lips as she picked her way across the grass. 'Roz is a wily old coot. Seen more crime scenes than all of us rolled together, and I'm sure she took notes the entire time. I wouldn't trust half of what she told you. Remember—the Devil can cite Scripture for his purpose.'

91

Amanda had a point, or at least Shakespeare did. Still, Will reminded her, 'Mrs. Levy's the one who told me about the Texicano visiting Evelyn. She took the picture of him.'

'She did, didn't she?'

Will felt the question hit him like a slap to the back of his head. Considering Mrs. Levy's artistic talent lent itself more to unflattering mugshots of household pets, it seemed strange that she just happened to have handy a photograph of the Texicano standing beside his black Cadillac. She was a sharp old lady. She'd been spying for a reason. 'We should go back and talk to her.'

'Do you really think she's going to tell us anything useful?'

Will silently conceded the point. Mrs. Levy seemed to like her games, and with Evelyn missing, they didn't really have time to play them. 'Does Evelyn know she killed her husband?'

'Of course she does.'

'And she still let her watch Emma?'

They had reached Faith's Mini. Amanda cupped her hands to the glass and peered inside. 'She killed a sixty-four-year-old abusive alcoholic, not a four-month-old baby.'

Will guessed somewhere in the world this kind of logic made sense.

Amanda headed toward the house. Charlie Reed was in the carport talking to a bunch of other crime scene unit techs. Some were smoking. One was leaning against a tan Malibu that was parked nose-out to Faith's Mini. They were all dressed in white Tyvek clean suits that made them look like various sizes of soiled marshmallows. Charlie's handlebar mustache was the only thing that distinguished him from the clean-shaven men. He saw Amanda and broke away from the group.

She said, 'Take me through it, Charlie.'

Charlie glanced back at a portly, dark man whose odd build made the Tyvek suit unflatteringly tight in all the critical areas. The man took a last puff on his cigarette and handed it to one of his co-workers. He introduced himself to Amanda in a clipped, British-sounding accent. 'Dr. Wagner, I am Dr. Ahbidi Mittal.'

She indicated Will. 'This is Dr. Trent, my associate.'

Will shook the man's hand, trying not to cringe at the effortless way Amanda rolled out a degree they both knew he'd obtained from a dubious online school.

Mittal offered, 'As a courtesy, I'm prepared to show you around the crime scene.'

Amanda gave a cutting glance to Charlie, as if he had any say in the matter.

'Thank you,' Will said, because he knew no one else would.

Mittal handed them each a pair of white booties for their shoes. Amanda grabbed Will's arm to steady herself as she slipped off her heels and covered her stocking feet. Will was left to hop around on his own. Even without his shoes, his feet were too big, and he ended up looking like Mrs. Levy with her heels hanging off the back of her slippers.

'Shall we start in here?' Mittal didn't wait for them to acknowledge his invitation. He led them around the back of the Malibu and into the house through the open kitchen door. Instinctively, Will ducked his head as he walked into the low-ceilinged room. Charlie bumped into him and mumbled an apology. The kitchen was small for four people, horseshoe shaped, with the open end facing the laundry room. Will caught the distinct odor of rusty iron that blood gave off when it congealed.

Faith was right—the intruders had been looking for something. The house was a mess. Silverware was scattered on the floor. Drawers had been thrown around. Holes were knocked in the walls. A cell phone and an older-looking BlackBerry were crushed on the floor. The wall phone had been smashed off the hook. Except for the black fingerprint powder and the yellow plastic markers the forensics team had used, nothing had been altered from what Faith said she'd first seen when she entered the house. Even the dead body was still in the laundry room. Faith must have been terrified, not knowing what was coming around the corner, terrified that her mother was injured—or worse.

Will should have been here. He should've been the kind of partner Faith knew she could call no matter what.

Mittal said, 'I've yet to write my report, but I am prepared to share my working theory.'

Amanda rolled her hand in a circle to move things along. 'Tell me what you've got.'

Mittal's lips pursed at the commanding tone. 'I assume that Captain Mitchell was preparing lunch when the crime commenced.' There were bags of cold cuts on the counter beside a knife and cutting board where Evelyn had obviously been slicing tomatoes. An empty Wonder bread sleeve was wadded up in the sink. The toaster had popped up long ago. Four slices of bread. Evelyn had probably known Faith would need lunch when she got home.

It was a normal enough scene, even pleasant, but for the fact that every item on the counter was spattered or smeared with blood. The toaster, the bread, the cutting board. More blood had dripped down to the floor and pooled onto the tiles. Two sets of red shoe prints crisscrossed the white porcelain, one small, one large; there had been a struggle.

Mittal continued, 'Captain Mitchell was startled by a noise, possibly the sliding glass door breaking, which likely made her cut her finger with the knife she was using to slice the tomatoes.'

Amanda noted, 'That's a lot of blood for a kitchen accident.'

Mittal obviously didn't want any editorial comments. He paused again before continuing, 'The infant, Emma, would've been here.' He pointed to the counter space beside the fridge, opposite the area where Evelyn had been preparing lunch. 'We found a small drop of blood on the counter here.' He pointed to the spot beside an older model CD player. 'There's a blood trail to and from the shed, so Captain Mitchell was most likely bleeding when she left the kitchen. Her handprint on the door supports this.'

Amanda nodded. 'She hears a noise, so she hides the baby to keep her safe, then comes back in with her S&W.'

Charlie's words came out in a rush, as if he could no longer hold his tongue. 'She must've wrapped a paper towel around the cut, but it bled through quickly. There's blood on the kitchen door and the wooden handle of the S&W.'

Will asked, 'What about the car seat?'

'It's clean. She must've carried it with her uninjured hand. We've got a blood trail back and forth across the carport where she carried Emma to the shed. It's Evelyn's blood. Ahbidi's people already typed it, so we can kinda puzzle it out from that.' He glanced up at Mittal. 'Sorry, Ahbi. I hope I'm not stepping on your toes.'

Mittal made an expansive gesture with his hands, indicating Charlie should continue.

Will knew that this was Charlie's favorite part of the job. There was a swagger to his walk as he went to the open doorway and clasped his hands together near his face as if he held a gun. 'Evelyn comes back into the house. Pivots, sees bad guy number one waiting in the laundry room and shoots him in the head. The force spun him around like a pinwheel. That's the exit wound you see at the back of his head.' Charlie turned back around, hands raised again in a classic Charlie's Angel pose, which was the best way to make sure you got shot in the chest. 'Then bad guy number two comes, probably from over there.' He pointed to the pass-through between the kitchen and dining room. 'There's a struggle. Evelyn loses her gun. See there?'

Will followed his pointing finger to a plastic marker on the floor. Now that Charlie had put the suggestion in his head, he could see the faint, bloody outline of a handgun.

'Evelyn grabs the knife off the counter. Her blood is on the handle, but it's not on the blade.'

Amanda interrupted, 'It's not just her blood on the knife?'

'No. According to her personnel file, Evelyn is

96

typed as O-positive. We've got B-negative coating the blade and here by the fridge.'

They all looked down at a dozen large, round drops of blood on the floor.

Mittal provided, 'It's a passive spatter. No arteries were compromised or there would be a spray pattern. All the samples were sent to the lab for DNA analysis. I imagine we're looking at a week for results.'

A smile played at Amanda's lips as she stared at the blood. 'Good girl, Ev.' There was a sound of triumph in her voice. 'Any of the dead guys B-negative?'

Charlie glanced at Mittal again. The man nodded his acquiescence. 'The Asian in the ugly shirt was O-positive, which is a fairly common type across races. It's Evelyn's type. It's my type. The other, the guy we're calling Ricardo because of his tattoo, was B-negative, but here's the kicker: he doesn't have any stab wounds. I mean, he bled at some point. He was obviously tortured. But the blood we're looking at here is a larger volume than anything—'

Amanda interrupted, 'So, we've got someone out there with a stab wound whose blood type is B-negative. Is that rare?'

'Less than two percent of the U.S. Caucasian population is B-negative,' Charlie told them. 'It's a quarter of that for Asians, and around one percent for Hispanics. Bottom line, it's a very rare blood type, which makes it probable that our dead B-negative Ricardo is genetically related to our missing and wounded B-negative.'

'So, we've got a wounded man out there, blood type B-negative.'

Charlie was ahead of her for once. 'I already put a be-on-the-lookout at all hospitals within a hundred miles for a stab wound of any kind—male, female, white, black, orange. We've already had three rule-outs from domestics just in the last half hour. More people get stabbed than I'd realized.'

Mittal made sure Charlie was finished, then pointed to the blood smeared across the floor. 'These shoe prints are conducive to a struggle between a small woman and a medium-sized man, probably around seventy kilos. We can tell from the variation of light to dark in the print that there is a medial roll to the foot, or supination.'

Amanda stopped the lesson. 'Take me back to the stab wound. Are we talking fatal?'

Mittal shrugged. 'The medical examiner's office would have to give you their opinion. As was stated earlier, there's no blood spray on the walls or ceiling, from which we can posit that none of the arteries were damaged. This spatter, then, could perhaps be the result of a head wound, where one would find a fair amount of blood with minimal damage.' He looked at Charlie. 'Do you concur?'

Charlie nodded, but added, 'A gut wound might bleed like this. I'm not sure how long you could last with that. If you trust the movies, not long. If a lung was punctured, then he'd have an hour, tops, before he suffocated. There's absolutely no arterial spray, so it's a seeping wound. I don't disagree with Dr. Mittal about the possibility of a head wound. . . .' He shrugged, then disagreed anyway. 'The blade was coated tip to hilt, which might indicate that the knife plunged into the body.' He saw the frown on Mittal's face and backpedaled. 'Then again, it could be that the victim grabbed the

98

knife, which cut his hand and coated the blade through transfer.' He showed his hand, palm up. 'In which case we'd have a B-negative out there with a wounded hand as well.'

Amanda had never embraced the equivocations of crime scene science. She tried to sum it up in absolutes. 'So, bad guy B-negative struggles with Evelyn. Then I suppose we bring in the second man, the Asian in the Hawaiian shirt, who later ended up dead in the bedroom. They managed to subdue Evelyn and take away her gun. And then there's a third man, Ricardo, who was a hostage at one point, and then became a shooter, and then, thanks to Agent Mitchell's quick action, became dead before he could injure anyone.' She turned to Will. 'My money is on Ricardo being hooked up in all of this, torture or not. He pretended to be a hostage to try to leverage Faith.'

Mittal looked uncomfortable with the finality in her tone. 'That is an interpretation.'

Charlie tried to smooth things over. 'There's always the chance that—'

There was a sound similar to the rush of a tropical waterfall. Mittal unzipped his clean suit and felt around in his pants pockets. He pulled out his cell phone and said, 'If you will excuse me,' before heading back into the garage.

Amanda turned to Charlie. 'Brass tacks?'

'They're not giving me full access, but there's no reason for me to disagree with what Ahbi's said so far.'

'And?'

'I don't want to sound racist,' Charlie began, 'but you don't often see Mexicans and Asians working together. Especially Los Texicanos.'

'Younger kids aren't as hung up on that sort of thing,' Will offered, wondering if that could be called progress.

Amanda didn't acknowledge either comment. 'What else?'

'The list by the phone.' Charlie pointed to a piece of yellow paper with a bunch of numbers and names. 'I took the liberty to call the number for Zeke. I left a message for him to get in touch with you.'

Amanda looked at her watch. 'What about the rest of house? Did forensics find anything?'

'Not that they've told me. Ahbi's not being overtly rude, but he's not going out of his way to volunteer anything, either.' Charlie paused before adding, 'It seems obvious whatever the bad guys were looking for wasn't found, otherwise they would've cleared out the minute Faith pulled up.'

'And we'd be planning Evelyn's funeral.' Amanda didn't dwell on the fact. 'Whatever they were searching for—what would you guess the size of this mysterious item to be?'

'No telling,' Charlie admitted. 'Obviously, they were looking everywhere—drawers, closets, cushions. I think they got angrier as they went through the house and started destroying on top of searching. They ripped open the beds, broke the baby's toys. There's a lot of fury in there.'

'How many searchers?'

'I'm sorry, Dr. Wagner.' Mittal was back. He tucked his phone into his pocket but left his white suit gaping open. 'That was the ME. He's been delayed by the discovery of another body at the apartment fire. What was your question?'

Charlie answered for her, perhaps sensing that

Amanda's tone might get them thrown out of the house. 'She was asking how many searchers you thought there were.'

Mittal nodded. 'An educated guess would be three to four men.'

Will saw the disgusted look on Amanda's face. It had to be more than three, otherwise all the suspects were dead and Evelyn Mitchell had kidnapped herself.

Mittal continued, 'They did not wear gloves. Perhaps they thought Captain Mitchell would relent without a struggle.' Amanda snorted a laugh and Mittal gave another one of his patented pauses. 'There are fingerprints on most surfaces, which of course we will share with the GBI.'

Charlie said, 'I've already called the lab. We've got two techs coming in to digitize them and put them in the database. From there it's only a matter of time before we know if they're in the system.'

Amanda indicated the kitchen. 'Once Evelyn was neutralized, they would've started their search in here. They were looking through drawers, so it's something that would fit in a drawer.' She looked up at Charlie, then Mittal. 'Any tire tracks? Footprints?'

'Nothing of consequence.' Mittal walked her over to the kitchen window and started pointing out things in the backyard that had been checked. Will studied the broken CDs on the floor. Beatles. Sinatra. No AC/DC. The player was white plastic, smudged with black fingerprint powder. Will used his thumbnail to press the eject button. The tray was empty.

Amanda's voice came back to him. 'Where did they keep Evelyn while they were tearing up the

101

house?'

Mittal started toward the living room. Will took up the rear as Charlie and Amanda followed the doctor through the path of debris. The setup was similar to Mrs. Levy's house, minus the sunken aspect of the living room. Opposite the couch and a wingback chair were a wall of bookshelves and a small plasma-screen television with a foot-sized crack in the center. Most of the books were strewn across the floor. The couch and chairs had been gutted, their frames broken. There was a stereo on the shelf by the TV, the old record-playing kind, but the speakers were busted and the arm had been wrenched off the turntable. A small pile of vinyl records had obviously met the hard edge of someone's heel.

There was a Thonet-style bentwood chair against the wall, the only thing in the room that seemed to have remained intact. The seat was thatched. The legs were scuffed. Mittal pointed to where chunks of veneer had been ripped off. 'It appears that duct tape was used. I found adhesive where Captain Mitchell's feet would've been.' He lifted up the chair and moved it away from the wall. A yellow plastic number marker had been placed beside a dark stain. 'One can surmise from the blood drops on the carpet that Captain Mitchell's hands were hanging down. The cut to her finger was still bleeding, but not with any significance. Perhaps my colleague is correct in assuming that she wrapped the wound in a paper towel.'

Amanda leaned down to look at the bloodstain, but Will was more interested in the chair. Evelyn's hands had been tied behind her back. He used his foot to tilt the chair forward so he could see the bottom of the thatched seat. There was a mark underneath, an arrowhead, drawn in blood.

Will looked out into the room, trying to figure out what the arrow was pointing to. The couch directly across from the chair was gutted, as was the wingback chair to the side. The hardwood floors meant nothing could be hidden under a carpet. Was Evelyn pointing to something in the backyard?

He heard a hiss of air through teeth. Will glanced up to find Amanda giving him such a searing look that he dropped the chair back into place without his brain being aware of what his foot was doing. She gave a slight shake of her head, indicating he should keep his mouth shut about the find. Will glanced at Charlie. They had all three seen the arrow under the chair while Mittal, oblivious, waxed poetic on the efficacy of fingerprinting on porous versus nonporous surfaces.

Charlie opened his mouth to speak, but Amanda talked over him. 'Dr. Mittal, in your opinion, was the glass door broken with a found object, such as a rock or lawn ornament?' She glared at Charlie, and Will thought if she was capable of shooting lasers from her eyes, they would've sealed Charlie's mouth shut. 'I'm just wondering how well this attack was planned. Did they bring something to break the glass? Did they surround the house? If so, did they know the layout ahead of time?'

Mittal frowned, because these were questions none of them were capable of answering. 'Dr. Wagner, these are not scenarios that can be forensically evaluated.'

'Well, let's just toss it around and see what sticks. Was a brick used to break the glass?'

Charlie started shaking his head. Will recognized the internal conflict. Like it or not, this was Mittal's crime scene, and there was evidence under the chair—possibly important evidence—that the man had missed. Charlie was obviously torn. As with most things that had to do with Amanda, there was the right thing to do and then there was the thing that she was ordering him to do. Each decision had its consequence.

Mittal was shaking his head, too, but only because Amanda wasn't making sense. 'Dr. Wagner, we have searched every inch of this crime scene, and I am telling you we have not found any more items of substance than what I have already detailed.'

Will knew for a fact they hadn't checked every inch. He asked, 'Has anyone checked the Malibu?'

That took Charlie's mind off his troubles. His brow furrowed. Will had made the same mistake with Faith's Mini. All of the violence had taken place inside the house, but the cars were still part of the crime scene.

Amanda was the first to move. She had made her way out to the carport and opened the driver's side door of the Malibu before anyone thought to ask her what she was doing.

Mittal said, 'Please, we've not yet processed—'

She gave him a withering look. 'Did you think to check the trunk?'

His stunned silence was enough of an answer. Amanda popped the trunk. Will was standing just inside the kitchen doorway, which gave him a raised view of the scene. There were several plastic

104

grocery bags in the trunk, their contents flattened down by the dead body on top of them. As in the kitchen, blood coated everything—soaking into the cereal box, dripping down the plastic wrap around the hamburger buns. The dead man was a big guy. His body was folded almost in two where he'd been bent to fit into the space. A deep gash in his bald head showed splintered bone and bits of brain. His jeans were wrinkled. His shirtsleeves were rolled up. There was a Los Texicanos tattoo on his forearm.

Evelyn's gentleman friend.

CHAPTER FOUR

The Georgia Diagnostic and Classification Prison was located in Jackson, about an hour south of Atlanta. The drive was usually a quick shot down I-75, but the Atlanta Motor Speedway was having some kind of exhibition event that slowed traffic to a crawl. Undeterred, Amanda kept hopping on and off the shoulder, jerking the wheel quickly to pass groups of sluggish cars. The SUV's tires made a strumming sound as they grazed the rumble strips meant to deter drivers from leaving the roadway. Between the noise and the vibration, Will found himself fighting an unexpected wave of motion sickness.

Finally, they made it through the worst of the traffic. At the speedway exit, Amanda took one last dash onto the shoulder, then popped the SUV back onto the road. The tires skipped. The chassis shook. Will rolled down the window for some fresh air to help settle his stomach. The wind slapped his face so hard that he felt his skin ripple.

Amanda pressed the button to roll the window back up, giving him the look she reserved for stupid people and children. They were going over a hundred miles an hour. Will was lucky he hadn't been sucked out the window.

She let out a long sigh as she stared back at the road. One hand rested in her lap, while the other was firmly wrapped around the steering wheel. She was wearing her usual power suit: a bright blue skirt and matching jacket with a light-colored blouse underneath. Her high-heel shoes exactly matched the color of her suit. Her fingernails were trim but manicured. Her hair was its usual helmet of salt-and-pepper gray. Most days, Amanda seemed to have more energy than all the men on her team. Now, she looked tired, and Will could see the worry lines around her eyes were more pronounced.

She said, 'Tell me about Spivey.'

Will tried to click his brain back over to his old case against Captain Evelyn Mitchell's team. Boyd Spivey was the former lead detective on the narcotics squad who was currently biding his time on death row. Will had talked to the man only once before Spivey's lawyers advised him to keep his mouth shut. 'I don't find it hard to believe he beat someone to death with his fists. He was a big guy, taller than me, carried about fifty more pounds, all of it muscle.'

'Gym rat?'

'I'd guess steroids gave him a boost.'

'How did that work for him?'

'They made him uncontrollably angry,' Will

106

recalled. 'He's not as smart as he thinks, but I wasn't able to get him to confess, so maybe I'm not either.'

'You still sent him to prison.'

'He sent himself to prison. His house in the city was paid for. His house at the lake was paid for. All three of his kids were in private school. His wife worked ten hours a week and drove a top-of-the-line Mercedes. His mistress drove a BMW. He kept his brand new Porsche 911 parked in her driveway.'

'Men and their cars,' she mumbled. 'He doesn't sound very smart to me.'

'He didn't think anyone would ask questions.'

'Generally, they don't.'

'Spivey was good at keeping his mouth shut.'

'As I recall, all of them were.'

She was right. In a corruption case, the usual strategy was to find the weakest member and persuade him or her to turn on his or her fellow conspirators in exchange for a lighter sentence. The six detectives belonging to Evelyn Mitchell's narcotics squad had proven immune to this strategy. None of them would turn on the other, and all of them routinely insisted that Captain Mitchell had nothing to do with their alleged crimes. They went out of their way to protect their boss. It was both admirable and incredibly frustrating.

Will said, 'Spivey worked on Evelyn's squad for twelve years—longer than any of them.'

'She trusted him.'

'Yes,' Will agreed. 'Two peas in a pod.'

Amanda cut him a sharp look. 'Careful.'

Will felt his jaw tighten so hard that the bone

107

ached. He didn't see how ignoring the most important part of this case was going to get them anywhere. Amanda knew as well as Will that her friend was guilty as hell. Evelyn hadn't lived large, but like Spivey, she'd been stupid in her own way.

Faith's father had been an insurance broker, solidly middle class with the usual kinds of debts that people had: car payments, mortgage, credit cards. Yet, during Will's investigation, he'd found an out-of-state bank account in Bill Mitchell's name. At the time, the man had been dead for six years. Though the account balance always hovered around ten thousand dollars, the activity showed monthly deposits since his death that totaled up to almost sixty thousand dollars. It was clearly a shell account, the kind of thing prosecutors called a smoking gun. With Bill dead, Evelyn was the only signatory. Money was taken out and deposited with her ATM card at an Atlanta branch of the bank. Her dead husband wasn't the one who was keeping the activities spread apart and the deposits shy of the limit that would throw up a red flag at Homeland Security.

As far as Will knew, Evelyn Mitchell had never been asked about the account. He'd figured it would come out during her trial, but her trial had never happened. There had been a press conference announcing her retirement, and that was the end of the story.

Until now.

Amanda flipped down the visor to block the sun. Clipped to the underside were a couple of yellow claim tickets that looked like they were from a dry cleaner. The sun wasn't doing her any favors. She didn't look tired anymore. She looked haggard.

She said, 'Something's bothering you.'

He resisted uttering the biggest 'duh' ever vocalized in the history of the world.

'Not that,' she said, as if she could read his mind. 'Faith didn't call you for help because she knew that she was going to do the wrong thing.'

Will looked out the window.

'You would've made her wait for backup.'

He hated the relief her words brought.

'She's always been headstrong.'

He felt the need to say, 'She didn't do the wrong thing.'

'That's my boy.'

Will watched the trees along the highway blend into a sea of green. 'Do you think there's going to be a ransom?'

'I hope so.' They both knew that a ransom pointed to a living hostage, or at least the opportunity to demand proof of life.

He said, 'This feels personal.'

'How so?'

He shook his head. 'The way the house was torn up. There's mad, and then there's furious.'

'I don't imagine the old girl sat by quietly while they performed their search.'

'Probably not.' Evelyn Mitchell was no Amanda Wagner, but Will could easily see her taunting the men who were tearing up her house. You didn't get to be one of the first female captains on the Atlanta police force by being sweet. 'They were obviously looking for money.'

'Why do you say that?'

'Clams—the last word Ricardo said to Faith before he died. You said it's slang for money. Ergo, they were looking for money.'

109

'In the silverware drawer?'

Another good point. Cash was nice, but it was cumbersome. A pile worth kidnapping an ex-Atlanta police captain for would fill several silverware drawers.

He said, 'The arrow was pointing into the backyard.'

'What arrow?'

Will suppressed a groan. She wasn't usually this obvious. 'The arrow drawn in Evelyn's blood underneath the chair she was duct-taped to. I know you saw it. You hissed at me like an air compressor.'

'You really should work on your metaphors.' She was silent for a beat, probably considering the most circuitous route to take him to nowhere. 'You think Evelyn has buried treasure in her backyard?'

He had to admit this was unlikely, especially considering the Mitchell backyard was on full display to the rest of the neighbors, most of whom were retired and seemed to have ample time to spy. Besides, Will couldn't picture Faith's mother out with a shovel and a flashlight in the middle of the night. Then again, it wasn't like she could put it in the bank.

'Safe deposit box,' Will tried. 'Maybe they were looking for a key.'

'Evelyn would have to go to the bank and sign in to get access. They'd compare her signature, ask for her ID. Our kidnapper had to know her picture would be on every television station the minute he took her.'

Will silently conceded the point. Besides, the same rule applied. A large amount of cash took up space. Diamonds and gold were more for

Hollywood movies. In real life, stolen jewels fetched pennies on the dollar.

She asked, 'What about the crime scene? Do you think Charlie got it right?'

Will went on the defense. 'Mittal did most of the talking.'

'Okay, you've covered Charlie's ass. Now answer my question.'

'The Los Texicanos in the trunk of the Malibu, Evelyn's gentleman friend. He throws it all out.'

She nodded. 'He wasn't stabbed. He died from a shot to the head, plus, he's B-positive. That still leaves us with our B-negative out there with a nasty wound.'

'That's not what I'm talking about.' Will resisted the urge to add, 'and you know it.' Amanda wasn't just tying his hands behind his back. She was blindfolding him and sending him toward the edge of a cliff. Her refusal to talk about or even acknowledge Evelyn Mitchell's sordid past wasn't going to help Faith and it sure as hell wasn't going to get her mother back in one piece. Evelyn had worked in narcotics. She was obviously in contact, almost daily, with a higher-up in Los Texicanos, the gang that ran the drug trade in and out of Atlanta. They should be back in the city talking to the gang units and putting together the last few weeks of Evelyn's life, not making a fool's errand to visit a guy who had nothing to lose and a history of stubborn silence.

'Come on, Dr. Trent,' Amanda chided. 'Don't make me pull teeth.'

Will let his ego get in the way for a few more seconds before saying, 'Evelyn's gentleman friend. His wallet was missing. He didn't have any ID or

111

money on him. The only thing in his pockets was the key to Evelyn's Malibu. She must've given it to him.'

'Keep going.'

'She was making lunch for two people. There were four slices of bread in the toaster. Faith was late. Evelyn didn't know what time she'd be home, but she would assume Faith would call when she was on her way. There were groceries in the trunk of the Malibu. The receipt says Evelyn used her debit card at the Kroger at 12:02. The gentleman was bringing in the groceries while she fixed lunch.'

Amanda smiled. 'I often forget how smart you are, but then something like this happens and it makes me realize why I hired you.'

Will ignored the backhanded compliment. 'So, Evelyn's making lunch. She starts to wonder where her gentleman friend is. She goes outside and finds his body in the trunk. She grabs Emma and hides her in the shed. If she'd grabbed Emma after cutting her hand, like Dr. Mittal said, there would've been blood somewhere on the car seat. Evelyn's strong, but she's not Hercules. The car seat, even without a baby in it, is pretty heavy. She couldn't dead lift one of those things off the counter with one hand—at least not safely. She'd have to cup the bottom with her free hand. Emma's little, but she's got some heft to her.'

Amanda supplied, 'Evelyn spent time in the shed. She moved the blankets around. There's no blood on them. She dialed the combination lock on the safe. There's no blood on the dial. The floor is clean. She was bleeding after she locked the door.'

'I'm not an expert on kitchen injuries, but you don't generally cut your ring finger when you're

112

slicing something. It's usually the thumb or the index finger.'

'Another good point.' Amanda checked the rearview mirror and changed lanes. 'Okay, what did she do next?'

'Like you said. Evelyn hides the baby, then gets her gun out of the safe, goes back into the house and shoots Kwon, who's waiting to ambush her from the laundry room. Then, she's overpowered by a second man, probably our mystery blood type B-negative. Evelyn's gun gets knocked out of her hand during the struggle. She stabs B-negative, but there's a third guy, Mr. Hawaiian Shirt. He gets Evelyn's gun off the floor and stops the struggle. He asks her where the thing is that they're looking for. She tells them to go to hell. She's duct-taped to the chair while they search the house.'

'That sounds plausible.'

It sounded confusing. There were so many bad guys that Will was having a hard time keeping track of them. Two Asians, one Hispanic, possibly two—maybe a third man, race unknown—a house being searched for God only knew what and a missing sixty-three-year-old ex-cop who had her share of secrets.

Then there was the even larger question that Will knew better than to ask: why hadn't Evelyn called for help? By Will's count, she'd had at least two opportunities to make a call or run for help: when she first heard the noise, and after she shot Hironobu Kwon in the laundry room. And yet, she had stayed.

'What are you thinking?'

Will knew better than to give an honest answer.

'I'm wondering how they got her out of the house without anyone seeing.'

Amanda reminded him, 'You're assuming Roz Levy is being forthcoming.'

'Do you think she's involved in this?'

'I think she's a wily old bitch who wouldn't piss on you if your hair was on fire.'

Will supposed the venom in her tone came from experience.

Amanda said, 'This wasn't spur-of-the-moment. Some planning went into it. They didn't all walk there. There was a car somewhere, maybe a van. There's a dogleg alley jutting into Little John Trail. They would've gone out the back, exiting into Evelyn's backyard. You follow the fence line between the neighbors and you're there in two minutes.'

'How many men do you think were there?'

'We've got three dead on scene. There's the injured B-negative and at least one able-bodied man. There's no way Evelyn would've gone to a second location without a fight. She would've risked being shot first. There had to be someone there who was strong enough to tie her up or subdue her.'

Will didn't add that they could've just as easily injured or killed her and removed the body. 'We'll know for sure when we get the fingerprints. They all must've touched something.'

Abruptly, Amanda changed the subject. 'Have you and Faith ever talked about your case against her mother?'

'Not really. I've never told her about the bank account, because there's no reason. She assumes I was wrong. A lot of people do. My case was never

114

made in court. Evelyn retired with full benefits. It's not a hard conclusion to jump to.'

She nodded as if she was giving her approval. 'The man in the trunk, the one you call Evelyn's gentleman friend. Let's talk about him.'

'If he was bringing in groceries, that implies they had a personal relationship.'

'That's certainly possible.'

Will thought about the guy. He'd been shot in the back of the head. His wallet and ID were not the only things missing from his person. He didn't have a cell phone. He didn't have the thick gold watch he'd been wearing in the picture Mrs. Levy had taken. His clothes were nondescript—Nikes with Dr. Scholl's orthopedic inserts, J. Crew jeans, and a Banana Republic shirt that had cost a lot of money considering he hadn't bothered to iron it. There was a smattering of gray in the black goatee on his chin. The stubble on his shiny head indicated he was hiding male pattern baldness rather than making a bold statement in style. Except for the Los Texicanos star on his forearm, he could've been a stockbroker having a midlife crisis.

Amanda said, 'I've checked with Narcotics. There've been some grumblings about the Asians making a play for the powder cocaine trade. It's been up for grabs since the BMF went down.'

The Black Mafia Family. They had controlled coke sales from Atlanta to LA, with Detroit in between. 'That's a lot of money. The Family was pulling down hundreds of millions of dollars a year.'

'Los Texicanos was calling the shots. They've always been suppliers, not distributors. It's a smart

115

way to play it. That's why they've survived all these years. Despite what Charlie thinks about race, they don't care if the dealer is black or brown or purple, so long as the money's green.'

Will had never worked a major drug case. 'I don't know much about the organization.'

'Los Texicanos started back in the mid-sixties at the Atlanta Pen. The population demographic back then was almost the exact reverse of what it is now—seventy percent white, thirty black. Crack cocaine changed that overnight. It worked faster than forced busing. There were still only a handful of Mexicans in the joint, and they ganged up to keep from getting their throats cut. You know how it goes.'

Will nodded. Just about every gang in America had started as a group of minorities, be they Irish, Jewish, Italian, or other, banding together for survival. It generally took a couple of years before they started doing worse than was done to them. 'What's the structure?'

'Pretty loose. No one's going to chart like MS-13.' She was referring to what was often called the most dangerous gang in the world. Their organizational structure rivaled the military's, and their loyalty was so fierce that they'd never been successfully infiltrated.

Amanda explained, 'In the early years, Los Texicanos was on the front page of the paper every single day, sometimes in both editions. Shootouts in the street, heroin, pot, numbers, prostitution, robbery. Their calling card was branding children. They didn't just go after the person who crossed them. They'd go after a daughter, son, niece, nephew. They'd cut open their faces, once across

116

the forehead, then a vertical line down the nose to the chin.'

Without thinking, Will put his hand to the scar along his jaw.

'There was one point during the Atlanta Child Murders investigation when Los Texicanos was at the top of our list. This was early on, the fall of '79. I was the glorified assistant of the senior liaison for Fulton, Cobb, and Clayton. Evelyn was on the Atlanta task force, mostly fetching coffee until it was time to talk to the parents, then it all fell to her. The general consensus was that the Texicanos were trying to send a broader message to the clientele. It seems ludicrous now, but at the time, we were hoping it was them.' She switched on the blinker and changed lanes. 'You were around four then, so you won't remember, but it was a very tense time. The entire metro area was terrified.'

'Sounds like it,' he said, surprised she knew his age.

'It wasn't long after the Child Murders that one of the top Texicanos was taken down during an internal struggle. They're tight-knit. We never found out what happened or who took over, but we know the new guy was much more business-oriented. No more violence for the sake of violence. He prioritized the business, taking out the riskier component. His motto was to keep the coke flowing and the blood off the streets. Once they went underground, we were glad to ignore them.'

'Who's in charge now?'

'Ignatio Ortiz is the only name we have. He's the face of the gang. There are two others, but they keep an incredibly low profile and you'll never find

117

all three of them together in the same place. Before you ask, Ortiz is in Phillips State Prison serving his third year of seven without parole for attempted manslaughter.'

'Attempted?' That didn't sound very gangbanger.

'Came home and found his wife tossing the sheets with his brother. Story goes he missed on purpose.'

Will assumed Ortiz had no trouble running his business from prison. 'Is he worth talking to?'

'Even if we had cause, he wouldn't sit with us in a room without his lawyer, who would insist that his client is just an average businessman who let his passion get the best of him.'

'Has he ever been arrested before?'

'A few times in his younger days, but nothing major.'

'So, the gang's still under the radar.'

'They come out every now and then to school the younger kids. Do you remember the Father's Day murder in Buckhead last year?'

'The guy who had his throat slit open in front of his kids?'

She nodded. 'Thirty years ago, they would've killed the children, too. One might say they've gotten softer in their old age.'

'I'd hardly call that soft.'

'Inside the joint, the Texicanos are known as throat slitters.'

'The gentleman in the trunk is high up on the food chain.'

'Why do you think that?'

'He's only got one tattoo.' Young gang members generally used their bodies as a canvas to illustrate their lives, etching tattoos of teardrops under their eyes for every murder, wrapping their elbows and shoulders in cobwebs to show that they'd done time. The tattoos were always rendered in blue ink culled from ballpoint pens, what was called 'joint ink,' and they always told a story. Unless their story was so bad that it didn't need to be told.

Will said, 'A clean body means money, power, control. The gentleman is older, probably early sixties. That puts him in on the ground floor of Texicanos. His age is his badge of honor. This isn't the kind of lifestyle that ensures longevity.'

'You don't get old by being stupid.'

'You don't get old by being in a gang.'

'We can only hope the APD shares the gentleman's identity with us when they manage to track it down.'

Will glanced at her. She stared ahead at the road. He had a niggling suspicion that Amanda already knew who this man was, and exactly what part he played in the Texicanos hierarchy. There was something about the way she'd folded Mrs. Levy's photograph in her pocket, and he was pretty sure that she had given the old woman some kind of coded message to keep her story to herself.

He asked, 'Do you ever listen to AC/DC?'

'Do I look like I listen to AC/DC?'

'It's a metal band.' He didn't tell her they'd created one of the bestselling albums in the history of music. 'They've got a song called 'Back in Black.' It was playing when Faith pulled up. I checked the CDs at the house. Evelyn didn't have it in her collection, and the player was empty when I ejected the tray.'

'What's it about?'

'Well, the obvious. Being back. Wearing black. It was recorded after the original lead singer of the group died from a drug and alcohol bender.'

'It's always sad when someone dies of a cliché.'

Will thought about the lyrics, which he happened to know by heart. 'It's about resurrection. Transformation. Coming back from a bad place and telling people who might've underestimated you, or made fun of you, that you're not taking it anymore. Like, you're cool now. You're wearing black. You're a bad guy. Ready to fight back.' He suddenly realized why he'd worn out the record when he was a teenager. 'Or something like that.' He swallowed. 'It could mean other things.'

'Hm' was all she would give him.

He drummed his fingers on the armrest. 'How did you meet Evelyn?'

'We went to Negro school together.'

Will nearly choked on his tongue.

She chuckled at his reaction to what must have been a well-used line. 'That's what they called it back in the stone ages—the Negro Women's Traffic School. Women were trained separately from men. Our job was to check meters and issue citations for illegally parked cars. Sometimes, we were allowed to talk to prostitutes, but only if the boys allowed us, and usually there was some crude joke about it. Evelyn and I were the only two whites in a group of thirty that graduated that year.' There was a fond smile on her lips. 'We were ready to change the world.'

Will knew better than to say what he was thinking, which was that Amanda was a hell of a lot older than she looked.

120

She obviously guessed his thoughts. 'Give me a break, Will. I joined in '73. The Atlanta you know today was fought for by the women in those classes. Black officers weren't even authorized to arrest whites until '62. They didn't have a precinct building. They had to hang out at the Butler Street YMCA until someone thought to call them. And it was even worse if you were a woman—two strikes, with the third hanging over your head.' Her voice took on a solemn tone. 'Every single day was a struggle to do right when everything around you was wrong.'

'Sounds like you and Evelyn went through a trial by fire.'

'You have no idea.'

'Then tell me about it.'

She laughed again, but this time at his fumble. 'Are you trying to interrogate me, Dr. Trent?'

'I'm wondering why you're not talking about the fact that Evelyn obviously had a close, personal relationship with an old-school Texicano who ended up murdered in the trunk of her car.'

She stared ahead at the road. 'It does seem odd, doesn't it?'

'How can we work this case if we're not going to at least admit what really happened?' She didn't respond. 'We'll keep it between us, all right? No one else has to know. She's your friend. I understand that. I spent a lot of time with her myself. She seems like a very agreeable person, and she obviously loves Faith.'

'There's a 'but' in there somewhere.'

'She was taking money like the rest of her team. She must've known the Texicanos from—'

Amanda cut him off. 'Speaking of Texicanos,

121

let's go back to Ricardo.'

Will clenched his fist, wanting to punch something.

Amanda let him stew in silence for a while. 'I've known you an awful long time, Will. I need you to trust me on a few things.'

'Do I have a choice?'

'Not really, but I'm giving you an opportunity here to give me a return on all that benefit of the doubt I've deposited into your account over the years.'

His inclination was to tell her exactly where she could put her benefit, but Will had never been the type of man to say the first thing that came into his head. 'You're treating me like a dog on a leash.'

'That's one interpretation.' She paused for a moment. 'Did it ever occur to you that I might be protecting you?'

He scratched the side of his jaw again, feeling the scar that had been ripped into his skin years ago. Will generally shied away from introspection, but a blind man could see that he had strangely dysfunctional relationships with all of the women in his life. Faith was like a bossy older sister. Amanda was the worst mother he'd never had. Angie was a combination of both, which was unsettling for obvious reasons. They could be mean and controlling and Angie especially could be cruel, but Will had never once thought that any of them truly wished him harm. And Amanda was right about at least one thing: she had always protected Will, even on the rare occasion when it put her job at risk.

He said, 'We need to call all the Cadillac dealerships in the metro area. The gentleman

122

wasn't driving a Honda. That's an expensive ride. There are probably only a handful of those Cadillacs on the road. I think it has a manual transmission. That's rare in a four-door.'

To his surprise, she said, 'Good idea. Set it up.'

Will reached into his pocket, remembering too late that he didn't have his phone. Or his gun and badge. Or his car for that matter.

Amanda tossed him her phone as she took the exit without so much as tapping the brake. 'What's going on with you and Sara Linton?'

He flipped open her phone. 'We're friends.'

'I worked a case with her husband a few years ago.'

'That's nice.'

'Those are some mighty big shoes to fill, friend.'

Will dialed information and asked for the number of the closest Cadillac dealership to Atlanta.

* * *

As he followed Amanda past the corridor that led to the death chamber, Will had to admit, if only to himself, that he hated visiting prisons—not just the D&C, but any prison. He could handle the constant threat of violence that made every inmate facility feel like a simmering pot that had been left too long on the stove. He could handle the noise and the filth and the dead-eyed stares. What he couldn't take was the feeling of helplessness that came from confinement.

The inmates ran their drug trade and other rackets, but at the end of the day, they had no power over the basic things that made them human

123

beings. They couldn't take a shower when they wanted. They couldn't go to the bathroom without an audience. They could be strip-searched or cavity-searched at any time. They couldn't go for a walk or take a book from the library without permission. Their cells were constantly checked for contraband, which could be anything from a car magazine to a roll of dental floss. They ate on someone else's schedule. The lights were turned off and on by someone else's clock. By far the worst part was the constant handling they received. Guards were always touching them—wrenching their arms behind their backs, tapping their heads during count, pushing them forward or yanking them back. Nothing belonged to them, not even their own bodies.

It was like the worst foster home on earth, only with more bars.

The D&C was the largest prison in Georgia and, among other things, served as one of the main processing centers for all inmates entering the state penal system. There were eight cellblocks with single and double bunk beds in addition to eight more dormitories that warehoused the overflow. As part of their intake, all state prisoners were subjected to a general medical exam, psych evaluation, behavioral testing, and a threat assessment to assign a security rating that determined whether they belonged in a minimum, medium, or maximum facility.

If they were lucky, this diagnosing and classification process took around six weeks before they were assigned to another prison or moved to the permanent facilities at D&C. Until then, the inmates were on twenty-three-hour lockdown, which meant that but for one hour a day, they were confined to their cells. No cigarettes, coffee, or soda were allowed. They could buy only one newspaper a week. No books were allowed, not even the Bible. There were no TVs. No radios. No phones. There was a yard, but inmates were allowed out only three days a week, and that was weather permitting and only for whatever time was left on their one hour a day. Only long-term residents were allowed visitors, and then it was in a room that was halved by a metal mesh that required you to yell to be heard over the voices of the other visitors. No touching. No hugging. No contact whatsoever.

Maximum security.

There was a reason suicide rates in prisons were three times higher than on the outside. It was heartbreaking to think about their living conditions, until you read some of their files. Rape of a minor. Aggravated sodomy with a baseball bat. Domestic violence. Kidnapping. Assault. Shooting. Beating. Mutilating. Stabbing. Slashing. Scalding.

But the really bad guys were sitting on death row. They'd been convicted of killings so heinous that the only way the state knew how to deal with them was to put them to death. They were segregated from the rest of the population. Their lives were even more limited than the intake prisoners'. Total lockdown. Total isolation. No hour a day in the sunshine. No shared meals. No stepping past the iron bars that held them in their cells except once a week for a shower. Days could pass without hearing another man's voice. Years could pass without feeling another person's touch.

This was where Boyd Spivey was housed. This

125

was where the former highly decorated detective was living while he waited to die.

Will felt his shoulders hunch as the gate leading to the death row cells swung closed behind him. Prison design lent itself to wide, open corridors where a running man could easily be taken out with a rifle from a hundred yards away. The corners were sharp ninety-degree angles that deliberately discouraged loitering. The ceilings were high to trap the constant heat from so many sweating bodies. Everything was meshed or barred—windows, doors, overhead lights, switches.

Despite the spring climate, the temperature inside hovered somewhere around eighty. Will instantly regretted the wicking nature of his running shorts under his heavy jeans, which clearly were not meant to be worn in tandem. Amanda, as always, seemed right at home, no matter the greasy-looking bars or the panic buttons that lined the walls every ten feet. D&C's permanent inmates were classified as violent offenders. A lot of them had nothing to lose and everything to gain by engaging in willful acts of violence. Taking the life of a deputy director of the GBI would be a big feather in any man's cap. Will didn't know how they felt about cops who took down other cops, but he didn't imagine that was much of a distinction for inmates looking to raise their status.

For this reason, they were escorted by two guards who were approximately the size of commercial refrigerators. One walked in front of Amanda and the other loomed behind Will, making him feel practically dainty. No one was allowed to carry guns into the prison, but each guard had a full array of weaponry on their belts:

pepper spray, steel batons, and worst of all a set of jangling keys that seemed to announce with every footstep that the only way out of this place was through thirty locked doors.

They turned a corner and found a man in a gray suit standing outside yet another locked door. As with every other door in the place, there was a large, red panic button beside the jamb.

Amanda extended her hand. 'Warden Peck, thank you for arranging this visit on such short notice.'

'Always glad to help, Deputy Director.' He had a gravelly old man's voice that fit perfectly with his weathered, mahogany face and slicked-back gray mane. 'You know you need only pick up the phone.'

'Would it be a bother to ask if you could print out a list of all the visitors Spivey's had since he entered the system?'

Peck obviously thought it was a bother, but he covered for it well. 'Spivey's been in four different facilities. I'll have to make some calls.'

'Thank you so much for going through the trouble.' She indicated Will. 'This is Agent Trent. He'll need to be in the observation room. He's got a somewhat checkered past with the prisoner.'

'That's fine. I should warn you that we got Mr. Spivey's death notice last week. He's to be executed on the first of September.'

'Does he know?'

Peck nodded gravely, and Will could see that he didn't like this part of his job. 'It's my policy to give the inmates as much information as we can as soon as we can. The news has sobered Mr. Spivey considerably. They generally become quite docile during this time, but don't be lulled into complacency. If at any point you feel a threat, stand and leave the room immediately. Don't touch him. Avoid being within reaching distance. For your safety, you'll be monitored through the cameras and one of my men will be outside the door at all times. Just keep in mind that these men are quick, and they have absolutely nothing to lose.'

'I'll just have to be quicker.' She winked at him as if this was some kind of frat party where the boys might get rowdy. 'I'm ready when you are.'

Will was led one door down to the observation room. The space was small and windowless, the sort of prison office that could've easily passed for a storage closet. There were three monitors stacked on a metal desk, each showing a different angle of Boyd Spivey in the adjacent room. He was shackled to a chair that was undoubtedly bolted to the floor.

Four years ago, Spivey hadn't exactly been handsome, but he'd carried himself with a cop's swagger that made up for his deficits. His reputation was as a practical joker, but a good cop—the guy you'd want to have your back when things went from bad to worse. His file was full of commendations. Even after he'd taken a deal to plead guilty for lesser time, there were men who worked in his station house who refused to believe that Spivey was dirty.

Now, everything about the man said 'con.' He was as hard looking as a piece of honed granite. His skin was pockmarked and puffy. A long, ratty ponytail draped down his back. Prison tattoos decorated his forearms and twisted around his

128

neck. His thick wrists were bolted to a chrome bar welded to the center of the table. His legs were crossed at the ankles. The chains around his leg irons were tightened into a straight line. Will guessed Boyd passed his days working out in his cell. His bright orange uniform was busting at the seams around his overly muscled arms and wide chest.

Will wondered if the extra weight was a good or bad thing as far as the man's impending execution was concerned. After several gruesome mishaps with the electric chair, including a man whose chest had burst into flames, Georgia had finally been ordered by the state supreme court to retire Old Sparky. Now, instead of being shaved, stuffed with cotton, and fried to a crisp, the condemned were strapped to a table and given a series of drugs that stopped their breathing, their hearts, and finally their lives. Boyd Spivey would probably get a larger dose than most. It would take a powerful combination of drugs to put down such a large man.

A crackly cough came through the tiny speakers on the desk. In the next room, Will could see Boyd staring straight ahead at Amanda, who was leaning against the wall despite the chair that was opposite his at the table.

The tone of Boyd's voice was surprisingly high for a man of his size. 'You too scared to sit across from me?'

Will had never known Amanda to show fear, and now was no exception. 'I don't mean to be rude, Boyd, but you've got an awful smell.'

He looked down at the table. 'They only let me shower once a week.'

129

Her voice had a teasing lilt. 'Now, that's cruel and unusual.'

Will checked the camera that was zoomed in on Boyd's face. There was a smile playing at his lips.

Amanda's high heels echoed in the concrete room as she walked over to the chair. The metal legs scraped across the floor. She sat down, primly crossing her legs, letting her hands rest in her lap.

Boyd let his eyes linger. 'You look good, Mandy.'

'I've been keeping myself busy.'

'With what?'

'You've heard about Evelyn.'

'We don't have TVs in here.'

She laughed. 'You probably knew I was coming here before I did. This place could put CNN out of business.'

He shrugged, as if it was out of his hands. 'Is Faith okay?'

'Tip-top.'

'I hear she K-fived both guys.'

A K-five indicated the center ring on a paper target, the kill shot. Amanda told him, 'One was to the head.'

'Ouch.' He faked a cringe. 'How's Emma?'

'A handful. I'm sorry I don't have a picture for you. I left my purse in the car.'

'The pedophiles would've stolen it anyway.'

'What an appalling lack of decorum.'

He smiled with his teeth. They were chipped and broken, the sort of souvenirs you got from fighting dirty. 'I remember the day Faith got her gold shield.' He sat back in his chair, shackles dragging across the table. 'Ev was beaming like a Maglite.'

130

'I think we all were,' Amanda admitted, and Will let it sink in that his boss knew Boyd Spivey a hell of a lot better than she'd let on in the car. 'How've you been, Boyd? They treating you okay?'

'Okay enough.' He smiled again, then stopped himself. 'Sorry about my teeth. Didn't see any point in getting them fixed.'

'It's no worse than the smell.'

He gave her a sheepish glance. 'It's been a long time since I've heard a woman's voice.'

'I hate to say it, but that's the nicest thing a man has said to me all year.'

He laughed. 'Hard times for us both, I guess.'

Amanda let the moment stretch out for a few more seconds.

He said, 'I guess we should get to the reason you're here.'

'We can do whatever you want.' Her tone implied she could talk to him all day, but Boyd got the message.

He asked, 'Who took her?'

'We think it was a group of Asians.'

His brow furrowed. Despite the orange jumper and the hellhole he called home, a piece of Boyd Spivey was still a cop. 'Yellow doesn't have traction in the city. Brown's been grooming black to do its bidding again.'

'Brown's involved in this, but I'm not sure how.'

He nodded, indicating he was taking all this in but didn't know what to make of it. 'Brown don't like getting their hands dirty.'

'Shit rolls downhill.'

'Did they send a sign?' Proof of life. Amanda shook her head. 'What do they want to trade her for?'

131

'You tell me.'

He was silent.

She said, 'We both know Evelyn was clean, but could there be blowback?'

He glanced at the camera, then looked down at his hands. 'I can't see it. She was under the umbrella. No matter what happened, ain't one man from the team wouldn't still lay down his life for her. You don't turn your back on family.'

Will had always thought Evelyn was protected on both sides of the law. Hearing it validated was no consolation.

Amanda told the man, 'You know Chuck Finn and Demarcus Alexander are already out?'

He nodded. 'Chuck stayed down South. Demarcus went out to LA where his mama's people live.'

Amanda must have already known the answer, but she asked him, 'Are they keeping their noses clean?'

'Chuck's got a belly habit for back-to-backs.' Meaning he was shooting heroin, then smoking crack chasers. 'Brother's gonna end up back in the joint if he don't die on the street first.'

'Has he pissed anybody off?'

'Not that I've heard. Chuck's a cotton shooter, Mandy. He'd fuck his own mama for the swill in a spoon.'

'And Demarcus?'

'I guess he's as clean as you can be with a felony rap hanging over your head.'

'I hear he's working on getting his electrician's license.'

'Good for him.' Boyd seemed genuinely pleased. 'Have you talked to Hump and Hop?' He meant

132

Ben Humphrey and Adam Hopkins, his fellow detectives who were currently serving time at Valdosta State Prison.

Amanda gauged her words. 'Should I talk to them?'

'It'd be worth a try, but I doubt they're still keyed in. They got four years left. Keeping their noses clean, and I don't guess they'd be too forthcoming with you considering your hand in their current incarceration.' He shrugged. 'Me, I got nothing to lose.'

'I heard you got your date.'

'September first.' The room went quiet, as if whatever air was left had been sucked out. Boyd cleared his throat. His Adam's apple bobbed in his neck. 'Gives you perspective on things.'

Amanda leaned forward. 'Like what?'

'Like not seeing my kids grow up. Never having the chance to hold my grandbabies.' His throat worked again. 'I loved being on the street, chasing down the bad guys. I had this dream the other night. We were in the raid van. Evelyn had that stupid song playing—you remember the one?'

' "Would I Lie to You?" '

'Annie Lennox. Stone cold. I could still hear it playing when I woke up. Pounding in my head, even though I ain't heard music in—what?—four years?' He shook his head sadly. 'It's like a drug, ain't it? You bust down that door, you clear out all the trash, and then you wake up the next day and do it again.' He opened his hands as much as he could with the shackles. 'They paid us for that shit? Come on. We shoulda been paying them.'

She nodded, but Will was thinking about the fact that they had managed to pay themselves in myriad other ways.

Boyd said, 'I was supposed to be a good man. But, this place . . .' He glanced around the room. 'It darkens your soul.'

'If you'd stayed clean, you'd be out by now.'

He stared blankly at the wall behind her. 'They got it on tape—me going after those guys.' There was no humor in the smile that came to his lips, just darkness and loss. 'I had it in my head that it went down different, but they played it at my trial. Tape don't lie, right?'

'Right.'

He cleared his throat twice before he could speak. 'There was this guy beating that guard with his fists, wrapping a towel around the brother's neck. Eyes glowing like something out of a freak show. Screaming like a goddamn animal. It got me to thinking about my time on the streets. All those bad guys I took down, all those men I thought were monsters, and then I look at that guy on the tape, that monster taking down that guard, and I realize that it's me.' His voice was almost a whisper. 'That was me beating that man. That was me killing two guys—over what? And that's when it hit me: I've turned into everything I fought against all those years.' He sniffed. There were tears in his eyes. 'You become what you hate.'

'Sometimes.'

Will couldn't tell if Boyd was feeling sorry for the men he'd killed or sorry for himself. Probably, it was a combination of both. Everyone knew they were going to die eventually, but Boyd Spivey had the actual date and time. He knew the method. He knew when he would eat his last meal, take his last crap, say his last prayer. And then they would

134

come for him and he would have to stand up and walk on his own two feet toward the last place he would ever lay down his head.

Boyd had to clear his throat again before he could speak. 'I hear Yellow's been encroaching down the highway. You should talk to Ling-Ling over in Chambodia.' Will didn't recognize the name, but he knew that Chambodia was the term used to describe the stretch of Buford Highway inside the Chamblee city limits. It was a mecca for Asian and Latino immigrants. 'You can't go straight to Yellow. Not without an invitation. Tell Ling-Ling Spivey said keep it on the DL.' The down low—don't tell anyone. 'Watch your back. Sounds to me like this thing is getting out of hand.'

'Anything else?'

Will saw Boyd's mouth move, but he couldn't make out the words. Will asked the guard, 'Did you hear what he said?'

The guard shook his head. 'No idea. Looked like 'amen' or something like that.'

Will checked Amanda's reaction. She was nodding.

'All right.' Boyd's tone indicated they were finished. His eyes followed Amanda as she got up from the chair. He asked, 'You know what I miss the most?'

'What's that?'

'Standing when a lady enters the room.'

'You always had good manners.'

He smiled, showing his busted teeth. 'Take care of yourself, Mandy. Make sure Evelyn gets back home to her babies.'

She walked around the table and stood a few feet from the prisoner. Will felt his stomach

135

clench. The guard beside him tensed. There was nothing to worry about. Amanda put her hand to Boyd's cheek, and then she left the room.

'Christ,' the guard breathed. 'Crazy bitch.'

'Watch it,' Will warned the man. Amanda may have been a crazy bitch, but she was *his* crazy bitch. He opened the door and met her out in the hallway. The cameras hadn't been focused on her face, but Will could tell now that she had been sweating inside the tiny, airless room. Or maybe it had been Boyd who brought out that reaction in her.

The two guards were back on point, standing either side of Amanda and Will. Over her shoulder, he saw Boyd being duckwalked down the hall in his hand and leg shackles. There was only one guard with him, a small man whose hand barely wrapped around the prisoner's arm.

Amanda turned around. She watched Boyd until he disappeared around the corner. She said, 'It's guys like that who make me want to bring back Old Sparky.'

The guards gave off deep belly laughs that echoed down the hallway. Amanda had been pretty soft on Spivey and she had to let them know it was all for show. Her act in the tiny room had been pretty convincing. Will had been momentarily fooled, even though the one time he'd heard Amanda ask about the death penalty, her response had been to say that the only issue she had with it was they didn't kill them fast enough.

'Ma'am?' one of the guards asked. He indicated the gate at the end of the hall.

'Thank you.' Amanda followed him toward the exit. She checked her watch, telling Will, 'It's coming up on four o'clock. We've got at least an hour and a half back to Atlanta if we're lucky. Valdosta is two and a half hours south of here, but it'll be closer to four with traffic. We'll never make it in time for a visit. I can pull some strings, but I don't know the new warden and even if I did, I doubt he'd be foolish enough to yank two men out of maximum security that late at night.' Prisons ran on routine, and anything that changed that routine brought the risk of sparking up violence.

Will asked, 'You still want me to go through my case files on the investigation?'

'Of course.' She said it like there had never been any question that they would talk about the investigation that led to Evelyn Mitchell's forced retirement. 'Meet me at the office at five tomorrow morning. We'll talk about the case on the drive down to Valdosta. That's about three hours each way. It shouldn't take more than half an hour each to talk to Ben and Adam—if they'll talk at all. That'll put us back in town by noon at the latest to talk with Miriam Kwon.'

Will had almost forgotten about the dead kid in the laundry room. What he clearly remembered was that Amanda had skated over the fact that she knew Boyd Spivey well enough for him to call her Mandy. Will had to assume that Ben Humphrey and Adam Hopkins were on the same familiar terms, which meant that yet again Amanda was working her own case within the case.

She told him, 'I'll make some calls to parole in Memphis and Los Angeles to reach out to Chuck Finn and Demarcus Alexander. All we can do is send them a message that Evelyn's in trouble and we're willing to listen if they're willing to talk.'

137

'They were all very loyal to Evelyn.'

She stopped at the gate, waiting for the guard to find the key. 'Yes, they were.'

'Who's Ling-Ling?'

'We'll get to that.'

Will opened his mouth to speak, but the air was pierced by a shrill alarm. The emergency lights flashed. One of the guards grabbed Will by the arm. Instinct took over, and Will jerked away from him. Amanda had obviously had a similar reaction, but she didn't stop there. She ran down the hall, her heels popping against the tile floor. Will jogged after her. He rounded the corner and nearly knocked into her when she came to a dead stop.

Amanda didn't speak. She didn't gasp or cry out. She just grabbed his arm, nails digging through the thin cotton of his T-shirt.

Boyd Spivey lay dead at the end of the hallway. His head was turned at an unnatural angle from his body. The guard beside him was bleeding from a large slit in his throat. Will went to the man. He dropped to his knees and pressed his hands to the wound, trying to stanch the flow. It was too late. Blood pooled onto the floor like a lopsided halo. The man's eyes locked on Will's, filling with panic, and then filling with nothing at all.

CHAPTER FIVE

Faith slowed the Mini as she neared her house. it was past eight o'clock. She had spent the last six hours going over and over what had happened at her mother's house, saying the same thing again

138

and again, as her lawyer, her union rep, three Atlanta cops, and one special agent from the GBI asked questions, took notes, and basically made her feel like a criminal. On some level, it made sense that they believed Faith was wrapped up in whatever had gotten her mother kidnapped. Evelyn had been a cop. Faith was a cop. Evelyn had shot and killed a man. Faith had shot two men—two possible witnesses—seemingly in cold blood. Evelyn was missing. If Faith had been on the other side of the table, she might've been asking the same questions.

Did she have any enemies? Had she ever taken a bribe? Had she ever been approached to do something illegal? Had she ever taken money or gifts to look the other way?

But Faith wasn't on that side of the table, and no matter how much she racked her brain, there was no reason she could think of that anyone would want to take her mother. The worst part about being trapped in the interrogation room was that every minute that ticked by reminded Faith that five able-bodied officers were wasting time in an airless interrogation room when they could all be out looking for her mother.

Who would do this? Did Evelyn have enemies? What were they looking for?

Faith was just as clueless now as when the interrogation began.

She pulled the car up to the curb in front of her house. All the lights were on, something she had never allowed in her life. The house looked like a Christmas decoration. A very expensive Christmas decoration. Four cars were parked in the driveway. She recognized Jeremy's old Impala that he'd

139

bought from Evelyn when she'd gotten the Malibu, but the two trucks and black Corvette were new to her.

'Shhh . . . ,' she shushed Emma, who was getting antsy now that the car had stopped. Defying all laws and basic common sense, Faith had put Emma in the front seat beside her. The drive from Mrs. Levy's was just a few minutes, but it wasn't laziness so much as neediness that made Faith want to keep her child close. She picked up Emma and held her tight. The baby's heart beat a soothing staccato against her chest. Her breathing was soft and familiar, like tissues being pulled out of a box.

Faith wanted her mother. She wanted to put her head on Evelyn's shoulder and feel her wiry, strong hands patting her back as she whispered that everything was going to be all right. She wanted to watch her mother tease Jeremy about his long hair and bounce Emma on her knee. Most of all, she wanted to talk to her mother about how awful today had been, to get her advice on whether or not to trust the union rep who was telling her she didn't need a lawyer, or to listen to the lawyer who was telling her the union rep was too tight with the Atlanta force.

'Oh, God,' she breathed into Emma's neck. Faith needed her mother.

Tears flooded into her eyes, and for once she did not try to stop them. She was alone for the first time since she'd stepped foot inside her mother's house hours ago. She wanted to fall apart. She *needed* to fall apart. But Jeremy wanted his mother, too. He needed Faith to be strong. Her son needed to believe her when she said that she

140

would do whatever it took to get his grandmother back in one piece.

Judging by the cars, there were at least three cops waiting inside with her son. Jeremy had been crying when she called him from the station—confused, worried, terrified for his grandmother as well as his mother. Amanda's warning came back to Faith. Standing in Mrs. Levy's living room, Faith had been surprised by Amanda's hug, but not by her words, whispered in a low warning: 'You've got two minutes to pull yourself together. If these men see you cry, all you will be to them for the rest of your career is a useless woman.'

Sometimes Faith thought that Amanda was fighting a battle that had been waged long ago, but sometimes she realized her boss was right. Faith used the back of her hand to wipe her eyes. She pushed open the car door and slipped her purse onto her free shoulder. Emma shifted, startled by the cold air. Faith pulled up her blanket and pressed her lips to the top of the baby's head. Her skin was warm. The fine hairs tickled Faith's lips as she walked up the driveway.

She thought of all the things she had to do before she could go to bed. The house would need to be straightened, no matter the circumstances. Emma needed to be put to bed. Jeremy would need reassurances, and probably dinner. She would have to talk to her brother Zeke at some point. If there was any grace in the world, he was somewhere over the Atlantic right now, flying home from Germany, so she wouldn't have to speak with him tonight. Their relationship had never been good. Thankfully, Amanda had handled the phone calls or Faith would've wasted

141

most of the afternoon yelling at Zeke rather than talking to the Atlanta police. Faith felt a modicum of relief as she climbed the front stairs. Only the threat of having to talk to her brother could make the way she'd spent the last six hours look inviting. She reached for the doorknob just as the door swung open.

'Where the hell have you been?'

Faith stood with her mouth open, staring up at her brother Zeke. 'How did you—'

'What happened, Faith? What did you do?'

'How—' Faith felt incapable of forming a complete sentence.

'Dude, chill.' Jeremy pushed past his uncle and took Emma from Faith's arms. 'You okay, Mom?'

'I'm fine,' she told him, but it was Zeke who had her attention. 'Did you come from Germany?'

Jeremy supplied, 'He's living in Florida now.' He pulled Faith into the house. 'Did you eat? I can make you something.'

'Yes—I mean, no. I'm fine.' She stopped worrying about Zeke for a moment and concentrated on her son. 'Are you okay?'

He nodded, but she saw he was putting on a brave face.

Faith tried to pull him closer, but he didn't budge, probably because Zeke was watching their every move. She told Jeremy, 'I want you to stay here with me tonight.'

He shrugged. *No big deal.* 'Sure.'

'We're going to get her back, Jaybird. I promise you.'

Jeremy looked down at Emma, jostling her in his arms. 'Jaybird' had been Evelyn's name for him until his entire elementary school heard her use it

142

one day and teased him into tears. He said, 'Aunt Mandy told me the same thing when she called. That she'll get Grammy back.'

'Well, you know Aunt Mandy doesn't lie.'

He tried to make a joke of it. 'I'd hate to be those guys when she finds them.'

Faith put her hand to Jeremy's cheek. There was stubble there, something she would never get used to. Her little boy was taller than her, but she knew that he wasn't as strong. 'Grandma's tough. You know she's a fighter. And you know she'll do whatever it takes to get back to you. To us.'

Zeke made a disgusted sound, and Faith gave him a nasty look over Jeremy's shoulder. He said, 'Victor wants you to call him. You remember Victor, right?'

Victor Martinez was the last person on earth she wanted to talk to right now. She told Jeremy, 'Go put Emma down for me, all right? And turn out some of those lights. Georgia Power doesn't need all of my paycheck.'

'You sound like Grandpa.'

'Go.'

Jeremy glanced back at Zeke, reluctant to leave. His instinct had always been to protect Faith.

'Now,' she told him, gently pushing him toward the stairs.

Zeke at least had the decency to wait until Jeremy was out of earshot. He crossed his arms over his chest, puffing up his already sizable frame. 'What the hell kind of mess did you get Mom into?'

'Glad to see you, too.' She pushed past him and walked down the hall toward the kitchen. Despite what she'd told Jeremy, Faith hadn't eaten

143

anything of substance since two o'clock, and she could feel that familiar throbbing headache and wave of nausea that signaled something wasn't right.

'If anything happens to Mom—'

'What, Zeke?' Faith spun around to face him. He had always been a bully, and just like all of his kind, standing up to him was the only way to stop it. 'What are you going to do to me? Throw away my dolls? Give me an Indian burn?'

'I didn't—'

'I've spent the last six hours being grilled by assholes who think I got my mother kidnapped and went on a murderous rampage. I don't need the same kind of crap from my asshole brother.'

She turned back around and walked toward the kitchen. There was a ginger-haired young man sitting at her table. His jacket was off. A Smith and Wesson M&P hung out of his tactical-style shoulder holster like a black tongue. The straps were tight around his chest, making his shirt blouse out. He was thumbing through the Lands' End catalogue that had come in the mail yesterday, pretending he hadn't just heard Faith screaming at the top of her lungs. He stood when she entered the room. 'Agent Mitchell, I'm Derrick Connor with the APD hostage negotiation task force.'

'Thank you for being here.' She hoped her tone sounded genuine. 'I take it there haven't been any phone calls?'

'No, ma'am.'

'Any updates?'

'No, ma'am, but you'll be the first to hear.'

Faith doubted that very seriously. Ginger wasn't just here to catch phone calls. Until the brass said otherwise, Faith had a dark cloud hanging over her head. 'There's another officer here?'

'Detective Taylor. He's checking the perimeter. I can get him for you if—'

'I'd just like some privacy, please.'

'Yes, ma'am. I'll be right outside if you need me.' Connor nodded to Zeke before leaving by the sliding glass door.

Faith groaned as she sat down at the table, feeling like she'd been on her feet for hours, even though she'd been sitting for most of the day. Zeke still had his arms crossed over his chest. He was blocking the doorway as if he thought she might try to bolt.

She asked, 'Are you still in the Air Force?'

'I got transferred to Eglin four months ago.'

Right around the time Emma was born. 'In Florida?'

'Last time I checked.' Her questions were obviously ratcheting up his anger. 'I'm in the middle of a two-week in-service at the VA hospital on Clairmont. It's a good thing I just happened to be in town or Jeremy would've been alone all day.'

Faith stared at her brother. Zeke Mitchell had always looked like he was standing at attention. Even at ten years old, he'd acted like an Air Force major, which was to say that he had been born with a giant steel rod shoved up his ass.

She asked, 'Does Mom know you were stateside?'

'Of course she does. We were supposed to have dinner tomorrow night.'

'You didn't think to tell me?'

'I didn't want the drama.'

Faith let out a long sigh as she sat back in the

chair. There it was—the defining word of their relationship. Faith had brought *drama* to Zeke's senior year by getting pregnant. Her *drama* had forced him to leave high school early and sign away ten years of his life to the military. There was more *drama* when she decided to keep Jeremy, and a heaping pile of *drama* when she'd cried uncontrollably at their father's funeral.

'I've been watching the news.' He said it like an indictment.

Faith pushed herself up from the table. 'Then you know I killed two men today.'

'Where were you?'

Her hands shook as she opened the cabinet and took out a nutrition bar. She had said it like it was nothing—she had killed two men today. Faith had noticed during the interrogation that the more she talked about it, the more anesthetized she became to the reality of the act, so that saying it now only made her feel numb.

Zeke repeated, 'I asked you a question, Faith. Where were you when Mom needed you?'

'Where were *you*?' She tossed the bar onto the table. Her mind was spinning out again. She should test her blood sugar before she ate anything. 'I was at a training seminar.'

'You were late.'

She assumed he was making a lucky guess. 'I wasn't late.'

'I talked to Mom this morning.'

Faith felt her senses sharpen. 'What time? Did you tell the police?'

'Of course I told the police. I talked to her around noon.'

Faith had gotten to their mother's house less

146

than two hours later. 'Did she seem okay? What did she say?'

'She said that you were late again, Faith, like you always are. That's how it is. The world bends to your schedule.'

'Christ,' she whispered. She couldn't take this right now. She was suspended from work for God only knew how long. Her mother could be dead. Her son was devastated and she couldn't get her brother out of her face long enough to catch her breath. Adding to the stress, her head felt like it was trapped in a vise. She fished around in her purse for her blood-testing kit. Slipping into a coma, while at the moment an attractive prospect, wasn't going to help anything.

Faith laid out the kit on the table. She hated being watched when she tested her blood, but Zeke didn't seem inclined to give her any privacy. Faith changed the needle in the pen, unwrapped a sterile wipe. Zeke watched her like a hawk. He was a doctor. She could almost hear his brain cataloguing the wrong way she was doing things.

Faith squeezed some blood onto the strip. The number flashed up. She showed Zeke the LED because she knew that he would ask.

He said, 'When was your last meal?'

'I had some cheese crackers at the station.'

'That's not enough.'

She got up and opened the refrigerator. 'I know.'

'It's high. Probably from the stress.'

'I know that, too.'

'What's your last A1C?'

'Six point one.'

He sat down at the table. 'That's not bad.'

'No,' she agreed, getting her insulin out of the fridge door. It was actually a hair above her target, which was pretty damn good considering Faith had just had a baby.

'Do you really think what you said?' He paused, and she could tell it took a lot out of him to ask the question. 'Do you think we'll get her back?'

She sat back down. 'I don't know.'

'Was she injured?'

Faith shook her head and shrugged at the same time. The police weren't sharing anything with her.

His chest rose and fell. 'Why would someone take her? Are you . . .' For a change, he tried to be sensitive. 'Are you messed up in something?'

'Why are you such a jerk all the time?' She didn't expect an answer. 'Mom ran a narc squad for fifteen years, Zeke. She made enemies. That was part of her job. And you know about the investigation. You know why she retired.'

'That was four years ago.'

'These things don't have a time limit. Maybe somebody decided they want something from her.'

'Like what? Money? She doesn't have any. I'm on all her accounts. She's got her pension from the city, some of Dad's retirement, and that's it. Not even Social Security yet.'

'It has to be related to a case.' Faith drew the insulin into the syringe. 'Her entire team went to prison. A lot of very bad people were pissed off to see their bought-and-paid-for cops taken out of the game.'

'You think Mom's guys are involved in this?'

Faith shook her head. They had always called Evelyn's team 'Mom's guys,' mostly because it was easier to keep track of them that way. 'I have no

148

idea who's involved or why.'

'Are you looking into all their old cases and interviewing perps?'

' 'Perps'? Where the hell did you get that from?' Faith lifted up her shirt just enough to jab the needle into her belly. There was no immediate rush; the drug didn't work that way. Still, Faith closed her eyes, willing the nausea to pass. 'I'm suspended, Zeke. They took my badge and my gun and told me to go home. Tell me what you want me to do.'

He folded his hands on the table and stared at his thumbs. 'Can you make some phone calls? Work some sources? I don't know, Faith. You've been a cop for twenty years. Call in some favors.'

'Fifteen years, and there's no one to call. I killed two men today. Did you not see the way that cop was looking at me? They think I'm involved in this. No one is going to do me any favors.'

His jaw worked. He was used to his orders being followed. 'Mom still has friends.'

'And they're all probably shitting their pants right now worried that whatever she's messed up in that got her kidnapped is going to blow back on them.'

He didn't like that. His chin tucked into his chest. 'All right. I guess there's nothing you can do. We're helpless. And so is Mom.'

'Amanda's not going to take this lying down.'

Zeke snorted in disbelief. He had never liked Amanda. It was one thing for his baby sister to try to boss him around, but he wasn't going to take it from someone who wasn't blood. It was a strange reaction considering Zeke, Faith, and Jeremy had all grown up calling her Aunt Mandy, an

149

endearment that Faith was fairly certain would get her fired if she used it today. Still, they had always thought that Amanda was part of their family. She was so close to Evelyn that at times she'd passed for a surrogate.

But she was still Faith's boss, and she still kept her foot firmly planted on the back of Faith's neck, just like she did with everyone else who worked for her. Or came into contact with her. Or smiled at her in the street.

Faith opened the nutrition bar and took a large bite. The only sound in the kitchen was her chewing. She wanted to close her eyes, but was afraid of the images she would see. Her mother tied up, mouth gagged. Jeremy's red-rimmed eyes. The way those cops had looked at her today, like the stink of her involvement was too much to stomach.

Zeke cleared his throat. She thought that the hostilities had passed, but his posture indicated otherwise. If there was one constant in her life, it was Zeke's enduring sense of moral superiority.

She tried to get it over with. 'What?'

'That Victor guy seemed surprised to hear about Emma. Wanted to know how old she was, when she was born.'

She choked, trying to swallow. 'Victor was here? In the house?'

'You weren't around, Faith. Someone had to stay with your son until I got here.'

The string of curses that came to Faith's mind was probably worse than anything Zeke had heard while stitching up soldiers in Ramstein.

He said, 'Jeremy showed him her picture.'

Faith tried to swallow again. She felt like rusty

150

nails were catching in her throat.

'Emma's got his coloring.'

'Jeremy's?'

'This some kind of pattern with you? You like being an unwed mother?'

'Hey, didn't they tell you when you got back that Ronald Reagan isn't president anymore?'

'Jesus, Faith. Be serious for once. The guy has a right to know he's a father.'

'Trust me, Victor's not interested in being a father.' The man couldn't even pick up his dirty socks off the floor or remember to leave the toilet seat down. God only knew what he'd forget with a baby.

Zeke repeated, 'He has a right to know.'

'So, now he knows.'

'Whatever, Faith. As long as *you're* happy.'

Any normal human being would've trounced off after dropping that bon mot, but Zeke Mitchell never walked away from a fight. He just sat there, staring at her, willing her to crank it back up. Faith reverted to old ways. If he was going to act like he was ten, then so was she. She ignored his presence, flipping through the Lands' End catalogue, ripping out the page that showed the underwear Jeremy liked so she could order it for him later.

She flipped to the thermal shirts, and Zeke tilted back in his chair, staring out the window.

This tension was nothing new between the two of them. Faith's selfishness was Zeke's favorite one-note song. As usual, she accepted his disapproval as part of her penance. He had good reason to hate her. There was no moving past an eighteen-year-old boy finding out his fourteen-year-old sister was pregnant. Especially when

151

Jeremy got older and Faith saw what it was like for teenage boys—not the walk in the park it had seemed when she was a teenage girl—Faith had felt guilty for what she'd done to her brother.

As hard as it was for her father, who was asked not to attend his men's Bible study, and her mother, who was ostracized by most every woman in the neighborhood, Zeke had endured a special hell because of Faith's unexpected pregnancy. He'd come home from school at least once a week with a bloody nose or black eye. When they asked him about it, he refused to talk. He sneered at Faith over the dinner table. He shot her looks of disgust if she walked by his room. He hated her for what she'd done to the family, but he would rain down hell on anyone who said a word against her.

Not that she could remember much from that time. Even now, it was one long, miserable blur of slobbering self-pity. It was hard to believe that so much had changed in twenty years, but Atlanta, or at least Faith's part of it, had been more like a small town back then. People were still riding high on the Reagan/Bush wave of conservative values. Faith was a spoiled, selfish teenager when it happened. All she could focus on was how miserable her own life was. Her pregnancy had been a result of her first—and, at the time, she vowed last—sexual encounter. The father's parents had immediately moved him out of state. There was no birthday party when she turned fifteen. Her friends abandoned her. Jeremy's father never wrote or called. She had to go to doctors who probed and prodded her. She was tired all the time, and cranky, and she had hemorrhoids and back pain and everything ached every time she moved.

Faith's father was away a lot, suddenly required to take business trips that had never before been part of his job description. The church had been the center of his life, but that center was abruptly ripped away when he was informed by the pastor that he no longer had the moral authority to be a deacon. Her mother had taken off work to be with her—whether forced or voluntary, Evelyn still would not say.

What Faith did remember was that she and her mother were both trapped at home every day, eating junk food that made them fat and watching soap operas that made them cry. For her part, Evelyn bore Faith's shame like a hermit. She wouldn't leave the house unless she had to. She woke every Monday morning at the crack of dawn to go to the grocery store across town so that she wouldn't run into anyone she knew. She refused to sit in the backyard with Faith even when the air conditioning broke and the living room turned into a kiln. The only exercise she took was a walk around the neighborhood, but that only happened late at night or early morning before the sun came up.

Mrs. Levy from next door left them cookies on the doorstep, but she never came in. Occasionally, someone would leave religious tracts in the mailbox that Evelyn burned in the fireplace. Their only visitor the entire time was Amanda, who didn't have the option of dropping off her de facto sister-in-law's social calendar. She would sit in the kitchen with Evelyn and talk in a low voice that Faith couldn't hear. After Amanda left, Evelyn would go into the bathroom and cry.

It was no wonder that one day Zeke came home from school not with a busted lip but with a copy of his enlistment papers. He had five more months to go until graduation. His ROTC service and SAT scores had already lined up a full ride to Rutgers. But he took his GED and entered the pre-med program almost a full year ahead of schedule.

Jeremy was eight years old the first time he met his uncle Zeke. They had circled each other like cats until a game of basketball had smoothed things over. Still, Faith knew her son and she recognized his reticence toward a man he felt wasn't treating his mother right. Unfortunately, he'd had a lot of opportunity over the years to hone this particular emotion.

Zeke dropped his chair back onto the floor, but still did not look at her.

Faith chewed the nutrition bar slowly, forcing herself to eat despite the nausea that gripped her stomach. She looked out the sliding door and saw the kitchen table, Zeke's posture, straight as a board, reflected back. There was a glow of red beyond the glass. One of the detectives was smoking.

The phone rang, and they both jumped. Faith scrambled to answer the cordless just as the detectives came in from the backyard.

'No news,' Will told her. 'I was just checking in.'

Faith waved away the cops. She took the phone with her into the living room, asking Will, 'Where are you?'

'I just got home. There was a jackknifed trailer on 675. It took three hours to clear.'

'Why were you down there?'

'The D&C.'

Faith felt her stomach lurch.

Will didn't bother with small talk. He told her about his prison visit, Boyd Spivey's murder. Faith put her hand to her chest. When she was younger, Boyd had been a frequent guest at family dinners and backyard barbecues. He'd taught Jeremy how to ride a bike. And then he'd flirted so openly with Faith that Bill Mitchell suggested the man find an alternative way to spend his weekends. 'Do they know who did it?'

'The security camera happened to be out in that one section. They've got the place in lockdown. All the cells are being tossed. The warden's not hopeful they'll find much of anything.'

'There was outside help.' A guard must have been bribed. No inmate would have the time it took to disable a camera mounted inside a prison corridor.

'They're talking to the staff, but the lawyers are already on scene. These guys aren't your everyday suspects.'

'Is Amanda all right?' Faith shook her head at her stupidity. 'Of course she's all right.'

'She got what she wanted. We get a back door into your mom's case because of this.'

The GBI had jurisdiction over all death investigations inside state prisons. 'I guess that's some kind of positive news.'

Will was quiet. He didn't ask her if she was doing okay, because he obviously knew the answer. Faith thought of the way he had held her hands that afternoon, making her pay attention as he coached her on what to say. His tenderness had been unexpected, and she'd had to bite the inside of her cheek hard enough to draw blood so that

155

she wouldn't break down and cry.

Will said, 'Do you know that I've never seen Amanda go to the bathroom?' He stopped himself. 'Not in person, I mean, but when we left the prison, she pulled over at the gas station and went inside. I've never seen her take a break like that. Have you?'

Faith was used to Will's odd tangents. 'I can't say that I have.' Amanda had been at those family dinners and barbecues with Boyd Spivey. She had joked with him the way cops do—questioning his manhood, praising his progress on the force despite his lack of mental prowess. She wasn't completely made of stone. Watching Boyd die would've taken something out of her.

Will said, 'It was very disconcerting.'

'I can imagine.' Faith pictured Amanda at the gas station, going into the stall, shutting the door, and allowing herself two minutes to mourn a man who had once meant something to her. Then she'd probably checked her makeup, fixed her hair, and dropped the key back with the gas station attendant, asking him if they locked the bathroom door to keep someone from cleaning it.

Will said, 'She probably sees urinating as a weakness.'

'Most people do.' Faith sat back on the couch. He had given her the best gift she could possibly receive right now: a moment of distraction. 'Thank you.'

'For what?'

'For being there today. For getting Sara to come. For telling me what to—' She remembered that the phone was tapped. 'For telling me that everything was going to be okay.'

156

He cleared his throat. There was a short silence. He was awful at this sort of thing, almost as bad as she was. 'Have you thought about what they were looking for?'

'That's all I can think about.' She heard the refrigerator door open and close. Zeke was probably making a list of foods she shouldn't stock in the house. 'What's next?'

He hesitated.

'Tell me.'

'Amanda and I are going down to Valdosta first thing.'

Valdosta State Prison. Ben Humphrey and Adam Hopkins. They were talking to everyone from her mother's old team. Faith should've expected this, but the news of Boyd's death had thrown her off. She should've known that Will was going to reopen the case.

Faith said, 'I should keep this line open in case someone calls.'

'All right.'

She hung up the phone because there was nothing more to say. He still thought her mother was guilty. Even after working with Faith for almost two years, seeing that she did things the right way because that was the kind of cop her mother had raised her to be, Will still thought Evelyn Mitchell was dirty.

Zeke loomed in the doorway. 'Who was that?'

'Work.' She stood up from the couch. 'My partner.'

'The asshole who tried to put Mom in prison?'

'The very same.'

'I still don't know how you can work with that douche.'

157

'I cleared it with Mom.'

'You didn't clear it with me.'

'Should I have sent the request to Germany or Florida?'

He stared at her.

Faith wasn't going to explain herself to her brother. It was Amanda who had asked her to partner with Will, and Evelyn had told Faith to do what was best for her career. She didn't have to point out that it was not a bad idea to get out of the Atlanta Police Department, where Evelyn's forced retirement was considered either a coast or a crime depending on whom you asked. 'Did Mom ever talk to you about the investigation?'

'Shouldn't you ask your partner about that?'

'I'm asking you,' Faith snapped. Evelyn had refused to discuss the case against her, and not just because Faith could've been called as a potential witness. 'If she said something, even something that was a little off but you didn't think about it at the time . . .'

'Mom doesn't shop talk with me. That's your job.'

There was the same tinge of accusation in his voice, as if Faith had the power to find their mother and was simply choosing not to exercise it. She looked at the clock on the wall. It was almost nine, too late to be doing this. 'I'm going to bed. I'll send down Jeremy with some sheets. The couch is pretty comfortable.'

He nodded, and Faith saluted his dismissal. She was halfway up the stairs when he spoke. 'He's a good kid.' Faith turned around. 'Jeremy. He's a good kid.'

She smiled. 'Yeah, he is.' She was almost to the

top of the stairs when the other shoe dropped.

'Mom did a good job.'

Faith continued up the stairs, refusing to take the bait. She checked on the baby. Emma smacked her lips when Faith leaned down to kiss her forehead. She was in that deep, blissful sleep that only babies know. Faith checked the monitor to make sure it was on. She stroked her hand down Emma's arm, letting the baby's tiny fingers wrap around her one, before leaving.

In the next room, Jeremy's bed was empty. Faith lingered at the door. She hadn't changed his room, though it would've been nice to have an office. His posters were still on the wall—a Mustang GT with a bikini-clad blonde leaning over the hood, another with a half-naked brunette draped across a Camaro, a third and fourth showing concept cars with the ubiquitous big-bosomed model. Faith could still remember coming home from work one day to find his 'Bridges of the Southeastern United States' posters replaced with these gems. Jeremy still thought that he'd cleverly tricked her into believing that puberty had brought on a sudden interest in automobiles.

'I'm in here.'

She found him in her room. Jeremy was lying on his stomach, head at the foot of her bed, feet in the air, iPhone in his hands. The sound on the TV was muted but the closed captioning was on.

She asked, 'Everything okay?'

He tilted the iPhone in his hands, obviously playing a game. 'Yeah.'

Faith remembered the fertile girlfriend. It was strange she wasn't here. They were usually attached at the hip. 'Where's Kimberly?'

159

'We're taking a break,' he said, and she almost sobbed with relief. 'I heard you and Zeke yelling.'

'There's a first time for everything.'

He tilted the phone the other way.

She said, 'I've been wanting one of those.' He got the hint and put the device in his pocket. 'I know you heard the phone ring. It was Will. He's working with Aunt Amanda.'

He stared at the TV. 'That's good.'

Faith started to untie his sneakers. In typical teenage boy logic, he'd thought keeping his feet raised off the bed would stop debris from raining down. 'Tell me what happened when Zeke got here.'

'Dude was being an asshole.'

'Tell me like I'm your mother.'

She saw him color slightly in the glow of the TV. 'Victor stayed with me. I told him he didn't have to, but he said he wanted to, so . . .'

Faith untied his other sneaker. 'You showed him Emma's picture?'

He kept staring at the set. Jeremy had really liked Victor—probably more than Faith had, which was only part of the problem.

She told him, 'It's all right.'

'Zeke was kinda shitty—I mean rude—to him.'

'In what way?'

'Just kinda poking his chest out and pushing him around.'

Just being Zeke. 'Nothing happened, right?'

'Nah, Victor's not the type.'

Faith assumed as much. Victor Martinez worked in an office, read *The Wall Street Journal,* wore bespoke suits, and washed his hands sixteen times a day. He was about as passionate as a box of hair.

160

It was Faith's lot in life that she would only ever be able to fall in love with the kind of man who would wear sleeveless T-shirts and punch her brother in the face.

She slid off Jeremy's shoe, frowning at the state of his sock. 'Toes go on the inside, college boy.' She made a mental note to get him more socks when she ordered his underwear. His jeans were looking ratty, too. So much for the three hundred dollars left in her checking account. Thank God they had suspended her with pay. Faith was going to have to dip into savings just to keep her son from looking like a hobo.

Jeremy rolled over onto his back to face her. 'I showed Victor Emma's Easter picture.'

She swallowed. Victor was a smart man, but it didn't take a genius to do the math. Even without that, Faith was blonde and fair. Emma had her father's dark coloring and rich brown eyes. 'The one where she's wearing the bunny ears?'

He nodded.

'That's a good one.' Faith could see the guilt well up in him like water spilling out of a glass. 'It's all right, Jay. He would've found out eventually.'

'Then why didn't you tell him?'

Because Faith was just the right mixture of emotionally stunted and controlling, which was something Jeremy would find out when his future wife screamed it in his face. For now, Faith said, 'It's not something I'm going to talk to you about.'

He sat up to face her. 'Grandma likes Will.'

Faith guessed he'd overheard her conversation with Zeke. 'She told you that?'

He nodded. 'She said he was an all right guy. That he treated her fairly, and that he had a hard

161

job to do but he wasn't mean about it.'

Faith didn't know whether her mother had been assuaging Jeremy's concerns or revealing her true opinion. Knowing her mother, it was probably a mixture of both. 'Did she ever talk to you about why she retired?'

He tugged at a loose thread on the bedspread. 'She said she was the boss, so it was her fault for not noticing what was going on.'

This was more than she'd ever told Faith. 'Anything else?'

He shook his head. 'I'm glad Aunt Amanda has Will helping her. She can't do everything by herself. And he's really smart.'

Faith stopped his hand and held it until Jeremy looked up at her. The television offered the only light in the room. It gave his face a green cast. 'I know you're worried about Grandma, and I know there's nothing I can say to make this better for you.'

'Thanks.' He was being sincere. Jeremy had always appreciated honesty.

She pulled him up from the bed and wrapped her arms around him. His shoulders were thin. He was gangly, not yet the man he was going to be no matter the fact that he ate his weight in macaroni and cheese every day.

He let her hug him for longer than usual. She kissed his head. 'Everything's going to be all right.'

'That's what Grandmamma always says.'

'And she's always right.' Faith squeezed him closer.

'Mom, you're suffocating me.'

Reluctantly, she let him go. 'Get some sheets for Uncle Zeke. He's going to sleep on the couch.'

Jeremy slid his feet back into his sneakers. 'Has he always been that way?'

Faith didn't pretend to miss his meaning. 'When we were little, every time he had to fart, he would run into my room and tear it loose.'

Jeremy started laughing.

'And then he said if I told on him, he'd gorge himself on beans and cheese and then hold me down and do it in my face the next time.'

That sent him over the edge. He bent over, holding his stomach as he brayed like a donkey. 'Did he do it?'

Faith nodded, which made him laugh even harder. She let him enjoy her humiliation a little longer before nudging him on the shoulder. 'Time to go to bed.'

He wiped tears from his eyes. 'Man, I've got to do that to Horner.'

Horner was his dorm mate. Faith doubted anyone would notice one more noxious odor in their shared quarters.

'Get Zeke a pillow from the closet.' She pushed him out of the room. He was still laughing as he walked down the hallway. It was a small price to pay to see the worry momentarily absent from her son's face.

Faith pulled back the comforter on her bed. Dirt from Jeremy's sneakers was smeared into the sheets. She was too tired to change the bed. She was too tired to put on her nightgown or even brush her teeth. She slipped off her shoes and got into bed wearing the same GBI regs she'd put on at five o'clock that morning.

The house was quiet. Her body was so tense that she felt like she was lying on a board. Emma's soft

163

snores came through on the baby monitor. Faith stared up at the ceiling. She'd forgotten to turn off the television. Light flashed like a strobe from the action movie Jeremy had been watching.

Boyd Spivey was dead. It seemed impossible to grasp. He was a big guy, larger than life, the sort of cop you imagined going out in a blaze of glory. He was the exact opposite of his partner. Chuck Finn was dour, full of gloomy predictions and terrified that he would be shot in the line of duty. His defense during the investigation was the only one Faith had found credible during the whole mess. Chuck had claimed he was just following orders. To those who knew him, it seemed entirely plausible. Detective Finn was the quintessential follower, which was exactly the personality type that men like Boyd Spivey knew how to exploit.

But Faith didn't want to think about Boyd or Chuck or any of her mother's team right now. The investigation had eaten up six months of her life. Six months of sleepless nights. Six months of worrying that her mother was going to have a heart attack or end up in prison or both.

Faith made herself close her eyes. She wanted to think of good times with her mother, to recall some moment of kindness or summon the pleasure of her company. What she saw instead was the man in her mother's bedroom, the black hole in the center of his forehead where Faith had shot him. His hands jerked up. The hostage stared at Faith in disbelief. His mouth gaped open. She saw the silver grill on his teeth, that his tongue was pierced with a matching silver ball.

Almeja, he had said.

Money.

Faith heard the floorboards creak in the hall. 'Jeremy?' She pushed herself up on her elbow and turned on the bedside lamp.

He gave her a sheepish look. 'Sorry, I know you're tired.'

'Do you want me to take the sheets down to Zeke?'

'No, it's not that.' He pulled his iPhone out of his pocket. 'Something came up on my Facebook page.'

'I thought you stopped using that when I made you friend me.' Faith had never been the kind of parent to completely trust her kid. Her own parents had trusted her and look where that had gotten them. 'What's going on?'

His thumbs moved across the screen as he talked. 'I got bored. I mean, not bored, but there was nothing to do, so . . .'

'It's okay, baby.' She sat up in bed. 'What is it?'

'Lots of people have been posting stuff. I guess they heard about Grandma on the news.'

'That's nice,' Faith said, though she found it a bit ghoulish and, to borrow a word from her brother, *dramatic*. 'What are they saying?'

'Mostly just that they're thinking about me and stuff like that. But there's this.' He turned the phone around and handed it to her.

Faith read the message aloud. ' "Hey, Jaybird, hope you're okay. I'm sure the bad guys will get fingered. Just remember what your grandma used to say: keep your mouth shut and your eyes open." ' Faith checked the screen name. 'GoodKnight92. Is that someone you went to Grady with?' Jeremy's high school's mascot was the knight, and he had been born in 1992.

He shrugged. 'Never heard of him.'

Faith noted that the post had come in at 2:32 that afternoon, less than an hour after Evelyn had been abducted. She tried not to sound concerned when she asked, 'When did he friend you?'

'Today, but a lot of people did. They kind of all came out of the woodwork.'

She gave him the phone. 'What does his profile say?'

'Just that he lives in Atlanta and works in distribution.' He thumbed through the screen and showed it to Faith.

Her eyes were so tired she had trouble focusing. Faith held the phone close to her face so she could read the words. There was nothing more, not even a picture. Jeremy was GoodKnight's only friend. Faith felt her cop's intuition telling her something was wrong, but she handed back the phone as if it was nothing. 'I'm sure it's someone you went to Morningside with. You were teased so bad about Grandma calling you Jaybird that you begged me to let you switch to another school.'

'It's weird, though—right?'

She wasn't going to let him worry. 'Most of your friends are weird.'

He wouldn't be soothed. 'How does he know that about Gran always saying that?'

'It's a pretty common saying,' Faith answered. 'Mouth shut, eyes open. I had a drill instructor at the academy who practically tattooed it on his forehead.' She forced a lightness into her tone. 'Come on. It's nothing. It's probably a cop's kid. You know the rule. Something bad happens and we're all family.'

That finally seemed to mollify him. Jeremy had

been dragged to his share of hospitals and strangers' homes when a police officer had been wounded or killed. He put the phone back into his pocket.

She asked, 'You sure you're okay?'

He nodded.

'You can sleep in here if you want.'

'That'd be weird, Mom.'

'Wake me if you need me.' Faith lay back down, slipping her hand under the pillow. Her fingers touched something wet. Familiar.

Jeremy immediately picked up on the change. 'What's wrong?'

Faith's breath was trapped in her chest. She didn't trust herself to speak.

'Mom?'

'Tired,' she managed. 'I'm just tired.' Her lungs ached for oxygen. She felt sweat break out all over her body. 'Get the sheets before Zeke comes up here.'

'Are you—'

'It's been a long day, Jeremy. I need to go to sleep.'

He was still reluctant. 'All right.'

'Can you shut my door?' She wasn't sure she could move even if she wanted to.

Jeremy gave her another worried look as he pulled the door closed. Faith heard the click of the latch, then the soft padding of his feet as he walked down the hall to the laundry room. It was only when she heard the third stair from the bottom squeak that Faith allowed herself to pull her hand out from under the pillow.

She opened her clenched fist. The sharp pain of fear receded and now all Faith could feel was

167

blinding fury.

The message on Jeremy's iPhone. His high school. His birth year.

Keep your mouth shut and your eyes open.

Her son had lain in this bed, his feet inches from what she had found.

I'm sure the bad guys will get fingered.

The words only made sense when Faith held her mother's severed finger in her hand.

CHAPTER SIX

Sara linton was no stranger to self-loathing. she'd felt ashamed when her father saw her steal a candy bar from the honor box at church. She'd felt humiliated when she caught her husband cheating on her. She'd felt guilty when she lied to her sister about liking her brother-in-law. She'd felt embarrassed when her mother pointed out that she was too tall to wear capri pants. What she'd never felt like was trashy, and the knowledge that she was no better than a reality TV star cut her to the core of her being.

Even now, hours later, Sara's face still burned at the thought of her confrontation with Angie Trent. There was only one other time in her life that she could recall a woman talking to her the way Angie had. Jeffrey's mother was a mean drunk, and Sara had caught her on a very bad night. The only difference in this instance was that Angie had absolutely every right to label Sara a whore.

Jezebel, Sara's mother would've said.

Not that Sara was going to tell her mother about

any of this.

She muted the television, the sound grating on her nerves. She'd tried reading. She'd tried cleaning up her apartment. She'd clipped the dogs' toenails. She'd washed dishes and folded clothes that were so wrinkled from being piled on her couch for so long that she'd had to iron them before they would fit in the drawers.

Twice, she'd headed toward the elevator to take Will's car back to his house. Twice she'd turned back around. The problem was his keys. She couldn't leave them in the car and she sure as hell wasn't going to knock on the front door and hand them to Angie. Leaving them in his mailbox was not an option. Will's neighborhood wasn't bad, but he lived in the middle of a major metropolitan city. The car would be gone in the time it took Sara to walk back home.

So she just kept assigning herself busywork, all the while dreading Will's arrival like a root canal. What would she say to him when he finally came to get his car? Words failed, though Sara had silently rehearsed plenty of speeches about honor and morality. The voice in her head had taken on the cadence of a Baptist preacher. This was all so sordid. It wasn't right. Sara was not going to be some tawdry other woman. She wasn't going to steal someone's husband, even if he was ripe for the taking. Nor was she going to engage in a catfight with Angie Trent. Most of all, she wasn't going to step into the middle of their incredibly dysfunctional relationship.

What kind of monster bragged about her husband trying to kill himself? It made Sara's stomach turn. And then there was the larger issue:

169

to what depths had Will sunk where slicing a razor up his arm seemed like the only solution? How obsessed was he with Angie that he would do such a terrible thing? And how sick was Angie that she'd held him while he did it?

These questions were best handled by a psychiatrist. Will's childhood obviously had not been a walk in the park. That fact alone could cause some damage. His dyslexia was an issue, but it didn't seem to stop his life. He had his quirks, but they were endearing, not off-putting. Had he worked through his suicidal tendencies or was he just good at hiding them? If he was past that point in his life, why was he still with that horrible woman?

And since Sara had decided nothing was going to happen between them, why was she still wasting her time thinking about these things?

He wasn't even her type. Will was nothing like Jeffrey. There was none of her husband's staggering self-confidence on display. Despite his height, Will wasn't a physically intimidating man. Jeffrey had been a football player. He knew how to lead a team. Will was a loner, content to blend into the background and do his job under the shadow of Amanda's thumb. He didn't want glory or recognition. Not that Jeffrey had been an attention seeker, but he was incredibly secure in who he was and what he wanted. Women had swooned in his presence. He knew how to do just about everything the right way, which was one of the many reasons Sara had thrown logic to the wind and married him. Twice.

Maybe she wasn't really interested in Will Trent at all. Maybe Angie Trent was partly right. Sara

170

had liked being married to a cop, but not for the kinky reasons Angie had implied. The black-and-white nature of law enforcement appealed to Sara on a deep level. Her parents had raised her to help people, and you couldn't get much more helpful than being a police officer. There was also a part of her brain that was drawn to the puzzle-solving aspects of a criminal investigation. She had loved talking to Jeffrey about his cases. Working in the morgue as the county coroner, finding clues, giving him information that she knew would help him with his job, had made her feel useful.

Sara groaned. As if being a doctor wasn't a useful thing. Maybe Angie Trent was right about the perversion. Next, Sara would start trying to imagine Will in a uniform.

She shifted her two greyhounds off her lap so that she could stand. Billy yawned. Bob rolled onto his back to get more comfortable. She glanced around her apartment. An antsiness took over. She felt overwhelmed by the desire to change something—anything—so that she felt more in control of her life.

She started with the couches, siding them at an angle from the television while the dogs looked down at the floor passing underneath them. The coffee table was too big for the new arrangement, so she shifted everything again, only to find that that didn't work, either. By the time she finished rolling up the rug and muscling everything back into its original place, she was sweating.

There was dust on the top of the picture frame over the console table. Sara got the furniture polish out and started dusting again. There was a lot of space to cover. The building she lived in was a converted milk-processing factory. Red brick walls supported twenty-foot ceilings. All the mechanical workings were exposed. The interior doors were distressed wood with barn door hardware. It was the sort of industrial loft you expected to find in New York City, though Sara had paid considerably less than the ten million dollars such a place would fetch in Manhattan.

No one thought the space suited her, which was what had drawn Sara to the apartment in the first place. When she'd first moved to Atlanta, she'd wanted something completely different from her homey bungalow back home. She was thinking lately that she'd gone overboard. The open plan felt almost cavernous. The kitchen, with its stainless steel everything and black granite tops, had been very expensive and very useless to someone like Sara, who had been known to burn soup. All the furniture was too modern. The dining room table, carved from a single piece of wood and large enough to seat twelve, was a ridiculous luxury considering she only used it to sort mail and hold the pizza box while she paid the delivery guy.

Sara put away the furniture polish. Dust wasn't the problem. She should move. She should find a small house in one of the more settled Atlanta neighborhoods and get rid of the low-lying leather couches and glass coffee tables. She should have fluffy couches and wide chairs you could snuggle into for reading. She should have a kitchen with a farmhouse sink and a cheery view to the backyard through the wide-open windows.

She should live somewhere like Will's house.

The television caught her eye. The logo for the evening news scrolled onto the screen. A serious-looking reporter stood in front of the Georgia Diagnostic and Classification Prison. Most insiders referred to it as the D&C, fully mindful of the play on words for Georgia's death row. Sara had seen the story of the two murdered men earlier and thought then what she thought now: here was yet another reason not to be involved with Will Trent.

He was working on Evelyn Mitchell's case. He had probably been nowhere near that prison today, but the minute Sara saw the story about a murdered officer, her heart had jumped into her throat. Even after they'd given the man's name as well as that of the dead inmate, her heart would not calm. Thanks to Jeffrey, Sara knew how it felt when the phone unexpectedly rang in the middle of the night. She remembered how every news story, every snippet of gossip, caused something inside of her to clench in fear that he would be going out on another case, putting his life in danger. It was a form of post-traumatic stress disorder. Sara hadn't realized until her husband was gone that she'd been living in dread for all those years.

The intercom buzzed. Billy gave a halfhearted growl, but neither dog got off the couch. Sara pressed the speaker button. 'Yes?'

Will said, 'Hi, I'm sorry I—'

Sara buzzed him in. She grabbed his keys off the counter and propped open the front door. She wouldn't invite him in. She wouldn't let him apologize for what Angie had said, because Angie Trent had every right to speak her mind, and what's more, she'd made some very good points. Sara would just tell Will that it was nice knowing him and good luck working things out with his wife.

If he ever got here. The elevator was taking its sweet time. She watched the digital readout show the car moving from the fourth floor down to the lobby. It took another forever for the numbers to start ascending. She whispered them aloud, 'Three, four, five,' and then finally the bell dinged for six.

The doors slid back. Will peered out behind a pyramid of two cardboard file boxes, a white Styrofoam carton, and a Krispy Kreme doughnut bag. The greyhounds, who only seemed to notice Sara around suppertime, ran out into the hall to greet him.

Sara mumbled a curse.

'Sorry I'm so late.' He turned his body so that Bob wouldn't knock him over.

Sara grabbed both dogs by their collars, holding the door open with her foot so that Will could come in. He slid the boxes onto her dining room table and immediately started petting the dogs. They licked him like a long-lost friend, their tails wagging, nails scratching against the wood floor. Sara's resolve, which had been so strong only seconds before, started to crack.

Will looked up. 'Were you in bed?'

She had dressed appropriately for her mood in an old pair of sweat pants and a Grant County Rebels football jersey. Her hair was pulled back so tightly that she could feel it tugging the skin on her neck. 'Here are your keys.'

'Thanks.' Will brushed the dog hair off his chest. He was still wearing the same black T-shirt from that afternoon. 'Whoa.' He pulled back Bob, who was making a play for the Krispy Kremes.

'Is that blood?' There was a dark, dried stain on

the right-hand sleeve of his shirt. Instinctively, Sara reached for his arm.

Will took a step back. 'It's nothing.' He pulled down the cuff. 'There was an incident at the prison today.'

Sara got that familiar, tight feeling in her chest. 'You were there.'

'I couldn't do anything to help him. Maybe you . . .' His words trailed off. 'The staff doctor said it was a mortal wound. There was a lot of blood.' He clamped his hand around his wrist. 'I should've changed shirts when I got home, but I've got a lot of work to do, and my house is kind of upside down right now.'

He had been home. Without reason, Sara had let herself think for just a moment that he hadn't seen his wife. 'We should talk about what happened.'

'Uh . . .' He seemed to purposefully miss her point. 'Not much to say. He's dead. He wasn't a particularly good guy, but I'm sure it'll be hard on his family.'

Sara stared at him. There was no guile on his face. Maybe Angie hadn't told Will about the confrontation. Or maybe she had, and Will was doing his best to ignore it. Either way, he was hiding something. But suddenly, after spending the last few hours working herself into a frenzy, Sara didn't care. She didn't want to talk about it. She didn't want to analyze it. The only thing she was certain of was that she did not want him to leave.

She asked, 'What's in the boxes?'

He seemed to note her shift in attitude, but chose not to acknowledge it. 'Case files from an old investigation. It might have something to do

175

with Evelyn's disappearance.'

'Not kidnapping?'

His grin indicated he'd been caught. 'I just have to know everything in these files by five tomorrow morning.'

'Do you need help?'

'Nope.' He turned to lift the boxes. 'Thanks for getting Betty home for me.'

'Being dyslexic is not a character flaw.'

Will left the boxes on the table and turned around. He didn't respond immediately. He just looked at her in a way that made Sara wish that she had bothered to bathe. Finally, he said, 'I think I liked it better when you were mad at me.'

Sara didn't respond.

'It's Angie, right? That's what you're upset about?'

These shifting levels of subterfuge were new to her. 'It seems like we were ignoring that.'

'Would you like to continue along that path?'

Sara shrugged. She didn't know what she wanted. The right thing to do would be to tell him that their innocent flirtation was over. She should open the door and make him leave. She should call Dr. Dale tomorrow morning and ask him out on another date. She should forget about Will and let time erase him from her memory.

But it wasn't her memory that was the problem. It was that tightness in her chest when she thought about him being in danger. It was that feeling of relief when he walked through the door. It was the happiness she felt just from being near him.

He said, 'Angie and I haven't been together—together—in over a year.' Will paused, as if to let that sink in. 'Not since I met you.'

176

All Sara could say was, 'Oh.'

'And then when her mother died a few months ago, I saw her for maybe two hours, and she was gone. She didn't even go to the funeral.' He paused again; this was obviously difficult for him. 'It's hard to explain our relationship. Not without making myself look pitiful and stupid.'

'You don't owe me an explanation.'

He put his hands in his pockets and leaned against the table. The overhead light caught the jagged scar above his mouth. The skin was pink, a fine line tracing the ridge between his upper lip and nose. Sara couldn't begin to calculate the amount of time she'd wasted wondering how the scar would feel against her own mouth.

Too much time.

Will cleared his throat. He looked down at the floor, then back up at her. 'You know where I grew up. How I grew up.'

She nodded. The Atlanta Children's Home had closed many years ago, but the abandoned building was less than five miles from where they stood.

'Kids went away a lot. They were trying to get more of us into foster care. I guess it's cheaper that way.' He shrugged, as if this was to be expected. 'The older ones didn't usually work out. They lasted maybe a few weeks, sometimes only a couple of days. They came back different. I guess you can imagine why.'

Sara shook her head. She didn't want to.

'There wasn't exactly a long line of people who wanted to foster an eight-year-old boy who couldn't pass the third grade. But Angie's a girl, and pretty, and smart, so she got sent out a lot.' Again, he shrugged. 'I guess I got used to waiting

177

for her to come back, and I guess I got used to not asking what happened while she was gone.' He pushed away from the table and picked up the boxes. 'So, that's it. Pitiful and stupid.'

'No. Will—'

He stopped in front of the door, the boxes held in front of him like a suit of armor. 'Amanda wanted me to ask you if you know anyone at the Fulton ME's office.'

Sara's brain took its time changing gears. 'Probably. I did some of my training there when I started.'

He shifted his grip. 'This is from Amanda, not me. She wants you to make some calls. You don't have to, but—'

'What does she want to know?'

'Anything that comes up on the autopsies. They're not going to share with us. They want to keep this case.'

He was turned toward the door, waiting. She looked at the back of his neck, the fine hairs at the nape. 'All right.'

'You've got Amanda's number. Just call her if anything comes up. Or call her if it doesn't. She's impatient.' He stood waiting for her to open the door.

Sara had spent most of the day wanting him out of her life, but now that he was leaving, she couldn't take it. 'Amanda was wrong.'

He turned back around to face her.

'What she said today. Amanda was wrong.'

He feigned shock. 'I don't think I've ever heard anyone say those words out loud before.'

'*Almeja*. The dying man's last words.' She explained, 'The literal translation is right—

"clams"—but it's not slang for "money." At least not the way I've heard it used.'

'What's it slang for?'

She hated the word, but she said it anyway. ' "Cunt." '

His brow furrowed. 'How do you know that?'

'I work in a large public hospital. I don't think a week's gone by since I started without someone calling me some variation of that word.'

Will dropped the boxes back on the table. 'Who called you that?'

She shook her head. He looked ready to take on her entire patient roster. 'The point is, the guy was calling Faith that name. He wasn't talking about money.'

Will crossed his arms. He was obviously riled. 'Ricardo,' he supplied. 'The guy in the backyard who shot at those little girls—his name was Ricardo.' Sara held his gaze. Will kept talking. 'Hironobu Kwon was the dead guy in the laundry room. We don't know anything about the older Asian, except that he had a fondness for Hawaiian shirts and spoke with a southside southern drawl. And then there's someone else who got injured, probably in a knife fight with Evelyn. You'll probably see the notice at the hospital when you go back to work. Blood type B-negative, possibly Hispanic, stab wound to the gut, possibly a wound on his hand.'

'That's quite a cast of characters.'

'Trust me, it's not easy keeping up with them, and I'm not even sure any of them are the real reason all of this is happening.'

'What do you mean?'

'This feels personal, like there's something else

179

at play. You don't wait around four years to rob somebody. It's got to be about something more than money.'

'They say it's the root of all evil for a reason.' Sara's husband had always loved money motivations. In her experience, he tended to be right. 'This injured guy—the one with the gut wound—is he in a gang?'

Will nodded.

'They generally have their own doctors. They're not bad—I've seen some of their handiwork at the ER. But a belly wound is pretty sophisticated to treat. They might need blood, and B-negative is hard to come by. They'd also need a sterile operating environment, medicines that you can't just grab at your local drugstore. They'd only be at a hospital pharmacy.'

'Can you give me a list? I can have it added to the alert.'

'Of course.' She went to the kitchen to find a pad and paper.

He stayed by the dining room table. 'How long could someone live with a stab wound in their belly? It bled a lot at the scene.'

'It depends. Hours, maybe days. Triage can buy some time, but anything close to a week would be a miracle.'

'You mind if I eat my dinner while you do that?' He opened the Styrofoam box. She saw two foot-long hot dogs soaked in chili. He sniffed, then frowned. 'I guess the guy at the gas station was going to throw them out for a reason.' Still, he picked up one of the hot dogs.

'Don't you dare.'

'It's probably fine.'

180

'Sit down.' She took out a frying pan from the cabinet and found a carton of eggs in the refrigerator. Will sat at the bar across from the stainless steel cooktop. The Styrofoam box was on the counter beside him. Bob poked it with his nose, then backed away.

She asked, 'Was that really your dinner—two hot dogs and a Krispy Kreme doughnut?'

'Four doughnuts.'

'What does your cholesterol look like?'

'I guess it's white like what they show in the commercials.'

'Very funny.' She wrapped the Styrofoam container in aluminum foil and threw it into the trash. 'Why do you think Faith's mother wasn't kidnapped?'

'I didn't actually say that. I just think a lot of things aren't adding up.' He watched Sara break eggs into a bowl. 'I don't think she left willingly. She wouldn't do that to her family. But I think she might know her kidnappers. Like, they had a previous working relationship.'

'How?'

He stood and walked to the dining room table, where he took out a handful of yellow folders from one of the boxes. He grabbed the bag of doughnuts before sitting back down at the kitchen bar. 'Boyd Spivey,' he said, opening the top file and showing her a mugshot.

Sara recognized the face and name from the news. 'That's the man who was killed at the prison today.'

Will nodded, opening the next file. 'Ben Humphrey.'

'Another cop?'

181

'Yep.' He opened another file. There was a yellow star stickered on the inside. 'This is Adam Hopkins. He was Humphrey's partner.' Another file, this one with a purple star. 'This is Chuck Finn, Spivey's partner, and this guy—' He fumbled open the last file. Green star. 'Is Demarcus Alexander.' He'd forgotten one. Will went back to the table and found another yellow folder. This one had a black star, which seemed prophetic when he said, 'Lloyd Crittenden. Died from a drug overdose three years ago.'

'All cops?'

Will nodded as he shoved half a doughnut into his mouth.

Sara poured the eggs into the pan. 'What am I missing?'

'Their boss was Evelyn Mitchell.'

Sara almost spilled the eggs. 'Faith's mother?' She went back to the photographs, studying the men's faces. They all had that same arrogant tilt to their chins, as if their present trouble was just a blip on the radar. She skimmed Spivey's arrest report, trying to decipher the typos. 'Theft during the commission of a felony.' She flipped back the page and read the details. 'Spivey issued a standing order to his team that they should remove ten percent off the top of every drug bust involving cash money exceeding two thousand dollars.'

'It added up.'

'To how much?'

'From what accounting could estimate, over the course of twelve years, they stole around six million dollars.'

She gave a low whistle.

'That's a little less than a million each, tax free.

182

Or at least it was. I'm sure Uncle Sam caught up with them their first day in prison.'

Even stolen money was taxable income. Most inmates got their notice from the IRS within the first week of their prison sentence.

Sara checked the front page of the arrest report, stopping on a familiar name. 'You were the investigating officer.'

'It's not my favorite part of the job.' He shoved the rest of the doughnut into his mouth.

Sara looked down at the file, pretending to read on. The typos hadn't been much of a red flag. Every police report she'd ever read was riddled with grammar and spelling mistakes. Like most dyslexics, Will treated spell check as sacrosanct. He'd substituted words that made no contextual sense, then signed his name at the bottom. Sara studied his signature. It was little more than a squiggle running at an angle from the black line.

Will was watching her closely. She realized she needed to ask a question. 'Who instigated the investigation?'

'An anonymous tip came into the GBI.'

'Why wasn't Evelyn charged?'

'The prosecutor refused to bring a case. She was allowed to retire with her full pension. They called it early retirement, but she was way past her thirty years. She wasn't working for the money. At least not the money she was getting from the city.'

Sara used a spatula to stir the eggs. Will ate another doughnut in two bites. The powdered sugar sprinkled onto the black granite countertop.

She said, 'Can I ask you something?'

'Sure.'

'How does Faith work with you after you

investigated her mother?'

'She thinks I'm wrong.' Bob was back. He propped his nose on the counter and Will started petting his head. 'I know that she cleared it with her mother, but we've never really talked about it beyond that.'

Sara would not have believed anyone else telling her the same thing, but she could easily imagine how this worked. Faith wasn't one to sit around talking about her feelings, and Will was just so damn decent that it was hard to assign him vengeful ulterior motives. 'What's Evelyn like?'

'She's old school.'

'Like Amanda?'

'Not exactly.' He took another doughnut out of the bag. 'I mean, she's tough, but she's not as intense.'

Sara understood what he meant. That generation didn't have a lot of avenues for proving themselves to their male counterparts. Amanda had taken the ball-breaking route with obvious relish.

'They came up together,' Will told her. 'They went to the academy together, then worked joint task forces through APD and the GBI. They're still good friends. I think Amanda dated Evelyn's brother, or her brother-in-law.'

Sara couldn't think of a more obvious conflict of interest. 'And Amanda was your senior officer when you were investigating Evelyn?'

'Yep.' He inhaled another doughnut.

'Did you know this at the time?'

He shook his head, keeping the doughnut in his cheek like a squirrel with a nut so that he could ask, 'You know the stove isn't on, right?'

184

'Crap.' That explained why the eggs were still liquid. She clicked the dial until the flame whooshed up.

He wiped his mouth with the back of his hand. 'I like to let them sit for a while, too. Gives them a woodsy character.'

'That's *E. coli.*' She checked the toaster, wondering why it hadn't popped up. Probably because there was nothing in there. Will smiled as she got a loaf of bread out of the cabinet. She said, 'I'm not much of a cook.'

'Do you want me to take over?'

'I want you to tell me about Evelyn.'

He leaned back in the chair. 'I liked her when I met her. I know that seems strange under the circumstances. I guess I was supposed to hate her, but you can't look at it that way. This is government work. Sometimes investigations get started for the wrong reason, and you find yourself sitting opposite somebody who's been jammed up for saying the wrong thing or ticking off the wrong politician.' He brushed the powdered sugar into a pile as he talked. 'Evelyn was very polite. Respectful. Her record was spotless until then. She treated me like I was just doing my job, not like I was a pedophile, which is what you normally get.'

'Maybe she knew she'd never be prosecuted.'

'I think she was worried about it, but her primary concern was her daughter. She worked really hard to keep Faith out of it. I never even met her until Amanda paired us up.'

'She's a good mother at least.'

'She's a classy lady. But she's also smart, strong, tough. I wouldn't bet against her on this.'

Sara had forgotten the eggs. She used the

spatula to scrape them off the bottom of the pan.

Will told her, 'Evelyn was duct-taped to a chair while they searched her house. I found an arrowhead drawn underneath the seat. She used her own blood to do it.'

'Where was it pointing?'

'Into the room. At the couch. Into the backyard.' He shrugged. 'Who knows? We didn't find anything.'

Sara thought about it. 'Just the head of an arrow? That's all?'

He fanned out the powdered sugar again and drew the shape.

Sara studied the symbol, silently debating how to proceed. She finally decided the truth was her only option. 'It looks like a *V* to me. The letter *V*.'

He was quiet in a way that changed the air in the room. She thought he was going to change the subject, or make a joke, but he told her, 'It wasn't perfect. It was smudged at the top.'

'Like this?' She drew another line. 'Like the letter *A*?'

He stared at the figure. 'I guess Amanda wasn't pretending when she said she didn't know what I was talking about.'

'She saw it, too?'

He brushed the powdered sugar into his hand and dropped it into the bag with the last doughnut. 'Yep.'

She put the plate of eggs in front of him. The toaster popped up. The bread was almost black. 'Oh, no,' she mumbled. 'I'm so sorry. You don't have to eat this. Do you want me to get the hot dogs out of the trash?'

He took the burned toast from her and dropped

186

it on the plate. It made a sound like a brick scraping concrete. 'Some butter would be nice.'

She had fake butter. Will dipped a knifeful out of the tub and coated the bread until it was soggy enough to fold in his hand. The eggs were closer to taupe than yellow, but he started in on them anyway.

Sara told him, 'The name 'Amanda' starts with an *A*. *Almeja* starts with an *A*. And now Evelyn might've drawn an *A* on the bottom of her chair.'

He put down the fork. His plate was clean.

She continued, '*Almeja* sort of sounds like 'Amanda.' The same number of syllables. The same first and last letter.' He would've missed the alliterative. Most dyslexics couldn't rhyme two words if you put a gun to their heads.

He edged his plate away. 'Amanda isn't telling me everything. She's not even admitting that the corruption case has anything to do with Evelyn's situation.'

'But she told you to go over all your case files.'

'Either she needs the information or she's trying to keep me busy. She knows this will take me all night.'

'Not if I help you.'

He picked up his plate and walked over to the sink. 'Do you want me to wash this before I go?'

'I want you to tell me about the crime scene.'

He rinsed his plate, then started to wash his hands.

'That's the cold,' Sara said, and then because it was pointless to tell him that because she was left-handed, she'd switched the hot water valve to the right-hand side, she leaned in and adjusted the temperature for him.

187

Will opened his hand so that she could squirt some soap onto his palm. 'Why do you smell like lemon furniture polish?'

'Why did you let me believe Betty belongs to your wife?'

He lathered the soap in his hands. 'There are some mysteries that will never be solved.'

She smiled. 'Tell me about the crime scene.'

Will told her what they had found: the upturned chairs and broken baby toys. He segued into Mrs. Levy and Evelyn's gentleman caller, Mittal's theory about the blood trail, and Will's own divergent theory about the same. By the time he got to the part where they had found the gentleman in the trunk, Sara had managed to get him to sit down at the dining room table.

She asked, 'Do you think Boyd Spivey was killed because he talked to Amanda?'

'It's possible, but not likely.' He explained, 'Think about the timing. Amanda called the warden two hours before we got to the prison. The prison doc said a serrated knife was used. That's not something you can make out of your toothbrush. The camera was disabled the day before, which indicates this was planned at least twenty-four hours in advance.'

'So, it was coordinated. Evelyn is taken. Boyd is killed a few hours later. Are the other men from her team safe?'

'That's a very good question.' He pulled his cell phone out of his pocket. 'Do you mind if I make some calls?'

'Of course not.' She got up from the table to give him some privacy. The frying pan was still warm, so she ran cold water over it. The eggs were

188

seared to the metal. She picked at the slime with her thumbnail before giving up and sticking it on the top rack of the dishwasher.

Sara opened Boyd Spivey's file again. Will had used a pink star to identify him, perhaps as a joke. The man looked the part of a corrupt cop. His moon-shaped face indicated steroid use. His pupils were barely discernible in his beady eyes. His height and weight were closer to a linebacker's.

She skimmed the details of Spivey's arrest while listening with half an ear as Will talked with someone at Valdosta State Prison. They discussed whether or not to move Ben Humphrey and Adam Hopkins into solitary confinement, and agreed that it would be best just to step up their monitoring.

Will's next call was more complicated. Sara assumed he was talking to someone at GBI headquarters about locating the remaining two men through their parole officers.

She opened Spivey's file and found his personnel record behind the arrest report. Sara read through the details of the man's professional life. Spivey had joined the academy fresh out of high school. He'd gone to night school at Georgia State in order to earn a BA in criminal science. He had three children and a wife who worked as a secretary at the Dutch consulate on the outskirts of the city.

Spivey's promotion onto Evelyn's team was a coup. The drug squad was one of the most elite in the country. They had all the best weapons and facilities, and enough high-profile bad guys in the Atlanta area to win them plenty of commendations and press time, which Spivey in particular seemed to enjoy. Will had collected newspaper clippings on

189

the team's most noteworthy busts. Spivey was front and center of every news story, even though Evelyn was the leader of the team. One photo showed a clean-shaven Spivey with enough ribbons on his chest to decorate a girl's bicycle.

And it still had not been enough.

'Hey.'

Sara looked up from her reading. Will had finished his phone calls.

'Sorry about that. I wanted to make sure they were safe.'

'It's fine.' Sara wasn't going to pretend she hadn't been listening. 'You didn't call Amanda.'

'No, I didn't.'

'Give me some more files to read.'

'You really don't have to do this.'

'I want to.' Sara was no longer being kind or trying to spend more time in his company. She wanted to know what had made a man like Boyd Spivey turn into such a lowlife.

Will stared at her long enough to make her think he was going to say no. Then he opened one of the boxes. There was an ancient Walkman nestled in a pile of audio cassette tapes. None of them had labels, unless you counted the colored, star-shaped stickers. Will explained, 'These are recordings of all the interviews I had with each suspect. None of them said much in the beginning, but they all ended up making deals to cut time off their sentences.'

'They ratted each other out?'

'Not a chance. They had some information on a couple of local councilmen to trade. It gave them some leverage with the prosecutor.'

Sara couldn't pretend to be shocked over

190

politicians with drug problems. 'How much leverage?'

'Enough to get them talking, not enough to make them give up the big fish.' He opened the next box and started pulling out files. As with everything else, they were color-coded. He handed her the green ones first. 'Witness testimony for the prosecution.' He stacked the red ones, which were fewer in number. 'Witnesses for the defense.' He took out the blue ones. 'High-dollar busts— anything where more than two thousand dollars was seized.'

Sara went right to work, carefully reading the next personnel file. Ben Humphrey had been the same kind of cop as Boyd Spivey: solidly built, good at his job, driven to get press, and, in the end, absolutely corrupt. The same proved to be true of Adam Hopkins and Demarcus Alexander, both of whom were praised for their bravery under fire during a bank robbery, both of whom paid cash for their vacation homes in Florida. Lloyd Crittenden had earned his shield after flipping his cruiser six times during the pursuit of a man who'd shot up a seedy bar with a sawed-off shotgun. He also had a mouth on him. There were two write-ups for insubordination, but Evelyn's yearly reviews had been nothing if not glowing.

The only outlier was Chuck Finn, who seemed more cerebral than his colleagues. Finn had been in the process of earning his PhD in Italian renaissance art when he was busted. His lifestyle wasn't as lavish as the others'. He'd used his ill-gotten gains to educate himself and travel the world. He must've complemented the team in more subtle ways. Evelyn Mitchell had obviously

191

handpicked each man for a reason. Some were leaders. Some, like Chuck Finn, were obviously followers. They all fit the same general profile: overachievers with a reputation in the department for doing whatever had to be done. Three were white. Two were black. One was part Cherokee Indian. All of them had given up everything for cold, hard cash.

Will flipped over the tape in the Walkman. He sat with his eyes closed, headphones tucked into his ears. She could hear the squeak of the wheels working in the tape player.

The next stack of folders detailed all of the high-dollar busts the team had made, and presumably skimmed from, over the years. Sara had thought these files would be the hardest to get through, but they all turned out to be fairly mundane. Such was the nature of the illegal drug trade that most of the men the team had arrested were either dead or incarcerated when Evelyn's squad was busted. Only a few were still on the street, but they were obviously active. Sara recognized some of the names from the nightly news. Two looked promising for their own reasons. She set their files aside for Will.

Sara checked the time. It was well past midnight and she had an early shift in the morning. As if on cue, her mouth opened in such a wide yawn that her jaw popped. She glanced at Will to make sure he hadn't seen. There was still a large stack of folders in front of her. She was only halfway through, but she couldn't make herself stop if she wanted to. It was like trying to put together all the clues in a mystery novel. The good guys were just as corrupt as the villains. The villains seemed to take the graft as a cost of doing business. Both probably had a long list of justifications for their illegal actions.

She tackled the next pile of folders. The six men on Evelyn's team had never gone to trial, but they must have been close to starting when the deals were made. The prosecution's list of potential witnesses had been highly screened, but no more so than those representing the defendants. The names would be familiar to Will, but still, Sara carefully read through each file. After a solid hour of comparing statements, she let herself move on to the last file, which she'd held back as a reward for not giving up.

Evelyn Mitchell's booking photo showed a trim woman with an unreadable expression on her face. She must have felt humiliated to be booked and processed after spending so much time on the other side of the table. Nothing about her expression gave that away. Her mouth was set in a tight line. Her eyes stared blankly ahead. Her hair was blonde, like Faith's, with gray streaking through at the temples. Blue eyes, 138 pounds, five-nine—a little taller than her daughter.

Her career was the sort that garnered pioneer awards from the local Women's Club, which Captain Mitchell had twice received. Her promotion to detective was preceded by a hostage negotiation that had resulted in the freeing of two children and the death of a serial child molester. Her lieutenant rank came almost ten years after passing the test with the highest grade yet recorded. Her captainship was the result of a gender-bias lawsuit filed with the EEOC.

Evelyn had worked her way up the hard way,

paying her dues on the street. She had two degrees, one from Georgia Tech, both with honors. She was a mother, a grandmother, a widow. Her children were in what Sara thought of as service—one to her community, the other to his country. Her husband had worked a solidly respectable job as an insurance salesman. In many ways, she reminded Sara of her own mother. Cathy Linton wasn't the sort of woman to carry a gun, but she was driven to do what she believed was right for herself and her family.

But she would've never taken a bribe. Cathy was painfully honest, the sort of person who would turn around and drive fifty miles back to a tourist trap in Florida because they had given her too much change. Maybe this explained why Faith could work with Will. If someone had told Sara that her mother had stolen almost a million dollars, she would've laughed in their face. It was the stuff of fairy tales. Faith didn't just think he was wrong about her mother. She thought he was deluded.

Will changed out another tape.

Sara motioned for him to take off his headphones. 'It doesn't add up.'

'What doesn't?'

'You said each team member netted just shy of a million dollars. You've accounted for sixty thousand, at best, in the out-of-state account that was opened in Bill Mitchell's name. Evelyn doesn't drive a Porsche. She doesn't have a mistress. Faith and her brother weren't in private schools, and the only vacations she took were to Jekyll Island with her grandson.'

'It adds up after today,' he reminded her. 'Whoever took Evelyn wants that money.'

194

'I don't buy it.'

Most cops defended their cases like they would defend their children. Will just asked, 'Why?'

'Gut feeling. Instinct. I just don't buy it.'

'Faith doesn't know about the bank account.'

'I won't tell her.'

He sat up, clasping his hands together. 'I've been listening to my early interviews with Evelyn. She talks about her husband, mostly.'

'Bill, right? He was an insurance agent.'

'He died a few years before the case was brought against Evelyn.'

Sara braced herself for a widow question, but Will went in another direction.

'The year before Bill died, he was sued by the family of a policyholder for a claim denial. They said Bill filled out some paperwork incorrectly. A father of three had a rare kind of heart defect. The company denied treatment.'

This wasn't a new story to Sara. 'They said it was a pre-existing condition.'

'Only it wasn't—at least not diagnosed. The family got a lawyer, but it was too late. The guy ended up dying because the wrong box was checked on a form. Three days later, his widow gets a letter in the mail from the insurance company saying that Bill Mitchell, the originating agent, made a mistake on the forms and her husband's treatment was approved.'

'That's awful.'

'Bill took it hard. He was a very careful man. His reputation was important to him, important to his work. He got an ulcer worrying about it.'

That wasn't technically how ulcers worked, but she told him, 'Go on.'

'He was eventually cleared. They found the original forms. The insurance company had screwed up, not Bill. Some data entry person had clicked the wrong box. No malfeasance, just incompetence.' Will waved this away. 'Anyway, what Evelyn said was that Bill never got past it. It made her crazy because he wouldn't let it go. They argued about it. She thought he was just feeling sorry for himself. She accused him of being paranoid. He said people at work treated him differently. A lot of people thought the company took the bullet and it was really Bill's mistake.'

Sara was dubious. 'An insurance company took the bullet?'

'People get crazy ideas,' Will said. 'Anyway, Bill felt like it wiped out all the good he'd done over the years. Evelyn said that when the cancer came— Bill died of pancreatic cancer three months after his diagnosis—she thought part of the reason he couldn't fight it was that he had this guilt hanging over his head. And that she had never forgiven him for that, for not fighting the cancer. He just kind of accepted it and then waited to die.'

Pancreatic cancer was not easily vanquished. The chances for long-term survival were less than five percent. 'Stress like that can certainly impair your immune system.'

'Evelyn was worried that the same thing was going to happen to her.'

'That she'd get cancer?'

'No. That the investigation would ruin her life, even if she was cleared. That it would hang over her head forever. She said that in all the years since her husband had died, she had never wanted him back more than she did that day so that she

196

could tell him that she finally understood.'

Sara considered the weight of the statement. 'That sounds like something an innocent person would say.'

'It does.'

'Does that mean you're leaning away from your original conclusion?'

'It's very kind of you to phrase your question so diplomatically.' He grinned. 'I don't know. My case was shut down before I could wrap it up to my satisfaction. Evelyn signed her papers and took her retirement. Amanda didn't even tell me it was over. I heard it on the news one morning—decorated officer retiring from the force to spend more time with her family.'

'You think she got away with it.'

'I keep coming back to one thing: she was in charge of a team that stole a whole lot of money. Either she turned a blind eye or she's not as good as she reads on paper.' Will picked at the plastic seam on one of the audiotapes. 'And there's still the bank account. It might not seem like much compared to millions, but sixty thousand is a chunk of change. And it's in her husband's name, not hers. Why not change it over now that he's dead? Why still keep it a secret?'

'All good points.'

He was quiet for a moment, the only sound in the room his thumbnail picking at the plastic seam. 'Faith didn't call me when it happened. I didn't have my cell, so it would've been pointless, but she didn't call me.' He paused. 'I thought maybe she didn't trust me because it was her mother involved.'

'I doubt she was even thinking about that. You

197

know how your brain just blanks out when something like that happens. Did you ask her about it?'

'She's got a lot more on her mind right now than holding my hand.' He gave a self-deprecating chuckle. 'Maybe I should write about it in my diary.' He started packing up the boxes. 'Anyway, I'll let you get to bed. Did you find anything I should know about?'

Sara pulled out the two files she'd set aside. 'These guys might deserve a closer look. They were in the high-dollar busts. One of them was also on Spivey's defense witness list. I flagged him because he has a history of kidnapping for leverage over rival gangs.'

Will opened the top file.

Sara supplied the name. 'Ignatio Ortiz.'

Will groaned. 'He's in Phillips State Prison on a manslaughter attempt.'

'So, it won't be hard to find him.'

'He runs Los Texicanos.'

Sara was familiar with the gang. She had treated her share of kids who were involved in the organization. Not many of them walked out of the ER in one piece.

Will said, 'If Ortiz is wrapped up in this, he'll never talk to us. If he's not, then he'll never talk to us. Whichever it is, driving to the prison would be three or four hours out of our day for nothing.'

'He was going to be called as a witness for Spivey's defense.'

'Boyd had a surprising number of thugs willing to testify that he hadn't touched their money. There was a whole roster of criminals willing to stand up for Evelyn's team.'

'Did you get anything from Boyd at the prison?'

Will frowned. 'Amanda interviewed him. They talked in some kind of code. One thing I picked up on was that Boyd said the Asians were trying to cut the Mexicans out of the supply side.'

'Los Texicanos,' Sara provided.

'Amanda told me their preferred method is slitting throats.'

Sara put her hand to her neck, trying not to shudder. 'You think that Evelyn was still doing business with these drug dealers?'

He closed Ortiz's file. 'I can't see how. She doesn't have any juice without her badge. And I can't picture her as a kingpin unless she's some kind of sociopath. Granny-Nanny by day, drug lord by night.'

'You said Ortiz is in prison for attempted manslaughter. Who'd he try to kill?'

'His brother. He found him in bed with his wife.'

'Maybe this is the brother.' Sara opened the next file. 'Hector Ortiz,' she told him. 'He's not a bad guy on paper, but he made the defense witness list. I pulled him because he has the same last name as Ignatio.'

Will unclipped the mugshot from the file to get a closer look. 'Is your gut still telling you that Evelyn is innocent?'

Sara looked at her watch. She had to be at work in five hours. 'My gut has turned in for the night. What is it?'

He held up Hector Ortiz's photograph. The man was bald with a salt-and-pepper goatee. His shirt was rumpled. He held up his arm to show a tattoo to the camera: a green and red Texas star with a rattlesnake wrapped around it.

Will said, 'Meet Evelyn's gentleman friend.'

SUNDAY

CHAPTER SEVEN

The open-handed slaps had turned into punches hours ago. Days ago? Evelyn wasn't sure. She was blindfolded, sitting in total darkness. Something dripped—faucet, gutter, blood—she didn't know. Her body was so riddled with pain that even when she squeezed her eyes shut and tried to block out every screaming muscle, every broken bone, nothing felt undamaged.

She panted out a laugh. Blood sprayed from her mouth. Her missing finger. There was one bone that wasn't broken, one piece of flesh that wasn't bruised.

They had started on her feet, beating the soles with a galvanized metal pipe. It was a form of torture they had apparently seen in a movie, which Evelyn knew because one of them had helpfully coached, 'The dude was swinging it back higher, like this.' The sensation Evelyn had felt could not be called pain. It was a searing of the skin that her blood carried like fire through her entire body.

Like most women, it was rape that had always terrified her, but she knew now that there were far worse dangers. There was at least an animalistic logic to the crime of rape. These men were not deriving pleasure from hurting her. Their reward came from the cheers of their friends. They were trying to impress each other, pulling a game of one-upmanship to see who could make her scream the loudest. And Evelyn *did* scream. She screamed so loud that she was sure that her vocal cords would rupture. She screamed from pain. She screamed from terror. She screamed from anger, fury, loss. She screamed most of all because these competing emotions felt like burning hot lava rushing up her throat.

At one point, they'd had a protracted discussion about where her vagus nerve was located. Three of them took turns, punching her in the general area of her kidneys until, like children hitting a piñata, one hit pay dirt. They'd laughed uncontrollably as Evelyn seized as if electrocuted. The feeling was one of primal terror. She had never in her life felt so close to death. She had urinated herself. She had screamed into the darkness until there was no sound coming out of her mouth.

And then they had broken her leg. Not a clean break, but the result of the heavy metal pipe pounding again and again against her leg until there was the resounding crunch of a single bone splintering into two.

One of them pressed his hand over the break, his putrid breath in her ear. 'This is what that stupid bitch did to Ricardo.'

That stupid bitch was her baby. They had no way of knowing how the words had given Evelyn hope. She had been knocked out, dragged from the scene, shortly after Faith's car had pulled into the driveway. Evelyn had come to in the back of a van. The engine noise had been rumbling in her ears, but she'd heard two distinct gunshots, the second following the first by a good forty seconds.

But now Evelyn knew the answer to the only question that kept her from just giving up. Faith was alive. She had gotten away. After that, every horror they visited on her was inconsequential. She thought of Emma in her daughter's arms, Jeremy

204

together with his mother. Zeke would be there. He was so full of anger, but he had always taken care of his sister. The APD would surround them like a shroud. Will Trent would lay down his life to protect Faith. Amanda would move heaven and earth to find justice.

'*Almeja . . .*' Evelyn's voice was raspy in the close space.

All that she could ask was for her children to be safe. No one could get her out of this. There was no promise of salvation. Amanda could not talk her through this pain. Bill Mitchell would not come riding up on his white horse to save her.

She had been so stupid. One mistake so many years ago. One terrible, stupid mistake.

Evelyn spit out a broken tooth. Her last right molar. She could feel the raw nerve responding to the cold in the air. She tried to cover the spot with her tongue as she breathed through her mouth. She had to keep the airway open. Her nose was broken. If she stopped breathing, or passed out with blood in her throat, she would choke to death. She should welcome the relief, but instead the thought of death still terrified her. Evelyn had always been a fighter. It was in her nature to dig in her heels the more she was pushed. And yet, she could feel herself starting to break—not from the pain, but from exhaustion. She could feel her resolve draining away like water through a sieve. If she gave in, they might get what they wanted. Her mouth might move, her voice might work, despite her mind willing her to be silent.

And then what?

They would have to kill her. She knew who they were, even though they had worn masks and blindfolded her. She knew their voices. Their names. Their smells. She knew what they were planning, what they had already done.

Hector.

She had found him in the trunk of her car. Even with a silencer, there was no such thing as a quiet gunshot. Evelyn had heard the noise twice in her life, and she instantly recognized the snip of gas passing through a metal cylinder.

At least she had protected Emma. At least she had made certain that her daughter's child was safe.

Faith.

Mothers were not supposed to pick favorites, but Zeke was the obvious choice. Driven. Smart. Capable. Loyal. He was her firstborn, a shy little boy who had clung to Evelyn's skirt when strangers visited the house. A toddler who sat with her while she cooked dinner and loved going to the store so he could help carry the bags. His little chest out. His arms overloaded. His teeth showing in a prideful, happy grin.

But it was Faith whom Evelyn felt closest to. Faith who had made so many mistakes. Faith whom Evelyn could always forgive because every time she looked at her daughter, she caught a glimpse of herself.

Their time together. Housebound. Those months of forced confinement. Forced exile. Forced misery.

Bill had never understood it, but then, it wasn't his nature to understand mistakes. He'd been the first to notice the swell of her stomach. He'd been the first to confront her about it. For nine long months, he was stoic and self-righteous, suddenly

206

making Evelyn understand where Zeke had gotten these tendencies. During the hardest time, he had all but disappeared from their lives. Even after it was all over, and Jeremy had brightened up their lives like the sun finally shining down after a summer storm, Bill had never been the same.

But then, Evelyn had never been the same, either. Nor had anyone. Faith was caught up in figuring out how to raise a child. Zeke, who had wanted nothing more than Evelyn's attention since he was a baby, had gone as far away as he could get from her without leaving the planet. Her little boy lost. Her heart split in two.

She couldn't bear to think about it anymore.

Evelyn straightened her spine, trying to take pressure off her diaphragm. She couldn't keep this up. She was breaking. These young men with their video games and film fantasies had an unlimited pool of ideas at their disposal. God only knew what they would resort to next. They had no problem laying their hands on drugs. Barbiturates. Ethanol. Scopolamine. Sodium Pentothal. Any one of them could act as a truth serum. Any one of them could pry the information out of her mouth.

Just the excruciatingly slow passage of time could make her talk. The unceasing agony. The relentless barrage of accusations. They were so angry, so hostile.

So barbaric.

She was going to die. Evelyn had known the minute she woke in the van that death was the only end to this. In the beginning, she thought it would be their death at her hands. She had quickly realized it was going to be the other way around. The only control she had over anything was her mouth. Through all of this, she had not once begged them to stop. She had not asked for mercy. She had not given them the power of knowing that they were so far into her head that every thought had a shadow lurking behind it.

But what if she told them the truth?

Evelyn had spent so many years hiding the secret that even thinking about unburdening herself brought her something akin to peace. These men were her torturers, not her confessors, but she was in no position to quibble. Perhaps her death would absolve her of her sins. Perhaps there would be a moment of relief when for the first time in a long while, Evelyn felt the weight of deceit finally lifting from her shoulders.

No. They would never believe her. She would have to tell them a lie. The truth was too disappointing. Too common.

It would have to be a believable lie, something so compelling that they would kill her without first waiting for verification. These men were hardened, but not experienced, criminals. They didn't have the patience to keep around an old woman who had defied them for so long. They would see killing her as the ultimate proof of their manhood.

Her only regret was that she wouldn't be there when they realized she'd tricked them. She hoped they heard her laughing at them from hell for the rest of their miserable, pathetic lives.

She laughed now, just to hear the sound, the desperation.

The door opened. A slash of light came under the blindfold. She heard men mumbling. They were talking about another TV show, another movie, that had a new technique they wanted to try out.

Evelyn inhaled deeply, even though her broken ribs stabbed into her lungs with every breath. She willed her heart to still. She prayed for strength to a God she'd stopped talking to the day her husband died.

The one with the putrid breath said, 'You ready to talk, bitch?'

Evelyn braced herself. She couldn't appear to give in too easily. She would have to let them beat her, make them think that they had finally won. It wasn't the first time that she'd let a man think he had complete control over her, but it sure as hell would be the last.

He pressed his hand into her broken leg. 'You ready to bring on the pain?'

This would work. This had to work. Evelyn would do her part, and her death would finish it, wash away her sins. Faith would never find out. Zeke would never know. Her children and grandchildren would be safe.

Safe but for one thing.

Evelyn closed her eyes and sent out a silent message to Roz Levy, praying that the old woman would keep her mouth shut.

CHAPTER EIGHT

Faith's eyes were closed, but she couldn't sleep. wouldn't sleep. The night had passed in inches, dragging along like Death's sickle being scraped across the floor. For hours, she had listened to every creak and groan of the house, straining to hear any movement downstairs that indicated Zeke was finally awake.

Her mother's finger was hidden in a half-empty box of Band-Aids in Faith's medicine cabinet. It was wrapped in a Ziploc bag she'd found in an old suitcase. Faith had debated about whether or not to put it on ice, but the thought of preserving her mother's finger had made bile come to the back of her throat. Besides, she hadn't wanted to go downstairs last night and face Zeke, or the detectives who were sitting at her kitchen table, or her son who would surely join them all if he heard his mother was up. Faith knew if she saw them, she would start crying, and if she started crying they would quickly figure out why.

Keep your mouth shut and your eyes open.

She was doing exactly that, though the cop inside of her was screaming that following the kidnapper's orders was an incredibly big mistake. You never gave them the upper hand. You never ceded to a request without getting something in return. Faith had coached families on these basic strategies dozens of times. She saw now that it was a different thing altogether when the threatened loved one was your own. If Evelyn's abductors had told Faith to douse herself in gasoline and light a match, she would've done it. Logic went out the window when there existed the very real possibility that she might never see her mother again.

Still, the cop in her wanted details. There were tests that could be done to determine whether or not Evelyn was alive when the finger was removed. There were other tests that would prove definitively whether or not the digit belonged to Evelyn in the first place. It looked like a woman's finger, but Faith had never spent much time studying her mother's hands. There was no wedding ring; Evelyn had stopped wearing that a few years ago. It was one of those things Faith didn't notice at first. Or maybe her mother was just a good liar. She'd laughed when Faith asked about her naked hand, saying, 'Oh, I took that off ages ago.'

Was her mother a liar? That was the central question. Faith lied to Jeremy all the time, but it was about things all mothers should lie to their children about: her dating life, what was happening at work, how she was managing her health. Evelyn had lied about Zeke being transferred back to the U.S. But, that was to keep the peace, and probably to prevent Zeke's disapproval from shadowing the happy occasion of Emma's birth.

Those sorts of lies didn't count. They were protective lies, not malignant lies that festered like a splinter under your skin. Had Evelyn lied to Faith in a way that counted? There was something bigger that Evelyn was hiding, something more than the obvious. Evelyn's house told that story. The circumstances of her kidnapping delivered chapter and verse. She had something in her possession that some very bad men wanted. There was a drug connection. There was at least one gang involved. Her mother had worked narcotics. Had she been sitting on a pile of cash all this time? Was there a secret vault hidden somewhere? Would Faith and Zeke find out when Evelyn's will was read that their mother was actually wealthy?

No, that wasn't possible. Evelyn would know that her children would turn over any illicit cash, no matter how much easier it would make their

211

lives. Mortgages. Car payments. Student loans. None of that would go away. Neither Zeke nor Faith would ever take dirty money. Evelyn had raised them better than that.

And she had raised Faith to be a better cop than to just sit around on her hands all night waiting for the sun to come up.

If Evelyn were here right now, what would she want Faith to do? The obvious answer was to call Amanda. The two women had always been close. 'Thick as thieves,' Bill Mitchell had often said, and not with flattery. Even after Faith's uncle Kenny had decided to make an ass of himself pursuing younger women on the beaches of South Florida, Evelyn had made it clear that she preferred to have Amanda at the family Christmas table rather than Kenny Mitchell. The two women shared a shorthand the way soldiers did when they came back from war.

But calling Amanda now was out of the question. She would come rushing in like a bull in a china shop. Faith's house would be turned upside down. A SWAT team would be in place. The kidnappers would take one look at the show of force and decide it was easier to put a bullet in their victim's head rather than negotiate with a woman who was hell-bent on revenge. Because that was exactly how Amanda would play it. She never went at anything quietly. It was always a hundred percent or nothing at all.

Will was good at going in soft. He'd perfected the technique. And he was her partner. She *should* call him, or at least get word to him. But what would she say? 'I need your help but you can't tell Amanda and we may end up breaking the law, but

212

please don't ask any questions.' It was an untenable position. He'd bent the rules for her yesterday, but she couldn't ask him to break them. There was no one else she would trust more to have her back, but Will had a sometimes vexing sense of right and wrong. Part of her was afraid that he would tell her no. And a larger part of her was afraid that she would end up getting him into the kind of trouble that he could never get out of. It was one thing for Faith to throw her career out the window. She couldn't ask Will to do the same.

She dropped her head into her hands. Even if she wanted to reach out, the phones were tapped in case a ransom demand was made. Her email was through her GBI account, which was more than likely being monitored. They were probably listening in on her cell phone calls, too.

And that was just the good guys. Who knew what Evelyn's kidnappers had managed to do? They knew Jeremy's nickname, his birth year, his school. They had sent a warning through his Facebook account. Maybe they had bugged the house, too. You could get spy-quality devices off the Internet. Unless Faith went around removing switch plates and taking apart the phones, there was no telling whether or not someone was listening. And the minute she started acting paranoid around her family, they would know that something was wrong. Not to mention the Atlanta detectives, who were watching her every move.

Finally, she heard the downstairs toilet flush. A few seconds later, the front door opened and closed. Zeke was probably going for a run, or maybe the detectives had decided to get their fresh air in the front yard instead of the back.

Faith's hamstrings vibrated with pain as she put her feet on the floor. She'd been curled up for so long that her body was stiff. Other than checking on Emma, she hadn't dared walk around last night for fear of Zeke coming upstairs to ask her what the hell she was doing. The house was old, the floorboards were squeaky, and her brother was a light sleeper.

She started with her chest of drawers, carefully opening each one, checking through her underwear and T-shirts and nightgowns to see if anything had been disturbed. Nothing looked out of place. Next, she went to the closet. Her work wardrobe consisted mostly of black suits with stretch in the pants so that she didn't have to worry about whether or not they would button in the morning. Her maternity clothes were in a box on the lower shelf. Faith dragged over a chair and checked that the tape was still sealed. The stack of blue jeans beside it looked undisturbed. Still, she checked all the pockets, then went back to her suits and did the same.

Nothing.

Faith climbed back onto the chair and stretched on tiptoe to reach the top shelf, where she'd stored the box of Jeremy's childhood memorabilia. It nearly fell on her head. She caught it at the last minute, holding her breath for fear of making too much noise. She sat on the floor with the box between her legs. The cardboard was unsealed. The tape had been peeled off months ago. While she was pregnant with Emma, Faith had been obsessed with going through Jeremy's childhood keepsakes. It was a good thing she lived alone or someone would've seriously questioned her emotional stability. Just the sight of his bronzed shoes and little knitted booties had turned her into a weeping mess. His report cards. His school papers. Mother's Day cards he'd drawn in crayon. Valentines he'd cut with his tiny blunted scissors.

Her eyes stung as she opened the box.

A lock of Jeremy's hair rested on top of his twelfth-grade report card. The blue ribbon looked different. She held it up to the light. Time had faded the pastel-colored silk, giving the creases a dingy cast. The hair had darkened to a golden brown. Something felt different. She couldn't tell whether or not the bow had been retied or if it had come loose in the box. She also couldn't remember whether she'd stacked his report cards first grade to twelfth or the other way around. It seemed counterintuitive that the last was first, especially since the lock of hair was on top. Or maybe she was just talking herself into a frenzy when nothing was wrong.

Faith lifted up the stack of report cards and looked underneath. His papers were still there. She saw the bronze shoes, the booties, the construction paper greeting cards he'd made in school.

Everything seemed accounted for, yet she couldn't shake the feeling that the box had been tampered with. Had someone else gone through Jeremy's things? Had they seen the hearts he'd drawn on a picture of Mr. Billingham, his first dog? Had they rifled through his report cards and laughed because Mrs. Thompson, his fourth-grade teacher, had called him a little angel?

Faith closed the box. She hefted it up over her head and slid it onto the shelf. By the time she

215

shoved the chair back in place, she was shaking with fury at the thought of some stranger's grimy hands on her boy's things.

She went to Emma's room next. The baby didn't normally sleep through the night, but yesterday had been unusually long and tumultuous. She was still asleep when Faith checked the crib. Her throat made a clicking noise as she breathed. Faith laid a hand on her chest. Emma's heart felt like a bird trapped under Faith's hand. Quietly, she searched the closet, the small box of toys, the diapers and supplies.

Nothing.

Jeremy was still asleep, but Faith went into his room anyway. She picked up his clothes from the floor to give some pretense of belonging. Part of her just wanted to stand there and stare at him. He was in what she thought of as his John Travolta pose, sprawled on his stomach, right foot hanging off the bed, left arm sticking straight out above his head. His thin shoulder blades stuck out like chicken wings. His hair covered most of his face. There was a spot of saliva on his pillow. He still slept with his mouth open.

His room had been spotless yesterday, but his mere presence had altered everything. Papers covered the desk. His backpack spilled onto the floor. Wires from various pieces of computer equipment were draped across the carpet. His laptop, which she had saved for six months to buy, was open on its side like a discarded book. Faith used her foot to tip it right side up before leaving the room. Then, she went back in one more time, but only to pull the sheet up over his shoulders so that he wouldn't get cold.

Faith threw Jeremy's clothes on top of the washer and made her way downstairs. Detective Connor was sitting in his usual chair at the kitchen table. His shirt was different from yesterday, and his shoulder holster wasn't as tight around his chest. His red hair was tousled, probably from sleeping with his head on the table. She had started thinking of him as 'Ginger' and was afraid to open her mouth for fear of the name slipping out.

He said, 'Good morning, Agent Mitchell.'

'My brother's out running?'

He nodded. 'Detective Taylor went to get breakfast. I hope you like McDonald's.'

The thought of food was enough to make Faith feel sick again, but she said, 'Thank you.'

Half the refrigerator's contents were gone, though that was probably down to Jeremy and Zeke, both of whom ate like eighteen-year-old boys. She took out the orange juice. The carton was empty. Neither her son nor her brother liked orange juice.

She asked Ginger, 'Did you guys have some juice?'

'No, ma'am.'

Faith shook the carton. It was still empty. She didn't think Ginger would lie about something like that. She had offered both detectives anything in the kitchen. Judging by her depleted stash of Diet Rite sodas, they had taken her up on the offer.

The phone rang. Faith checked the clock on the stove. It was exactly seven in the morning. 'This will probably be my boss,' she told Ginger. Still, he waited until she had answered the phone.

Amanda said, 'No news.'

Faith waved away the detective. 'Where are

you?'

She didn't answer the question. 'How's Jeremy holding up?'

'As well as can be expected.' Faith didn't offer more. She checked to make sure Ginger was in the living room, then opened the silverware drawer. The spoons were turned in the wrong direction, the flat handles to the right rather than the left. The forks were upside down. The tines pointed toward the front of the drawer instead of the back. Faith blinked, not sure about what she was seeing.

Amanda said, 'You know about Boyd?'

'Will told me last night. I'm sorry. I know he did some bad things, but he was . . .'

Amanda didn't make her finish the sentence. 'Yes, he was.'

Faith opened the junk drawer. All the pens were gone. She kept them bundled together with a red rubber band, tucked in the bottom right-hand corner. They were always in this drawer. She rifled through the coupons, scissors, and unidentified spare keys. No pens. 'Did you know that Zeke was stateside?'

'Your mother was trying to protect you.'

Faith opened the other junk drawer. 'Apparently, she tried to protect me from a lot of things.' She reached into the back and found the pens. The rubber band was yellow. Had she changed it out? Faith had a vague recollection of the band breaking a while back, but she would've sworn on a stack of Bibles that she'd used the red rubber band from the broccoli she'd bought at the store that same day.

'Faith?' Amanda's tone was terse. 'What's going on with you? Has something happened?'

218

'I'm fine. It's just . . .' She tried to think of an excuse. She was really doing this—she was locked into not telling Amanda that the kidnappers had been in touch. That they had left something of Evelyn's under Faith's pillow. That they knew far too much about Jeremy. That they had messed with her silverware. 'It's early. I didn't sleep well last night.'

'You need to take care of yourself. Eat the right foods. Sleep as much as you can. Drink lots of water. I know it's hard, but you have to keep up your strength right now.'

Faith felt her temper flare. She didn't know if she was talking to her boss or to Aunt Mandy right now, but either one of them could kiss her ass. 'I know how to take care of myself.'

'I'm very glad to hear you think that, but from where I'm standing, it's not the case.'

'Did she do something, Mandy? Is Mom in trouble because—'

'Do you need me to come by the house?'

'Aren't you in Valdosta?'

Amanda went silent. Faith had obviously crossed a line. Or maybe it was a simple case of her boss being smart enough to remember that their conversation was being recorded. Right now, Faith didn't care. She stared at the yellow rubber band, wondering if she was losing her mind. Her blood sugar was probably low. Faith's vision was slightly blurry. Her mouth was dry. She opened the fridge again and reached for the orange juice carton. Still empty.

Amanda said, 'Think of your mother. She would want you to be strong.'

If she only knew that Faith was about to lose her

219

shit over a yellow rubber band. She mumbled, 'I'm fine.'

'We'll get her back, and we'll make sure that whoever did this pays for what they've put us through. You can take that to the bank.'

Faith opened her mouth to say she didn't give a damn about retribution, but Amanda had already ended the call.

She tossed the orange juice carton into the trash. There was a bag of emergency candy in the cabinet. Faith pulled it out, and Jolly Ranchers scattered onto the floor. She looked at the bag. The bottom had been ripped open.

Ginger was back. He leaned down to help her pick up the candy. 'Everything all right?'

'Yes.' Faith tossed a handful of candy onto the counter and left the kitchen. She hit the light switch in the living room but nothing happened. Faith flipped the toggle down, then up again. Still nothing. She checked the bulb in the lamp. One turn made the light come on. She did the same to the bulb in the other lamp. She felt the heat singe her fingers as the light came on.

Faith fell heavily into the chair. Her temper kept revving up and down like scales on a piano. She knew that she needed to eat something, to test her blood and make the proper adjustments. Her brain wouldn't work properly until she was leveled out. But now that she was sitting down, she didn't have the strength to move.

The couch was across from her. Zeke had folded his sheets into a perfect square and placed them on top of his pillow. She could see the red stain on the beige cushion where Jeremy had spilled Kool-Aid fifteen years ago. She knew that if she flipped the cushion over, she would find a blue stain from a Maui punch Popsicle he had dropped two years later. If she turned over the cushion she was sitting on, there would be a tear where his soccer cleat had cut the material. The rug on the floor was worn from both their tracks back and forth to the kitchen. The walls were an eggshell they had painted during Jeremy's spring break last year.

Faith considered the very real possibility that she was losing her mind. Jeremy was too old for these kinds of games, and Zeke had never been one for psychological warfare. He would rather beat her to death than unscrew a couple of light bulbs. Regardless, neither one of them was in the mood for pranks. This couldn't just be Faith's blood sugar. The pens, the silverware, the lamps— it was little things that only Faith would notice. The sort of stuff that would make someone else think you were crazy if you told them about it.

She looked up at the ceiling, then let her eyes travel down to the shelves mounted on the wall behind the couch. Bill Mitchell had been a collector of kitsch. He had hula girl salt and pepper shakers from Hawaii. He had Mount Rushmore sunglasses, a foam Lady Liberty crown, and an enameled silver spoon set depicting some of the more notable scenery of the Grand Canyon. His most prized collection had been his snow globes. Every road trip, every flight, every time he left the house, Bill Mitchell looked for a snow globe to mark the occasion.

When her father died, there was no question in the family that these would go to Faith. As a child, she had loved shaking the globes and watching the snow fall. Order into chaos. It was something Faith

221

had shared with her father. In a rare splurge, she'd had custom shelves built for the globes and made Jeremy so scared of breaking one that for an entire month he took the long way to the kitchen just so he didn't accidentally brush against the shelves.

As she sat in the living room that morning, Faith looked up at the shelves to find that all of thirty-six globes had been turned around to face the wall.

CHAPTER NINE

Sara wondered if it was a southern peculiarity for little children to get sick in the half hour between Sunday school and church services. Most of her early patients that morning had fallen into that golden time period. Tummy aches, earaches, general malaise—nothing that could be pinned down by a blood test or an X-ray, but was easily cured by a set of coloring books or a cartoon on the television.

Around ten o'clock, the problems had turned more serious. The cases came in rapid succession, and were the kind Sara hated because they were largely preventable. One child had eaten rat poison he'd found under the kitchen cabinet. Another had gotten third-degree burns from touching a pan on the stove. There was a teenager she'd had to forcibly commit to the lockdown ward because his first hit of marijuana had pushed him into a psychotic break. Then a seventeen-year-old girl had come in with her skull split open. Apparently, she was still drunk when she drove home this morning. The girl had ended up wrapping her car around a parked Greyhound bus. She was still in surgery, but Sara guessed that even if they managed to control the swelling in her brain, she would never be the same person again.

By eleven, Sara wanted to go back to bed and start the day over.

Working at a hospital was a constant negotiation. The job could suck away as much of your life as you permitted. Sara had agreed to work at Grady knowing this truth, embracing it, because she didn't want a life after her husband had died. Over the last year, she'd been cutting back on her time in the ER. Keeping regular hours was a struggle, but Sara fought the uphill battle every day.

It was really a form of self-preservation. Every doctor carried around a cemetery inside them. The patients she could help—the little girl whose stomach she'd pumped, the burned toddler whose fingers she'd saved—were momentary blips. It was the lost ones that Sara remembered most. The kid who'd slowly, painfully succumbed to leukemia. The nine-year-old who'd taken sixteen hours to die from antifreeze poisoning. The eleven-year-old who'd broken his neck diving headfirst into a shallow swimming pool. They were all inside of her, constant reminders that no matter how hard she worked, sometimes—oftentimes—it was never enough.

Sara sat down on the couch in the doctors' lounge. She had charts to catch up on, but she needed a minute to herself. She'd gotten less than four hours of sleep last night. Will wasn't the direct reason her brain would not turn off. She'd kept thinking about Evelyn Mitchell and her corrupt band of brothers. The question of the woman's guilt weighed heavily on her mind. Will's words kept coming back to Sara: either Evelyn Mitchell was a bad boss or a dirty cop. There was no in-between.

Which was probably why Sara hadn't found the time this morning to call Faith Mitchell and check on her. Technically, Faith was Delia Wallace's patient, but Sara felt an odd sort of responsibility for Will's partner. It tugged at her the same way Will seemed to tug at her every waking thought these days.

All of the tedium. None of the pleasure.

Nan, one of the student nurses, plopped down on the couch beside Sara. She scrolled through her BlackBerry as she talked. 'I want to hear all about your hot date.'

Sara forced a smile onto her face. That morning when she got to the hospital, there'd been a large bouquet of flowers waiting for her in the doctors' lounge. It seemed Dale Dugan had bought out the entire city's supply of baby's breath and pink carnations. Everyone in the ER had made a comment to Sara before she'd even managed to change into her lab coat. They all seemed caught up in the romance of the widow being swept off her feet.

Sara told the girl, 'He's very nice.'

'He thinks you're nice, too.' Nan gave a sly grin as she typed an email. 'I ran into him at the lab. He's super cool.'

Sara watched the girl's thumbs move, feeling three hundred years old. She couldn't remember if she'd ever been that young. Neither could she imagine Dale Dugan sitting down and having a

224

nice gossip with this giddy young nurse.

Nan finally looked up from the device. 'He said you're fascinating, and that you had a great time, and that you shared a very nice kiss.'

'You're emailing him?'

'No.' She rolled her eyes. 'He said that in the lab.'

'Great,' Sara managed. She didn't know how to deal with Dale, who was either deluded or a pathological liar. Eventually, she would have to talk with him. The flowers alone were a very bad sign. She would have to rip off the Band-Aid quickly. Still, she couldn't help wondering why the man she wanted was unavailable and the available man was unwanted. Thus continued her quest to turn her life into a television soap opera.

Nan started typing again. 'What do you want me to tell him that you said?'

'I haven't said anything.'

'But you could.'

'Uh . . .' Sara stood up from the couch. This was much easier when you could just slip a note into somebody's locker. 'I should go get lunch while things are quiet.'

Instead of heading toward the cafeteria, Sara took a left toward the elevators. She almost got mowed down by a gurney flying down the corridor. Stab wound. The knife was still sticking out of the patient's chest. EMTs screamed vitals. Doctors snapped orders. Sara pressed the elevator down button and waited for the doors to open.

The hospital had been founded in the 1890s, and was housed in four different locations before finding its final home on Jesse Hill Jr. Drive. Constant mismanagement, corruption, and plain

225

incompetence meant that at any given time in its storied history, the hospital was about to go under. The U-shaped building had been added onto, remodeled, torn down, and renovated so many times that Sara was certain no one could keep count anymore. The land around the facility was sloped toward Georgia State University, which shared its parking decks with the hospital. The ambulance bays for the emergency department backed onto the interstate, at what was called the Grady Curve, and were a full story above the main front entrance on the street side. During Jim Crow, the hospital was called the Gradys, because the white wings were on one side, looking onto the city, and the African American wings were on the other, looking onto nothing.

Margaret Mitchell had been rushed here, and died five days later, after being hit by a drunk driver on Peachtree Street. Victims from the Centennial Olympic Park bombing had been treated here. Grady was still the only Level 1 trauma center in the area. Victims with most serious, life-threatening injuries were all flown here for treatment, which meant the Fulton County medical examiner's office had a satellite location to process intakes down in the morgue. At any given time, there were two or three bodies waiting for transport. When Sara had first taken the job as Grant County coroner, she had trained at the Pryor Street medical examiner's office downtown. They were constantly shorthanded. She'd spent many a lunch hour making body runs to Grady.

The elevator doors opened. George, one of the security guards, got off. His girth filled the hall. He had been a football player until a dislocated ankle had convinced him to pursue an alternative career path.

'Dr. Linton.' He held the doors back for her.

'George.'

He winked at her and she smiled.

A young couple was already in the car. They huddled together as the elevator moved down one floor. That was the other thing about working at a hospital. Everywhere you turned, you ran into someone who was having one of the worst days of their life. Maybe this was the change Sara needed in her life—not to sell her apartment and move into a cozy bungalow, but to return to private practice, where the only emergency during the day was deciding which pharmaceutical rep was going to buy lunch.

The temperature was colder two stories down in the sub-basement. Sara pulled her lab coat closed as she walked past the records department. Unlike the old days when she'd interned at Grady, there was no need to stand in line for charts. Everything was automated, a patient's information only as far away as the computerized tablets that worked on the hospital's intranet. X-rays were on the larger computer monitors in the rooms, and all medications were coded to patient armbands. As the only publicly funded hospital left in Atlanta, Grady was constantly teetering on bankruptcy, but at least it was trying to go out in style.

Sara stopped in front of the thick double doors that separated the morgue from the rest of the hospital. She waved her badge in front of the reader. There was a sudden whoosh of changing air pressure as the insulated steel doors swung open.

The attendant seemed surprised to find Sara in his space. He was as close to goth as you could get while wearing blue hospital scrubs. Everything about him announced that he was too cool for his job. His dyed black hair was pulled into a ponytail. His glasses looked like they had belonged to John Lennon. His eyeliner was something out of a Cleopatra movie. To Sara, the paunch at his stomach and the Fu Manchu made him look more like Spike, Snoopy's brother. 'You lost?'

'Junior,' she read off his nametag. He was young, probably Nan's age. 'I was wondering if someone from the Fulton ME's office was here.'

'Larry. He's loading up in the back. Is there a problem?'

'No, I just want to pick his brain.'

'Good luck finding it.'

A skinny Hispanic man came out of the back room. His scrubs hung on him like a bathrobe. He was around Junior's age, which was to say that he had probably been in diapers a few weeks ago. 'Very funny, *jefe*.' He punched Junior in the arm. 'Whatchu need, Doc?'

This wasn't going as planned. 'Nothing. Sorry to bother you guys.' She started to turn away, but Junior stopped her.

'You're Dale's new lady, right? He said you were a tall redhead.'

Sara bit her lip. What was Dale doing hanging around all these ten-year-olds?

Junior's face broke out into a grin. 'Dr. Linton, I presume.'

She would've lied but for her badge hanging off her jacket. And her name embroidered over the

228

breast pocket. And the fact that she was the only doctor with red hair working in the hospital.

Larry offered, 'I'd be pleased to help Dale's new squeeze.'

'Hells yeah,' Junior chimed in.

Sara plastered a smile onto her face. 'How do you two know Dale?'

'B-ball, baby.' Larry feigned a hoop shot. 'What is the nature of your emergency?'

'No emergency—' she said, before realizing he was just being funny. 'I had a question about the shooting yesterday.'

'Which one?'

This time he wasn't joking. Asking about a shooting in Atlanta was like asking about the drunk at a football game. 'Sherwood Forest. The officer-involved shooting.'

Larry nodded. 'Damn, that was freaky. Guy had a belly full of H.'

'Heroin?' Sara asked.

'Packed into balloons. The gunshot split 'em open like . . .' He asked Junior, 'Shit, man, what're them things with sugar in 'em?'

'Dip Stick?'

'No.'

'Is it chocolate?'

'No, man, like in the paper straw.'

Sara suggested, 'Pixie Stix?'

'Yeah, that's right. Dude went out on an epic high.'

Sara waited through some fist bumping between the two. 'This was the Asian man?'

'No, the Puerto Rican. Ricardo.' He put an exotic spin on the *r*'s.

'I thought he was Mexican.'

229

'Yo, 'cause we all look alike?'

Sara didn't know how to answer him.

Larry laughed. 'That's cool. I'm just playin' ya. Sure, he's Puerto Rican, like my moms.'

'Did they get a last name on him?'

'No. But, he got the Neta tattooed on his hand.' He pointed to the webbing between his thumb and index finger. 'It's a heart with an *N* in the middle.'

'Neta?' Sara had never heard the name before.

'Puerto Rican gang. Crazy dudes want to break off from the U.S. My moms was all up in that shit when we left. All "we gotta get out from the rule of the colonial oppressors." Then she gets here and she's all, "I gotta get me one'a them big-screen plasma TVs like your aunt Frieda." Word.' Another fist bump with Junior.

'You're sure that's a gang symbol—the *N* inside a heart?'

'One of 'em. Everybody who joins up has to bring in more people.'

'Like Wiccans,' Junior provided.

'Exactly. Lots of 'em drop out or move on. Ricardo there can't be big-time. He don't got the fingers.' Larry held up his hand again, this time with his index finger crossed in front of his middle finger. 'Usually looks like this, with the Puerto Rican flag around the wrist. They're all about independence. At least that's what they say.'

Sara remembered what Will had told her. 'I thought Ricardo had the Los Texicanos tattoo on his chest?'

'Yeah, like I said, a lot of 'em drop out or move on. Brother must've moved on and up. Neta ain't got pull here like Texicanos.' He hissed air through his teeth. 'Scary stuff, man. Them Texicanos don't screw around.'

'Does the ME's office know all of this?'

'They sent the pictures to the gang unit. Neta's the top organization in PR. They'll be in the Bible.'

The Gang Bible was the book used by police officers to track gang signs and movements. 'Was there anything on the Asian men? The other victims?'

'One was a student. Some kind of math whiz. Won all kinds of prizes or some shit.'

Sara remembered Hironobu Kwon's photo from the news. 'I thought he was at Georgia State?' State wasn't a bad school, but a math prodigy would end up at Georgia Tech.

'That's all I know. They're doing the other guy right now. That apartment fire got us backed up big-time. Six bodies.' He shook his head. 'Two dogs. Man, I hate when it's dogs.'

Junior said, 'I feel ya, bro.'

'Thank you,' Sara said. 'Thank you both.'

Junior pounded the side of his fist against his chest. 'Be good to my man Dale.'

Sara left before more fists were bumped. She dug her hand into her pocket, trying to find her cell phone as she walked down the hallway. Most of the staff carried so many electronic devices that they were all likely going to die of radiation poisoning. She had a BlackBerry she received lab reports and hospital communiqués on as well as an iPhone for personal use. Her hospital cell phone was a flip-style that had previously belonged to someone with very sticky hands. Two pagers were clipped to her coat pocket, one for the emergency department and one for the pediatrics ward. Her personal phone was slim and usually the last thing she found, which was the case this time.

She scrolled through the numbers, pausing on Amanda Wagner's name, then scrolling back up to Will Trent. His phone rang twice before he picked up.

'Trent.'

Sara was inexplicably tongue-tied by the sound of his voice. In the silence, she could hear wind blowing, the sound of children playing.

He said, 'Hello?'

'Hi, Will—sorry.' She cleared her throat. 'I was calling because I talked to someone at the ME's office. Like you asked.' She felt her face turning red. 'Like Amanda asked.'

He mumbled something, probably to Amanda. 'What'd you find out?'

'The Texicanos victim, Ricardo. No last name as of yet, but he was probably Puerto Rican.' She waited while he relayed this information to Amanda. She asked the same question Sara had. Sara answered, 'He had a tattoo on his hand for a gang, the Neta, which is in Puerto Rico. The man I talked with said Ricardo probably switched affiliations when he came to Atlanta.' Again, she waited for him to tell Amanda. 'He also had a belly full of heroin.'

'Heroin?' His voice went up in surprise. 'How much?'

'I'm not sure. The man I spoke with said the powder was packed in balloons. When Faith shot him, the heroin was released. That alone would've killed him.'

Will told Amanda as much, then came back on the line. 'Amanda says thank you for checking into this.'

232

'I'm sorry there's not more.'

'That's great what you came up with.' He clarified, 'I mean, thank you, Dr. Linton. This is all very useful information to have.'

She knew he couldn't talk in front of Amanda, but she didn't want to let him go. 'How's it going on your end?'

'The prison was a bust. We're standing outside Hironobu Kwon's house right now. He lived with his mother in Grant Park.' He was less than fifteen minutes away from Grady. 'The neighbor says his mother should be home soon. I guess she's probably making arrangements. She lives across the street from the zoo. We had to park about a mile away. Or, I did. Amanda made me drop her off.' He finally paused for breath. 'How are you doing?'

Sara smiled. He seemed to want to stay on the phone as much as she did. 'Did you get any sleep last night?'

'Not much. How about you?'

She tried to think of something flirty to say, but settled on, 'Not much.'

Amanda's voice was too muffled to understand, but Sara got the tone. Will said, 'So, I'll talk to you later. Thank you again, Dr. Linton.'

Sara felt foolish as she ended the call. Maybe she should go back up to the lounge and gossip with Nan.

Or maybe she should talk to Dale Dugan and nip this in the bud before they both got any more embarrassed. Sara took out her hospital BlackBerry and looked up Dale's email address, then started to enter it into her iPhone. She would ask him to meet her in the cafeteria so they could

233

talk this through. Or maybe she should suggest the parking lot. She didn't want to cause more gossip than was already circulating.

Up ahead, the elevator bell dinged and she caught sight of Dale. He was laughing with one of the nurses. Junior must've told him she was down here. Sara chickened out. She opened the first door she came to, which happened to be the records department. Two older women with matching, tightly groomed perms sat behind desks piled with charts. They were typing furiously on their computer keyboards and barely looked up at Sara.

One of them asked, 'Help you?' turning the page on the chart opened beside her.

Sara stood there, momentarily unsure of herself. She realized that somewhere in the back of her mind, she had been thinking about the records office since she got on the elevator. She dropped her iPhone back into her coat pocket.

'What is it, darlin'?' the woman asked. They were both staring at Sara now.

She held up her hospital ID. 'I need an old chart from nineteen . . .' She did the math quickly in her head. 'Seventy-six, maybe?'

The woman handed her a pad and paper. 'Give me the name. That'll make it easier.'

Sara knew even as she wrote down Will's name that what she was doing was wrong, and not just because she was breaking federal privacy laws and risking immediate termination. Will had been at the Atlanta Children's Home from infancy. There wouldn't have been a family physician managing his care. All of his medical needs would have been handled through Grady. His entire childhood was

234

stored here, and Sara was using her hospital ID to gain access to it.

'No middle name?' the woman asked.

Sara shook her head. She didn't trust herself to speak.

'Gimme a minute. These won't be in the computer yet or you'd be able to pull them up on your tablet. We've barely dipped our toe into 1970.' She was out of her chair and through the door marked 'File Room' before Sara could tell her to stop.

The other woman went back to her typing, her long red fingernails making a sound like a cat running across a tile floor. Sara looked down at her shoes, which were stained with God knows what from this morning's cases. In her mind, she went over the possible culprits, but as hard as she tried, she could not shake the feeling that what she was doing was absolutely and without a doubt the most unethical thing she had ever done in her life. What's more, it was a complete betrayal of Will's trust.

And she couldn't do it. She wouldn't do it.

This wasn't the way Sara operated. She was normally a forthright person. If she wanted to know about Will's suicide attempt, or any details about his childhood, then she should ask him, not sneak around his back and look at his medical chart.

The woman was back. 'No William, but I found a Wilbur.' She had a file tucked under her arm. 'Nineteen seventy-five.'

Sara had used paper charts the majority of her career. Most healthy kids had a chart with twenty or so pages by the time they reached eighteen

235

years of age. An unhealthy kid's file could run around fifty. Will's chart was over an inch thick. A decaying rubber band held together faded sheets of yellow and white paper.

'No middle name,' the woman said. 'I'm sure he had one at some point, but a lot of these kids fell through the cracks back then.'

Her partner supplied, 'Ellis Island and Tuskegee rolled up into one.'

Sara reached for the file, then stopped herself. Her hand hovered in the air.

'You all right, darlin'?' The woman glanced back at her office mate, then to Sara. 'You need to sit down?'

Sara dropped her hand. 'I don't think I need that after all. I'm sorry to waste your time.'

'Are you sure?'

Sara nodded. She could not remember the last time she had felt this awful. Even her run-in with Angie Trent hadn't produced this amount of guilt. 'I'm so sorry.'

'No need to apologize. Felt good to get up.' She started to tuck the file under her arm but the rubber band broke, sending papers flying onto the floor.

Automatically, Sara bent down to help. She gathered the pages together, willing herself not to read the words. There were lab reports printed in dot matrix, reams of chart notations, and what looked like an ancient Atlanta police report. She blurred her vision, praying she wouldn't pick up a word or a sentence.

'Look at this.'

Sara looked up. It was a natural thing to do. The woman held a faded Polaroid picture in her hand.

236

The shot was a close-up of a child's mouth. A small silver ruler was beside a laceration running the width of the philtrum, the midline groove between the top of the lip and nose. The injury wasn't from a tumble or bump. The impact had been significant enough to rend the flesh in two, revealing the teeth. Thick black sutures pulled together the wound. The skin was puffy and irritated. Sara was more accustomed to seeing this kind of baseball stitching in a morgue, not on a child's face.

'I bet he was in that poly-what's-it study,' the woman said. She showed the photo to her friend.

'Polyglycolic acid.' She explained to Sara, 'Grady piloted a study on different types of absorbable sutures they were working on at Tech. Looks like he's one of the kids that had an allergic reaction. Poor little thing.' She went back to her typing. 'I guess it was better than sticking a bunch of leeches on him.'

The other woman asked Sara, 'You all right, hon?'

Sara felt as if she was going to be sick. She straightened up and left the room. She didn't stop walking until she had bolted up two flights of stairs and was outside, breathing fresh air.

She paced in front of the closed door. Her emotions pinballed back and forth between anger and shame. He was just a child. He'd been admitted for treatment and they had experimented on him like an animal. To this day, he probably had no idea what they had done. Sara wished to God she didn't know herself, though it served her right for prying. She should've never asked for his chart. But she had, and now Sara couldn't get that picture out of her head—his beautiful mouth

237

crudely pulled together with a suture that couldn't meet the basic standards for government approval.

The faded Polaroid would be burned into her memory until she died. She had gotten exactly what she deserved.

'Hey, you.'

She spun around. A young woman was standing behind her. She was painfully thin. Her greasy blonde hair hung to her waist. She scratched at the fresh needle tracks on her arms. 'Are you a doctor?'

Sara felt her guard go up. Junkies lurked around the hospital. Some of them could be violent. 'You should go inside if you need treatment.'

'It's not me. There's a guy over there.' She pointed to the Dumpster in a corner behind the hospital. Even in full daylight, the area was shadowed by the looming façade of the building. 'He's been there all night. I think he's dead.'

Sara moderated her tone. 'Let's go inside and talk about this.'

Anger flashed in the girl's eyes. 'Lookit, I'm just trying to do the right thing. You don't gotta go all high and mighty on me.'

'I'm not—'

'I hope he gives you AIDS, bitch.' She limped off, mumbling more insults.

'Christ,' Sara breathed, wondering how her day could get any worse. How she missed the manners of good country people, when even the junkies called her 'ma'am.' She started back toward the hospital, then stopped. The girl could've been telling the truth.

Sara walked back toward the Dumpster, not getting too close in case the girl's accomplice was

238

hiding inside. The trash wasn't collected over the weekend. Boxes and plastic bags spilled out of the metal container and littered the ground. Sara took a step closer. There was someone lying underneath a blue plastic bag. She saw a hand. A deep gash splayed open the palm. Sara took another step closer, then stopped. Working at Grady had made her hyper-cautious. This could still be a trap. Instead of going to the body, she turned around and jogged toward the ambulance bay so that she could get help.

Three EMTs were standing around talking. She directed them toward the back and they followed her with a gurney. Sara pulled away the trash. The man was breathing but unconscious. His eyes were closed. His brown skin had a yellow, waxy look. His T-shirt was soaked in blood, obviously from a penetrating wound in his lower abdomen. Sara pressed her fingers to his carotid and saw a familiar tattoo on his neck: a Texas star with a rattlesnake wrapped around it.

Will's missing Type B-negative.

'Let's move it,' one of the EMTs said.

Sara ran beside the gurney as they rolled the man into the hospital. She listened to the medics run down vitals as she pulled back the gauze over his belly. The entrance to the wound was thin, probably from a kitchen knife. The edge was rough from the serration. There was very little fresh blood, indicating a closed bleed. The gut was distended, and the telltale odor of rotting flesh told her that there was not much that she would be able to do for him in the ER.

A tall man in a dark suit jogged alongside her. He asked, 'Is he going to make it?'

Sara looked for George. The security guard was nowhere to be found. 'You need to stay out of the way.'

'Doctor—' He held up his wallet. She saw the flash of gold shield. 'I'm a cop. Is he going to make it?'

'I don't know,' she said, pressing the gauze back in place. Then, because the patient might hear, she said, 'Maybe.'

The cop dropped back. She glanced up the hall, but he was gone.

The trauma team set up immediately, cutting off the man's clothes, drawing blood, connecting lines to hook him up to various machines. A cut-down tray was laid out. Surgical packs were opened. The crash cart appeared.

Sara called for two large-bore IVs to force fluids. She checked the ABCs: airway clear, breathing okay, circulation as good as could be expected. She noticed the pace slow considerably as people began to realize what they were dealing with. The team thinned. Eventually, she was down to just one nurse.

'No wallet,' the nurse said. 'Nothing in his pockets but lint.'

'Sir?' Sara tried, opening the man's eyes. His pupils were fixed and dilated. She checked for a head injury, gently pressing her fingers in a clockwise pattern around his skull. At the occipital bone, she felt a fracture that splintered into the brainpan. She looked at her gloved hand. There was no fresh blood from the wound.

The nurse pulled the curtain closed to give the man some privacy. 'X-ray? CT the belly?'

Sara was technically doing the regular

240

attending's job. She asked, 'Can you get Krakauer?'

The nurse left, and Sara did a more thorough exam, though she was sure Krakauer would take one look at the man's vitals and agree with her. There was no emergency here. The patient could not survive general anesthesia and he likely would not survive his injuries. They could only load him up with antibiotics and wait for time to decide the patient's fate.

The privacy curtain pulled back. A young man peered in. He was clean-shaven, wearing a black warm-up jacket and a black baseball hat pulled down low on his head.

'You can't be back here,' she told him. 'If you're looking for—'

He punched Sara in the chest so hard that she fell back onto the floor. Her shoulder slammed against one of the trays. Metal instruments clattered around her—scalpels, hemostats, scissors. The young man pointed a gun at the patient's head and shot him twice at point-blank range.

Sara heard screaming. It was her. The sound was coming out of her own mouth. The man pointed the gun at her head and she stopped. He moved toward her. She groped blindly for something to protect herself. Her hand wrapped around one of the scalpels.

He was closer, almost on top of her. Was he going to shoot her or was he going to leave? Sara didn't give him time to decide. She slashed out, cutting the inside of his thigh. The man groaned, dropping the gun. The wound was deep. Blood sprayed from the femoral artery. He fell to one knee. They both saw the gun at the same time. She kicked it away. He reached for Sara instead, grabbing the hand that held the scalpel. She tried to pull back but his grip tightened around her wrists. Panic took hold as she realized what he was doing. The blade was moving toward her neck. She used both her hands, trying to push him away as he inched the blade closer and closer.

'Please . . . no . . .'

He was on top of her, pressing her into the ground with the weight of his body. She stared into his green eyes. The whites were crisscrossed with a road map of red. His mouth was a straight line. His body shook so hard that she felt it in her spine.

'Drop it!' George, the security guard, stood with his gun locked out in front of him. 'Now, asshole!'

Sara felt the man's grip tighten. Both their hands were shaking from pushing in opposite directions.

'Drop it now!'

'Please,' Sara begged. Her muscles couldn't take much more. Her hands were starting to weaken.

Without warning, the pressure stopped. Sara watched the scalpel swing up, the blade slice into the man's flesh. He kept his hand wrapped tightly around hers as over and over again he plunged the scalpel into his own throat.

CHAPTER TEN

Will had been trapped in the car so long with Amanda that he was worried he was going to develop Stockholm syndrome. He was already feeling himself weaken, especially after Miriam Kwon, mother of Hironobu Kwon, had spit in Amanda's face.

In Ms. Kwon's defense, Amanda hadn't exactly been tender toward the woman. They had practically ambushed her on her front lawn. She'd obviously just come from arranging her son's funeral. Pamphlets with crosses on them were clutched in her hand as she approached the house. Her street was lined with cars. She'd had to park some distance away. She looked exhausted and limp, the way any mother would look after choosing the coffin in which her only son would be buried.

After mumbling the perfunctory condolences on behalf of the GBI, Amanda had gone straight for the jugular. From Ms. Kwon's reaction, Will gathered the woman hadn't been expecting her dead son's name to be sullied in such a manner, despite the nefarious circumstances surrounding his death. It was the nature of Atlanta news stations that every dead young man under the age of twenty-five was celebrated as an honor student until proven otherwise. According to his criminal record, this particular honor student had been a fan of Oxycontin. Hironobu Kwon had been arrested twice for selling the drug. Only his academic promise had saved him from serious jail

243

time. The judge had ordered him to rehab three months ago. Apparently, that hadn't worked out too well.

Will checked the time on his cell phone. The recent change to daylight savings time had switched the phone into military hours. He couldn't for the life of him figure out how to change it back to normal. Thankfully, it was half past noon, which meant he didn't have to count on his fingers like a monkey.

Not that he didn't have ample time to perform mathematical equations. Despite traveling almost five hundred miles this morning, they had nothing to show for it. Evelyn Mitchell was still missing. They were about to hit the twenty-four-hour mark since her abduction. The dead bodies were stacking up, and the only clue Will and Amanda had been given thus far had come from the mouth of a death row inmate who had been murdered before the state could kill him.

Their trip to Valdosta State Prison may as well have never happened. Former drug squad detectives Adam Hopkins and Ben Humphrey had stared at Amanda as if gazing through a piece of glass. Will had expected as much. Years ago, they had each refused to talk to Will when he'd shown up on their respective doorsteps. Lloyd Crittenden was dead. Demarcus Alexander and Chuck Finn were probably just as unreachable. Both ex-detectives had left Atlanta as soon as they were released from prison. Will had talked to their parole officers last night. Alexander was on the West Coast trying to rebuild his life. Finn was in Tennessee, wallowing in the misery of drug addiction.

'Heroin,' Will said.

Amanda turned to him, looking as if she'd forgotten that he was in the car. They were heading north on Interstate 85, toward another bad guy who was more than likely going to refuse to talk to them.

He told her, 'Boyd Spivey said that Chuck Finn had a belly habit for heroin. According to Sara, Ricardo was packed full of heroin.'

'That's a very tenuous connection.'

'Here's another one: Oxy usually leads to heroin addiction.'

'These straws are mighty thin. You can't throw a brick without hitting a heroin addict these days.' She sighed. 'If only we had more bricks.'

Will tapped his fingers against his leg. He'd been holding back something all morning, hoping he'd catch Amanda off guard and get the truth. Now seemed as good a time as any. 'Hector Ortiz was Evelyn's gentleman friend.'

The corner of her mouth turned up. 'Is that so?'

'He's Ignatio Ortiz's brother, though I gather from your expression that this isn't a news flash.'

'Ortiz's cousin,' she corrected. 'Are these observations courtesy of Dr. Linton?'

Will felt his teeth start to grind. 'You already knew who he was.'

'Would you like to waste the next ten minutes discussing your feelings or do you want to do your job?'

He wanted to spend the next ten minutes throttling her, but Will decided to keep that to himself. 'What was Evelyn doing mixed up with the cousin of the guy who runs all the coke in and out of the southeastern United States?'

'Hector was a car salesman, actually.' She glanced at him. There was something like humor in her eyes. 'He sold Cadillacs.'

That explained why the man's name hadn't come up on Will's vehicle search. He was driving a dealer car. 'Hector had a Texicanos tattoo on his arm.'

'We all make mistakes when we're young.'

Will tried, 'What about the letter *A* that Evelyn drew under the chair?'

'I thought we were calling that an arrowhead?'

'*Almeja* rhymes with "Amanda."'

'It kind of does, doesn't it?'

'It's slang for "cunt."'

She laughed. 'Why, Will, are you calling me a cunt?'

If she only knew how many times he'd been tempted.

'I suppose I should reward your good police work.' Amanda pulled a folded sheet of paper from the sun visor. She handed it to Will. 'Evelyn's phone calls from the last four weeks.'

He scanned the two pages. 'She's been calling Chattanooga a lot.'

Amanda gave him a curious look. Will glared back at her. He could read, just not quickly and certainly not under scrutiny. The Tennessee Bureau of Investigation's eastern field office was in Chattanooga. He'd called them constantly to coordinate meth cases while he was working in North Georgia. The 423 area code appeared at least a dozen times in Evelyn's phone records.

He asked, 'Is there something you want to say to me?'

For once, she was silent.

246

Will pulled out his cell phone to call the number.

'Don't be stupid. It's Healing Winds, a rehab facility.'

'Why was she calling there?'

'I had the same question.' She signaled, pulling into the next lane. 'They're not allowed to give out patient information.'

Will checked the dates against the numbers. Evelyn had only started calling the facility in the last ten days, the same time period in which Mrs. Levy said that Hector Ortiz's visits with Evelyn had picked up.

Will said, 'Chuck Finn lives in Tennessee.'

'He lives in Memphis. That's a five-hour drive from Healing Winds in Chattanooga.'

'He has a serious drug addiction.' Will waited for her to respond. When she didn't, he said, 'Guys get clean, sometimes they want to unburden themselves. Maybe Evelyn was afraid he would start talking.'

'What an interesting theory.'

'Or maybe it took clearing his mind for Chuck to realize that Evelyn was still sitting on her share of the cash.' He pushed on. 'It's hard to find work with a rap sheet like Chuck's. He was kicked off the force. He spent serious time in prison. He's got his habit to battle. Even if he's clean, no one would go out of their way to hire him. Not in this economy.'

Amanda dropped another dollop of information. 'There were eight sets of prints in Evelyn's house, excluding hers and Hector's. They've identified three. One set belonged to Hironobu Kwon, another belonged to Ricardo the

247

heroin mule, and another set belonged to our Hawaiian shirt aficionado. His name is Benny Choo. He's a forty-two-year-old enforcer for the Yellow Rebels.'

'Yellow Rebels?'

'It's an Asian gang. Don't ask me where they got the name. I suppose they're very proud to be hillbillies. Most of them are.'

'Ling-Ling,' Will guessed. That was who they were going to see. 'Spivey said you should talk to Ling-Ling.'

'Julia Ling.'

Will was surprised. 'A woman?'

'Yes, a woman. My laws, how the world has changed.' Amanda glanced in the rearview mirror and darted into the next lane. 'The nickname comes from the now-disproven perception that she's not very smart. Her brother likes to rhyme things. 'Ding-a-ling' turned into 'Ling-a-Ling,' shortened to "Ling-Ling."'

Will had no idea what she was talking about. 'That makes sense.'

'Madam Ling is the outside boss of the Yellow Rebels. Her brother Roger still pulls the strings from inside, but she runs the day-to-day. If Yellow is making a play for Brown, then it's being made by Roger via Ling-Ling.'

'What's he in for?'

'He's serving life for the rape and murder of two teenage girls. Sixteen and fourteen. They were tricking for him. He didn't think they were pulling their weight, so he strangled them to death with a dog leash. But not before raping both of them and ripping off their breasts with his teeth.'

Will felt a shudder working its way up his spine.

'Why isn't he on death row?'

'He took a deal. The State was worried about him making an insanity plea—which, between you and me, wouldn't be much of a stretch, because the man is absolutely nuts. This wasn't the first time Roger was caught with human flesh between his teeth.'

The shudder made his shoulders flex. 'What about the victims?'

'They were both runaways who fell into drugs and prostitution. Their families were more about divine retribution than an eye for an eye.'

Will was familiar with the concept. 'They probably ran away for a reason.'

'Young girls usually do.'

'Roger's sister still supports him?'

She gave him a meaningful look. 'Don't be fooled, Will. Julia talks a very good game, but she could slit your throat and not lose a wink of sleep. These people are not to be messed with. There are procedures that have to be followed. You must show them the utmost respect.'

Will repeated Boyd's words. ' "You can't go to Yellow without an invitation." '

'You have such a remarkable memory.'

Will checked out the number for the next exit. They were heading toward Buford Highway. Chambodia. 'Maybe Boyd was only half right. Heroin is a lot more addictive than coke. If the Yellow Rebels flood the market with cheap heroin, then Los Texicanos will lose its cocaine customer base. That points to a power struggle, but it doesn't explain why two Asian men and a Texicano were in Evelyn Mitchell's house looking for something.' Will stopped. She'd sidetracked him again.

'Hironobu Kwon and Benny Choo. What's Ricardo's last name?'

She smiled. 'Very good.' She offered the information like another reward. 'Ricardo Ortiz. He's Ignatio Ortiz's youngest son.'

Will had interviewed ax murderers who were more forthcoming. 'And he was muling heroin.'

'Yes, he was.'

'Are you going to tell me if any of these guys are connected or do I have to find that out on my own?'

'Ricardo Ortiz was thrown into juvie twice, but he never crossed paths inside with Hironobu Kwon. Neither of them have visible connections to Benny Choo, and as I said, Hector Ortiz was just a simple car salesman.' She zipped in front of a delivery truck, cutting off a Hyundai in the process. 'Believe me, if I saw a connection between any of these men, we'd be working it.'

'Except for Choo, they're all young guys, early twenties.' Will tried to think of where they might've met. AA meetings. Nightclubs. Basketball courts. Church, maybe. Miriam Kwon wore a gold cross around her neck. Ricardo Ortiz had a cross tattooed on his arm. Stranger things had happened.

Amanda said, 'Check the number Evelyn called the day before she was taken. 3:02 p.m.'

Will traced his finger under the first column, finding the time. He moved across. The number had an Atlanta area code. 'Am I supposed to recognize this?'

'I'd be surprised if you did. It's the precinct number for Hartsfield.' Hartsfield-Jackson, Atlanta's airport. 'Vanessa Livingston is the commander.

250

I've known the old gal a long time. She partnered with Evelyn after I left APD.'

Will waited, then asked, 'And?'

'Evelyn asked her to check for a name on the flight manifests.'

'Ricardo Ortiz,' Will guessed.

'You must've gotten your sleep last night.'

He'd stayed up until three listening to the rest of the recordings, apparently for no reason but to find out things that Amanda already knew. 'Where did Ricardo fly in from?'

'Sweden.'

Will frowned. He hadn't been expecting that.

Amanda merged onto the exit ramp for I-285. 'Ninety percent of all heroin in the world comes from Afghanistan. Your tax dollars at work.' She slowed for the curve as they went through Spaghetti Junction. 'The bulk of the European supply runs through Iran, up into Turkey and farther points north.'

'Like Sweden.'

'Like Sweden.' She accelerated again as they merged into fast-moving traffic. 'Ricardo was there for three days. Then he took a flight from Gothenburg to Amsterdam, then straight into Atlanta.'

'Filled with heroin.'

'Filled with heroin.'

Will rubbed his jaw, thinking about what had happened to the young man.

'Someone beat the hell out of him. He was full of balloons. Maybe he couldn't pass them.'

'That would be a question for the ME.'

Will had assumed that she'd gotten all of this information from the medical examiner's office.

251

'You didn't ask him?'

'They've kindly promised me their full report by end of business this evening. Why do you think I asked you to have Sara reach out?' She added, 'How's that going, by the way? I'm assuming from your good night's sleep that there's not a lot of progress.'

They were coming up on the Buford Highway exit. U.S. Route 23 ran from Jacksonville, Florida, to Mackinaw City, Michigan. The Georgia stretch was around four hundred miles, and the part that went through Chamblee, Norcross, and Doraville was one of the most racially diverse in the area, if not the country. It wasn't exactly a neighborhood—more like a series of desolate strip malls, flimsy apartment buildings, and gas stations that offered expensive rims and quick title loans. What it lacked in community it made up for in raw commerce.

Will was fairly certain Chambodia was a pejorative term, but the name for the area had stuck, despite DeKalb County's push to call it the International Corridor. There were all kinds of ethnic subsets, from Portuguese to Hmong. Unlike most urban areas, there didn't seem to be a clear line of segregation between any of the communities. Subsequently, you could find a Mexican restaurant beside a sushi place, and the farmer's market was the sort of melting pot that people thought of when they pictured the United States.

The strip was much closer to the land of opportunity than the amber waves of grain in the heartland. People could come here with little more than a work ethic and build a solidly middle-class

252

life. For as long as Will could remember, the demographics were in constant flux. The whites complained when the blacks moved in. The blacks complained when the Hispanics moved in. The Hispanics complained when the Asians moved in. One day they would all be grumbling about the influx of whites. The gerbil wheel of the American dream.

Amanda pulled into the middle strip that served as the turning lane for both sides of the highway. Will saw a bunch of signs stacked one on top of the other like a Jenga game. Some of the characters were unrecognizable, more like pieces of art than letters.

'I've had a car sitting on Ling-Ling's shop all morning. She hasn't had any visitors.' Amanda floored the gas, narrowly missing a minivan as she made the turn. Horns blared, but she talked over them. 'I made some phone calls last night. Roger was transferred to Coastal three months ago. They had him at Augusta for six months prior, but he evened out on his meds, so they sent him back into the cattle shoot.' Augusta Medical Hospital provided Level 4 mental health services to inmates on a transient basis. 'Roger's first day at Coastal ended with a nasty incident involving a bar of soap wrapped in a tube sock. Apparently, he's not happy with his new accommodations.'

'You're going to offer to transfer him?'

'If it comes to that.'

'Are you going to use Boyd's name?'

'That might not be a wise idea.'

'What do you think Roger's going to give us?' Will did a mental head slap. 'You think he's behind Evelyn's kidnapping.'

'He may be clinically insane, but he'd never be stupid enough to do something like that.' She gave Will a meaningful look. 'Roger's extremely intelligent. Think chess, not checkers. There's no gain for him in taking Evelyn. His whole organization would be disrupted.'

'Okay, so, you think Roger knows who's involved?'

'If you want to know about a crime, ask a criminal.' Her cell phone started to ring. She checked the number. Will felt the car slow. Amanda pulled to the side of the road. She answered the phone, listened, then hit the unlock button on the door. 'A little privacy, please?'

Will got out of the SUV. The weather had been spectacular the day before, but now it was cloudy and warm. He walked toward the edge of the strip mall. There was a shack of a restaurant near the street entrance. He guessed from the rocking chair painted on the sign that it was some kind of country-cooking establishment. Strangely, Will didn't feel his stomach rumble at the thought of food. The last thing he'd had to eat was a bowl of instant grits that he'd forced down this morning. His appetite was gone, which was something he'd only experienced once before in his life—the last time he'd been around Sara Linton.

Will sat down on the curb. Cars whirred by behind him. Fragments of beats bounced from their radios. A glance toward Amanda told him she was going to be a while. She was gesturing with her hands, never a good thing.

He took out his phone and scrolled through the numbers. He should call Faith, but he didn't have anything he could report and their conversation last night hadn't ended well. Whatever happened with Evelyn wasn't going to make things better. No matter what tricky verbal maneuvering Amanda was doing, there were still some hard facts she couldn't talk around. If the Asians were really making a play for the Texicanos drug market, then Evelyn Mitchell had to be at the center of it. Hector might've called himself a car salesman, but he still had the tattoo that connected him to the gang. He still had a cousin in prison running that same gang. His nephew had been shot dead at Evelyn's house, and Hector himself was dead in Evelyn's trunk. There was no reason for a cop, especially a retired one, to be mixed up with these kind of bad guys unless there was something dirty going on.

Will looked down at his phone. Thirteen hundred hours. He should go into the setup menu and try to figure out how to switch it back to the normal time display, but Will didn't have the patience right now. Instead, he scrolled to Sara's cell phone number, which had three eights in it. He had stared at it so many times over the last few months that he was surprised the numbers weren't burned into his retinas.

Unless you counted the unfortunate misunderstanding with the lesbian who lived across the street, Will had never been on a real date before. He'd been with Angie since he was eight years old. There had been passion at one time, and for a short while, something that felt close to love, but he could not ever recall a point in his life when he felt happy to be with her. He lived in dread of her showing up on his doorstep. He felt enormous relief when she was gone. Where she got him was the in-between, those rare moments of peace when he got a glimpse of what a settled life could be. They would have meals together and go to the grocery store and work in the yard—or Will would work and Angie would watch—and then at night they'd go to bed and he would find himself lying there with a smile on his face because this was what life was like for the rest of the world.

And then he would wake up in the morning and she'd be gone.

They were too close. That was the problem. They had lived through too much, seen too many horrors, shared too much fear and loathing and pity, to look at each other as something other than victims. Will's body was like a monument to that misery: the burn marks, the scars, the various slings and arrows he had suffered. For years, he had wanted more from Angie, but Will had recently come to the hard realization that there was nothing more that she could give.

She wasn't going to change. He knew that truth even when they finally got married, which had come about not through careful planning but because Will had bet Angie that she wouldn't go through with it. Gambling aside, she was never going to see being with Will as anything other than a safe haven at best and a sacrifice at worst. There was a reason she never touched him unless she wanted something. There was a reason he didn't try to call her when she disappeared.

He slid his thumb inside his sleeve and felt the beginnings of the long scar that traced up his arm. It was thicker than he remembered. The skin was still tender to the touch.

Will pulled away his hand. Angie had flinched

the last time her fingers had accidentally brushed against his bare arm. Her reactions to him were always intense, never half measures. She liked to see how far she could push him. It was her favorite sport: how bad did she have to be before Will finally had enough and abandoned her just like everyone else had in her life?

They had teetered on that line many times, but somehow, she always managed to yank him back at the last second. Even now, Will felt the pull. He hadn't seen Angie since her mother had died. Deidre Polaski was a junkie and a prostitute who'd overdosed herself into a vegetative coma when Angie was eleven. Her body had held on for twenty-seven years before finally giving up. Four months had passed since the funeral. Not much in the scheme of things—Angie had disappeared for a whole year once—but Will felt a warning in his spine that told him something was wrong. She was in trouble or she was hurt or she was upset. His body knew it just like it knew that it needed to breathe.

They had always been connected like this, even back when they were kids. Especially when they were kids. And if there was one thing Will knew about his wife, it was that she always came to him when things were bad. He didn't know when she would show up, whether it would be tomorrow or next week, but he knew one day soon he'd come home from work and find Angie sitting on his couch, eating his pudding cups and making derogatory comments about his dog.

That was why Will had gone to Sara's house last night. He was hiding from Angie. He was fighting the inevitable. And, if he was being honest, he had been aching to see Sara again. That she had bought his excuse about his house being upside down made him think that maybe she had wanted him there, too. As a kid, Will had trained himself to not want things he couldn't have—the latest toys, shoes that actually fit, home-cooked meals that didn't come out of a can. His power to deny himself disappeared where Sara Linton was concerned. He could not stop thinking about how her hand had felt on his shoulder when they'd stood in the street yesterday. Her thumb had stroked the side of his neck. She had lifted her heels off the ground so that they were the same height, and for just a second, he'd thought that she was going to kiss him.

'Christ,' Will groaned. He visualized the carnage at Evelyn Mitchell's house, the blood and brain matter spattered across her kitchen and laundry room. And then he tried to blank his mind completely, because he was pretty sure thinking about sex and then picturing scenes of violence was how serial killers got their start.

The SUV jerked into reverse. Amanda rolled down the window. Will stood.

She told him, 'That was a source at APD. Looks like our Type B-negative showed up by the Dumpster at Grady. Unconscious, barely breathing. They found his wallet in one of the trash bags. Marcellus Benedict Estevez. Unemployed. Lives with his grandmother.'

Will wondered why Sara hadn't called him about this. Maybe she had already left work. Or maybe it wasn't her job to keep him in the loop. 'Did Estevez say anything?'

'He died half an hour ago. We'll swing by the

258

hospital after this.'

Will thought that was a pointless trip considering the guy was dead. 'Did he have something on him?'

'No. Get in.'

'Why are we—'

'I don't have all day, Will. Wipe the dirt out of your vagina and let's get going.'

Will got into the SUV. 'Did they confirm Estevez is blood type B-negative?'

She punched the gas. 'Yes. And his fingerprints have been positively identified as one of the eight sets found in Evelyn's house.'

He was missing something again. 'That was a long conversation for just that little bit of information.'

For once, she was forthcoming. 'We got a call-back on Chuck Finn. Why didn't you tell me that you talked to his parole officer last night?'

'I suppose I was being petty.'

'Well, you certainly showed me. The parole officer did a spot check on Chuck this morning. He's been gone for two days.'

'Wait a minute.' Will turned toward her. 'Chuck's PO told me last night that he was accounted for. He said that Chuck never missed a sign-in.'

'I'm sure the Tennessee parole office is as overburdened and understaffed as ours is. At least he had the balls to come clean this morning.' She gave him a meaningful look. 'Chuck Finn signed himself out of treatment two days ago.'

'Treatment?'

'He was at Healing Winds. He's on his third month of sobriety.'

259

Will felt a slight vindication.

'Healing Winds is also where Hironobu Kwon got treatment. They were there at the same time.'

Will had to be silent for a moment. 'When did you find all of this out?'

'Just now, Will. Don't pout. I know an old gal who works in records down at the drug court.' Apparently, Amanda knew an old gal everywhere. 'Kwon was sent to Hope Hall for his first offense.' The drug court's inpatient treatment facility. 'The judge wasn't inclined to give him a second chance on the state's dime, so the mother stepped in and said she'd secured him a place at Healing Winds.'

'Where he met Chuck Finn.'

'It's a large facility, but you're right. It would be quite a stretch to say that these two particular men just happened to be there at the same time.'

Will was shocked to hear her concede the point, but he kept going. 'If Chuck told Hironobu Kwon that Evelyn had money sitting around . . .' He smiled. Finally, something was making sense. 'What about the other guy? The Type B-negative who showed up at Grady? Does he have any connection to Chuck or Hironobu?'

'Marcellus Estevez has never been arrested. He was born and raised in Miami, Florida. Two years ago, he moved to Carrollton to attend West Georgia College. He dropped out last quarter. He hasn't had contact with his family since.'

Another kid in his mid-twenties who had gotten mixed up with some very bad people. 'You seem to know an awful lot about Estevez.'

'APD has already spoken with his parents. They filed a missing persons report as soon as the school informed them that their son wasn't attending

260

class.'

'Since when is Atlanta sharing information with us?'

'Let's just say I reached out to some old friends.'

Will was beginning to form an image of a network of steely old ballbusters who either owed Amanda a favor or had worked with Evelyn at some point in their long careers.

She said, 'The point is that we don't know how Type B, Marcellus Estevez, ties into this. Except for Hironobu Kwon and Chuck Finn, there's no hint of a connection between anyone else in the house. They all went to different high schools. Not all of them were in college, but the ones who were didn't go together. They didn't meet in prison. None of them share a gang affiliation or a social club. They all have different backgrounds, different ethnicities.'

Will felt like she was being honest at least about this. In any investigation involving multiple perpetrators, the key was always to find out how they knew each other. Human beings were largely predictable in their habits. If you found out where they met, how they knew each other, or what had brought them together, then you could generally find someone outside the group, just hovering around the periphery, who wanted to talk.

He told her what he'd been thinking since he first saw Evelyn's upturned house. 'This feels like a personal vendetta.'

'Most vendettas are.'

'No, I mean it feels like it's about something more than money.'

'That will be one of the many questions we ask these imbeciles once we have the cuffs on them.'

261

Amanda twisted the steering wheel, taking a sudden turn that jerked Will to the side. 'I'm sorry.'

He couldn't remember a time Amanda had ever apologized for anything. He stared at her profile. Her jaw was more prominent than usual. Her skin was sallow. She was looking downright beaten. And she had given him more information in the last ten minutes than she had in the last twenty-four hours. 'Is something else going on?'

'No.' She stopped in front of a large commercial warehouse with six loading docks. There were no cargo trucks, but several vehicles were parked in front of the large bay doors. Any one of the vehicles would've cost more than Will's pension—BMWs, Mercedes, even a Bentley.

Amanda circled the lot, making sure there would be no surprises. The space was large enough for an eighteen-wheeler to turn around, and sloped toward the docks to facilitate loading and unloading. She made a lazy U-turn, going back the way they had come. The tires squealed as she cut the wheel hard, taking a space as far from the building as she could get without parking on the grass. Amanda cut the engine. The SUV was directly across from what appeared to be the front office. About fifty yards of wide-open space separated them from the building. A set of crumbling concrete steps led to a glass door. The railing had rusted so badly it keeled to the side. The sign over the entrance had a set of kitchen cabinets bolted to the front. A Confederate flag waved in the breeze. Will read the first word on the sign, then guessed at the rest, 'Southern Cabinets? That's an unusual drug front.'

She narrowed her eyes at him. 'It's like watching a dog walk on its hind legs.'

Will got out of the car. He met Amanda behind the SUV. She used the key-fob remote to pop open the trunk. In Valdosta this morning, they had locked up their weapons before going into the prison. The black SUV was regulation GBI, which meant the entire back end was taken up by a large steel cabinet with six drawers. Amanda pressed the combination into the pushbutton lock and pulled open the middle drawer. Her Glock rested in a dark purple velvet bag that had the Crown Royal logo stitched into the hem. She dropped it into her purse while Will clipped his paddle holster onto his belt.

'Hold on.' She reached into the back of the drawer and pulled out a five-shot revolver. This particular type of Smith and Wesson was called an 'old-timer,' because mostly old-timers carried them. The gun was lightweight, with an internal hammer that made it easy to conceal. Despite the 'Lady Smith' logo etched above the trigger, the recoil could leave a nasty bruise the entire length of your hand. Evelyn Mitchell's S&W was a similar model, with a cherry handle instead of Amanda's custom walnut. Will wondered if the two women had bought their guns together on a shopping trip.

Amanda said, 'Stand straight. Try not to react. We're just in view of the camera.'

Will fought to follow her orders as she reached under the back of his jacket and shoved the revolver down his pants. He stared ahead at the warehouse. It was metal, wider than it was deep, about half the length of a football field. The whole building was on a concrete foundation that raised

263

the height of the ground floor by at least four feet, the standard height of a loading dock. Except for the steep flight of concrete steps leading up to the front door, there was no way in and out. At least not unless you were willing to pull yourself up onto the loading dock and muscle open one of the large metal doors.

He asked, 'Where are the guys you had sitting on this place?'

'Doraville needed an assist. We're on our own.'

He watched the camera over the door track back and forth. 'This doesn't seem like a bad idea at all.'

'Stand up straight.' She slapped him on the back, making sure the gun was snug. 'And for God's sake, don't hold in your stomach or it'll fall straight through to the ground.' She had to go up on the tips of her toes to pull the trunk closed. 'I don't know why you wear your belt so loose. It's pointless to even have one if you're not going to use it right.'

Will walked behind her as she headed toward the entrance. The walk was a brisk one, fifty yards of wide-open space. The camera had stopped its sweep to track their progress. They might as well have targets on their chests. He concentrated on the top of Amanda's head, the way her hair swirled at the crown like a spiral ham.

The glass door opened when they reached the concrete steps to the entrance. Amanda shielded her eyes from the sun, staring up at an angry-looking Asian man. He was huge, his body seemingly comprising equal parts fat and muscle. The guy stood wordlessly, holding open the front door as he watched them make their way up the steps. Will followed Amanda inside. His eyes took their time adjusting in the tiny, airless front office. The fake paneling on the wall had buckled from humidity. The carpet was brown in ways that would repulse a more fastidious man. The whole place smelled of sawdust and oil. Will could hear machines running in the warehouse: finish nailers, compressors, lathes. Guns N' Roses played on the radio.

Amanda told the man, 'Mrs. Ling should be expecting me.' She smiled at the camera mounted above the doorway.

The man didn't move. Amanda dug into her purse like she was looking for her lipstick. Will didn't know if she was reaching for her gun or if she just needed lipstick. His answer came when the door was opened by a tall, lithe woman with a grin on her face.

'Mandy Wagner, it's been ages.' The woman seemed almost pleased. She was Asian, roughly Amanda's age with short salt-and-pepper hair. She was as thin as a teenager. Her sleeveless shirt showed well-toned arms. She spoke in a distinctive, slow southern drawl. There was something catlike in the languid way she moved, or maybe the smell of pot clinging to her body had something to do with that. She was wearing moccasins with beads on the top, the sort of souvenir you'd find at a tourist trap outside an Indian reservation.

'Julia.' Amanda gave a convincing smile. 'It's so good to see you.' They hugged, and Will saw the woman's hand linger at Amanda's waist.

'This is Will Trent, my associate.' She put her hand over Julia's as she turned to Will. 'I hope you don't mind his tagging along. He's in training.'

265

'How fortunate to learn from the best,' Julia cooed. 'Tell him to leave his gun on the counter. You too, Mandy. You still using that old Crown Royal bag?'

'Keeps the lint out of the firing pin.' The gun made a thud as she dropped the bag on the counter. The dour man checked the contents, then nodded at his boss. Will wasn't as quickly compliant. Giving up his gun was not something he was comfortable with.

'Will,' Amanda said. 'Don't embarrass me in front of my friends.'

He unclipped the paddle holster from his belt and put his Glock on the counter.

Julia Ling laughed as she waved them through the door. The warehouse was even bigger than it looked from the outside, but the operation was small, the sort of thing that would've fit into a two-car garage. There were at least a dozen men putting together cabinets. Will couldn't tell whether they were Asian, Hispanic, or anything else, because their hats were pulled down and their faces were turned away. Whoever they were, they were obviously working. The smell of glue was pungent. Sawdust littered the floor. A gigantic Confederate flag served as a divider between the work area and the vacant-looking rear of the building. The stars were yellow instead of white.

Julia led them through another door and they found themselves in a small but well-furnished back office. The carpet underfoot was plush. There were two couches with overstuffed pillows. A plump Chihuahua sat in a recliner by the window, its eyes closed to what little sun came through the panes. Heavy metal bars framed the view to the

266

service alley behind the building.

'Will has a Chihuahua,' Amanda said, because Will hadn't been emasculated enough today. 'What's its name again?'

Will felt barbed wire sticking in his throat. 'Betty.'

'Really?' Julia picked up the dog and sat on the couch with it. She patted the cushion beside her, and Amanda sat down. 'This is Arnoldo. He's a chunky little thing. Is yours long-haired or short?'

Will didn't know what else to do. He reached around to pull out his wallet, too late remembering Amanda's revolver. It shifted dangerously, and he sat on the couch across from the women, opening his wallet to show Betty's picture.

Julia Ling made a tsk-ing sound with her tongue. 'Isn't she adorable?'

'Thank you.' Will took back the picture and dropped his wallet into his coat pocket. 'Yours is nice, too.'

Julia had already tuned Will out. She ran her hand along Amanda's leg. 'What brings you here, buttercup?'

Amanda did a good job of blocking out Will, too. 'I trust you've heard about Evelyn?'

'Yes,' Julia said, drawing out the word. 'Poor Almeja. I hope they are kind to her.'

Will fought to keep his mouth from dropping open. Evelyn Mitchell was Almeja.

Amanda laid her hand over Julia's. Instead of taking it off her knee, she left it there. 'I don't suppose you've heard anything on her whereabouts?'

'Not a peep, but you know I'd come straight to you if I did.'

'Obviously, we're doing everything we can to make sure she's returned home safely. I would pull some considerable strings to make this come out right.'

'Yes,' Julia repeated. 'She's a grandmother now, right? Again, I mean. Such a fertile family.' She laughed as if there was a joke between them. 'How is that dear, sweet child doing?'

'This is a difficult time for everyone in the family.'

'Yes.' It seemed this was her favorite word.

'I'm sure you've heard about Hector.'

'Bless his heart. I was thinking of trading down for a Cadillac.'

'I thought business was going well?'

'It's not really the time to drive something so flashy.' She lowered her voice. 'Carjackings.'

'Awful.' Amanda shook her head.

'These young boys are such a problem.' She tsked her tongue. Will thought he understood at least this part of the conversation. Julia Ling was referring to the young men who had broken into Evelyn's house. 'They see all the gangsters on TV and think it's so easy. Scarface. The Godfather. Tony Soprano. You can see their little brains spinning. Before long, they get these notions into their heads and they pop off without considering the consequences.' She tsked her tongue again. 'I just lost one of my workers through this kind of careless action.'

She meant Benny Choo, the man in the Hawaiian shirt. Will had been right. Julia Ling had sent her strongarm in to clean up the mess Ricardo and his friends had made. And then Faith had killed him.

268

Amanda must have known this, too, but she treaded carefully. 'Your line of business isn't without its risks. Mr. Choo understood this as well as anyone.'

Julia Ling hesitated long enough to make Will worry for Faith, then finally let out a slow, 'Yes. The cost of doing business. I think we'll let Benny rest in peace.'

Amanda appeared as relieved as Will felt. 'I hear your brother's coping with his new surroundings.'

'Yes,' she said. ' 'Coping' is a good word for it. Roger's never liked the heat. Savannah is practically *tropical*.'

'You know, there's a vacancy at the D&C. Perhaps I could see if they'll take Roger? Might be nice to give him a change of scenery.'

She pretended to think about it. 'Still a little too warm.' She smiled. 'How about Phillips?'

'Well, that *is* a nice facility.' It was also where Ignatio Ortiz was serving his manslaughter rap. Amanda shook her head like she was very sorry to say that that particular holiday had already been booked by another family. 'Doesn't seem like the right fit.'

'Baldwin is a better drive for me.'

'Baldwin isn't really suited to Roger's temperament.' Most likely because the prison only handled minimum to medium security inmates. 'Augusta? It's close but not too close.'

She wrinkled her nose. 'With the sex offender release site?'

'Good point.' Amanda seemed to think on it, though she must've already cleared the deal with the state attorney's office. 'You know, Arrendale

269

has started taking in some maximum security prisoners. Only with good behavior, of course, but I'm sure that Roger could swing that.'

She gave a chuckle. 'Oh, Mandy. You know Roger. He's always getting into trouble.'

Amanda's offer was firm. 'Still, I'd think about Arrendale. We could certainly make sure his transition was a pleasant one. Evelyn has a lot of friends who want nothing more than to see that she's returned home safely. Roger might as well get something for himself in the process.'

Julia stroked the dog. 'I'll see what he says the next time I go visit him.'

'A phone call might be better.' Amanda added, 'I'm sure he'll want to hear about Benny from you rather than a stranger.'

'God rest his soul.' She squeezed Amanda's leg. 'It's horrible to lose people you care about.'

'It is.'

'I know that you and Evelyn were close.'

'We still are.'

'Why don't you get rid of Tonto here and we can comfort each other?'

Amanda's laughter sounded genuinely delighted. She patted Julia's knee, then stood up from the couch. 'Oh, Jules. It's been nice seeing you again. I wish we could do this more.'

Will started to stand, but then remembered the revolver. He put his hands in his pockets to keep his pants tight enough to hold it in place. All he needed was to break up whatever game Amanda was playing by dropping a gun through the leg of his pants.

Amanda said, 'Let me know about Arrendale. It really is a lovely place. The windows are four

270

inches wider in the close-security wing. Lots of sunshine and fresh air. I think Roger will love it.'

'I'll let you know his decision. I think we can all agree that uncertainty is bad for business.'

'Tell Roger I am at his beck and call.'

Will opened the door for Amanda. They walked back through the shop together. The crew had obviously taken a break. The machines were idle, the stations vacant. The radio had been turned down to a low hum. He mumbled to Amanda, 'That was interesting.'

'We'll see if she does her part.' He could tell she was hopeful. The bounce was back in her walk. 'I'd bet my left one Roger knows exactly what happened at Ev's house yesterday. Julia probably told him herself. She would've never let us step foot in here if she wasn't willing to deal. We'll know something within the hour. Mark my word.'

'Ms. Ling seems eager to please you.'

She stopped and looked up at him. 'Do you really think so? I can never tell if she's just being affectionate or . . .' Amanda shrugged in lieu of finishing the sentence.

He thought she was joking, then realized she wasn't. 'I guess. I mean—' He felt himself start to sweat. 'You've never—'

'Grow up, Will. I *did* go to college.'

He could still hear her chuckling as they walked toward the front office. Will guessed that he was doomed to have this woman play him like a banjo for the rest of his life. She was almost as bad as Angie.

He was reaching for the doorknob when he heard the first pop, almost like a champagne bottle

271

being uncorked. Then he felt his ear sting, saw the door splinter in front of him, and knew that it was a bullet. And another. And another.

Amanda was faster than Will. She had pulled the gun from the back of his pants, swung around, and fired off two shots, before he hit the floor.

The sound of a machine gun ripped the air. Bullets sprayed inches from his head. There was no telling where the threat was coming from. The back of the warehouse was dark. It could be Ling-Ling, the men who had been working on the cabinets, or both.

'Go!' Amanda yelled. Will shouldered open the door to the front office. Of course their guns were gone from the counter. The disapproving Asian who'd let them in was dead on the floor. Will felt something hard hit him in the back of the head. He was stunned for a few seconds before he realized that Amanda had thrown her purse at him.

Will tucked the bag under his arm and slammed open the front door. The sudden, sharp sunlight blinded him so badly that he tripped down the concrete stairs. The old railing bent under his weight, softening what could've been a catastrophic fall. Quickly, he righted himself and headed straight across the parking lot toward the parked SUV. The contents of Amanda's purse scattered behind him as he searched for the key fob. He thumbed the button and the trunk was open by the time he got to the back of the vehicle. Will pressed the numbers on the combination lock. The drawer rolled open.

In Will's experience, you were either a shotgun person or a rifle person. Faith preferred the shotgun, which was counterintuitive considering

272

her diminutive stature and the fact that the kick from a shogun could tear your rotator cuff. Will liked the rifle. It was clean, precise, and extremely accurate, even at a hundred fifty feet—a good thing, considering this was the approximate distance between the SUV and the entrance to the building. The GBI provided agents with the Colt AR-15A2, which Will rolled up to his shoulder as the front door shattered open.

Will put his eye to the scope. Amanda handled the sunlight better than he had. Without missing a beat, she bolted down the concrete stairs, firing backward, her shots missing the stocky-looking man who was chasing her. He had on dark sunglasses. A machine gun was in his hands. Instead of taking the easy shot at Amanda's retreating back, he held up the gun in the air as he jumped down the flight of stairs. It was a cowboy move, which gave Will equal opportunity to pull one of his own. He pressed back on the trigger. The man jerked midair and dropped to the ground.

Will lowered the rifle. He looked for Amanda. She was walking back toward the man on the ground. She held her gun down at her side. She must've been out of ammunition. Will pressed his eye to the scope again to give Amanda cover in case anyone else came out of the building. She kicked away the machine gun. He could see her mouth moving.

Without warning, Amanda dove behind the concrete steps. Will took his eye away from the scope so he could locate the new threat. It was the man on the ground. Impossibly, he was still alive. He had Will's Glock in his hand. It was pointed toward the SUV. He fired off three shots in rapid

273

succession. Will knew the heavy-gauge steel cabinet would shield him, but he still ducked as metal pinged against metal.

The shooting stopped. Will's heart was pumping so hard that he could feel his pulse throbbing in his stomach. He chanced a look back at the building. The shooter must've been hiding behind the Mercedes, probably on the other side of the gas tank. Will lined up the rifle, hoping the guy would do something stupid like poke up his head. The Glock came up instead. Will shot, and the gun quickly receded.

'Police!' Will yelled, because it had to be done. 'Show me your hands!'

The guy shot blindly toward the SUV, missing by several yards.

Will mumbled some choice words. He looked at Amanda as if to ask what the plan was. She shook her head, not to tell him no, but in exasperation. If Will had made the first shot, they wouldn't be having this conversation.

He couldn't think of a way to gesture to her that he had made the shot—not without getting fired—so he pointed to the magazine jutting out from his rifle to pose the question. Was she out of bullets? Her revolver held five rounds. Unless she'd gotten her speed loader out of her purse, there was not much she could do.

Even from this distance, he saw her annoyed expression. Of course she had gotten her speed loader out of her purse. She had probably stopped to put on some lipstick and make some phone calls, too. He checked the Mercedes again, scanning the sights along the contour of the big sedan. When he looked back at Amanda, she had already spun open the S&W, dropped the empty shells on the ground, and reloaded. She waved her hand at him to get on with it.

'Sir!' Will yelled. 'I am giving you one more warning to surrender.'

'Fuck you!' The man shot at Will again, hitting the side door panel of the SUV.

Amanda did a crouched walk to the edge of the concrete stairs, then bent her head to the ground to try to see where the man was hiding. She sat back up. She didn't look at Will. She didn't pause to line up the shot. She simply rested her hand on the third step from the bottom and squeezed the trigger.

Television had done a great disservice to bad guys. They didn't show that bullets could go through Sheetrock walls and metal car doors. They also didn't explain that a ricochet was nothing like a rubber ball. Bullets came out at a very high velocity, and they wanted to go forward. Shooting a bullet into the ground does not mean it will pop back up in the air. Shooting one into the ground underneath a car means it skips across the pavement, pierces the tire, and, if you are sitting the right way, lodges into your groin.

Which is exactly what happened.

'Jesus Christ!' the man screamed.

Will ordered, 'Show me your hands!'

Two hands shot up. 'I give! I give!'

This time, Amanda kept her gun trained on the man as she walked over to the car. She kicked away the Glock, then jammed her knee into the man's back, all the while keeping her eye on the office door.

She was watching the wrong door. One of the

275

cargo bays flew open. A black van screeched out, sailing through the air. Sparks flew as it skipped across the asphalt. Rubber burned. The wheels slid in place before they got purchase. Will saw two young men in the cab. They were wearing black warm-up jackets and matching black baseball caps. The van momentarily blocked his view of Amanda. Will raised the rifle, but he couldn't shoot—not without risking the bullet cutting through the van and hitting Amanda. Two more quick pops sounded. Gunfire. The van screeched away.

Will ran into the parking lot to line up a shot. He stopped. Amanda was on the ground.

'Amanda?' He felt his chest tighten. His throat didn't want to work. 'Amanda? Are you—'

'Dammit!' she screamed, rolling over so that she could sit up. Her face and chest were covered in blood. 'God*damn* it.'

Will dropped to one knee. He put his hand on her shoulder. 'Are you shot?'

'I'm fine, you idiot.' She slapped away his hand. 'This one's dead. They tapped him twice in the head while they were driving off.'

Will could see as much. The man's face was gone.

'That's a damn good shot out of a moving car.' She glared at him as he helped her up. 'Much better than yours. When was the last time you were on the range? This is unacceptable. Absolutely unacceptable.'

Will knew better than to argue with her, but if he was the arguing type, he might've mentioned what a bad idea it'd been to leave their guns on the counter, or how stupid it was to go into this place without backup.

'I swear to God, Will, when this is over—' She didn't finish her sentence. She paced off, stepping on the plastic compact from her purse. 'Goddamn it!'

Will knelt down in front of the dead man. Out of habit, he checked for a pulse. There was a hole in the black warm-up jacket, about two inches from his heart. It was big enough for Will's finger to poke through. He tugged down the zip, revealing the top of a military-grade tactical assault vest. The bullet's full metal jacket had expanded on impact, smashing into the shock plate, flattening out like a dog trying to crawl underneath a couch.

K-5, right in the center of the chest.

Amanda was back. She stared down at the dead man without saying a word. She must have been standing downblast when he was shot. Bits of gray matter stuck to her face. There was a piece of bone in the collar of her blouse.

Will stood up. He couldn't think of anything to do but offer his handkerchief.

'Thank you.' She wiped her face with a steady hand. The blood smeared like clown makeup. 'Thank God I have a change of clothes in the car.' She looked up at him. 'Your jacket is ripped.'

He looked at his sleeve. There was a small tear where his shoulder had met asphalt.

'You should always keep a change of clothes in your car. You never know what's going to happen.'

'Yes, ma'am.' Will rested his hand on the butt of his rifle.

'Ling-Ling's gone.' Amanda wiped her forehead. 'She came out of her office with that stupid dog under her arm. Guns blazing. I'm under no impression that she was trying to save me, but it

277

seemed rather obvious that they were trying to kill her, too.'

Will tried to process this new piece of information. 'I assumed the shooters were working for Ling-Ling.'

'If Julia wanted us dead, she would've taken both of us out in her office. Didn't you see the sawed-off shotgun under the couch cushion?'

Will nodded, though he hadn't seen the gun and the thought of it now brought out a cold sweat. 'The shooters worked in her shop. I recognized them from when we first went in. They were putting together cabinets. Why would they try to kill Julia? Or us, for that matter?'

'Isn't it obvious?' Amanda finally realized it wasn't. 'They didn't want her talking to me. They certainly don't want her talking to Roger. She must know something.'

Will tried to put the pieces together. 'Julia said that the young boys were getting ahead of themselves. Trying to be gangsters. I don't imagine a bunch of twenty-something-year-old, testosterone-filled guys want to be ordered around by a middle-aged woman.'

'And here I was thinking that men loved that.' Amanda looked down at the dead man. 'He's sweating like a pig. No doubt he was on something.'

Something that had made him capable of taking the impact of a .223-caliber 55-grain full metal jacket to the chest and popping up seconds later like a Toaster Strudel.

Amanda prodded the man with the toe of her shoe, pushing him over so she could check for his wallet. 'These youngsters certainly don't like to leave witnesses.' She slid out the driver's license. 'Juan Armand Castillo. Aged twenty-four. Lives on Leather Stocking Lane in Stone Mountain.' She showed Will the license. Castillo looked like a schoolteacher, not the kind of guy who would chase a GBI agent into a parking lot with a machine gun.

She unzipped Castillo's jacket the rest of the way. Her Glock was tucked into his pants. She took it out, saying, 'Well, at least he didn't shoot at me with my own gun.'

Will helped her unloop the side clasps on the Kevlar vest.

'He smells, too.' Amanda lifted up the shirt, checking his chest. 'No tattoos.' She checked his arms. 'Nothing.'

'Try the hands.'

Castillo's fists were clenched. She uncurled the fingers with her bare hand, which was technically against every procedure in the book, but Will was an accomplice already, so it didn't really matter.

She said, 'Nothing.'

Will scanned the parking lot. There were only two cars now, the Bentley and the Mercedes. 'Do you think someone else is inside?'

'The Bentley is Ling-Ling's. I imagine she keeps another car close by that she's using right now to go as far underground as possible. The Merc belongs to Perry.' She explained, 'The dead man in the front office.'

'You certainly seem to know a lot about these people. Mandy.'

'I'm in no mood for that, Will.'

'Julia Ling is high up in the pecking order. She's practically the beak.'

279

'Is there a reason you're talking like Foghorn Leghorn?'

'I'm just saying that it takes either a large set of balls or an extreme amount of stupidity to try to take out someone with Julia Ling's kind of juice. Her brother's not going to just roll over. You told me yourself that he's practically insane. Shooting at his sister is an open act of war.'

'Finally, a salient point.' She handed back his handkerchief. 'Did you get a good look at the men in the van?'

He shook his head. 'Young, I guess. Sunglasses. Hats. Jackets. Nothing else I could swear to.'

'I'm not asking you to swear. I'm asking you to—' The air was pierced by the sound of sirens. 'Took them long enough.'

Will guessed the first gunshot had been fired less than five minutes ago. By his calculations, that was pretty good response time.

He asked, 'Did *you* get a look at them?'

She shook her head. 'I suppose we should be looking for someone with drive-by experience.'

She was right about the shots. Nailing someone in the head, twice, from a moving vehicle, even at a short distance, was not something you got lucky at. It took practice, and obviously Castillo's killer hadn't worried about missing.

Will asked, 'Why didn't they shoot you?'

'Are you complaining or asking a question?' Amanda rubbed something off her arm. She looked down at Castillo. 'I guess we're down to two now. At least our odds are getting better.'

She was talking about the fingerprints found at Evelyn's house. 'It's three.'

She shook her head, still looking down at the

280

corpse.

He counted it out on his fingers. 'Evelyn killed Hironobu Kwon. Faith took care of Ricardo Ortiz and Benny Choo. Marcellus Estevez died at Grady, and Juan Castillo here makes five.' She didn't say anything. He worried about his math. 'Eight sets of prints at Evelyn's house minus five dead guys equals three.'

She watched the squad cars speeding down the road. 'Two,' she told him. 'One tried to kill Sara Linton an hour ago.'

CHAPTER ELEVEN

Dale Dugan rushed into the doctors' lounge. 'i came as soon as they let me.'

Sara closed her eyes as she shut her locker. She had spent nearly two hours going over her statement with the Atlanta police. Then the hospital administration had swarmed around her for another hour, ostensibly to help, but Sara had quickly realized that they were more concerned that they would be sued. Once she'd signed a paper absolving them of all responsibility, they left as quickly as they had arrived.

Dale asked, 'Can I get you anything?'

'Thank you, but I'm fine.'

'Can I drive you home?'

'Dale, I—' The door slammed open. Will stood there, a panicked look on his face.

For a few suspended seconds, nothing mattered anymore. Sara was blind to everything else in the room. Her peripheral vision was gone. Everything tunneled to Will. She didn't see Dale leave. She didn't hear the constant throng of ambulance sirens and ringing phones and screaming patients.

She just saw Will.

He let the door close, but didn't move toward her. There was sweat on his brow. His breath was labored. She didn't know what to say to him, what to do. She just stood there staring at him as if this was another ordinary day.

He asked, 'Is that a new outfit?'

She laughed, the sound getting caught in her throat. She'd changed into scrubs. Her clothes were in police evidence.

The corner of his mouth went up in a forced smile. 'It brings out the green in your eyes.'

Sara bit her lip to keep tears from falling. She had wanted to call him as soon as it happened. Her cell phone had been in her hands, his number up on the screen, but she had tucked the phone into her purse because Sara knew if she saw Will before she was ready, she would shatter like a delicate piece of china.

Amanda Wagner knocked as she entered the room. 'I hate to interrupt, Dr. Linton, but could we have a word with you?'

Anger flashed across Will's face. 'She doesn't—'

'It's all right,' Sara interrupted. 'There's not much that I can tell you.'

Amanda smiled as if this was some sort of social gathering. 'Anything at all would be appreciated.'

Sara had talked about it so much over the last few hours that she recited the events as if by rote. She gave them the abbreviated version of her statement, not going into a detailed description of the female junkie, which, on paper, had sounded

282

like every junkie Sara had ever seen. Nor did she describe the trash around the Dumpster or the EMTs, or list the procedures she followed. She cut to what mattered: the young man who'd peered at her from behind the curtain. He had punched her in the chest. He had shot her patient twice in the head. He was thin, Caucasian, mid-to-late twenties and wearing a black warm-up jacket and baseball cap. In the short time that elapsed between her first sight of him and his death, he had not uttered one word. The only sound she'd heard was a grunt, and then the air whistling from his neck as his breath seeped out.

She finished, 'His hand was gripped around my hand. I couldn't stop it. He's dead. They're both dead.'

Will seemed to have trouble speaking. 'He hurt you.'

Sara could only nod, but her mind conjured the image she had seen in the bathroom mirror: an oblong, ugly bruise over her right breast where the man had punched her.

Will cleared his throat. 'All right. Thank you for your cooperation, Dr. Linton. I know you probably want to get home.' He turned to leave, but Amanda made no move to follow.

'Dr. Linton, I noticed a soda machine in the waiting room. Would you like something to drink?'

Sara was taken off guard. 'I'm—'

'Will, could you get a Diet Sprite for me and— I'm sorry, Dr. Linton. What did you want?'

Will's jaw tightened like a ratchet. He wasn't stupid. He knew that Amanda was trying to get her alone, just like Sara knew that Amanda wouldn't give up until she got what she wanted. She tried to

283

make this easier for Will, saying, 'A Coke would be nice.'

He didn't give in that easy. 'Are you sure?'

'Yes. I'm sure.'

He wasn't happy, but he left the room.

Amanda checked the hallway, making sure Will was gone. She turned back to Sara. 'I'm rooting for you, you know.'

Sara didn't have a clue what she was talking about.

'Will,' she explained. 'He's got one too many bitches in his life, and I'm not going anywhere.'

Sara was in no mood to joke. 'What do you want, Amanda?'

She got to the point. 'The bodies are still downstairs in the morgue. I need you to examine them and give me your professional opinion.' She added, 'A *coroner's* opinion.'

Sara felt a cold chill at the thought of seeing the man again. Every time she blinked, she could see his expressionless face hovering over her. She couldn't grip her hand without feeling his fingers wrapped around her own. 'I can't cut them open.'

'No, but you can answer some questions for me.'

'Such as?'

'Drug use, gang affiliations, and whether or not one of them has a stomach full of heroin.'

'Like Ricardo.'

'Yes, like Ricardo.'

Sara didn't give herself time to think about the request. 'All right. I'll do it.'

'Do what?' Will was back. He must've run the entire way. He was out of breath again. He held two sodas in one hand.

'There you are,' Amanda said, as if she was

284

surprised to see him. 'We were about to go down to the morgue.'

Will looked at Sara. 'No.'

'I want to do this,' Sara insisted, though she was not sure why. For the last three hours, all she could think about was going home. Now that Will was here, the thought of returning to her empty apartment was unimaginable.

'We don't need these.' Amanda took the soda cans and dropped them into the trash. 'Dr. Linton?'

Sara led them down the corridor toward the elevators, feeling like a lifetime had passed since she'd made the same walk this morning. A loaded gurney rolled by, EMTs shouting stats, doctors giving orders. Sara held out her arm, guiding Will back against the wall so that the patient could get past. Her hand hovered just in front of his tie. She could feel the silk material sway against her fingertips. He was wearing a suit, his normal work attire, but without the usual vest. His jacket was dark blue, the shirt a lighter shade of the same color.

The cop. Sara had forgotten the cop. 'I didn't—'

'Hold that thought,' Amanda said, as if she was afraid the walls had ears.

Sara fumed at herself as they waited for the elevator. How had she forgotten about the cop? What was wrong with her?

The doors opened. The elevator was packed. It took an interminable amount of time for the old pulleys and lifts to groan into action. They went down a floor and most of the people exited. Two young orderlies rode with them to the sub-basement. They got off and headed toward the

285

stairwell, probably for an illicit tryst.

Amanda waited until they were well beyond earshot. 'What is it?'

'There was a man when we came in from the Dumpster. I nearly ran him over. I told him to get out of the way, and he flashed a badge. It looked like a badge. I'm not sure anymore. He acted like a cop.'

'In what way?'

'He acted like he had every right to question me, and he was irritated when I didn't answer immediately.' Sara gave her a meaningful look.

'Sounds like a cop to me,' Amanda wryly admitted. 'What did he want?'

'To know whether or not the patient was going to make it. I told him maybe, even though it was obvious...' Sara let her voice trail off, willing herself to remember. 'He was wearing a dark suit, charcoal. White shirt. He was very thin, almost gaunt. He reeked of cigarette smoke. I could smell it even after he left.'

'Did you see which way he went?'

She shook her head.

'White? Black?'

'White. Gray hair. He was older. He looked older.' She put her hand to her face. 'His cheeks were sunken. His eyes were heavily lidded.' She remembered something else. 'He was wearing a hat. A baseball hat.'

'Black?' Will asked.

'Blue,' she said. 'Atlanta Braves.'

'We'll probably get some nice images of the top of it from the security cameras,' Amanda commented. 'We'll have to share this information with the APD. They may want to see if you can work with a sketch artist.'

Sara would do whatever it took. 'I'm sorry I didn't remember earlier. I don't know what—'

'You were in shock.' Will seemed ready to say more. He glanced at Amanda, then indicated the double doors at the other end of the hallway. He said, 'I think it's this way.'

In the morgue, Junior and Larry were nowhere to be seen. Instead, there were two gurneys, each with a body, each with a white sheet covering the dead. Sara assumed one was the man she had found outside by the Dumpster and the other was the man who had shot the first, then tried to kill her.

There was an older woman leaning against the door to the walk-in freezer. She looked up from her BlackBerry as they walked into the room. Her hospital badge was tucked into her pants pocket. No white lab coat, just a well-tailored black pantsuit. She was clearly on the administration side of the hospital. She was older, more gray than black in her hair. She pushed away from the freezer and walked over. Her posture was ramrod straight, her sizable chest out in front of her like the prow of a ship.

She didn't stop for introductions. She pulled a small spiral-bound notebook out of her jacket pocket and read, 'The shooter's name is Franklin Warren Heeney. APD found his wallet on him. Local boy, lives in Tucker with his parents. Dropped out of Perimeter College his sophomore year. No employment records. No adult arrest history, but at thirteen, he spent six months in juvie for breaking windows. He has one child, a daughter, six years old, who lives with an aunt out

287

in Snellville. The baby mama is in county lockup for shoplifting and a Baggie of meth they found in her purse. That's all I could get on him.' She indicated the other body. 'Marcellus Benedict Estevez. As I said on the phone, his wallet was found in the trash by the Dumpster. I assume you've already looked into him?' Amanda nodded, and the woman closed her notebook. 'That's all I have for now. Nothing else has come down on the wire.'

Amanda nodded again. 'Thank you.'

'I bought you an hour before the body boys come. Dr. Linton, the films you ordered for Estevez are in the transport packet. I've gathered together some tools that might be useful. I'm sorry it can't be more.'

She had done plenty. Sara looked over the four Mayo trays laid out beside the bodies. Whoever the woman was, she had some medical knowledge and was high enough up the Grady food chain to raid the supply closet without setting off alarms. 'Thank you.'

The woman nodded her goodbyes, then left the room.

Will's tone was sharp when he asked Amanda, 'Let me guess, one of your old gals?'

Amanda ignored him. 'Dr. Linton, if we could get started?'

Sara had to force herself to move or she would've just stood rooted to the floor until the building fell down around her. There was a pack of sterile gloves hanging from a cleat on the wall. She took out a pair and forced them over her sweating hands. The powder rolled into tiny balls that stuck to her palm like dough.

288

Without preamble, she pulled back the sheet covering the first body, revealing Marcellus Estevez, the man she had found by the Dumpster. He had two closely spaced bullet holes in his forehead. Powder burns tattooed the skin. She smelled cordite, which was impossible considering the man had been shot hours ago.

Amanda said, 'Two rounds to the center of the forehead, just like our drive-by at the warehouse.'

Will's voice was low. 'You don't have to do this.'

'I'm fine.' Sara forced herself to get on with it, starting with the easy stuff. 'He's approximately twenty-five years of age,' she mumbled. 'Five-eight or nine. Around one hundred eighty pounds.' She pressed open his eyes, feeling herself fall into the routine of examination. 'Brown. Jaundiced. His wound was septic. Necropsy will probably show infiltration into the larger organs. He was in systemic shutdown when we found him.' She rolled down the sheet so she could look at the belly again, this time with an eye toward forensic evaluation rather than treatment.

The man was nude; his clothes had been cut off when they'd brought him into the ER. Sara could clearly see the penetrating stab wound in the lower left quadrant of his abdomen. She pressed on either side of the cut to see if she could discern the path of the blade. 'The small intestines were pierced. It looks like the knife went in at an upward angle. Right-handed thrust from a supine position.'

Amanda asked, 'He was on top of her?'

'I would assume. We're talking about Evelyn here, right?' Will was still being stoic, but Amanda nodded. 'The blade entered at an oblique angle to the abdominal Langer's lines, or the natural direction of the skin. If I reorient the edges like this'—she twisted the skin into the position it had been in when the man was stabbed—'you can see the point of penetration suggests Evelyn was on her back, most likely on the floor, with her attacker on top of her. He was slightly bent at the waist. The knife went in like this.' Sara reached for a scalpel on the tray, but changed her mind and grabbed a pair of scissors instead. She illustrated the action, holding her hand down at her hip with the scissors angled upward. 'It was more defensive than deliberate. Maybe they struggled and fell at the same time. The knife went in. The man rolled over while the blade was still lodged—you can see how the wound is incised significantly more at the lateral edge, indicating movement.'

'Kitchen knife?' Amanda asked.

'Statistically, it's the most likely weapon, and the struggle took place in the kitchen, so it makes sense. They'll have to do a comparison at the ME's office to be sure. Did they find the weapon at the scene?'

'Yes,' she answered. 'Are you sure about this? She was on her back?'

Sara could see that Amanda was not pleased with the evaluation. She wanted her friend to be a fighter, not someone who got lucky. 'The majority of fatal stab wounds are in the left chest region. If you want to kill someone, you go for the heart, overhanded, straight into the chest. This was defensive.' She indicated the man's sliced palm. 'But Evelyn didn't go easily. At some point, she must've come at him directly, because he grabbed the blade of the knife.'

290

Amanda seemed only slightly placated by this information. 'Is there anything in his stomach?'

Sara reached under the gurney and pulled out the transportation packet destined for the Fulton County medical examiner. Krakauer had filled in most of the information while Sara was being interviewed by the police. The form was standard. The ME performing the autopsy needed to know drugs on board, procedures followed, which marks came from the hospital and which had more nefarious origins. Sara found a thermal reproduction of the X-rays on the last page.

She said, 'The belly looks clear of any foreign objects. They'll know for sure when they cut him open, but I'm assuming that the amount of heroin we're talking about, something worth dying for, would be easy to spot.'

Will cleared his throat. He seemed reluctant as he asked, 'Would Evelyn have a lot of blood on her from stabbing this guy?'

'It's not likely. Most of the bleeding happened inside the belly, even after the knife was pulled out. There's the defensive wound on his hand, but the ulnar and radial arteries are intact and none of the digital arteries were compromised. If the cut on his hand was deeper or if one of the fingers was sliced open or off, you could expect a significant amount of blood loss. But that's not the case with Estevez, so I'm guessing Evelyn would've had a minimal amount of blood on her clothes.'

Will said, 'There was a lot of blood on the floor. You could see footprints back and forth across the tiles.'

'How big was the space?'

'Kitchen sized,' he said. 'Bigger than yours, but

291

not by much, and enclosed. The house is older, ranch-style.'

Sara thought about it. 'I'd have to see the crime scene photos, but I'm fairly certain that if there was enough blood on the floor to show a struggle, that blood didn't come from Estevez's hand or belly. At least not all of it.'

'Could Estevez just get up on his own and walk off after sustaining his injuries?'

'Not without help. Any type of damage to the abdominal wall makes it difficult to breathe, let alone move.' Sara put her hand to her stomach. 'Think about how many muscles have to fire just to sit up.'

Amanda asked Will, 'What are you getting at?'

'I'm just wondering who struggled with Evelyn if this guy couldn't get up after being stabbed and there wasn't a lot of blood from his wound.'

Sara followed his logic. 'You think Evelyn was injured.'

'Maybe. They did blood typing on scene, but they didn't look at all of it, and DNA won't be back for another few days.' He shrugged. 'If Evelyn was hurt, and Estevez didn't bleed much, that could explain the extra blood.'

'I'm sure if she's injured it's nothing serious.' Amanda waved away Will's theory as if swatting a fly. Any logical person would've already accepted the very real possibility that Evelyn Mitchell's chances of survival were very slim considering how much time had elapsed. Amanda seemed to be holding on to the opposite theory.

Sara wasn't going to be the one to tell her otherwise.

There was a large magnifying glass on one of the

292

trays. Sara pulled down the overhead light and went back to the examination, checking the dead man head to toe for trace evidence, needle marks, anything unusual that might lead them to a clue. When it was time to roll him over, Will put on a pair of surgical gloves and helped flip the body.

'Well, that's interesting,' Amanda said with her usual flair for understatement.

Estevez had a large tattoo of an angel on his back. The image covered the width of his shoulders and reached the bottom of his sacrum, and was so intricate that it more closely resembled a carving. 'Gabriel,' Sara said. 'The archangel.'

Will asked, 'How do you know that?'

She pointed to the horn in the angel's mouth. 'There's no biblical foundation, but some religions believe that Judgment Day comes when Gabriel blows his horn.' Sara knew that Will had never been to church. 'It's the sort of thing they teach kids in Sunday school. And it tracks with his name—Marcellus Benedict. I believe those are the names of two different popes.'

Amanda asked, 'How recently would you say this tattoo was worked on?'

The skin at the small of his back was still irritated from the needle. 'A week, maybe five days?' She leaned in closer to look at the scrollwork. 'This was done in stages. Whoever did this took a long time. Probably months. It's not the kind of thing you'd forget, and I imagine it'd be very expensive.'

Will held the dead man's hand in his. 'Did you see this under the fingernails?'

'I saw they're dirty,' she admitted. 'That's fairly typical for a man this age. I can't do any scrapings.

293

The ME's office would have a fit and anything I found would be inadmissible because we haven't established the chain of evidence.'

Will put his nose close to the man's fingers. 'It smells like oil to me.'

Sara smelled for herself. 'I can't tell. The police told me that they checked the outside security cameras. They're not static. They sweep back and forth across the back lot, which the bad guys obviously knew because they managed not to get caught leaving the body. The time stamp says that Estevez was by the Dumpster at least twelve hours. The smell could be anything.' She rolled over the hand to show Will. 'This is more interesting. Estevez obviously worked with his hands. There's a hardening of the skin on the ball of the thumb and here on the side of the index finger. He held some kind of tool for long periods of time. It would've had some weight to it and moved around a bit.'

He asked Amanda, 'You said he was unemployed?'

'The state shows he's been collecting unemployment insurance for almost a year.'

Sara thought of something else. 'Can you hand me that?' She pointed to the magnifying glass. Will picked it up and waited as Sara forced open Estevez's mouth. The jaw was stiff. The tendon popped when she pried open the lips. 'Hold it here,' she told Will, indicating he should focus on the upper teeth. 'Do you see these tiny indentations in the bottom edges of his top front teeth?' Will leaned in closer, then let Amanda take a look. 'These are repetitive impressions. They come from constantly gripping something between his teeth. You see this sort of thing with seamstresses who bite thread or finish carpenters who put nails in their mouth.'

'Or cabinetmakers?' Will asked.

'That's possible.' Sara looked at Estevez's hand again. 'These calluses could come from holding a nail gun. I'd have to see the tool for comparison, but if you told me he worked as a carpenter, I'd agree that his hands show signs of working in that industry.' She picked up the man's left hand. 'Do you see these scars on his index finger? These line up with common injuries for carpenters. Hammers slip. A nail pinches the skin. Threads from screws scrape off the top dermal layer. Do you see this scar down the center line of his nail?' Will nodded. 'It cuts through his cuticle, too. Carpenters use carpet knives to cut edges or score wood. Sometimes the blade skips down the fingernail or shaves the skin off the side of the finger. A lot of times they'll use their nondominant hand to smooth out putty or caulk, which causes wearing at the tip. His fingerprints would be different week-to-week, sometimes day-to-day.'

Amanda said, 'So, he's been at this job for a while?'

'I'd say whatever job he's been working at that caused these marks has been going on for two to three years.'

'What about Heeney, the shooter?'

Sara reached under the sheet to check the other man's hands. She did not want to look at his face again. 'He was left-handed, but I would hazard he worked in the same industry as Estevez.'

Will said, 'There's one connection, at least. They both worked for Ling-Ling.'

Sara asked, 'Who's Ling-Ling?'

295

'A missing person of interest.' Amanda checked her watch. 'We should hurry this along. Dr. Linton, can you examine our other friend here?'

Sara didn't give herself time to think about it. She pulled back the sheet in one quick motion. It was the first time she'd looked at Franklin Warren Heeney's face since he'd tried to kill her. His eyes were open. His lips were wrapped around the tube that had been inserted into his throat to help him breathe. A crusty layer of blood circled his neck where the flesh gaped open. He was still dressed from the waist down, but his jacket and shirt had been cut open so that the ER staff could try to save his life. The exercise had been perfunctory; the man had sliced open his own jugular. He'd lost nearly half his blood volume before they'd managed to pick him up off the floor and put him on the table. Sara knew this because she had been the doctor working on him.

She looked up. Both Amanda and Will were staring at her.

'Sorry,' she apologized. She had to clear her throat before she could talk again. 'He's around the same age as Estevez. Mid-to-late twenties. Underweight for his build.' She pointed to the needle tracks on his arm. The IV port she'd inserted was still taped to his skin. 'Recent user, at least intravenously.' She found an otoscope and checked inside the man's nose. 'There's significant scarring in the nasal passages, probably from snorting powder.' She shoved the scope in farther. 'He's had surgery to repair the septum, so you're looking at coke or meth, maybe Oxy. They're all extremely corrosive to cartilage.'

Will asked, 'What about heroin?'

'Oh, heroin, of course.' Sara apologized again. 'Sorry, most of the heroin users I see are smokers or needle junkies. The snorters usually go straight to the morgue.'

Amanda crossed her arms. 'What about his stomach?'

Sara didn't have to check the file. No X-rays had been taken. The man had expired before any tests could be ordered. Instead of continuing the exam, Sara found herself looking at his face again. Franklin Heeney hardly resembled a choirboy, but the acne-scarred skin and sunken cheeks were recognizable to someone out in the world. He had a mother. He had a father, a child, perhaps a sister or brother, who right at this moment was probably hearing that their loved one was dead.

Their loved one who had killed a man in cold blood and punched Sara so violently that the breath had gone out of her body. She felt the bruise on her chest start to throb at the memory. She had a mother, too—a sister, a father—all of whom would be horrified if they heard what had happened to Sara today.

Amanda asked, 'Dr. Linton?'

'Sorry.' In the time it took to walk over to the box of gloves and put on a fresh pair, she had managed to pull herself back together. She ignored Will's look of concern and pressed her fingers into the dead man's belly. 'I don't feel anything unusual. The organs are in their proper position and are normal size. No swelling or compaction in the bowel or stomach.' She snapped off the gloves and threw them into the trash. The water in the sink was cold, but Sara washed her hands anyway. 'I can't send him to X-ray because they'll need a

297

patient ID, and frankly, I'm not going to make a living person wait to satisfy a curiosity. The ME's office will have to give you a definitive answer.' She squirted antibacterial gel into her palm, fighting to keep her voice steady. 'Is that all?'

'Yes,' Amanda said. 'Thank you, Dr. Linton.'

Sara didn't acknowledge the answer. She ignored Will. She ignored the two bodies. She kept her eyes on the door until she had passed through it. In the hallway, she concentrated on the elevator, the button she would press, the numbers that would light up over the door. She only wanted to think about the steps ahead, not the ones behind her. She had to get out of this place, to get home and wrap herself in a blanket on the couch and pull the dogs around her and forget this miserable day.

There were footsteps behind her. Will was running again. He caught up with her quickly. She turned around. He stopped a few feet away.

He said, 'Amanda's putting out an APB on the tattoo.'

Why was he just standing there? Why did he keep rushing up to her and doing absolutely nothing?

He said, 'Maybe we'll find—'

'I really don't care.'

He stared at her. His hands were in his pockets. The sleeve of his jacket was tight around his upper arm. There was a small tear in the material.

Sara leaned her shoulder against the wall. She hadn't noticed before, but there was a fresh cut at the top of his earlobe. She wanted to ask him about it, but he would probably tell her that he'd cut himself shaving. Maybe she didn't want to know what had happened. The Polaroid of his damaged mouth still burned in her memory. What else had they done to him? What else had he done to himself?

Will said, 'Why is it that none of the women in my life call me when they need help?'

'Doesn't Angie call you?'

He looked down at the floor, the space between them.

She said, 'I'm sorry. That wasn't fair. It's been a really long day.'

Will didn't look up. Instead, he took her hand. His fingers laced through hers. His skin was warm, almost hot. He traced his thumb along the inside of her palm, the webbing between her fingers. Sara closed her eyes as he slowly explored every inch of her hand, caressing the lines and indentations, pressing his thumb gently against the pulse beating in her wrist. His touch was palliative. She felt her body starting to relax. Her breathing took on an easy cadence that matched his.

The doors to the morgue swished open. Sara yanked away her hand at the same time as Will. Neither of them looked at each other. They were like two kids caught in the back of a parked car.

Amanda held her cell phone in the air, triumphant. 'Roger Ling wants to talk.'

CHAPTER TWELVE

Faith felt as close to a nervous breakdown as she'd ever been in her life. Her teeth kept chattering despite the sweat dripping down her body. She'd thrown up her breakfast and had to force down lunch. Her head ached so badly that it hurt to even close her eyes. Her blood sugar levels were just as fragile. She'd had to call her doctor's office to find out what to do. They had threatened to put her in the hospital if she didn't get her numbers under control. Faith had promised to report back, then she'd gone into the bathroom, turned on the shower as hot as she could stand it, and sobbed for half an hour.

The same series of thoughts kept running through her mind like tires wearing a groove in a gravel road. They had been in her house. They had touched her things. Touched Jeremy's things. They knew when he was born. They knew his schools. They knew his likes and dislikes. They had planned this—all of it, down to the last detail.

The threat was like a death sentence. Mouth shut. Eyes open. Faith didn't think her eyes could open any wider or her mouth could close any tighter. She'd searched the house twice. She was constantly checking her phone, her email, Jeremy's Facebook page. It was three o'clock in the afternoon. She had been trapped in the house like a caged animal for nearly ten hours.

And still, nothing.

'Hey, Mom?' Jeremy came into the kitchen. Faith was sitting at the table, staring at the backyard, where Detective Taylor and Ginger were talking earnestly to the ground. She could tell from their bored demeanors that they were just waiting for the word from their boss so they could get back to their real jobs. As far as they were concerned, this case had come to a screeching halt. Too many hours had passed. No one had made contact. She could read the truth in their eyes. They honestly believed that Evelyn Mitchell was dead.

'Mom?'

Faith rubbed Jeremy's arm. 'What is it? Is Emma up?' The baby had slept too long last night. She was fussy and irritable, and had screamed for nearly a full hour before finally relenting to her afternoon nap.

'She's fine,' Jeremy answered. 'I was gonna go for a walk. Get out of the house for a minute. Take some fresh air.'

'No,' she told him. 'I don't want you leaving the house.'

His expression told her how hard her voice was.

She squeezed his arm. 'I want you to stay here, all right?'

'I'm tired of being cooped up inside.'

'So am I, but I want you to promise me you won't leave the house.' She played at his emotions. 'I've already got Grandma to worry about. Don't make me add you to my list.'

His reluctance was obvious, but he told her, 'All right.'

'Just do something with your uncle Zeke. Play cards or something.'

'He pouts when he loses.'

'So do you.' Faith shooed him out of the kitchen. She charted his path through the house and up to

301

his room by the familiar squeaks in the floorboards and on the stairs. She should put Zeke to work on her list of handyman repairs. Of course, that would involve actually talking to him, and Faith was doing her best to avoid her brother. Miraculously, he seemed to be doing the same. He'd been in the garage for the last three hours, working on his laptop.

Faith pushed herself up from the table and started pacing in hopes that she could work out some of her nervous energy. That didn't last long. She leaned over the table and tapped the keyboard on her laptop to wake it up. She moused up to reload Jeremy's Facebook page. The rainbow wheel started to spin. Jeremy was probably playing some game upstairs that was slowing down the wireless network.

The phone rang. Faith jumped. She startled any time there was an unexpected noise. She was as nervous as a cat. The back door slid open. Ginger waited while she took the receiver off the hook. She could tell from his tired expression that he felt this was not only perfunctory, but beneath his talents.

She put the phone to her ear. 'Hello?'

'Faith.'

It was Victor Martinez. She waved away Ginger. 'Hey.'

'Hi.'

Now that the easy part was out of the way, neither of them seemed capable of talking. She hadn't spoken to Victor in thirteen months, not since she'd sent him a text that he needed to get his stuff out of her house or she was going to leave it on the street.

Victor broke the silence. 'Is there any news on your mother?'

'No. Nothing.'

'It's been over twenty-four hours, right?'

She didn't trust herself to speak. Victor had a habit of pointing out the obvious, and his love of crime shows meant that he knew as well as Faith that time was against them.

'Is Jeremy all right?'

'Yes. Thank you for bringing him home yesterday. And staying with him.' She thought to ask, 'You didn't see anything unusual when you were here, right? No one hanging around the house?'

'Of course not. I would've told the police.'

'How long were you here before they arrived?'

'Not long. Your brother came about an hour later and I left.'

Faith's exhausted brain struggled to do the math. Evelyn's kidnappers hadn't hesitated. They'd driven straight here from her house. They were familiar enough with the space to walk right upstairs to her room and plant the finger under Faith's pillow. Maybe they were watching the house even before that. Maybe they had listened to Faith's phone calls or checked her calendar on her laptop and knew that she would be away. Nothing in the house was password protected because she had always assumed that she was safe here.

Faith had missed something Victor said. 'What?'

'I said, your brother's kind of an asshole.'

Faith snapped, 'It's not exactly an easy time for him, Victor. Our mother is missing. God knows whether she's dead or alive. Zeke dropped everything to be with Jeremy. I'm sorry if you

303

thought he was rude. It's kind of hard to be friendly right now.'

'Hold on, all right? I'm sorry. I shouldn't have said that.'

Her breathing was revved up again. Faith tried to get her control back. She wanted to yell at someone. That person probably didn't need to be Victor.

'Are you there?' he asked.

Faith couldn't drag this out any longer. 'I know that Jeremy showed you Emma's picture.'

He cleared his throat.

'What you're thinking about her . . .' Faith pressed her fingers to her closed eyelids. 'You're right.'

He was silent for what felt like an eternity. Finally, he said, 'She's beautiful.'

Faith dropped her hand. She looked up at the ceiling. Her hormones were so out of whack that the stupidest thing could set her off. She cradled the phone against her shoulder and tried to reload Jeremy's Facebook page again.

'I'd like to meet her when this is all over.'

Faith watched the wheel spin on the computer screen as the processor worked. She couldn't think about seeing Victor with Emma. Holding her in his arms. Stroking her hair. Pointing out that looking into her light brown eyes was like looking into a mirror. Faith could only think about right now, and how every second that ticked by made it less likely that Evelyn Mitchell would see her grand-daughter's first birthday.

'Your mom's a fighter,' Victor said. Then, almost ruefully, 'Just like you.'

The page finally loaded. GoodKnight92 had

posted a comment eight minutes ago.

'I have to go.' Faith hung up the phone. Her hand hovered over the laptop. She stared at the words on the screen. They had a familiar ring.

You must be feeling cooped up. Why don't you get out of the house and take some fresh air?

They had contacted Jeremy again, and her son, her little boy, had been ready to walk out the front door and put his life on the line so that he could get his grandmother back.

She raised her voice, calling, 'Jeremy?'

Faith waited. There were no footsteps overhead, no squeaks on the stairs or floorboards.

'Jeremy?' she called again, going into the living room. An eternity passed. Faith grabbed the back of the couch so she wouldn't fall down. Her voice trilled in panic. 'Jeremy!'

Her heart stopped at the thumping sound from upstairs, heavy footsteps across the floor. But it was Zeke who called from the top of the landing. 'Jesus, Faith, what's wrong?'

Faith could barely speak. 'Where's Jeremy?'

'I told him he could go for a walk.'

Ginger came in from the kitchen, a puzzled look on his face. Before he could say anything, Faith grabbed the gun out of his shoulder holster and bolted from the room. She didn't remember opening the front door or running down the driveway. It wasn't until she was in the middle of the street that Faith stopped. She saw a figure up ahead. He was about to turn the corner onto the next street. Tall, lanky, baggy jeans and a yellow Georgia Tech sweatshirt.

'Jeremy!' she yelled. A car pulled up to the intersection, stopping a few feet from her son.

'Jeremy!' He didn't hear her. He walked toward the car.

Faith ran all out, arms pumping, bare feet pounding the pavement. She gripped the gun so tightly in her hand that it felt like part of her skin.

'Jeremy!' she screamed. He turned around. The car was in front of him. Dark gray. Four doors. New-model Ford Focus with chrome trim. The window rolled down. Jeremy turned back to the car, bent down to look inside. 'Stop!' Faith yelled, her throat clenching around the word. 'Get away from the car! Get away from the car!'

The driver was leaning toward Jeremy. Faith saw a teenage girl behind the wheel, mouth agape, obviously terrified by the armed madwoman running down the street. The car screeched off as Faith reached her son. She bumped into him, almost pushing him down.

'Why?' she asked, gripping his arm so tight that her fingers hurt.

He pulled away, rubbing his arm. 'Jesus, Mom, what is wrong with you? She was lost. She needed directions.'

Faith was dizzy from fear and adrenaline. She bent over and put her hand on her knee. The gun was at her side. So was Ginger.

He snatched the weapon back. 'Agent Mitchell, that was not cool.'

His words filled her with anger. 'Not cool?' She thumped her open palm against his chest. 'Not cool?'

'Agent.' His tone of voice implied she was acting hysterical, which only served to amp up her fury another notch.

'How about letting my son walk out the door

when you were assigned to watch him? Was that not cool, too?' She pushed him again. 'How about you and your partner standing around holding your dicks while my boy is gone?' Another push. 'Is that cool?'

Ginger held up his hands in surrender.

'Faith,' Zeke said. She hadn't noticed her brother standing there, maybe because for once he wasn't making things worse. 'Let's just go back to the house.'

She held out her hand to Jeremy, palm up. 'iPhone.'

He looked appalled. 'What?'

'Now,' she ordered.

'That's got all my games on it.'

'I don't care.'

'What am I supposed to do?'

'Read a book!' she screamed, her voice screeching. 'Just stay offline. Do you hear me? No Internet!'

'Jesus.' He glanced around for support, but Faith didn't care if God Himself came down and told her to give the kid a break.

She said, 'I'll tie you to my waist with a rope if I have to.'

He knew she wasn't bluffing; she'd done it before. 'This isn't fair.' He slapped the phone in her hand. She would've thrown it to the ground and crushed it with her foot if the damn thing hadn't cost so much.

'No Internet,' Faith repeated. 'No phone calls. No communication of any kind, and you stay in the fucking house. Do you hear me?' He walked toward the house, giving her his back. Faith wasn't going to let him off that easy. 'Do you hear me?'

'I heard you!' he yelled. 'God!'

Ginger shoved his gun back into the holster, adjusting the straps like a haughty cheerleader. He followed Jeremy down the street. Faith limped along after them. Her feet were bruised from the rocky asphalt. Zeke fell in beside her. His shoulder brushed against hers. Faith braced herself for some kind of tirade, but he was mercifully silent as they walked up the driveway and entered the house.

Faith threw Jeremy's iPhone onto the kitchen table. No wonder he wanted to leave. The space was beginning to feel like a prison. She leaned heavily against the chair. What had she been thinking? How could any of them be safe here? Evelyn's kidnappers knew the layout of the house. They had obviously targeted Jeremy. Anyone could've been in that car. They could've rolled down the window, pointed a gun at Jeremy's head, and pulled the trigger. He could've bled out in the middle of the street and Faith wouldn't have known until his stupid Facebook page loaded that something was wrong.

'Faith?' Zeke was standing in the middle of the kitchen. His tone indicated this wasn't the first time he'd said her name. 'What's wrong with you?'

Faith crossed her arms low on her stomach. 'Where have you been staying? You weren't sleeping at Mom's. I would've seen your stuff.'

'Dobbins.' She should've known. Zeke had always loved the soulless anonymity of base housing, even if Dobbins Air Reserve was an hour drive from the VA hospital where he was doing his in-service.

'I need you to do me a favor.'

He was instantly skeptical. 'What?'

308

'I want you to take Jeremy and Emma back to the base with you. Today. Right now.' The Atlanta police couldn't protect her family, but the United States Air Force could. 'I don't know how long it'll be for. I just need you to keep them on the base. Don't let them off until I tell you.'

'Why?'

'Because I need to know that they're safe.'

'Safe from what? What are you planning?'

Faith checked the backyard to make sure the detectives weren't listening. Ginger stared at her, his jaw rigid. She turned her back to him. 'I need you to trust me.'

Zeke snorted a laugh. 'Why would I start doing that?'

'Because I know what I'm doing, Zeke. I'm a police officer. I was trained to do this kind of thing.'

'What kind of thing? Run into the street barefooted like you're escaping from the loony bin?'

'I'm going to get Mom back, Zeke. I don't care if it kills me. I'm going to get her back.'

'You and what army?' he scoffed. 'You gonna call in Aunt Mandy and go smear lipstick all over them?'

She punched him in the face. He looked more shocked than hurt. Her knuckle felt like it might be broken. Still, she got some satisfaction when she saw a thin line of blood drip onto his upper lip.

'Christ,' he muttered. 'What the hell was that for?'

'You'll need to take my car. You can't fit a car seat in the Corvette. I can give you some money for gas and groceries and I—'

309

'Wait.' His voice was muffled by his hand as he felt the bridge of his nose for damage. He looked at her—really looked at her—for the first time since she'd walked through her own front door. Faith had hit her brother before. She'd burned him with a match. She'd beaten him with a clothes hanger. To her recollection, this was the first time any violence between them actually seemed to work.

'All right.' He used the toaster to check his reflection. His nose wasn't broken, but a deep, purple bruise was working its way underneath his eye. 'But I'm not taking your Mini. I'm going to look retarded enough as it is.'

CHAPTER THIRTEEN

Will had never been quick to anger, but once he got there, he held on to it like a miser with a pot of gold. He didn't throw things or use his fists. He didn't rage or even raise his voice. Actually, the opposite happened. He went quiet—completely silent. It was as if his vocal cords were paralyzed. He kept it all on the inside because, in his vast experience with angry people, Will knew that letting it out meant that someone could end up very badly hurt.

Not that this particular expression of anger didn't have its drawbacks. His stubborn silence had gotten him suspended from school on more than one occasion. Years ago, Amanda had transferred him to the nether regions of the north Georgia mountains for his refusal to respond to her

310

questions. Once, he'd stopped speaking to Angie for three whole days for fear of saying things to her that could never be taken back. They'd lived together, slept together, dined together, done everything together, and he hadn't uttered one word to her for a full seventy-two hours. If there had been a category in the Special Olympics for functionally illiterate mutes, Will would've had no problem cinching the gold.

This was all to say that not speaking to Amanda during the five-hour drive down to Coastal State Prison was nothing in the scheme of things. The worrying part was that the intensity of Will's anger would not dissipate. He had never hated another human being as much as he did when Amanda told him that, by the way, Sara had almost been murdered. And that hatred would not go away. He kept waiting to feel that click of it letting up, the pot going from a boil to a simmer, but it wouldn't come. Even now as Amanda paced back and forth in front of him, going from one end of the empty visitors' waiting room to the other like a duck in a shooting gallery, he felt the rage burning inside him.

The worst part was that he wanted to speak. He yearned to speak. He wanted to lay it all out for her and watch her face crumble as she realized that Will truly and irrevocably despised her for what she had done to him. He had never been a petty man, but he really, really wanted to hurt her.

Amanda stopped pacing. She put her hands on her hips. 'I don't know what you've been told, but sulking is not an attractive trait in a man.'

Will stared at the floor. Grooves had been worn into the linoleum by the women and children who had wiled away their weekends waiting to visit the men inside the cells.

She said, 'As a rule, I only let someone call me that word once. I think you picked an appropriate time.'

So, he hadn't been completely mute. When Amanda had told him about Sara, he'd called her the word that rhymes with her name. And not in Spanish.

'What do you want, Will, an apology?' She huffed a laugh. 'All right, I'm sorry. I apologize for not letting you get distracted so that you could do your job. I apologize for making sure your head didn't get blown off. I apologize—'

His mouth moved of its own accord. 'Could you just shut up?'

'What was that?'

He didn't repeat himself. He didn't care whether or not she heard him, or if his job was in jeopardy, or if she was going to unleash a new kind of hell on him for standing up to her. Will could not remember the last time he had experienced the kind of agony he'd suffered this afternoon. They'd sat outside that damn warehouse for a full hour before the Doraville police released them. Will understood intellectually why the detectives wanted to talk to them. There were two dead bodies and bullet holes everywhere. There was a stockpile of illegal machine guns on a shelf in the back. There was a large safe in Julia Ling's office with the door swinging open and hundred-dollar bills scattered on the floor. You didn't just roll up on a scene like that and release the only two witnesses. There were forms to be filled out, questions to be answered. Will had to give a statement. He'd had to wait while Amanda gave hers. It seemed like she had taken her time. He'd sat in the car, watching her talk to the detectives, feeling like an earthquake was going off in his chest.

His cell phone had been in and out of his hand a dozen times. Should he call Sara? Should he leave her alone? Did she need him? Wouldn't she call him if she did? He had to see her. If he saw her, he would know how to react, to do what she needed. He would wrap his arms around her. He would kiss her cheek, her neck, her mouth. He would make everything better.

Or, he would just stand there in the hallway like a jackass, molesting her hand.

Amanda snapped her fingers for his attention. Will didn't look up, but she talked anyway. 'Your emergency contact is Angela Polaski. Or I should say Angie Trent, I suppose, since she's your wife.' She paused for effect. 'She *is* still your wife?'

He shook his head. He had never wanted to punch a woman so badly in his life.

'What did you expect me to do, Will?'

He kept shaking his head.

'So, I tell you that your—I don't know, what is Dr. Linton to you these days? Mistress? Girlfriend? *Pal?*—is in trouble, and then what? We drop everything so you can go make googly eyes at her?'

Will stood up. He wasn't going to do this. He would hitchhike back to Atlanta if he had to.

She sighed like the world was against her. 'The warden will be here any minute. I need you to pull up your big-girl pants so I can prep you for your conversation with Roger Ling.'

313

Will looked at her for the first time since they'd left the hospital. 'Me?'

'He asked for you specifically.'

This was some kind of trick, but he couldn't see where it was going. 'How does he even know my name?'

'I imagine his sister filled him in.'

As far as Will knew, Julia Ling was still on the run. 'She called him at the prison?'

She crossed her arms over her chest. 'Roger Ling is in solitary confinement for hiding a razor blade in his rectum. He doesn't get phone calls. He doesn't get visitors.'

Isolation had never deterred the prison message system. There were so many illegal cell phones inside the walls that last year during a statewide prisoner strike, *The New York Times* had been flooded with calls from inmates making their demands.

Still, Will said, 'Roger Ling asked for me specifically?'

'Yes, Will. The request came through his lawyer. He asked for you specifically.' She allowed, 'Of course, they called me first. No one knows who the hell you are. Except for Roger, apparently.'

Will sat back down in the chair. He felt his jaw ratcheting tight. The silence wanted to come back. He could feel it like a shadow looming behind him.

She asked, 'Who do you think the cop is who confronted Dr. Linton in the hospital?'

He shook his head. He didn't want to think about Sara anymore. He felt sick every time he thought about what she'd been through today. Alone.

Amanda repeated herself. 'Who do you think

the cop is?' Again, she snapped her fingers to get his attention.

He looked up. He wanted to break her hand.

'This isn't about me. This is about Faith and getting back her mother. Now, who do you think the cop is?'

He cleared the glass out of his throat. 'How do you know all of these people?'

'What people?'

'Hector Ortiz. Roger Ling. Julia Ling. Perry the bodyguard who drives a Mercedes. Why are you on a first-name basis with all these people?'

She was silent, obviously debating about whether or not to answer. Finally, she relented. 'You know I came up in the job with Evelyn. We were cadets together. We were partners before they got tired of us busting all their cases.' She shook her head at the memory. 'These are the bad guys who were on the other side. Drugs. Rape. Murder. Assault. Hostage negotiation. RICO cases. Money laundering. They've been around as long as we have.' She added ruefully, 'Which is a very, very long time.'

'You've worked cases against them?'

There were fifty chairs in the room, but she sat down right beside him. 'Ignatio Ortiz and Roger Ling didn't just vault to the top. There are bodies they climbed over. Lots and lots of dead bodies. And the sad part is that they were human beings once. They were nice, normal people who went to church every Sunday and clocked into their jobs during the week.' Amanda shook her head again, and Will could tell that her words invoked memories she'd rather forget.

Still, she told him, 'You know the word

315

underbelly refers to the part of society that's never seen, but it also means the vulnerable part. The weak part. That's what monsters like Roger Ling and Ignatio Ortiz prey on. Addiction. Greed. Poverty. Desperation. Once these guys figured out how to exploit these people, they never looked back. They cut their teeth doing carhops for dealers when they were twelve. They murdered before they were old enough to legally buy a drink in a bar. They've slit throats and beaten old women to death and done whatever it takes to get to the top and hold on to that power. So, when you ask me why I'm on a first-name basis with them, it's because I *know* them. I know who they are. I have stared into the darkness of their souls. But I guarantee you it doesn't go the other way. They don't have a damn idea who I am, and I've spent my career keeping it that way.'

Will was finished treading carefully. 'They know Evelyn.'

'Yes,' Amanda allowed. 'I think they do.'

He sat back in his chair. It was a stunning admission. He didn't know how to respond. Unfortunately—or maybe fortunately—she didn't give him the chance.

She clasped her hands together. Sharing time was over. 'Let's talk about this cop who confronted Sara in the hospital.'

Will was still trying to wrap his brain around what had just happened. For just a moment, he'd forgotten all about Sara.

'Chuck Finn,' she prompted.

Will leaned his head against the wall. The concrete block felt cold against his scalp. 'He used to be a cop. You don't lose that no matter how

316

much heroin you shoot up. He's tall. He's probably lost a lot of weight from his habit. Sara wouldn't have recognized him from his mugshot. I'm assuming he's a smoker. Most junkies are.'

'So, at the hospital: you think Chuck Finn discerned from Sara that Marcellus Estevez might live, so he sent Franklin Heeney in to kill him.'

'Don't you?'

Amanda wasn't quick with her response. He could tell what she'd said about Evelyn Mitchell still weighed heavily on her. 'I don't know what I think anymore, Will. And that's the God's honest truth.'

She sounded tired. Her shoulders were slumped. There was a sort of detachment about her. He went back over their conversation, wondering what had finally made her admit that Evelyn Mitchell wasn't squeaky clean. He had never in his life seen Amanda give up on anything. Part of him felt sorry for her, and another part of him realized that he might not ever have this chance again.

He struck while her defenses were down. 'Why didn't they shoot you outside the warehouse?'

'I'm a deputy director with the GBI. That's a lot of heat.'

'They've already kidnapped a decorated police officer. They shot at you inside the warehouse. They killed Castillo. Why didn't they kill you?'

'I don't know, Will.' She rubbed her eyes with her fingers. 'I think we must be caught in the middle of some kind of war.'

Will stared at the Meth Project poster on the wall. A toothless woman with scabby skin stared back. He wondered if that was what the junkie had looked like, the woman who had told Sara that

317

there was a guy laid out by the Dumpster. How long had it taken before Marcellus Estevez was dead and Franklin Heeney was struggling with Sara on the floor, threatening to cut open her face with a scalpel?

Minutes. Maybe ten at the most.

Will couldn't help it. He put his elbows on his knees and dropped his head in his hands. 'You should've told me.' He could hear a distant voice in his head screaming at him to shut up. But he couldn't. 'You had no right to keep that from me.'

Amanda gave a heavy sigh. 'Maybe I should have. Or maybe I was right to hold it back. If it's the first one, I'm sorry. If it's the second, then you can be mad at me later. I need you to talk this through with me. I need to figure out what is going on. If not for my sake, then for Faith's.'

Her voice sounded as desperate as he felt. The day had utterly defeated her. Will couldn't help it. As much as he hated her right now, he couldn't be cruel.

And somewhere in all of this, the click happened. He hadn't noticed it, but sometime during the last ten minutes, his anger had started to seep out, so that now when he thought about it, when he considered what Amanda had done about Sara, Will felt a festering anger rather than a burning hate.

He took a deep breath and slowly let it go as he sat back up. 'Okay. We have to assume that all the dead guys worked in Julia Ling's shop—some of them on the books, some of them off, all of them doing both sides of her business.'

'You think Ling-Ling sent Ricardo Ortiz to Sweden to pick up some heroin?'

318

'No, I think Ricardo got ahead of himself. I think he got all the young guys worked up, thinking they could take over Ling-Ling's business. He took it on himself to go to Sweden.' Will looked at his watch. It was almost seven o'clock. 'He was tortured, probably by Benny Choo.'

'Then why didn't they just cut the drugs out of him and be done with it?'

'Because he told them that he knew where they could get more money.'

'Evelyn.'

'It's what I said earlier.' He turned toward her. 'Chuck Finn mentioned in one of his Healing Winds group sessions with Hironobu Kwon that his old boss was sitting on a pile of money. Cut to yesterday morning. Ricardo has a belly full of heroin and Benny Choo beating his ass. His friend Hironobu Kwon says he knows where they can get some cash to buy themselves out of the situation.' Will shrugged. 'They go to Evelyn's. Benny Choo tags along to keep them from doing a runner. Only, they can't find the money, and Evelyn won't give it up to them.'

'Perhaps they weren't expecting to find Hector Ortiz there. Ricardo would recognize his father's cousin.'

Will wanted to ask what Hector Ortiz was doing at Evelyn's in the first place, but he didn't want to make Amanda lie to him right now. 'Ricardo Ortiz would know that killing Hector would bring some heat. He's already turned his back on his own father by smuggling in the heroin. Ling-Ling is out for his blood because she's found out that Ricardo turned on her, too. Ricardo's gang can't find the money in Evelyn's house. She's not talking.

319

Ricardo has to see at this point that his life isn't worth much. He's packed full of balloons he can't pass. He's been beaten nearly to death. Benny Choo's got a gun to his head.' Will ran through Faith's statement about her confrontation with Choo and Ortiz. 'Ricardo's last word was 'Almeja.' That's what Julia Ling called Evelyn, right? How would Ricardo know that?'

'I suppose if your theory holds that this all came from Chuck Finn, then that's where he got it.'

'Why would Evelyn's name be the last word on Ricardo's lips?'

'It's her street name. I'd be surprised if Ricardo knew her real one.' She explained, 'It's not just the bangers who give themselves nicknames. You work narcotics long enough, they come up with something street to call you by. Sometimes, that spills over into the squad. 'Hip' and 'Hop' were obviously shortened from their last names. Boyd Spivey was Sledge, as in hammer. Chuck Finn was called Fish, I suppose because they couldn't remember the name for a lemming.' She smiled; another private joke. 'Roger Ling took credit for coming up with 'Almeja,' which seemed curious at the time until we realized he doesn't speak a bit of his parents' language. Mandarin, in case you're curious.'

'What about you?'

'I don't work narcotics.'

'But they know you.'

'Wag,' she told him. 'Short for Wagner.'

Will didn't believe her. 'Why did Roger Ling ask to speak with me?'

She gave a startled laugh. 'You can't really think that you're the only man in this prison right now

320

who despises me.'

There was a loud buzz and a clanging of gates opening and closing. Two guards came into the waiting room, followed by a younger man with Harry Potter spectacles and a floppy haircut to match. He was definitely not one of Amanda's old gals. There were velvet patches on the elbows of his corduroy jacket. His tie was made of a knit cotton. His shirt had a stain over the pocket. He smelled of pancakes.

'Jimmy Kagan,' he said, shaking their hands. 'I'm not sure what strings you pulled, Deputy Director, but this is the first time in my six years as warden here that I've been called back to work this late at night.'

Amanda had easily transitioned back to her old self. It was like seeing an actor slip into character. 'I appreciate your cooperation, Warden Kagan. We all have to do our part.'

'I didn't have much of a choice,' Kagan admitted, indicating the guards should open the door into the main prison. He led them down a long hallway at a fast clip. 'I'm not going to disrupt my entire system no matter who you get on the phone. Agent Trent, you'll have to go back into the cells. Ling has been in solitary for the last week. You can talk to him through the slot in the door. I'm sure you know the type of person you're dealing with, but I'll tell you straight up I wouldn't be in the same room with Roger Ling if you held a gun to my head. I'm actually terrified that's going to happen to me one day.'

Amanda raised an eyebrow at Will. 'You make it sound as if the primates are running the zoo.'

Kagan gave her a look that said he thought she

was either deluded or insane. He told Will, 'At any given time in the U.S. penal system, at least half the inmate population have been diagnosed with some kind of mental illness.'

Will nodded. He'd heard the statistic before. All the prisons in the country combined bought more Prozac than any other single institution.

Kagan said, 'Some of them are worse than others. Ling is worse than the worst. He should be in a mental ward. Locked down. Throw away the key.'

Another gate opened and closed.

Kagan listed the rules. 'Don't get close to the door. Don't think you're safe just because you're an arm's length away. This man is very resourceful, and he has a lot of time on his hands. The razor blade we found up his ass was wrapped in a hand-tied pouch Ling made from strings he pulled out of his bedsheets. It took him two months. He braided a Yellow Rebel star into it as some kind of joke. Must've dyed it with urine.'

Kagan stopped at yet another door and waited for it to open. 'I have no idea how he got the razor blade. He's in his cell twenty-three hours a day. His yard time is isolated—he's the only one in the cage. He doesn't have contact visits, and the guards are all terrified of him.' The door opened and he continued walking. 'If it was up to me, I'd leave him to rot in the hole. But it's not up to me. He'll be confined another week unless he pulls something awful. And believe me, he is capable of the awful.'

The warden stopped at a set of metal doors. The first one clanged open and they went inside. 'The last time we locked him in the hole, the guard who

322

sent him there was attacked the next day. We never found the responsible party, but the man lost one of his eyes. It was plucked out by hand.'

The door behind them shut and the one in front of them banged open.

Kagan said, 'We'll have the cameras on you, Mr. Trent, but I have to warn you that our response time clocks in at sixty-one seconds, just over a minute. We can't get it any tighter than that. I have a full raid team suited up and on standby if anything happens.' He patted Will on the back. 'Good luck.'

There was a guard waiting to take Will through. The man looked filled with the kind of dread you'd see on a death row inmate's face. It was like staring into a mirror.

Will turned to Amanda. He had broken his silence in the waiting room so that she could coach him on what to say to Roger Ling, but he just now realized she hadn't offered any advice. 'You want to help me here?'

She said, 'Quid pro quo, Clarice. Don't come back without some useful information.'

Will remembered again that he hated her.

The guard motioned him through. The door closed behind them. The man said, 'Keep close to the walls. If you see something coming at you, cover your eyes and close your mouth. It's probably shit.'

Will tried to walk as if his testicles hadn't receded into his body. The lights were out in the cells, but the hall was well lit. The guard kept to the wall, away from the prisoners opposite. Will followed suit. He could feel a new set of eyes tracking him as he passed each cell. There was a skittering noise behind him as kites, tiny pieces of paper with strings attached to them, slid across the concrete floor in his wake. In his mind, Will listed out all the possible contraband in the cells. Shivs made from toothbrushes and combs. Blades fashioned from pieces of metal lifted out of the kitchen. Feces and urine mixed in a cup to create gas bombs. Threads from a sheet braided into a whip with razor blades tied at the ends.

Another set of double gates. The first one opened. They walked through. The first one closed. Seconds ticked by. The second set groaned open.

They came to a solid door with a piece of glass at eye level. The guard took out a heavy ring of keys and found the right one. He stuck it into a lock on the wall. There was a *ka-thunk* as a bolt opened. He turned around and looked at the camera overhead. They both waited until there was a responding click from the guard watching them in a remote viewing room. The door slid open.

Solitary confinement. The hole.

The hallway was about thirty feet deep and ten feet wide. Eight metal doors were on one side. A concrete block wall was on the other. The cells faced inside the prison, not out. There would be no windows. No fresh air. No sunlight. No hope.

As Kagan had pointed out, these men had nothing but time.

Unlike the rest of the prison, all of the overhead lights were on in solitary. The glow of fluorescent bulbs gave Will an instant headache. The hallway was warm and muggy. There was something like pressure in the air, a weighted, heavy feeling. He had the sensation of being in the middle of a field

324

waiting for a tornado to hit.

'He's in the last one,' the guard said. He kept to the wall again, his shoulder rubbing against the concrete block. Will could see the paint had been rubbed off from years of guards sliding their shoulders across. The doors opposite were bolted up tight. Each had a viewing window at the top, narrow, eye level, like at a speakeasy. There was a slit at the bottom for passing meals and tightening handcuffs. All of the doors and panels were secured with heavy bolts and rivets.

The guard stopped at the last door. He put his hand to Will's chest and made sure his back was flat against the wall. 'I don't need to tell you to stay there, right, big guy?'

Will shook his head.

The man seemed to gather his courage before walking to the cell door. He wrapped his hand around the slide bolt that kept the viewing panel covered. 'Mr. Ling, if I pull back this slat, are you going to give me any trouble?'

There was the muffled sound of laughter behind the door. Roger Ling had the same heavy southern accent as his sister. 'I think you're safe for now, Enrique.'

The guard was sweating. He gripped the bolt and pulled back, stepping out of the way so quickly that his shoes squeaked across the floor.

Will felt a bead of sweat roll down his neck. Roger Ling was obviously standing with his back pressed against the door. Will could see the side of his neck, the bottom of his ear, a hint of the orange prison garb that covered his shoulder. The lights were on inside, brighter than they were in the hallway. Will saw the rear of the cell, the edge of a

325

mattress on the floor. The space was smaller than a normal cell, less than eight feet deep, probably four feet wide. There would be a toilet but nothing else. No chair. No table. Nothing to make you feel like a human being. The usual smells of a prison—sweat, urine, feces—were more pungent here. Will realized there was no screaming. Normally, a prison was as noisy as an elementary school, especially at night. The kites had done their job. The whole place had ground to a stop because Roger Ling had a visitor.

Will waited. He could hear his heart pumping, the sound of breath going in and out of his lungs.

Ling asked, 'How's Arnoldo doing?'

Julia Ling's Chihuahua. Will cleared his throat. 'He's fine.'

'Is she letting him get fat? I told her not to let him get fat.'

'He seems . . .' Will struggled for an answer. 'She's not letting him starve.'

'Naldo's a cool little dude,' Ling said. 'I always say a Chihuahua is only as high strung as his owner. You agree with that?'

Will hadn't given it much thought, but he said, 'I guess that makes sense. Mine's pretty laid back.'

'What's her name again?'

There was a point to this after all. Ling was confirming that he was talking to the right man. 'Betty.'

He had passed the test. 'Good to meet you in person, Mr. Trent.' Ling shifted, and Will saw most of his neck. A tattoo of a dragon went up his vertebrae. The wings were spread across his shaved head. The eyes were bright yellow.

Ling said, 'My sister's pretty freaked out.'

326

'I can imagine.'

'Those little shits tried to kill her.' His voice was hard, exactly the kind of tone you'd expect from a man who'd mutilated and killed two women. 'They wouldn't be actin' so tough if I wasn't locked up in here. I'd be bringin' them some pains in their brains. You feel me?'

Will looked at the guard. The man was tensed like a bulldog ready to fight. Or flee, which seemed the smarter option. Will thought about the raid team waiting, and wondered what Roger Ling could do in sixty-one seconds. A lot, probably.

Ling said, 'You know why I asked to speak with you?'

Will was honest. 'I have no idea.'

' 'Cause I don't trust nothin' that bitch has to say.'

Obviously, he meant Amanda. 'That's probably smart.'

He laughed. Will listened to the sound echoing through the cell. There was no joy in the noise. It was chilling, almost maniacal. Will wondered if Ling's victims had heard this laughter while they were being strangled to death with Arnoldo's leash.

Ling said, 'We gotta end this. Too much blood on the street is bad for business.'

'Tell me how to make that happen.'

'I got word from Ignatio. He understands Yellow isn't behind this. He wants peace.'

Will wasn't exactly a gang expert, but he doubted that the leader of Los Texicanos would turn the other cheek over his son being beaten and killed. He told Ling as much. 'I would assume Mr. Ortiz wants vengeance.'

'Nah, man. No vengeance. Ricardo dug his own grave. Ignatio knows that. Make sure Faith knows that, too. She did what she had to do. Family is family, am I right?'

Will didn't like this man knowing Faith's name, and he sure as hell didn't trust his assurances. Still, he said, 'I'll tell her.'

Ling echoed his sister's words. 'These young guys are crazy, man. Got no sense of the value of life. You bust your ass to make the world good for them. You give them brand new cars and send them to private schools, and the minute they're on their own, pow, they turn around and pop you one.'

Will thought 'pow' was a bit of an understatement, but he kept that thought to himself.

'Ricardo was at Westminster,' Ling said. 'You know that?'

Will was familiar with the private school, which cost upwards of twenty-five thousand dollars a year. He also knew from Hironobu Kwon's file that he'd attended Westminster on a math scholarship. So, another connection.

Ling said, 'Ignatio thought he could buy his son a different life, but them spoiled rich kids got him hooked on Oxy.'

'Was Ricardo in rehab?'

'Shit, little dude *lived* in rehab.' He shifted again. Will could hear the material of his stiff orange shirt rub against the metal door. 'You got kids?'

'No.'

'Not that you know of, right?' He laughed as if this was funny. 'I got three. Two ex-wives always

328

bitchin' at me for money. I give it to 'em, though. They keep my boys in line, don't let my daughter dress like no whore. Keep their noses clean.' His shoulder raised in a shrug. 'What can you do, though? It's in the blood sometimes. No matter how many times you show them the right way, they get to a certain age and they get ideas into their heads. They think maybe they don't have to work their way up. They see what other people got and think they can just walk in and take it.'

Ling seemed to know a lot about Ignatio Ortiz's parenting woes. Odd, especially considering the two were locked down in separate prisons that were almost an entire state away from each other. Boyd Spivey had been wrong. Yellow wasn't making a play for Brown. Yellow was working for Brown.

Will said, 'You have a business relationship with Mr. Ortiz.'

'That's a fair statement.'

'Ignatio asked Julia to give his son a job on the legit side of the business.'

'It's good for a young man to have a trade. And Ricardo took to it. He had an eye for the work. Most of 'em, they're just putting together boxes, slapping on doors. Ricky was different. He was smart. Knew how to get the right people on the job. Could've run his own shop one day.'

Will started to understand. 'Ricardo got a crew together—Hironobu Kwon and the others worked at your sister's shop. Maybe they saw the money coming in from the less legitimate side of the business and thought that they deserved a bigger piece. Ortiz would never approve of some upstart gang taking a piece of the Los Texicanos pie, even

329

if it was his own son.'

'Starting a business is harder than it looks, especially with a franchise. You gotta pay the fees.'

'You heard about Ricardo's trip to Sweden.'

'Hell, everybody heard.' He chuckled as if it was funny. 'Problem with being that age is you don't know when to keep your mouth shut. Young, dumb, and full of come.'

'Your people talked to Ricardo about his trip.' Will didn't say that they were probably torturing the young man during the discussion. 'Ricardo mentioned that there might be a way to buy himself out of his problem.' Will imagined Ricardo would've been willing to trade his own mother by the time they were finished torturing him. 'He told you that he could get his hands on some money. A lot of money. Almost a million dollars. Cash.'

'That sounds like a deal no businessman can say no to.'

Everything was lining up. Ricardo had taken his crew to Evelyn's, where they met with a hell of a lot more resistance than they'd anticipated. They had killed Hector. Even if Amanda was right and Hector Ortiz was just a car salesman, there was no getting around that he was Ignatio Ortiz's cousin. 'Ricardo took them to Evelyn's house to get the money. Only, they didn't count on her fighting back. They took too many casualties. They had to regroup. And then Faith rolled up.'

Ling asked, 'You heard this story before?'

Will kept talking. 'They took Evelyn somewhere else to question her.'

'Sounds like a plan, man.'

'Only, she hasn't given up the money. If she had, I wouldn't be here.'

330

He laughed. 'I don't know about that, brother. You seem to be missing something in your story.'

'What do you mean?'

'Think about it.'

Will was still at a loss.

'The only way you can kill a snake is to cut off its head.'

'Okay.' He still wasn't following.

'Far as I can tell, that ol' snake's still out there twitchin'.'

'You mean Evelyn?'

'Shit, you think that old bitch could get a bunch of kids to follow her? Whore couldn't even keep her *own* house in order.' He tsked his tongue the same way his sister had. 'Nah, this is man's work, bro. How do you think they got one over on my sister? Bitches don't got the balls for this kind of work.'

Will wasn't going to argue the point. Gangs were the ultimate boys' club—more patriarchal than the Catholic Church. Julia Ling had only been in charge at her brother's pleasure. Generals don't go into battle. They send their pawns to the front lines. Hironobu Kwon was shot within minutes of breaching the house. Ricardo Ortiz had been left behind. Benny Choo had held a gun to his head. The man had been beaten. He was abandoned. He was expendable.

Someone else had tipped them off about Evelyn. Someone else was leading the gang.

Will said, 'Chuck Finn.'

Ling laughed as if the name surprised him. 'Chuckleberry Finn. I thought that brother would be dead by now. Fish sleeping with the fishes.'

'Is he behind this?'

331

Roger didn't answer. 'And old Sledge taken down, too. From what I hear, they did the brother a favor. Go out like a man instead of waiting to be put down like a dog. Can't say some good ain't come outta this.'

'Who's behind—'

'Yo, this is over.' Roger Ling banged on the cell door. 'Enrique, close it up.'

The guard started to slide back the panel. Will reached out to stop him. Like a snake striking, Ling's hand snared out, clamping around Will's wrist. He pulled so hard that Will's shoulder slammed into the door. The side of his face was pressed against the cold metal surface. He felt hot breath on his ear. 'You know why you're here, bro?'

Will pulled back as hard as he could. He pushed with his leg, tried to brace his foot against the bottom of the door.

Ling's grip was tight, but his voice implied effortlessness. 'Tell Mandy that Evelyn's gone.' His voice got lower. 'Tap-tap. Two in the head. Ding-dong, Almeja is dead.'

Ling released him. Will fell backward, his shoulders banging into the concrete wall. His heart was going like a metronome. He looked back at the cell door. There was a squeal of metal sliding across metal. The viewing panel closed, but not before Will saw Roger Ling's eyes. They were flat black, soulless. But there was something else there. A flash of triumph mixed in with bloodlust.

'When?' Will yelled. 'When did it happen?'

Ling's voice was muffled behind the door. 'Tell Mandy to wear something pretty to the funeral. I always did like her in black.'

332

Will brushed himself off. As he walked up the corridor, he wondered which was worse: feeling Roger Ling's hot breath on his neck or having to tell Amanda and Faith that Evelyn Mitchell was dead.

CHAPTER FOURTEEN

Faith grabbed a grocery buggy from the line outside the store. She found an old list in her purse and clutched it in her hand as she walked into the building, pretending like this was just another day at the market. The Atlanta police had taken her Glock to process for ballistics, but they didn't know about Zeke's Walther P99 that he kept loaded in his glove compartment. The weight dragged on her purse strap as she hefted it over her shoulder. The German-made weapon was well suited for her brother, who'd never seen combat. It was bulky and expensive, the sort of thing you'd carry for show. It could also drop a man at one hundred yards, and, at the end of the day, that was all Faith needed it for.

She started out in the produce section, taking more time than usual to test the freshness of the oranges piled on display. She dropped a few into a plastic bag, then moved toward the bakery.

She should've left the house hours ago, but she wanted to wait until she got the call from Zeke that Jeremy and Emma were safely ensconced in the visiting officers' quarters at Dobbins Air Reserve Base. Just getting them all loaded into Jeremy's Impala had taken forever. Zeke had yelled at the car seat. Jeremy was still pouting about his confiscated iPhone. Emma hadn't cried, because her big brother was there to soothe her, but Faith had bawled like a baby the minute their car had disappeared at the end of the street.

Faith had assumed that the men who took her mother were as skilled as they were brazen. Tactically, they had always had the advantage, whether it was taking Evelyn or breaking into Faith's house. But with two cops sitting in her kitchen and her six-foot-four brother stomping around like a bully spoiling for a fight, there was no way they would try the house again.

They had gone for Jeremy, the weakest link save for Emma. Faith felt her breath catch as she thought about her children. She had been so worried about her mother that she'd let the rest of her family slip. That wasn't going to happen again. She was going to keep all of them safe or die trying.

Faith felt a presence over her shoulder. Someone was watching her. She'd felt eyes on her from the moment she left the house. Casually, Faith turned around. She saw a kid in a Frito-Lay uniform stacking bags onto the shelves. He smiled at her. Faith smiled back, then pushed her cart down the aisle.

When Faith was a little girl, the Charles Chip man would come every Monday to fill their brown metal tins with potato chips. Tuesdays and Thursdays, the Mathis Dairy truck idled in front of their house while Petro, the driver, put fresh milk in the metal rack by the door in the carport. A half-gallon was ninety-two cents. Orange juice was fifty-two cents. Buttermilk, her father's favorite, was forty-seven cents. If Faith was good, her mother would let her count out the change to pay Petro. Sometimes, Evelyn would get chocolate milk, fifty-six cents, for special occasions. Birthdays. Good report cards. Winning games. Dance recitals.

Cosmetics. Vitamins. Shampoo. Greeting cards. Books. Soap. Faith kept piling things into her buggy, willing whoever was there to make contact. She slowed her pace. The cart was nearly full. She checked Jeremy's iPhone. There were no new messages on his Facebook wall, no emails from GoodKnight92. Faith backtracked through the store, returning the shampoo and the vitamins, perusing the magazines again. She looked at her watch. She'd been here almost an hour and no one had approached her. Ginger would probably start wondering what was taking her so long. The young detective hadn't seemed fazed when she'd told him that she was going to the grocery store by herself. He was still licking his wounds over Faith taking his gun. She wasn't sure how much farther she could push him without getting a hard shove back.

She angled her buggy around an old man who had stopped in the middle of the cereal aisle. Faith knew that they wanted her in the parking lot. They wanted her alone. She should just give in and get it over with. She put her hand on her purse, ready to take it out of the buggy. Logic intervened. They couldn't abduct her in the middle of the grocery store. They might try, but Faith wouldn't go anywhere. They would either have to bargain with her or shoot her. She wasn't leaving this store without a deal that would get her mother back.

Faith stopped outside the restroom and left her

buggy by the door. This was her third trip to the toilet since she'd gotten to the grocery store. She wasn't just trying to draw them out. One of the many benefits of her diabetes acting up was that her bladder felt constantly full. She pushed open the ladies' room door and held her breath at the stench. Grime covered the stainless steel walls and tile floor. The air felt greasy. Given a choice, she would've waited until she got home, but Faith didn't have that luxury.

She checked all four stalls, then went into the handicap space because it was still the least filthy. Her thighs ached as she hovered over the seat. It was a balancing act. She had to keep her purse tucked to her stomach because there was nowhere to hang it and she was afraid the fake leather would become glued to the floor.

The door opened. Faith looked under the stall. She saw a pair of women's shoes. Short heels. Fat ankles stuffed into brown support hose. The faucet turned on. The hand towel dispenser cranked. The faucet turned off. The door opened again, then slowly closed.

Faith closed her eyes and mumbled a prayer of relief. She finished going to the bathroom, flushed the toilet, then hiked her purse back onto her shoulder. The stall door didn't exactly lock. The thumb latch was missing. She had to stick her pinky into the square opening and twist the metal spindle to get the door open.

'Hola.'

Instantly, Faith catalogued everything she could about the man standing in front of her. Medium build, a few inches taller than Faith, around one hundred eighty pounds. Brown skin. Dark hair.

Blue eyes. Band-Aid around his left index finger. Tattoo of a snake on the right side of his neck. Faded blue jeans with holes at the knees. Black warm-up jacket with a bulge at the front that could only be a gun. The brim of his black baseball cap was pulled low. She could still see his face. The smattering of facial hair. The mole on his cheek. He was about Jeremy's age, but as far from her docile, loving son as could be. Hate seemed to radiate off him. Faith knew his type, had dealt with it many times before. Hair-trigger finger. Full of spite. Too young to be smart, too stupid to grow old.

Faith put her hand in her purse.

He pressed the bulge under his jacket. 'Wouldn't do that if I was you.'

Faith could feel the cold steel of the Walther. The muzzle was pointing toward the man. Her finger was close to the trigger. She could shoot the gun through her purse before he even thought to lift his jacket. 'Where is my mother?'

' "*My* mother," ' he repeated. 'You say that like she only belongs to you.'

'Leave my family out of this.'

'You ain't the one in the driver's seat here.'

'I need to know that she's alive.'

He tilted up his chin and clicked his tongue once against the back of his teeth. The gesture was familiar, the same response Faith had gotten from just about every thug she'd ever arrested. 'She's safe.'

'How do I know that?'

He laughed. 'You don't, bitch. You don't know nothin'.'

'What do you want?'

337

He rubbed his fingers against his thumb. 'Money.'

Faith didn't know if she could pull the bluff again. 'Just tell me where she is and we'll end this. No one has to get hurt.'

He laughed again. 'Yo, you think I'm that stupid?'

'How much do you want?'

'All of it.'

A stream of curses came to mind. 'She never took any money.'

'She done spun me out this story, bitch. We past that. Gimme the fucking money, and I'll give you what's left of her.'

'Is she alive?'

'Not for long, you don't do what I say.'

Faith felt a bead of sweat roll down her back. 'I can have the money tomorrow. By noon.'

'What, you waitin' for the bank to open?'

'Safe deposit box.' She was making this up as she went along. 'Boxes. There are three of them. All over the city. I need time.'

He smiled. One of his teeth was capped in a silver-colored metal. Platinum, probably worth more money than Faith had in her checking account. 'I knew you'd deal. I told Mommy that little baby girl wouldn't throw her over.'

'I need to know she's alive. None of this happens unless I know for sure that she's okay.'

'I wouldn't say she's okay, but the bitch is still breathing last time I checked.' He took an iPhone out of his pocket, a newer model than she could afford for Jeremy. He held his tongue between his teeth as his thumbs worked across the screen. He found what he was looking for and showed Faith

338

the phone. The screen showed the image of her mother holding a newspaper.

Faith stared at the photo. Her mother's face was swollen, barely recognizable. Her hand had a bloody rag wrapped around it. Faith pressed her lips together. Bile stung the back of her throat. She fought against the tears stinging her eyes. 'I can't tell what she's holding.'

He used his fingers to enlarge the image. 'It's a newspaper.'

'I know it's a *USA Today,*' she snapped. 'That doesn't prove she's alive right now. It just proves that sometime after the papers were delivered this morning, you made her hold one up.'

He looked at the screen. She could tell he was worried. He bit his bottom lip the same way Jeremy did when she'd caught him doing something wrong.

The man said, 'This is proof of life. You need to deal with me if you wanna keep it that way.'

Faith noticed that his grammar had improved. His voice had gone up an octave, too. There was something familiar about his tone, but she couldn't place it. She just needed to keep him talking. 'You think I'm stupid?' she demanded. 'This doesn't prove anything. My mother could already be dead. I'm not going to just hand you a pile of money because you have some stupid picture. You could've Photoshopped that. I don't even know if it's really her.'

He stepped closer, puffing out his chest. His eyes were almond shaped, deep blue with speckles of green. Again, she had the sensation of knowing him.

'I've arrested you before.'

339

'Shit,' he snorted. 'You don't know me, bitch. You don't know a goddamn thing about me.'

'I need proof that my mother's alive.'

'She won't be for long if you keep this shit up.'

Faith felt that familiar snap inside of her. All the anger and frustration of the last few days came rushing out. 'Have you ever even done this before? Are you some kind of amateur? You don't show up like this without real proof. I've been a fucking cop for sixteen years. You think I'm going to buy this cheap trick?' She pushed him back hard enough to let him know she meant it. 'I'm leaving.'

He slammed her face into the door. Faith was stunned by the blow. He jerked her around. His left arm pressed into her throat. His right hand gripped her face, fingers pressing into her skull. Spit flew from his mouth. 'You want me to leave another present under your pillow? Maybe her eyes?' He pressed his thumb harder against her eye socket. 'Maybe her tits?'

The door pushed against Faith's back. Someone was trying to get into the restroom.

'Excuse me?' a woman said. 'Hello? Is this open?'

The man stared at Faith, a hyena studying its prey. His hand shook from the effort of gripping her face. Her teeth cut into the inside of her cheek. Her nose started to bleed. He could break her skull if he wanted to.

'Tomorrow morning,' he said. 'I'll send you instructions.' He leaned in so close that Faith's eyes blurred on his features. 'You don't tell anybody about this. You don't tell your boss. You don't tell that freak you work with. You don't tell your brother, or anyone else in your precious

340

family. Nobody. You hear me?'

'Yes,' she whispered. 'Yes.'

Impossibly, his grip tightened. 'I won't kill you first,' he warned her. 'I'll cut off your eyelids. Are you listening to me?' Faith nodded. 'I'll make you watch while I skin your son. Piece by piece, I'll cut away his flesh until all you see is his muscles and bones and all you hear is him crying like the bitch little spoiled baby that he is. And then I'll go to work on your daughter. Her skin'll be easier, like wet paper peeling back. Do you understand me? You get what I'm saying?' She nodded again. 'Don't push me, bitch. You have no idea how little I've got left to lose.'

He let go of her as quickly as he'd grabbed her. Faith fell to the floor. She coughed, tasting blood in her throat. He kicked her out of the way so that he could open the door. She reached out to her purse. Her fingers felt the impression of the gun. She should get up. She had to get up.

'Ma'am?' a woman said. She peered around the door, looking down at Faith. 'Do you want me to call a doctor?'

'No,' Faith whispered. She swallowed the blood in her mouth. The inside of her jaw was ripped open. More blood trickled from her nose.

'Are you sure? I could call—'

'No,' Faith repeated. There was no one to call.

CHAPTER FIFTEEN

Will pulled into his driveway and waited for the garage door to open. All the lights were off in his house. Betty was probably floating on her full bladder like a balloon in the Macy's Thanksgiving Day parade. At least he hoped she was. Will was in no mood to clean up a mess.

He felt like he had killed Amanda. Not literally, not with his bare hands like he'd dreamed of doing for most of the day. Telling her what Roger Ling said, that Evelyn Mitchell was dead, was just as good as shooting her in the chest. She had deflated in front of him. All of her bravado was gone. All the arrogance and meanness and pettiness had rushed out of her, and the woman in front of him had been nothing but a shell.

Will had had the sense to wait until they were outside the prison building to relay the news. She hadn't cried. Instead, to his horror, her knees had buckled. That was when he put his arm around her. She was surprisingly bony. Her hip was sharp under his hand. Her shoulders were frail. She seemed ten, twenty years older by the time he fastened her seatbelt around her lap and closed the car door.

The trip back had been excruciating. Will's silence on the way down paled in comparison. He had offered to pull over but she'd told him not to stop. Just outside of Atlanta, he'd seen her hand grip the door. Will had never been to her house before. She lived in a condo in the middle of Buckhead. It was a gated community. The

342

buildings were all regal looking with keyed corners and large, heavily trimmed windows. She had directed him to a unit in the back.

Will had idled the car, but she didn't get out. He was debating whether or not to help her again when she said, 'Don't tell Faith.'

He'd stared at her front door. She had a flag hanging from the front post. Spring flowers. A seasonal motif. Amanda had never struck him as a flag person. He couldn't imagine her standing on the porch in her heels and suit, leaning on tippy-toe to clip the appropriate flag onto the pole.

'We have to verify this,' she'd said, though what Roger Ling had told Will was merely a confirmation of a truth Will realized he had been sensing for most of the day.

Amanda must've known it, too. That was the only explanation for her earlier capitulation inside the prison waiting room. She had admitted that Evelyn was tainted because she'd known there was no reason to protect her anymore. The twenty-four-hour mark had come and gone. There had been no contact from the kidnappers. There was blood all over Evelyn's kitchen floor, a lot of it— maybe most of it—from Evelyn. The young men they were dealing with had proven themselves to be remorseless killers, nothing more than assassins, even when it was against members of their own crew.

The odds that Evelyn Mitchell had even made it through the night were close to nil.

Will had told her, 'Faith has to know.'

'I'll tell her when I know for sure.' Her voice sounded flat, lifeless. 'We meet at seven tomorrow morning. The whole team. If you're a minute late,

343

then don't bother coming.'

'I'll be there.'

'We're going to find her. I have to see her with my own eyes.'

'Okay.'

'And if what Roger said is true, we'll find the boys who did this, and we will rain down hell on them. Every last one. We will hound them into the ground.'

'Yes, ma'am.'

Her voice was so low and tired he could barely hear her. 'I will not rest until every single one of them is put to death. I want to watch them slip the needle in and see their feet twitch and their eyes roll and their chests freeze. And if the state won't kill them, then I'll do it myself.' Amanda had pushed open the door and gotten out of the car. Will could see the effort it took her to keep her back straight as she walked up the stairs. If it were up to Amanda, if there was a way for her to will her friend to be alive, then there would be no question of Evelyn's survival.

But that just wasn't the case.

The garage door finally finished opening. Will pulled in and pressed the button to close the door. The garage had not been an original part of the house. Will had added on the structure in the neighborhood's more transitional days, back when junkies knocked on his door wondering if this was still a crack den. The entrance was awkward and led into the spare bedroom. Betty raised her head from the pillow when she saw Will. There was a puddle in the corner that neither one of them was ready to talk about.

Will turned on the lights as he walked through

344

the house. There was a chill in the air. He cracked open the kitchen door so Betty could go outside. She hesitated.

'It's all right,' he told her, using as soothing a tone as he could muster. Her injuries were healing, but the dog still remembered last week when a hawk had swooped into the yard and tried to pick her up. And Will could still remember the groomer's uncontrollable laughter when he'd told the man that a hawk had mistaken his dog for a rat.

Betty finally went outside, but not without a wary glance over her shoulder. Will put his car key on the hook and placed his wallet and gun on the kitchen table. The pizza from yesterday was still in the refrigerator. Will took out the box but couldn't do anything more than stare at the gelatinous slices.

He wanted to call Sara, but this time his motivations were purely selfish. He wanted to tell her what had happened today. He wanted to ask her if it was right to wait to tell Faith that her mother was dead. He wanted to describe to her the way it felt to see Amanda brought so low. That it scared him to see her fallen so far from her pedestal.

Instead, he returned the pizza box to the fridge, made sure the back door was still cracked open, and went to take a shower. It was almost midnight. He'd been up since five this morning, having slept only a few hours the night before. Will stood under the stream of hot water, trying to wash away his day. The grime of Valdosta State Prison. The warehouse where he'd been shot at. Grady, where he'd felt dizzy with fear. Coastal, where he'd sweated so much that rings were still under the arms of his shirt.

Will thought about Betty while he dried his hair. She'd been stuck in the house all day. The puddle was a responsibility they both shared. As late as it was, he couldn't see himself sleeping. He should take her for a walk. They could both do with stretching their legs.

He pulled on a pair of jeans and a dress shirt that was too worn to wear to work anymore. The collar was frayed. One of the buttons was broken, dangling by a thread.

He walked into the kitchen to get Betty's leash.

Angie was sitting at the table. 'Welcome home, baby. How was your day?'

Will would've rather driven to Coastal and faced Roger Ling again than have to talk to his wife right now.

She stood. Her arms went around his shoulders. She put her mouth close to his. 'Aren't you going to tell me hello?'

Her hands stroking his neck felt nothing like Sara's. 'Stop.'

She pulled away, feigning a pout. 'Is that any kind of welcome for your wife?'

'Where have you been?'

'Since when do you care?'

He thought about it. She had posed a legitimate question. 'I don't, really. I just—' The words came out easier than he'd thought. 'I don't want you here.'

'Hmm.' She tucked her chin down, crossed her arms. 'Well, I suppose this was inevitable. I can't leave you alone after all.'

She had closed the back door. He opened it. Betty ran in. She saw Angie and growled.

346

Angie said, 'Looks like none of the women in your life are happy to see me.'

He felt the hair on the back of his neck go up. 'What are you talking about?'

'Sara didn't tell you?' Angie paused, but he couldn't answer her. 'It's Sara, right? That's her name?' She gave a breathy laugh. 'I have to say, Will, but she's a little plain for you. I mean she's all right up top, but she's got no ass to speak of and she's almost taller than you are. I thought you liked your women more womanly.'

Will still couldn't talk. His blood had frozen in his veins.

'She was here when I got home yesterday. Lingering in the bedroom. Didn't she tell you?'

Sara hadn't told him. Why hadn't she told him?

'She colors her hair. You know that, right? Those highlights aren't natural.'

'What did you . . . ?'

'I'm just letting you know she's not the perfect little angel you think she is.'

Will forced the words out of his mouth. 'What did you say to her?'

'I asked her why she was fucking my husband.'

His heart stopped. This was the reason Sara had been crying yesterday afternoon. This explained her initial coldness when he showed up at her house last night. Will's heart clenched like a vise was around it. 'You are not allowed to to talk to her ever again.'

'You're trying to protect her?' She laughed. 'Jesus, Will. That's hilarious considering I'm trying to protect you.'

'You don't—'

'She's got a thing for cops. You know that,

347

right?' She shook her head at his stupidity. 'I looked into her husband. He was quite a catch. Fucked anything that moved.'

'Like you.'

'Oh, come on. Try harder than that, baby.'

'I don't want to try.' He finally said the words that he'd been thinking for the last year. 'I just want it over. I want you out of my life.'

She laughed in his face. 'I *am* your life.'

Will stared at her. She was smiling. Her eyes practically glowed. Why was it that she only ever seemed happy when she was trying to hurt him? 'I can't do this anymore.'

'His name was Jeffrey. Did you know that?' Will didn't answer. Of course he knew Sara's husband's name. 'He was smart. Went to college—a real one, not some correspondence school where they charge extra to mail your diploma. He ran a whole police department. They were so fucking in love that she looks cross-eyed in the pictures.' Angie grabbed her purse out of the chair. 'You wanna see them? They were in the newspaper in that shithole town every other week. They did a fucking collage on the front page when he died.'

'Please, just go.'

Angie dropped her purse. 'Does she know you're stupid?'

He held his tongue between his front teeth.

'Oh, of course she does.' She almost sounded relieved. 'That explains it. She feels sorry for you. Poor little Willy can't read.'

He shook his head.

'Let me tell you something, Wilbur. You're not a great catch. You're not handsome. You're not smart. You're not even average. And you're sure as

348

hell not good in the sack.'

She had said this so many time before that the words no longer had meaning. 'Is there a point to this?'

'I'm trying to keep you from getting hurt. That's the point.'

He looked down at the floor. 'Don't do this, Angie. Just this one time—don't do it.'

'Do what? Tell you the truth? Because you've obviously got your head so far up your ass that you can't see what's going on here.' She put her face inches from his. 'Don't you know that every time she kisses you, every time she touches you or fucks you, or holds you, she's thinking about him?' She paused as if she expected an answer. 'You're just a replacement, Will. You're just there until somebody better comes along. Another doctor. A lawyer. Someone who can read a newspaper without his lips getting tired.'

Will felt his throat tighten. 'You don't know anything.'

'I know people. I know women. I know them a hell of a lot better than you.'

'I'm sure you do.'

'Damn right I do. And I know you best of all.' She paused to survey the damage. Obviously, it wasn't enough. 'You're forgetting I was there, baby. Every visiting day, every adoption rally, there you were standing in front of that mirror combing your hair, checking your clothes, primping yourself up so that some mommy and daddy might see you and take you home with them.' She started shaking her head. 'But they never did, did they? No one ever took you home. No one ever wanted you. And you know why?'

He couldn't breathe in. His lungs started to ache.

'Because there's something about you, Will. Something wrong. Something off. It makes people's skin crawl. It makes them want to get as far away from you as they can.'

'Just stop. All right? Stop it.'

'Stop what? Pointing out the obvious? What do you see happening with her? You're gonna get married and have babies and live some kind of normal life?' She laughed as if this was the most ludicrous thing she'd ever heard. 'You ever consider the fact that you like what we have?'

He tasted blood on the tip of his tongue. He imagined a wall between them. A thick concrete wall.

'There's a reason you wait for me. There's a reason you don't go on dates and you don't go to bars or pay for pussy like every other man in the world.'

The wall got higher, stronger.

'You like what we have. You know you can't be with somebody else. Not really be with them. You can't walk out on that ledge. You can't open yourself up to someone like that, because you know at the end of the day they will *always* leave you. And that's what your precious Sara is going to do, baby. She's an adult. She's been married before. She had a real life with somebody else. Someone who was worthy of being loved and knew how to love her back. And she's gonna see real fast that you're not capable of that. And then she's gonna drop you on your ass and be gone.'

The taste of blood got stronger in his mouth.

'You're just so fucking desperate for somebody

350

to give you a little attention. You've always been that way. Clingy. Pathetic. Needy.'

He couldn't stand her being this close to him. He walked over to the sink and filled a glass with water. 'You don't know anything about me.'

'Have you told her what happened to you? She's a doctor. She knows what a cigarette burn looks like. She knows what happens when somebody holds two live wires to your skin.' Will drank the water in one gulp. 'Look at me.' He didn't look up, but she kept talking anyway. 'You're a project for her. She feels sorry for you. Poor little orphan Will. You're Helen Keller and she's whoever the fuck that bitch is who taught her how to read.' She grabbed his chin and made him face her. Will still looked away. 'She just wants to cure you. And when she gets tired of trying to fix you, when she realizes that there's no magic pill that'll take away the stupid, she's going to drop you back into the trash where she found you.'

Something broke inside of him. His resolve. His strength. His flimsy walls. 'And then what?' he yelled. 'I'll come crawling back to you?'

'You always do.'

'I'd rather be alone. I'd rather rot alone in a hole than be stuck with you.'

She turned her back to him. Will put the glass in the sink, used the back of his hand to wipe his mouth. Angie didn't cry much, at least not for real. Every kid Will grew up with had a different survival tactic. Boys used their fists. Girls turned bulimic. Some, like Angie, used sex, and when sex didn't work, they used tears, and then when tears didn't work, they found something else to cut into your heart.

351

When Angie turned around, she had Will's gun in her mouth.

'No—'

She pulled the trigger. He closed his eyes, held up his hands to block his face from the pieces of brain and skull.

But nothing happened.

Slowly, Will dropped his arms, opened his eyes.

The gun was still in her mouth. Dry fire. The echo of the hammer clicking was like a needle piercing his eardrum. He saw the magazine on the table. The bullet he kept in the chamber was beside it.

Will's voice trembled. 'Don't you ever—'

'Does she know about your father, Will? Have you told her what happened?'

His whole body was shaking. 'Don't ever do that again.'

She dropped the gun back on the table. Her hands cupped his face. 'You love me, Will. You know you love me. You felt it when I pulled that trigger. You know you can't live without me.'

Tears came into his eyes.

'We're not whole people unless we're together.' She stroked his cheek, his eyebrow. 'Don't you know that? Don't you remember what you did for me, baby? You were willing to give up your life for me. You'd never do that for her. You'd never cut yourself for anybody but me.'

He pulled away from her grasp. The gun was still on the table. The magazine felt cold in his hand. He shoved it home. He pulled back the slide to chamber a round. He held out the gun to her, muzzle pointing to his chest. 'Go ahead and shoot me.' She didn't move. He tried to take her hand.

352

'Shoot me.'

'Stop.' She held up her hands. 'Stop it.'

'Shoot me,' he repeated. 'Either shoot me or let me go.'

She took the gun and dismantled it, throwing the pieces onto the counter. When her hands were free, she slapped him hard across the face. Then again. Then her fists started to fly. Will grabbed her arms. She twisted around, turning her back to him. Angie hated being held down. He pressed his body into hers, forcing her against the sink. She fought furiously, screaming, scratching with her fingernails.

'Let me go!' She kicked back at him, grinding her heel into his foot. 'Stop it!'

Will tightened his grip. She leaned into him. All the anger and frustration of the last two days pooled into one place. He could feel his body responding to her, yearning to release. She managed to turn back around. Her hand went behind his neck, pulling him closer. She put her lips to his. Her mouth opened.

Will stepped back. She moved to put her arms around him again but he took another step away. He was breathing too hard to speak. This was their dance. Anger. Fear. Violence. Never compassion. Never kindness.

He took Betty's leash off the hook. The dog pranced at his feet. Will's hands were shaking so badly he could barely clip the leash to her collar. He took his keys off the hook and tucked his wallet into his back pocket. 'I don't want you here when I get back.'

'You can't leave me.'

He reassembled the gun and clipped the paddle

353

holster to his jeans.

'I need you.'

He turned around to face Angie. Her hair was wild. She looked desperate, ready to do anything. He was so tired of this. So tired. 'Don't you understand? I don't want to be needed. I want to be wanted.'

She didn't have a good answer to that, so she went with a threat. 'I swear I'll kill myself if you walk out that door.'

Will left the room.

She followed him down the hallway. 'I'll take pills. I'll slit my wrists. That's one of your favorites, isn't it? I'll slit my wrists, and you'll come home and find me. How's that gonna make you feel, Wilbur? How're you gonna feel if you come home from fucking your precious little doctor and I'm dead in the bathroom?'

He picked up Betty from the floor. 'Annie Sullivan.'

'What?'

'That's the woman who taught Helen Keller.'

Will went into the garage and closed the door behind him. The last thing he saw was Angie standing in the hallway, fists clenched in front of her. He got into his car. He waited for the garage door to open. He backed the car into the driveway and waited for the door to close.

Betty settled down into the seat beside him as he drove away. He cracked the window so she could enjoy the night air. Will didn't think about where he was going until he pulled into the parking lot in front of Sara's building. He grabbed the dog and carried her to the front entrance. Sara was on the top floor. He pressed the buzzer. He didn't have to say anything. There was a responding buzz, and the lock clicked open.

Betty squirmed as they got into the elevator. He put her down at his feet. When they reached the top floor, she ran out into the hall. Sara's door was open. She was standing in the middle of the room. Her hair was loose and down around her shoulders. She was wearing jeans and a thin white T-shirt that didn't do much to conceal what was underneath.

Will closed the door. There were so many things he wanted to tell her, but when he finally managed to speak, none of it came out. 'Why didn't you tell me you saw Angie?'

She didn't answer. She just stood there looking at him. Will couldn't stop himself from looking back. Her shirt was tight. He could see the swell of her breasts, her nipples pressing into the thin material.

He said, 'I'm sorry.' His voice broke. He would never forgive himself for bringing Angie into Sara's life. It was the most awful thing he had ever done to anyone. 'What she said to you. I never wanted . . .'

Sara walked toward him.

'I'm so sorry.'

She took his hand and turned it so that the palm was facing up. Her fingers moved nimbly over the buttons on his sleeve.

Will wanted to pull away. He needed to pull away. But he couldn't move. He couldn't make his muscles work. He couldn't stop her hands or her fingers or her mouth.

She pressed her lips to his bare wrist. It was the gentlest kiss he had ever known. Her tongue flicked lightly along the skin, tracing the scar up his arm. Will felt like a current was going through his body, so that by the time she kissed his mouth, he was already on fire. Her body curved into his. The kiss deepened. Her hand wrapped around the back of his head, nails scraping through his hair. Will was dizzy. He was in free fall. He couldn't stop touching her—her narrow hips, the curve at the small of her back, her perfect breasts.

His breath caught when her hand slipped inside his shirt. Her fingers brushed over his chest, down his belly. She didn't flinch. She didn't falter. Instead, she put her forehead to his, looked him in the eye, and told him, 'Breathe.'

Will let out a breath he felt like he'd been holding his entire life.

MONDAY

CHAPTER SIXTEEN

Sara woke to hear the shower running. she turned over in bed. Her hand traced along the indentation left in the pillow. The sheets were twisted around her body. Her hair was a mess. She could still smell Will in the room, taste him in her mouth, remember what his arms felt like when they'd wrapped around her.

She could not recall the last time good reasons had made her not want to get out of bed in the morning. Obviously, it had happened when Jeffrey was alive, but for the first time in four and a half years, Jeffrey was the last thing on Sara's mind. She wasn't making comparisons. She wasn't weighing differences. Her worst fear had always been that her husband's ghost would follow her into the bedroom. But that hadn't been the case. There was only Will, and the absolute joy she felt when she was with him.

Sara had a vague recollection that her clothes were somewhere between the kitchen and the dining room. She pulled a black silk robe out of the closet and made her way down the hall. The dogs gave her a lazy look from the couch as she walked into the living room. Betty was sleeping on a pillow. Billy and Bob were piled into a crescent shape around her. Will had to be at work in an hour or Sara would've joined him in the shower. Yesterday, she had told the hospital staff that she didn't need time off after her ordeal, but this morning, she was glad they had insisted. She needed to process what had happened. And

359

she wanted to be home when Will got off work.

Her clothes were neatly folded on the counter. Sara smiled, thinking she'd at last found a good use for her dining room table. She turned on the coffeemaker. There was a yellow Post-it note on the wall above the dog bowls. Will had drawn a smiley face in the center. She saw another note with the same graphic above the leashes. There was something to be said for a man who fed and walked the dogs while Sara was sleeping. She stared at the blue ink, the arc of a smile and two dots for eyes.

Sara had never pursued a man before. She had always been on the receiving end of the wooing. But she'd realized last night that nothing would ever happen if she didn't make the first move. And she had wanted something to happen. She had wanted Will more than anything she'd wanted in a long while.

He'd been tentative at first. He was obviously self-conscious about his body, which was laughable considering how beautiful it was. His legs were strong and lean. His shoulders were roped with muscle. His abs would be perfectly at home on an underwear billboard in the middle of Times Square. It wasn't just that, though. His hands knew exactly where to touch her. His mouth felt wonderful. His tongue felt wonderful. Everything about him was wonderful. Being with him felt like a key sliding into a lock. Sara had never dreamed that she would ever again be so open with another man.

If there was any comparison to be made, it was between Sara and her old self. Something was altered inside of her, and not just her moral compass. She felt different with Will. She didn't have to immediately know everything about this man she'd shared her bed with. She didn't feel the need to demand answers about the obvious abuse he had suffered. For the first time in her life, Sara felt patient. The girl who had gotten kicked out of Sunday school for arguing with the teacher and driven her parents, her sister, and eventually her husband crazy with her unyielding desire to understand every last detail about everything on earth was finally learning how to relax.

Maybe seeing the Polaroid of Will's sutured mouth had taught her a lesson about prying. Or maybe it was just the nature of life that you learned from past mistakes. For now, Sara was content to just be with Will. The rest would come in time. Or it wouldn't. Either way, she felt remarkably content.

There was an insistent knock at the door, probably Abel Conford from across the hall. The lawyer had anointed himself czar of the parking lot. Every board meeting Sara attended started with Abel complaining about visitors parking in the wrong spaces.

Sara pulled her robe tight as she opened the door. Instead of her neighbor, she found Faith Mitchell.

'I'm sorry to barge in on you.' Faith pushed her way into the apartment. She was wearing a bulky navy blue jacket with the hood pulled over her head. Dark sunglasses obscured half her face. Her jeans and Chuck Taylors completed the ensemble. She looked like a PTA mom's idea of a cat burglar.

Sara could only ask, 'How did you get in?'

'I badged one of your neighbors.'

361

'Great,' Sara mumbled, wondering how long it would take for everyone in the building to think she was being arrested. 'What's going on?'

Faith took off the sunglasses. There were five tiny bruises circling her face. 'I need you to call Will for me.' She went to the window and looked down at the parking lot. 'I thought about this all night. I can't do it alone. I don't think I'm capable.' She shielded her eyes with her hand, though the sun had yet to come up. 'They don't know I'm here. Ginger fell asleep. Taylor left last night. I sneaked out. Through the back yard. I took Roz Levy's car. I know they've tapped my phones. They're watching me. They can't know that I'm doing this. They can't know that I talked to anybody.'

She was a poster child for hypoglycemia. Sara suggested, 'Why don't you sit down?'

Faith kept her perch over the parking lot. 'I sent my children away. They're with my brother. He's never even changed a diaper. This is too much responsibility for Jeremy.'

'Okay. Let's talk about it. Come over here and sit down with me.'

'I have to get her back, Sara. I don't care what it takes. What I have to do.'

Her mother. Will had told Sara about his trip to Coastal State Prison, his conversation with Roger Ling. 'Faith, sit down.'

'I can't sit or I'll never get up again. I need Will. Can you please just call him?'

'I'll get him for you. I promise, but you have to sit down.' Sara guided her over to the stool by the kitchen counter. 'Did you eat breakfast?'

She shook her head. 'My stomach's too upset.'

362

'How's your blood sugar?'

She stopped shaking her head. Her guilty expression was answer enough.

Sara made her voice firm. 'Faith, I'm not going to do anything until we get your numbers in order. Do you understand me?'

Faith didn't argue, perhaps because part of her knew that she needed help. She felt around in her jacket pockets and pulled out a handful of hard candy that she dropped on the counter. Next came a large gun, then her wallet, a set of keys with a gold cursive *L* on the chain, and finally, her blood-testing kit.

Sara scrolled through the tester's memory, checking the stats. Faith had obviously been playing candy roulette for the last two days. It was a common trick among diabetics, using candy to fight the lows, gritting out the highs. It was a good way to get through a difficult period, but it was an even better way to end up in a coma. 'I should take you to the hospital right now.' Sara gripped the monitor in her hand. 'Do you have your insulin?'

Faith dug into her pockets again and put four disposable insulin pens on the counter. She started babbling. 'I got them from the pharmacy this morning. I didn't know how much to take. They showed me, but I've never used them before and they're so expensive I didn't want to mess up. My ketones are okay. I used a strip last night and this morning. I should probably get a pump.'

'An insulin pump wouldn't be a bad idea.' Sara slid a testing strip into the monitor. 'Did you eat supper last night?'

'Sort of.'

'I'll take that as a no,' Sara mumbled. 'What

363

about snacks? Anything?'

Faith leaned her head in her hand. 'I can't think straight with Jeremy and Emma gone. Zeke called this morning. He says they're settled in but I can tell he's annoyed. He's never been good around kids.'

Sara took Faith's finger and lined up the lancet. 'We are going to have a long talk when this is over about your noncompliance. I know that saying right now is stressful for you is an incredible under-statement, but your diabetes isn't something you can magically put on hold. Your vision, your circulation, your motor skills . . .' Sara didn't finish the sentence. She'd lectured so many diabetics about this same issue that she felt like she was reading from a script. 'You have to take care of yourself or you're going to end up blind or in a wheelchair or worse.'

Faith said, 'You look different.'

Sara patted down her hair, which was sticking straight up in the back.

'You're practically glowing. Are you pregnant?'

Sara laughed, surprised by the question. An ectopic pregnancy in her twenties had led to a partial hysterectomy. Will wasn't that much of a miracle worker. 'You're one-thirty?'

'One thirty-five.'

Sara dialed out the correct dosage on the pen. 'You're going to inject this, then I'm going to cook breakfast for you, and you're not doing anything else until you've eaten every bite.'

'That stove cost more than my house.' Faith leaned over the counter for a better look. Sara pushed her back down. 'How much money do you make?'

She took Faith's hand and wrapped her fingers around the insulin pen. 'You do this, and I'll go get Will.'

'You can call him from here. I know what you're going to say.'

Sara didn't stop to explain herself, especially since Faith was obviously having trouble processing information. She grabbed her clothes off the counter and went into the bedroom. Will was standing in front of the dresser putting on his shirt. She saw his broad chest reflected in the mirror, the dark stain of electrical burns traveling down the flat of his belly and disappearing into his jeans. Sara had put her mouth on every inch of him last night, but standing here in the light of day, she felt awkward around him.

He looked at her reflection. Sara pulled her robe tighter around her waist. He had made the bed. The pillows were stacked neatly against the headboard. This wasn't how she'd envisioned her morning.

He asked, 'What's wrong?'

She put her folded clothes on the bed. 'Faith is here.'

'Here?' He turned around. He sounded almost panicked. 'Why? How did she know?'

'She doesn't know. She asked me to call you. She's terrified her phone's being tapped.'

'Does she know about her mother?'

'I don't think so.' Sara put her hand to her chest, cinching the robe again, feeling every bit of her nakedness underneath. 'She said that people are watching her. She's acting paranoid. Her blood sugar is off the charts. She's taking her insulin now. She should settle once we get some food into her.'

'Do I need to get breakfast?'

'I can make her something.'

'I can—' He stopped, looking extremely uncomfortable. 'Maybe I should do that. For Faith, I mean. You could cook me something after.'

So much for the honeymoon period. At least she knew now why Bob had smelled like scrambled eggs the other night. 'I'll stay in here to give you some privacy.'

'Could you . . .' He hesitated. 'It might be better if you were there. I'm going to have to tell her about her mother.'

'I thought Amanda said to wait.'

'Amanda says a lot of things I don't agree with.' He indicated that she should leave the room ahead of him. Sara walked down the hall. She could feel Will close behind her. Despite what had happened the night before—some of it in this very hallway— he felt like a stranger to her. Sara gripped her robe tighter, wishing she had stopped to change into some real clothes.

Faith was still sitting at the kitchen bar. Some of her nervous energy had dissipated. She saw Will and said, 'Oh.'

He looked embarrassed. Sara felt the same. Maybe that explained his standoffish mood. It seemed wrong for them to be together given what had happened to Evelyn Mitchell.

Still, Faith said, 'It's all right. I'm happy for you.'

Will didn't acknowledge the comment. 'Dr. Linton says you need to eat.'

'I need to talk to you first.'

Will looked at Sara. She shook her head.

'You need breakfast first.' Will opened the dishwasher and took out the frying pan. He found

366

the eggs and bread in their proper place. Faith watched him make breakfast. She didn't speak. Sara didn't know if she was crashing or if she just didn't know what to say. Probably a little of both. For her part, Sara had never felt so uncomfortable in her own home. She watched Will break the eggs and butter the toast. His jaw was rigid. He didn't look up at her. She might as well have stayed in the bedroom.

Will took three plates out of the cabinet and loaded them up with food. Sara and Faith sat at the bar. Though there was a third chair, Will stood, leaning against the counter. Sara picked at her food. Faith ate half her eggs and a slice of toast. Will cleaned his plate, then finished Faith's toast as well as Sara's, before scraping the rest into the trash and stacking the plates in the sink. He rinsed the bowl that had held the eggs, ran some water in the frying pan, then washed his hands.

Finally, he said, 'Faith, I have to tell you something.'

She shook her head. She must've known what was coming.

He stood with his back against the counter. He didn't lean over and take her hands. He didn't come around and sit beside her. He just told her the news straight out. 'Last night, I was at Coastal State Prison. I talked to a man who's pretty high up in the drug trade. Roger Ling.' He kept his eyes focused on hers. 'There's no other way to say this. He told me that your mother was killed. Shot in the head.'

She didn't respond at first. She sat there with her elbows on the counter, hands hanging down, mouth open. Eventually, she said, 'No, she's not.'

'Faith—'

'Did you find the body?'

'No, but—'

'When was this? When did he tell you?'

'Late, around nine o'clock.'

'It's not true.'

'Faith, it's true. This guy knows what he's talking about. Amanda says—'

'I don't care what Amanda says.' She dug around in her pockets again. 'Mandy doesn't know what she's talking about. Whoever this guy is who you talked to was lying.'

Will glanced at Sara.

'Look,' Faith said. She had an iPhone in her hands. 'Do you see this? It's Jeremy's Facebook page. They've been sending messages.'

Will pushed away from the counter. 'What?'

'I met one of them last night. At the grocery store. He did this.' She indicated the bruises on her face. 'I told him I had to have proof of life. He emailed me through Jeremy's Facebook account this morning.'

'What?' Will repeated. The color had drained from his face. 'You met him alone? Why didn't you call me? He could've—'

'Look at this.' She showed him the phone. Sara couldn't see the image, but she heard the sound.

A woman's voice said, 'It's Monday morning. Five thirty-eight.' She paused. There was background noise. 'Faith, listen to me. Don't do anything they say. Don't trust them. Just walk away from this. You and your brother and the kids are my family. My only family . . .' Suddenly, the voice grew stronger. 'Faith, this is important. I need you to remember our time together before Jeremy—'

Faith said, 'It stops right there.'

Will asked, 'What's she talking about? The time before Jeremy?'

'When I was pregnant.' Her cheeks colored, though almost twenty years had passed. 'Mom stayed with me. She was . . .' Faith shook her head. 'I wouldn't have made it through without her. She just kept telling me to be strong, that it would be over eventually and then everything would be all right.'

Sara put her hand on Faith's shoulder. She could not imagine the pain that the other woman was going through.

Will stared at the iPhone. 'What's on the television set behind her?'

'*Good Day Atlanta.* I checked with the station. This is the weather segment they aired half an hour ago. You can see the time over the station logo. I got the file two minutes later.'

He handed Sara the phone, but still would not look her in the eye.

Curiosity had always been her weakness. Sara's reading glasses were on the counter. She slipped them on so she could see the small details. The screen showed Evelyn Mitchell sitting beside a large plasma-screen TV. The sound was off, but Sara saw the weather woman pointing to the five-day forecast. Evelyn was looking off-camera, probably at the man filming her. Her face was a bloody mess. She moved stiffly, as if in a great deal of pain. Her words slurred as she began, 'It's Monday morning.'

Sara let the video play out, then put the phone down.

Faith was watching Sara closely. 'How does she

look?'

Sara took off her glasses. She could hardly render a medical opinion based on a grainy video, but it was obvious to anyone that Evelyn Mitchell had been very badly beaten. Still, she said, 'She looks like she's holding up.'

'That's what I thought.' Faith turned to Will. 'I told them I'd meet them at noon, but the email says twelve-thirty. Mom's house.'

'Your mother's house?' he repeated. 'It's still an active crime scene.'

'Maybe it's been released. APD isn't telling me anything. Let me find the email.' Faith moved her thumbs across the screen again and handed the phone to Will. 'Oh,' she said, reaching for the device. 'I forgot—'

'I've got it.' Will took Sara's glasses off the counter and slipped them on. He stared at the phone for a few seconds. Sara couldn't tell if he'd read the email or was just making a lucky guess when he said, 'They want the money.'

Faith took the phone away from him. 'There is no money.'

Will just stared at her.

'It's not true,' Faith said. 'It was never true. You couldn't prove anything. She wasn't dirty. Boyd and the rest of them were on the take, but Mom never took anything.'

'Faith,' Will said. 'Your mother had a bank account.'

'So what? Everyone has a bank account.'

'An out-of-state bank account. It's in your father's name. She still has it. There's been about sixty grand in and out of it as far as I can tell. There might be other accounts in other states,

370

other names. I don't know.'

Faith shook her head. 'No. You're lying.'

'Why would I lie about that?'

'Because you can't admit that you were wrong about her. She wasn't dirty.' Tears filled her eyes. She had the look of someone who knew the truth but could not accept it. 'She wasn't.'

There was another knock at the door. Sara guessed that Abel Conford had finally noticed the extra cars in the parking lot. Wrong again.

'Good morning, Dr. Linton.' Amanda Wagner did not look pleased to be standing in the hallway. Her eyes were red. The makeup had been wiped off her nose. Her skin was darker where foundation and blush covered her cheeks.

Sara opened the door wider. She tightened her robe again, wondering where the nervous tic had come from. Perhaps it was because she was completely naked underneath and the black silk was as thin as crepe paper. She hadn't planned on hosting a party this morning.

Faith seemed incensed to see Amanda. 'What are you doing here?'

'Roz Levy called. She said you stole her car.'

'I left a note.'

'Which she strangely did not interpret as the proper way to ask for permission. Fortunately, I was able to talk her out of calling the police.' She smiled at Will. 'Good morning, Dr. Trent.'

Will feigned a sudden fascination with the tiles on Sara's kitchen floor.

'Wait a minute,' Faith said. 'How did you know where I was?'

'Roz LoJacked the car. I called in a few favors at dispatch.'

'LoJack? It's a nine-hundred-year-old Corvair. It's worth five dollars.'

Amanda took off her coat and handed it to Sara. 'I'm sorry to intrude on your morning, Dr. Linton. I love what you've done to your hair.'

Sara forced a smile onto her face as she hung the coat in the closet. 'Would you like some coffee?'

'Yes, thank you.' She turned to Will and Faith. 'Should I be hurt that I wasn't invited to this party?'

No one seemed up to answering her. Sara took three mugs down from the cabinet and poured coffee into each of them. She heard Evelyn Mitchell's voice on the iPhone as Faith played the video for their new guest.

Amanda asked her to play it again, then a third time, before asking, 'When did this come in?'

'A little over half an hour ago.'

'Read me the message that came with it.'

Faith read, ' "Twelve-thirty at 339 Little John. Bring the cash in a black duffel bag. Do not alert anyone. We are watching you. If you deviate from these instructions, she will be dead and so will you and your family. Remember what I said." '

'Roger Ling.' Amanda's voice was one of restrained fury. 'I knew that bastard was lying. You can't trust a goddamn word any of them say.' She seemed to realize the greater meaning of her words. Her mouth opened in surprise. 'She's *alive*.' She laughed. 'Oh, God, I knew the old girl wouldn't give up without a fight.' She put her hand to her chest. 'How could I think for a minute that . . .' She shook her head. The smile on her face was so wide that she finally covered it with her hand.

Will asked the more important question. 'Why would they want to meet at your mother's house? It's not secure. They won't have the advantage. It doesn't make sense.'

Faith answered, 'It's familiar. It's easy to keep an eye on.'

Will said, 'But there's no way that the crime scene's been released. It'll take days to process everything.'

Amanda supplied, 'The kidnappers must know something we don't.'

'It could be a test,' Will countered. 'If we clear out the forensic team, it'll be obvious that Faith called the police. Or us.' He told Faith, 'You pull up to the house and you're out in the open. You go inside and you're walking right into their hands. What's to stop them from shooting you and taking the money? Especially if we can't put in a tactical team to secure the area.'

'We can make do,' Amanda insisted. 'There are only three routes in and out of that neighborhood. They make a move in either direction and we'll have pistols at the ready.'

Will ignored the bravado. He opened the drawer by the refrigerator and took out a pen and pad of paper. He held the pen awkwardly in his left hand, resting the barrel between his middle and fourth finger. Sara watched as he covered the page with a large T, then drew two irregularly shaped squares—one on the arm of the T, one at the base. His spatial recollection was better than Sara would have guessed, but then, he'd probably been to Faith's house several times.

He explained, 'Faith's house is on the corner

here. Evelyn is here on Little John.' He traced an L-shaped line between the two houses. 'We've got all this open space. They could block the intersection here and take her. They could park a van at the same spot and shoot her from a distance. She could pull into the driveway here, and up comes their black van. Two in the head, just like Castillo at the warehouse, or they could grab her and be on the interstate or Peachtree Road within five minutes. Or they could make it easy and set up here—' He drew an oblong square beside Evelyn's house. 'Roz Levy's carport. She's got a knee wall here where they could set up with a rifle. The bathroom window to Evelyn's house faces Mrs. Levy's. It's down an incline. You can see straight through to the kitchen door from Mrs. Levy's without anyone knowing. Faith comes in the door with the bag of cash and they drop her.'

Amanda took the pen and turned the base of the T into a circle. 'Little John loops around. The whole neighborhood folds back on itself.' She drew more arcs. 'This is Nottingham. Friar Tuck. Robin Hood. Beverly. Lionel.' She drew large X's at the end points. 'Beverly dumps out onto Peachtree here, where every car in the world eventually passes; the other end throws you back into the infinite loop of Ansley Park. Lionel does the same. They're bottlenecks. Most of the houses along these routes have on-street parking. We could have ten cars at each point and no one would notice.'

Will said, 'I'm not worried about their exit routes. I'm worried about Faith going into that house alone. If they really are watching the place, they'll know the minute someone shows up who shouldn't be there. They've had almost three full days to get the lay of the neighborhood, possibly more. Even if the CSU guys leave, they'll be counting the number who go in and the number who go out.'

Amanda turned over the paper. She drew a rough diagram of a house, pointing out the rooms. 'Faith comes in through the kitchen. The foyer is here, looking into the living room. Here's the bookcase on the left—my left. Takes up the entire wall. Sofa backs up to here. The wingback chair is here on the right. A couple of other chairs are here and here. Stereo console here. Sliding glass doors opposite the foyer.' She tapped the pen to what must've been the master bedroom. 'They'll keep Ev in here until Faith comes with the money, then they'll bring her into the living room. It's the obvious area for the exchange.'

'Nothing is obvious here.' He grabbed the pen. 'We can't cover the front windows because we don't know who's watching the house. We can't cover the back because the yard is wide open to the neighbors' and they'll see movement at any window. We still don't know how many kids are left on this team. There could be one, there could be a hundred.' He threw down the pen. His tone was firm. 'I don't like it, Faith. You can't go in there. Not on their terms. We'll find another way to do this. We'll suggest another location that we can secure ahead of time so that we can make sure you're safe.'

Amanda's tone betrayed her irritation. 'Don't be so fatalistic, Will. We've got six hours. All of us know the layout of the house, so that's our advantage as well as theirs. I know every old broad in that neighborhood. It's a residential street.

We've got joggers, deliverymen, cable trucks, meter readers, postal carriers, and afternoon strollers we can tap into. I can dribble in four teams over the next few hours and no one will be the wiser. We're not a bunch of Keystone Kops. We can figure out a way to do this.'

'I'll do it,' Will offered, and Sara felt her heart jump into her throat.

'You can hardly pass for Faith.'

'We'll send them an email to let them know I'm going to make the exchange. Roger Ling knows what I look like. Even if he's not involved in this, he's obviously enjoying the show. He knows who these guys are. He can tell them to trust me.'

Sara felt a wave of relief to see Amanda start shaking her head even before he'd finished talking.

He insisted, 'It's safer this way. Safer for Faith.'

As usual, Amanda didn't hold back. 'That's one of the most idiotic things I've ever heard come from your mouth. Think about what we've seen over the last couple of days. This is amateur hour. Julia Ling practically laid it out for us. We're dealing with a bunch of young, stupid boys who think they know how to play cops and robbers. We'll either have them on the ground or in it before they know what hit them.'

Will wasn't swayed. 'They may be young, but they're fearless. They've killed a lot of people. They've taken a lot of stupid risks.'

'None more stupid than sending you in instead of Faith. *That's* the way to get people killed.' Amanda decided, 'We'll do it my way. We'll figure out how to strategically place our people. We'll have eyes on Faith at all times. We'll wait until the kidnappers show up with Evelyn. Faith will do the swap, and then we'll nab them when they try to make their escape.'

Will wouldn't give in. He was adamant. 'She can't do this. She can't go in there alone. Either let me do it or we'll find another way.'

Faith said, 'If I'm not alone, then my mother is dead.'

Will looked down at the floor. He obviously thought that there was still the real possibility that Evelyn Mitchell was dead. Sara found herself silently agreeing with him. This didn't sound like a plan to get Evelyn back. It sounded like a plan to get Faith killed. Amanda was so hellbent on saving her friend that she couldn't see the collateral damage.

Sara had forgotten about the coffee. She kept one for herself, then passed the other mugs to Amanda, then Will.

'Thank you.' Will awkwardly took his. It was as if he was making sure that their hands didn't touch.

Faith said, 'He doesn't drink coffee. I'll take it.'

Sara felt her cheeks start to burn. 'You probably shouldn't be drinking caffeine right now.'

Will cleared his throat. 'That's okay. I like it sometimes.' He took a sip from the mug. He practically grimaced as he swallowed.

Sara couldn't take much more of this. The only way she could be more out of place is if she pulled out an accordion and started singing polka tunes. 'I should give y'all some privacy.'

Amanda stopped her. 'If you don't mind, Dr. Linton, I'd like a fresh ear on this.'

They were all looking at her. Impossibly, Sara felt even more naked than before. She looked at Will for help, but his blank expression was

377

probably the same one he gave to the woman at the bank or the guy who picked up his recyclables.

There was nothing to be done about it. She sat down beside Faith.

Amanda took the other seat. 'All right, let's go over what we know so we're all on the same page. Will, run it down for us.'

He put down the coffee mug and started talking. He told Faith about everything that had happened since Evelyn had been taken, detailing the crime scene, their visit with Boyd Spivey at the D&C and his silent ex-colleagues at Valdosta State Prison. Faith's lips parted in surprise when he told her about Roz Levy's photographs of Evelyn's gentleman friend. Still, she kept silent as he detailed Sara's ordeal at the hospital and the shootout at Julia Ling's warehouse. Sara felt that familiar tightness in her chest when he got to this last part. The cut on his ear. A bullet had whizzed by, less than an inch from his skull.

Will said, 'Ricardo Ortiz and Hironobu Kwon knew each other from school. They both went to Westminster. They were most likely working in Ling-Ling's cabinet shop together. They got it into their heads to start their own business. They obviously pulled together a crew from the other guys working in the shop. Ricardo went to Sweden and picked up some heroin for them to sell. According to Roger Ling, the boys were all bragging about it. Benny Choo, strongarm for the Yellow Rebels, picked up Ricardo and basically beat the crap out of him. He was about to pull the plug, but Ricardo, or maybe Hironobu, told him where they could get some serious money.'

Faith had been quietly taking all this in, but now

378

she mumbled, 'Mom.'

'Right,' Will confirmed. 'Chuck Finn and Hironobu Kwon were in the same rehab facility for at least a month. Chuck must've told Hironobu about the money. Ricardo was about to die, so Hironobu says, 'I know where I can get almost a million in cash.' Benny Choo takes him up on the offer.'

Amanda picked up the story. 'That's what they were looking for at Evelyn's. They thought she had money at the house. When she didn't give it up, they took her.'

Sara thought it was convenient that Amanda had skipped over the fact that Hector Ortiz, the cousin of one of the most powerful drug lords in Atlanta, was dead in Evelyn's trunk. She should've kept her mouth shut, but this was her house, they had barged in without notice, and Sara was tired of being polite. 'That doesn't explain why Hector Ortiz was there.'

Amanda raised one eyebrow. 'No, it doesn't, does it?'

Sara didn't work for this woman. She wasn't going to walk on eggshells. 'You're not going to answer the question?'

There was a crocodile smile on Amanda's lips. 'The more important issue here is that they did all of this because they want money. We can negotiate with people who want money.'

Will said, 'It's not about money.'

'We don't have time for your woman's intuition,' Amanda snapped.

His voice sounded tired, but he didn't back down. 'They're trying to get Faith trapped in that house for a reason. If we go in without knowing

379

that reason, then it's not going to end well. Not for any of us.' What he said sounded perfectly reasonable, but Sara could tell Amanda wasn't buying it. Still, he kept trying. 'Look, if it was just about money, they would've made a ransom demand the first day. They wouldn't be doing this back-and-forth through Facebook. They wouldn't risk meeting Faith face-to-face in the grocery store. It would be a simple transaction. Make the call. Pick up the money. Leave the hostage somewhere, and you're home free.'

Again, a reasonable assumption. Again, Amanda ignored it.

She said, 'There is no secret endgame here. They want cash. We'll give them cash. We'll shove it so far down their throats they'll be shitting paper all the way to prison.'

'He's right.' Faith had been staring blankly ahead for most of this exchange, but with her hypoglycemia finally leveled out, she was back to thinking like a detective. 'What about the bank account?'

Amanda stood up to get more coffee. 'The account doesn't matter.'

Will seemed ready to disagree, but for his own reasons, he kept silent.

Amanda told Faith, 'Your father was a gambler.'

Faith shook her head. 'That's not true.'

'He played poker every weekend.'

'For quarters.' She kept shaking her head. 'Dad was an insurance salesman. He hated risk.'

'He wasn't risking anything. He was very careful.' Amanda went back around the kitchen island and sat down by Faith. 'How many times did he and Kenny go to Vegas when you were little?'

Faith was still unconvinced. 'That was for work conventions.'

'Bill was methodical about it. He was methodical about everything. You know that. He knew how to bluff and he knew when to walk away. Kenny wasn't as smart, but that's a story for another time.' She looked at Will. 'Bill didn't pay taxes on the money. That's why the bank account was a secret.'

Sara could see her own confusion reflected in Will's face. Past a certain amount, you couldn't just walk out of a Vegas casino, or any legal casino in America, for that matter, without paying taxes.

Faith didn't pick up on this. 'I can't see Dad taking that kind of risk. He hated gambling. He was all over Kenny about it.'

'Because Kenny was an idiot with his money,' Amanda countered. The bitter edge to her voice reminded Sara that the two had dated for many years. 'For Bill, it was just fun, blowing off steam, and sometimes he won a lot of money, and sometimes he lost a little, but he always knew when to walk away. It wasn't an addiction for him. It was sport.'

Will finally spoke up. 'Why didn't Evelyn tell me that when I was investigating her?'

Amanda smiled. 'She didn't tell you a hell of a lot about anything when you were investigating her.'

'No,' he agreed. 'But she could've easily gotten rid of the suspicion if—'

'There was no suspicion,' Amanda interrupted. She directed her words toward Faith. 'Your mother was the one who turned in the team. That's why they called her Almeja. She was a snitch.'

381

'What?' Faith's confusion was almost palpable. She looked at Will as if he had the answers. 'Why didn't she tell me?'

Amanda said, 'Because she wanted to protect you. The less you knew, the safer you were.'

Will said, 'Then why are you telling her now?'

Amanda was obviously annoyed. 'Because you won't get off that stupid account, even though I've told you time and again that it doesn't matter.'

Will had put his coffee mug on the counter. He slowly turned the handle so that it was parallel to the backsplash.

Faith asked what Sara was thinking. 'How did she find out they were taking money?'

Amanda shrugged, 'Does it matter?'

'Yes,' Will answered, He obviously wanted to hear the story so that he could find the holes.

Amanda took a deep breath before starting, 'There was a bust on the southside, one of the projects in East Point. Evelyn led the raid team into the apartment. Early morning. The bad guys were still asleep, hungover from the night before, with a pile of money sitting on the coffee table and enough coke to take down an elephant.' Amanda started to smile, clearly enjoying the story. 'They rounded them up and perp walked them the street. They had their hands behind their backs, sitting on their knees, staring at the doors on the squad cars to remind them who was in charge. In comes the media, which Boyd could never resist. He lines up the team for photos, with the bad guys in the background. Charlie's Angels territory. Your mother always hated that part. She usually left— went back to the office to do the paperwork— when the press came. This time, the street was blocked, so she went back into the apartment and looked around for herself.' Amanda pursed her lips. 'First thing she notices is that the cash pile doesn't look like it did before. She said it was stacked into a pyramid when they busted down the door. You know your mom was always the first one in.' Faith nodded. 'She said she noticed the pyramid right off, because Zeke used to—'

'Pyramid everything.' Faith explained, 'When he was ten or eleven, he started stacking stuff—books, Legos, Matchbox cars—into pyramids.'

'Your mother thought he was autistic. Maybe she was right.' Amanda continued, 'Anyway, she noticed the pile, is the point here. That the pyramid was a square when she went back into the apartment. She started watching the team more closely after that, keeping her ear to the ground, tracking which cases made it and which fell apart because evidence was lost or witnesses went missing. And then when she was sure, she came to me.'

Will said, 'You told me the tip was anonymous.'

'Evelyn had to be investigated just like everyone else. These weren't choirboys we were dealing with. Boyd and the crew were raking in tons of cash. They were also being paid to look the other way. You don't cut into that kind of business without risking your life. Ev had to be protected. So we decided that we'd call it an anonymous tip and put her through the ringer just like everyone else.'

Faith said, 'But they must've suspected the tip came from Mom. She was the only one who wasn't in on it.'

'There's a big leap between suspecting and

383

knowing.' Her tone became strained. 'And Boyd Spivey protected her. He let it be known that she was off limits. He stood up for her at every turn. I suppose that's why they took him out. They could take the GBI and the APD on their tails, but someone with Boyd's juice could get to them in ways we can't.'

Faith was quiet, probably thinking about the dead man who had protected her mother. For her part, Sara was thinking about the time and money that went into putting a hit on a man who lived on death row. The whole thing had been carefully planned and executed by people who knew Evelyn Mitchell's weak points: Boyd Spivey, her muscle; Faith, her daughter; Amanda, her best friend. This was sounding more and more like a revenge attack and less like a money grab. Sara could tell that Will had made the same connections. But as usual, when he finally spoke, he didn't make mention of the obvious.

Instead, he asked Amanda, 'Did you redact the bank account out of my report?'

'We're not the IRS.' She shrugged. 'No reason to punish someone for doing the right thing.'

Sara could tell Will was angry, but he still said nothing. He didn't even seethe. He just tucked his hands into his pockets and leaned his back against the counter. She had never had an argument with him. At this point, she wasn't sure she ever would, but Sara could imagine that it would be a grand exercise in futility.

For her part, Faith seemed oblivious to the holes in Amanda's story. Considering her blood sugar had been spiking and plummeting like a Ping-Pong ball for the last few days, it was surprising she could even sit up straight. That was why Sara was sure she'd heard wrong when Faith finally spoke.

'They left her finger under my pillow.'

Amanda didn't blink an eye. 'Where is the finger?'

'In my medicine cabinet.' Faith put her hand to her mouth. She looked as if she was going to be sick. Sara jumped up and grabbed the trashcan, but Faith waved her away. 'I'm all right.' She took a few deep breaths. Sara got a glass out of the cabinet and filled it with water.

Faith drank greedily, her throat making gulping sounds.

Sara refilled the glass and put it in front of her. She leaned back against the counter and kept an eye on Faith. Will was leaning a few feet down from her. His hands were still in his pockets. She felt the distance between them like a cold rush of air.

Faith took a sip of water before telling them, 'They tried to get Jeremy. I sent him away with my brother. Emma, too. And then I went to the grocery store and the guy cornered me in the bathroom.'

Amanda asked, 'What did he look like?'

Faith gave them a very detailed description of his height, weight, clothing, grammar. 'I think he was Hispanic. He had blue eyes.' She looked at Sara. 'Is that normal?'

'It's not common, but it's not rare.' Sara explained, 'Mexico was settled by Spaniards. Some of them married Native Americans. Not all Mexicans have brown skin and dark hair. Some have blond hair and lighter skin. Some have blue

385

or green eyes. It's a recessive gene, but it shows up.'

Amanda asked, 'But this guy had blue eyes?'

Faith nodded.

'No tattoos?'

'A snake on his neck.'

It was Amanda's turn to nod. 'We can put that on the wire. At the very least, we can get a list of Hispanic men eighteen to twenty who have blue eyes.' She seemed to remember something. 'No luck on the search for tattoo parlors. Whoever did Marcellus Estevez's tattoo of the archangel Gabriel is either out of state, off the books, or isn't talking.'

'There was something familiar about him,' Faith said. 'I thought maybe I'd arrested him, but he told me no.'

'I'm sure he was telling the truth.' Amanda pulled out her BlackBerry and started typing as she talked. 'I'll have records look through your reports. I know someone in the APD who can sneak in the back door for your cases before you started working with us.'

'I doubt you'll find anything.' Faith rubbed her temples. 'He's Jeremy's age. Maybe he knows him. Maybe they went to school together. I don't know.'

Amanda finished her email. 'Did you ask Jeremy?'

Faith nodded her head. 'I gave him a rough description last night. He doesn't know anybody who fits the bill. At least no one he can recall.'

Will asked, 'Is there anything else you can remember?'

Obviously, there was something. Faith looked reticent. 'It's something really stupid. Maybe . . .'

386

She looked at Sara. 'My blood sugar has been crazy. It's making me hallucinate.'

Sara asked, 'In what way?'

'I just—' She shook her head. 'It's stupid. The silverware drawer was wrong.' She laughed at herself. 'It's really stupid. Never mind.'

'Go on,' Sara told her. 'What was wrong with it?'

'The forks were turned the wrong way. And the spoons. And my pens were in the wrong drawer. I always put them in the same place, and . . . And then I went into the living room and the snow globes were all turned toward the wall. They usually face out. I'm really careful with them. They belonged to my father. I dust them every week. Jeremy isn't allowed to touch them. Zeke wouldn't go near them. I just . . .' She shook her head. 'I don't know. Maybe I did it last night and I don't remember. Maybe I just thought they were turned around. But I remember turning them back around, so . . .' She put her head in her hands. 'My mind has been off-kilter since all of this happened. I'm not sure what's real and what's not. Maybe I'm just going crazy. Could I be hallucinating?'

Sara told her, 'Your numbers are erratic, but they don't point to metabolic derangement. You're not that dehydrated, but you're certainly under a lot of stress. Do you feel like you have a cold or infection?' Faith shook her head. 'I'd expect confusion, which you've shown, and paranoia, which is understandable, but not full-on hallucinations.' She felt the need to add, 'Turning the snow globes around sounds more like something a kid would do for attention. You're sure your son didn't do it?'

'I haven't asked him. It's embarrassing even to

387

talk about. I'm sure it's nothing.'

Amanda was shaking her head. 'Jeremy wouldn't do something like that, especially with what's been going on. He wouldn't want to cause you more stress. And he's almost twenty years old. He's too mature for that sort of thing.'

'Maybe I just imagined it,' Faith said. 'Why would these guys turn around all the snow globes?' She seemed to remember something else. 'And unscrew the light bulbs.'

Amanda sighed. 'It doesn't matter, Faith. What matters is that we've got to get a plan together.' She checked her watch. 'It's almost seven o'clock. We need to put our thinking caps on.'

Faith said, 'Will's right. They're watching Mom's house. I know they're watching mine. If we bring in the APD—'

'I have no intention of doing something so stupid,' Amanda interrupted. 'We still don't know if Chuck Finn is involved in this or not.' Faith opened her mouth to protest, but Amanda held up her hand to stop her. 'I know you think that Chuck was pushed into a life of crime while the others willingly jumped in, but guilty doesn't come in shades. He took the money. He spent it. He confessed to his crimes and he's out on the street somewhere with a very serious habit that costs a great deal of money. You also need to remember that Chuck still has friends on the Atlanta force, and where he doesn't have friends, he might have the money to buy them. I know you don't want to hear this, but there's no getting around that he either gave Hironobu Kwon the tip-off or he's pulling the strings on this new group of young guns.'

388

Faith countered, 'That doesn't sound like Chuck.'

'Skimming money off busts didn't sound like Chuck, either, but here we are.' She told Will, 'You mentioned the vantage point from Roz Levy's house. There's no way they could set up there. She'd shoot them the second they set foot in the driveway.'

'It's true,' Faith agreed. 'Mrs. Levy watches the street like a hawk.'

Will countered, 'Unless someone's getting shot or kidnapped next door.'

Amanda ignored the observation. 'The point, Will, is that we can exploit the position just as easily as the kidnappers can. Short of shipping you in the world's largest box, we need to figure out how we're going to get you and your rifle into Roz Levy's carport without being seen.' She looked at Faith. 'Are you sure you weren't followed here?'

Faith shook her head. 'I was careful. I wasn't followed.'

'Good girl,' Amanda told her. She was back in her element, almost giddy with the task at hand. 'I need to make some phone calls to find out what's going on at Evelyn's house. Our bad guys wouldn't have suggested a meeting there if they thought the Atlanta Crime Scene Unit was going to be steady at work. We'll see if Charlie can make some inquiries, too. Failing that, I think I've got a few more favors in my pocket with some old gals in Zone Six who would love nothing more than to show the kids how it's done. Dr. Linton?'

Sara was surprised to hear her name. 'Yes?'

'Thank you for your time. I trust you'll keep this little party to yourself?'

389

'Of course.'

Faith stood behind Amanda. 'Thank you,' she said. 'Again.'

Sara hugged her. 'Be careful.'

Will was next. He held out his hand. 'Dr. Linton.'

Sara looked down, wondering if she was having one of Faith's hallucinations. He was actually shaking her hand goodbye.

He said, 'Thank you for your help. I'm sorry we imposed on you this morning.'

Faith mumbled something Sara couldn't hear.

Amanda opened the closet. Sara guessed the smile on her face wasn't there because she was happy to see her coat. 'I know a lot of Evelyn's neighbors. They're mostly retired and I think that with the exception of that old battle-ax across the street, they'll be okay with us using their places. I'll need to get my hands on some cash. I think I can make that happen, but we'll be tight for time.' She slipped on her coat. 'Faith, you'll need to go home and wait until you hear from us. I imagine at some point we'll need you to run to a bank or two. Will, go home and change that shirt. The collar's frayed and you're missing a button. And while you're at it, you'd better start building a Trojan horse or come up with a plan to romance Roz Levy. She was ready to have Faith arrested an hour ago. God knows what bee is up her wrinkled old butt this morning.'

'Yes, ma'am.'

Sara opened the front door for them. Amanda started toward the elevator. Will, ever the gentleman, stepped aside so that Faith could leave first.

390

Sara shut the door after Faith.

'What—' Will began, but she put her finger to his lips.

'Sweetheart, I know you've got work to do and I know it's going to be dangerous, but whatever you get into today will not be nearly as life-threatening as what'll happen if you ever do to me what you did to me last night and then think you can get off with a handshake the next morning. Okay?'

He swallowed.

'Call me later.' She kissed him goodbye, then opened the door so that he could leave.

CHAPTER SEVENTEEN

Will subscribed to a lot of car magazines. Mostly, he bought them for the pictures, but sometimes he felt compelled to read the articles. That's how he knew that Roz Levy's avocado green 1960 Chevrolet Corvair 700 sedan was worth considerably more than Faith's five-dollar appraisal.

The car was a beauty, the sort of classic American carmakers used to be known for. The rear-mounted, air-cooled, horizontally opposed, aluminum flat-six engine had been engineered to directly take on the increasingly more popular compact-sized European models coming onto the market. The design was renowned for its innovative swing-axle rear suspension, which received its own chapter in Ralph Nader's *Unsafe at Any Speed*. The spare tire was mounted in the forward luggage compartment, where the engine was normally located in other cars, nestled right next to a gasoline heater for the passenger area. Though winter was over, the tank was still filled with gas, which Will knew because his face had been pressed against the metal canister while Faith drove him to Mrs. Levy's house. The sloshing of gasoline had been like ocean waves crashing against the shore. Or, a highly volatile accelerant churning less than a rusty millimeter from his face.

The car had been built well before the 2001 National Highway Traffic Safety Administration deadline that required all manufacturers to install a glow-in-the-dark emergency release strap in case someone got trapped in the trunk of the car. Will wasn't sure whether he would be able to reach a handle even if one existed. The trunk was deep but not wide, more like a pelican's mouth. He was folded into a space meant to hold a spare tire and maybe a couple of suitcases—1960s suitcases, not the modern wheelie kinds that people nowadays used to pack their entire houses in for a weekend trip to the mountains.

In short, there existed the very real possibility that he might die in here before Roz Levy remembered that she was supposed to let him out.

There was a thin sliver of light coming through the cracked rubber seal around the hinge. Will lifted up his cell phone to check the time. He'd been in the trunk for almost two hours and had at least another half hour to go. His rifle was jammed between his legs in a way that was no longer pleasant. His paddle holster was turned so that his Glock dug into his side like an insistent finger. The bottle of water Faith had given him had long been recycled back into the plastic bottle. It was

392

approximately six thousand degrees inside the metal tomb. He had lost feeling in his hands and feet. He was beginning to think that this was a very bad idea.

It was the words 'Trojan horse' that had gotten him thinking. One call to Roz Levy proved that she wasn't going to make this easy for them. She was still pissed about Faith taking her car. She'd refused to let any of them inside of her house. Unusually, Will was the person who suggested the idiotic thing for him to do. Faith would return the Corvair to the carport. He would hide in the trunk until a few minutes before the appointed time. Mrs. Levy would take out her trash, releasing the trunk lid along the way. Will would then crawl out and give Faith cover.

The fact that Roz Levy agreed to this alternate plan so easily made him suspect that she wasn't going to play along, but by then another hour had passed and they didn't really have a choice in the matter.

There were other Trojan horses, too—most of them more clever than Will's. The good thing about Amanda's old gals was that they were old and they were women, which went against type in this particular situation. Whoever was watching the neighborhood would be expecting testosterone-pumped young guns with trigger fingers and short haircuts. Amanda had sent in six of her friends to various houses around the block. They'd had bakeware and cake stands in their hands, their purses dangling from their arms. Some of them carried Bibles. They would look like visitors to anyone who was paying attention.

The outside perimeter was covered by a cable

truck, a mobile pet groomer's van, and a bright yellow Prius that no self-respecting cop would ever drive. Between the three vehicles, they could monitor all traffic coming in and out of the two roads that led to the Mitchell section of the neighborhood.

Even with all of this, Will still was not happy with the plan. It was the lesser of two evils, the greater evil being no police presence at all. He didn't like the idea of Faith being so vulnerable, even though she was armed and had proven to anyone who was paying attention that she would not hesitate to shoot somebody. He felt in his gut that Amanda was wrong. This wasn't about money. Maybe on the surface it was. Maybe even the kidnappers themselves thought it was about cold, hard cash. But at the end of the day, their behavior belied that motivation. This was personal. Someone was working out a grudge. Chuck Finn seemed like the most likely culprit. His underlings wanted the cash. Chuck wanted revenge. It was a win-win for everyone but Faith.

And for the idiot trapped in a 1960 Corvair.

Will winced as he tried to shift his position. His back ached. His nose itched. His ass felt like he had been pressing his full weight against a piece of hardened steel for two hours. In retrospect, shoving Will into a trunk sounded more like the kind of idea Amanda would have. Painful. Humiliating. Bound to end badly for Will. He must've had some sort of death wish. Or maybe he just wanted to spend a couple of hours simmering in the heat because it was the only way he'd have time to think about what he'd gotten himself into. And he didn't mean the car.

Will had never smoked a cigarette. He'd never done an illegal drug of any kind. He hated the taste of alcohol. As a kid, he'd seen how addictions could ruin lives, and as a cop, he saw how it could end them. He'd never been tempted to imbibe. He'd never understood how people could be so desperate for the next high that they were willing to trade away their lives and everything that mattered for another hit. They stole. They prostituted themselves. They abandoned or sold their children. They murdered people. They would do anything to avoid getting dopesick, that point at which the body craved the drug so badly that it turned on itself. Muscle cramps. Stabbing pains in the gut. Blinding headaches. Cotton mouth. Heart palpitations. Sweaty palms.

Will's physical discomfort wasn't solely caused by the tight quarters in Mrs. Levy's Corvair.

He was dopesick for Sara.

To his credit, he realized that his response to her was completely disproportionate to what a normal human being should be feeling right now. He was going to make a fool of himself. More so than he already had. He didn't know how to be around her. At least not when they weren't having sex. And they'd had a lot of sex, so it had taken Sara some time before she finally got the full-on view of Will's astounding stupidity. And what a show he had put on for her. Shaking her hand like a realtor at an open house. He was surprised that she hadn't slapped him. Even Amanda and Faith had been at a loss for words as they'd all waited for the elevator in the hall. His idiocy had actually rendered them speechless.

Will was beginning to wonder if there was

something physically wrong with him. Maybe he was diabetic like Faith. She was always yelling at him about his afternoon sticky bun, his second breakfast, his love of cheesy nachos from the downstairs vending machine. He went through his symptoms. He was sweating profusely. His thoughts were racing. He was confused. He was thirsty and he really, really needed to urinate.

Sara hadn't seemed mad at him when she'd told him goodbye. She had called him sweetheart, which he'd only been called once before, and that time was by her, too. She had kissed him. It wasn't a passionate kiss—more like a peck. The sort of thing you saw on 1950s television shows right before the husband put on his hat and went off to work. She had told him to call her later. Did she really want him to call her or had she just been making a point? Will was used to the women in his life making points at his expense. But what defined later? Did that mean later tonight or later tomorrow? Or later in the week?

Will groaned. He was a thirty-four-year-old man with a job and a dog to take care of. He had to get himself back under control. There was no way he was going to call Sara. Not later tonight or even later next week. He was too unsophisticated for her. Too socially awkward. Too desperate to be with her. Will had learned the hard way that the best thing to do when you really wanted something was to put it out of your mind, because you were never going to get it. He had to do that now with Sara. He had to do that before he got himself shot or he ended up getting Faith killed because he was acting like a lovesick schoolgirl.

The worst part was that Angie had been right

about everything.

Well, maybe not everything.

Sara didn't color her hair.

His phone vibrated. Will struggled not to castrate himself with his rifle while he pressed the Bluetooth piece into his ear. The trunk was well insulated, but he still kept his voice to a whisper. 'Yeah?'

'Will?' That's all he needed—Amanda's voice in his head. 'What are you doing?'

'Sweating,' he whispered back, wondering if she could've asked a more pointless question. He'd had this idea of springing out of the trunk like a superhero. After all this time, he realized he'd probably do well not to roll out onto the ground like a tongue.

'We're set up at Ida Johnson's.' Evelyn's backyard neighbor. Will wasn't sure how Amanda had sweet-talked the woman into letting a bunch of cops sit in her house. Maybe she'd promised that Faith wouldn't shoot any more drug dealers in her yard again. 'I just heard a call on the scanner. There was a drive-by shooting in East Atlanta. Two dead. Ahbidi Mittal and his team just left Evelyn's house so they can process the car. High profile. A woman and her kid. White, blonde, middle class, pretty.'

So, now they knew how the kidnappers planned to get Evelyn's house cleared out. Amanda had made some discreet calls earlier and found out that the CSU team had at least another three days on the house. They knew that Evelyn's abductors had some drive-by experience. Obviously, these particular bad guys weren't afraid of killing innocent bystanders, and they knew exactly the

397

right victim profile to make sure every news station in Atlanta halted programming to cover the events live at the scene.

The most troubling part to Will was that this proved they had no problem murdering a mother and her child.

Amanda said, 'Evelyn's backyard is dug up.'

Maybe it was the heat. Will had the image of a dog looking for a bone.

'She must've told them the money was in the backyard. Holes are everywhere.'

That had been one of Will's early guesses. He saw how stupid it was now. People didn't hide money like that anymore. Even Evelyn had a bank account. Everything was on a file in a computer these days.

He kept his tone low. 'Did Mrs. Levy see them digging?'

Amanda was uncharacteristically silent.

'Amanda?'

'She's not answering her phone right now, but I'm sure she's just taking a nap.'

He couldn't swallow. It wasn't funny anymore now that it might actually happen.

'She'll have her alarm set to wake her.'

Will wondered how the old woman was going to hear her alarm if she couldn't hear a phone. And then he stopped worrying, because he was going to pass out from heat stroke long before that happened.

Amanda said, 'I've got two friends with me and another old gal in the street. She'll keep an eye on Faith while she's on route to the house. Bev's with the Secret Service. She requisitioned a mail truck.'

Will wished that he were more surprised by this

398

information. If Amanda told him that she called an old gal at the White House and borrowed the nuclear codes, he would just nod.

'Everything's lining up.' Amanda always got chatty right before a case was about to break, and now was no exception. 'Faith is waiting at her house. She went to three different banks this morning to support her safe deposit box story. We had one of the managers hand her the cash at the last drop. All the bills are registered. There's a tracker in the lining of the duffel.' She was silent for a moment. 'I think she'll be okay. Sara got her evened out for now. I'm worried that she's not taking care of herself.'

Will was worried about that, too. He'd always thought of Faith as indestructible. She seemed capable of handling any crisis. Maybe that had come from being thrust into motherhood before she was ready. Mrs. Levy's words about the pregnancy scandal rocking the neighborhood kept coming back to him. Faith obviously still carried some shame. She had blushed when she explained her mother's words to Sara, though Evelyn was obviously just using what might be her last words to her daughter to lift away some of that guilt. Faith's entire life had been shattered by her pregnancy. Somehow, she had managed to pick up the pieces. Evelyn had been there to offer her support, but Faith had done all the heavy lifting. Getting her GED. Joining the Academy. Going back to college. Raising her kid. She was one of the strongest women Will had ever met. In some ways, she was even stronger than Amanda.

And she deserved the truth.

Will whispered, 'Why did you lie to Faith about

399

her father being a gambler?'

Amanda didn't answer.

He started to ask her again. 'Why did you—'

'Because he was,' Amanda said. 'I would think after this morning, you would recognize that there are other things a man can gamble with besides money.'

Will swallowed the last bit of saliva in his mouth. He wasn't up to Amanda's riddles right now. 'Evelyn was on the take.'

'She made a big mistake a long time ago, and she's been paying for it ever since.'

He struggled to keep his voice quiet. 'She took money—'

'I'll make you a promise, Will. If we get Evelyn out of this, then she'll tell you the whole truth about everything. You can have a whole hour with her. She'll answer any question you have.'

He glanced around the trunk, the slit of light coming through the cracked rubber seal. 'And if we don't?'

'Then it won't matter, will it?' He heard talking in the background. 'I need to go. I'll call you when I have news.'

Will shifted the rifle again so that he could end the call. He closed his eyes and tried to clear his mind. A bead of sweat glided down his back. There was a stinging sensation near the base of his spine where Sara had scratched him.

He shook his head, trying to clear the image from his mind so that his rifle didn't file a complaint for sexual assault. Will thought about the rifle sitting in the witness stand, using its trigger to wipe a tear from its scope.

He shook his head again. The heat was really

400

getting to him. He started going over the case to focus his mind. Amanda always wanted him to talk it out from the beginning. It was the best way to see what they had missed. In the heat of the moment, it was hard to put together the pieces. Now, Will went through the last few days step-by-step, examining all the angles, reviewing all the lies and half-truths the bad guys had told them as well as the lies and half-truths Amanda had spun.

As before, Will's mind kept coming back to Chuck Finn. It was a process of elimination. Chuck was the only man from Evelyn's former team who was not accounted for. He had been at Healing Winds with Hironobu Kwon. He obviously knew Roger Ling, who called him Chuckleberry Finn.

Roger had also talked about cutting off the head of the snake. There had to be one person in charge. Chuck could very well be that person. He ticked a lot of boxes: He had a personal vendetta against Evelyn Mitchell for turning him in. His life in prison wasn't a cakewalk. He'd gone from being a well-respected police officer to having to watch his back in the shower room.

The man had probably developed his habit inside the joint, then reveled in it the minute he'd been paroled. Heroin and crack added up to an expensive habit. Even if Chuck was clean now, his money would be long gone. Of all the detectives Will investigated, Chuck was the one who had the least to show for his crimes. He'd shot his wad on luxury travel, seeing every corner of the world in the style of a multimillionaire. The trip to Africa alone had cost around a hundred thousand dollars. The only person Will interviewed who seemed to really be upset about the charges against Chuck

401

Finn was his travel agent.

Will guessed he would find out soon enough whether or not Chuck was really behind all of this. He heard the carport door open, the shuffle of bedroom slippers across the concrete. The trunk cracked open, daylight pouring in like water. He saw Mrs. Levy pad by with a white garbage bag in her hand. There was the clatter of a plastic Herbie Curbie garbage can as she threw away the trash.

Will clutched the rifle in one hand and held down the trunk lid with the other. His movement was as predicted—more like a lazy tongue flopping onto the concrete than Superman leaping into action. Roz Levy passed right by him. She looked straight ahead, cool as a cucumber. Her hand reached out, effortlessly making the small movement to close the trunk. Without a glance down at Will, she was back inside the house, door closed, and he was left thinking that it was entirely possible this old woman had been calm enough not just to kill her husband but to lie to Amanda's face about it for the last decade.

Will lay on the concrete for a few seconds, relishing the feel of cold on his skin, gulping in the crisp, fresh air tinged with the odor of leaking oil from the Corvair's back end. He got up on his elbows. His memory of the carport, while accurate, was next to useless. It was a wide-open space front to back, like the underpass of a bridge, only more dangerous. Roz Levy's house was on one side of the structure. On the other was the brick knee wall, about four feet high, with an ornate metal column at each end to support the roof. Will could see into the street from under the car, but there was no vantage point from which to tell whether or not he was being watched.

He looked to his side. The Herbie Curbie was equidistant between the half wall and the car. Will guessed the blur of movement would be obvious to anyone watching, but he didn't really have a choice. He got up into a low squat. He held his breath, thinking there was no time to waste, and darted behind the large trashcan.

No bullets. No shouts. Nothing but his heart pounding in his chest.

There were at least three more feet to go to the knee wall. Will braced himself to move, then stopped because there was probably a better way to do this than sit against the wall with a neon sign pointing to his head. Slowly, he pushed the trash container, duckwalking behind it, and closing the gap between the car and the wall. At least he had some visual cover, if not protection, from anyone out in the street. Across the yard was another matter. The brick wall might protect him from shots fired from Evelyn's house, but he was basically an easy target to anyone who walked up on him from the backyard.

Will couldn't squat like this forever. He bent down on one knee and chanced a look over the wall. The space was clear. Evelyn's house was on a lower elevation. He could not have lined up the bathroom window any better if he'd planned it. It was high in the wall, probably inside the shower. The opening was narrow enough to fit a small child through, though unfortunately not a grown man. Especially an overgrown man. The shade was pulled up. Will could see clear down the hallway. With the rifle scope to his eye, he could make out the wood grain in the door that led to Evelyn's

403

carport. It was closed. Black powder dusted the white where the CSU techs had taken fingerprints.

They had already talked this out. When Faith came into the house, she was supposed to enter through that door.

Will's phone vibrated. He pressed the Bluetooth piece. 'I'm in position.'

'The black van was just spotted on Beverly. They came from the Peachtree side.'

Will tightened his hand on the grip. 'Where's Faith?'

'She just left her house. She's on foot.'

He didn't have to say anything. They both knew this was not part of the plan. Faith was supposed to drive, not go for a stroll.

He heard the rattling of an engine in the street. The black van pulled close to the curb. They weren't exactly incognito. Bullet holes pocked the side panels. Will slid the lever on the side of the rifle to fire. He aimed down on the middle section of the van as the side door slid open. He scanned the inside, surprised by what he found.

Will whispered to Amanda, 'There are only two of them. They have Evelyn.'

'You're authorized to take your shot.'

He didn't see how that was going to happen. The two young men on either side of Evelyn Mitchell each had their weapons aimed at her head. It looked impressive, but if one of them pulled the trigger, it wouldn't just take out Evelyn—the bullet would go straight through her skull and into his buddy's head. Amanda would've called this doing the Lord's work if her best friend in the world weren't in the middle of these two Einsteins.

404

They jerked Evelyn down from the van, making sure that her body gave them cover. She screamed in pain, the sound piercing the quiet afternoon. She wasn't tied up, but Evelyn Mitchell could hardly run off to safety. One of her legs was crudely splinted with two broken-off broom handles. Duct tape kept them in place. She was obviously severely wounded. Her abductors obviously did not care.

Both boys were wearing black jackets and black baseball hats. Their heads swiveled around as they looked for possible threats. They walked single file, with Evelyn sandwiched between them. The one in back kept a Glock jammed into her ribs, spurring her on the way you would a horse. She obviously couldn't walk on her own. Glock's arm was wrapped around her waist. She leaned back into him with every step, her face a mask of pain. The one in front kept his knees bent as he walked. Evelyn's hand dug into his shoulder for balance. The man didn't falter. He kept sweeping a Tec-9 back and forth across the front of the house. His finger was on the notoriously sensitive trigger. Will hadn't seen a Tec-9 since the now-expired federal assault-weapons ban had forced the manufacturer out of business. The gun had been used during the Columbine massacre. It was a semiautomatic, but that hardly mattered when you had fifty rounds in the magazine.

For just a second, Will took his eye away from the scope and checked the street. It was empty. No Chuck Finn. No more young guns in black jackets and black baseball hats. He looked back through the scope. His stomach dropped. There couldn't just be two of them.

Amanda's voice was terse. 'Do you have the shot?'

Will's sights were lined up on Tec-9's chest. Maybe the two kids weren't complete amateurs after all. Tec-9 was directly in front of Evelyn, guaranteeing that any bullet that went through him would go through Evelyn, too. The same held true for Glock, who was pressed behind her. A head shot was out of the question. Even if there was a way to take down Tec-9, Glock would have a round in Evelyn before Will could realign his sights. Will may as well kill the prisoner as kill one of her captives. 'No shot,' he whispered to Amanda. 'It's too risky.'

She didn't argue with him. 'Keep the line open. I'll let you know when Faith reaches the house.'

Will tracked the three figures until they disappeared inside the carport. He pivoted, lining up the rifle to the kitchen door, holding his breath as he waited. The door was kicked open. Will kept his finger resting on the trigger guard as Evelyn Mitchell stumbled into the kitchen. Glock was still behind her. He lifted and carried her, the strain showing on his face. Tec-9 was still in front, still walking low. The top of his hat showed at Evelyn's chest level. Will studied her face. One of her eyes was swollen shut. The skin on her cheek was ripped open.

They were in the foyer. Evelyn winced when Glock loosened his grip around her waist to set her down. She was a thin woman, but she was practically dead weight. The kid behind her was breathing heavy. He pressed his head into her back. Like Tec-9, he was still more teenager than man.

The light in the foyer changed. The space darkened. They must have pulled down the blinds covering the front windows. They were vinyl, meant to filter the light, not completely block it. Will could still clearly see all three figures. Evelyn was half carried, half pushed again, this time into the living room. He saw the black hat, the Tec-9 waving in the air. Then they were gone. His line of sight cleared straight through to the kitchen.

'They're in the living room,' he told Amanda. 'All of them.' He didn't point out that her obvious plan was already off the rails. Evelyn wasn't being kept in the back bedroom. They wanted her front and center when Faith entered the house.

Amanda said, 'They're using Ev as a shield while they close the curtains in the back. I can't get a shot.' She muttered a curse. 'I can't see anything.'

'Where's Faith?'

'She should be here soon.'

Will tried to relax his body so his shoulders didn't ache. No Chuck Finn. No stashing Evelyn. The two boys had not checked the house for lurking cops. They hadn't secured the scene. They hadn't barricaded the front door or taken any precautions to make sure their escape was just as easy as their entry.

Every item they failed to check off the list was like a noose tightening around Faith's neck.

All Will could do now was wait.

CHAPTER EIGHTEEN

Before she left the house, Faith used Jeremy's Iphone to make a video for her children. She told them that she loved them, that they were everything to her, and that no matter what happened today, they should always know that she cherished every hair on their precious heads. She told Jeremy that keeping him was the best decision she had made in her life. That he was her life. She told Emma the same, and added that Victor Martinez was a good man, and that she was glad that her daughter would get to know her father.

Dramatic, Zeke would've called it. She had made a video for him, too. Her words to her brother had surprised her, mostly because the phrase 'you asshole' hadn't come up once. She told him that she loved him. She told him that she was sorry for what she'd put him through.

And then she'd tried to leave a video for her mother. Faith had stopped and started the recording at least a dozen times. There was so much to say. That she was sorry. That she hoped Evelyn wasn't disappointed with the choices that Faith had made. That every small bit of good inside of Faith had come from her parents. That her only goal in life ever had been to be as good a cop, as good a mother, as good a woman, as her own mother.

In the end, she had given up, because the likelihood that Evelyn Mitchell would ever see the recording was very slim.

Faith was not completely delusional. She knew

that she was walking into a trap. Earlier, in Sara's kitchen, Amanda hadn't been listening to Will but Faith had. She saw the logic in what he was saying, that there was more to this than just a money grab. Amanda was infused with the thrill of the chase, the opportunity to tell these upstart bastards who'd had the gall to take her best friend that they weren't going to get away with it. Will, as usual, was more clearheaded about the situation. He knew how to ask the right questions, but, just as importantly, he knew how to listen to the answers.

He was a logical man, not given to emotion—at least Faith didn't think he was. There was no telling what went on in that head of his. God help Sara Linton and the Herculean task in front of her. The handshake this morning wouldn't be the worst of it. Even if Sara managed to get Angie Trent out of the picture, which Faith doubted was possible, there was still Will's immutable stubbornness. The last time Faith had seen a man shut down so quickly was when she'd told Jeremy's father that she was pregnant.

Or maybe Faith was wrong about Will. She was about as good at reading her partner as he was at reading a book. The only thing Faith could swear by was Will's uncanny ability to understand emotional behavior in others. Faith supposed this came from being raised in care, having to quickly discern whether the person in front of him was friend or foe. He was a maestro at massaging facts out of the subtle clues that normal people tended to ignore. She knew it was just a matter of time before Will figured out what had happened with Evelyn all those years ago. Faith had only figured it out herself this morning when, for what might be the last time, she went through Jeremy's things.

Of course, she couldn't completely leave it to Will's investigative telepathy. Faith, ever the control freak, had written a letter outlining everything that had happened and why. She'd mailed it to Will's house from the last bank she visited. The Atlanta police would look at the videos on Jeremy's iPhone, but Will would never tell them what Faith had written in the letter.

This much she trusted to her core: Will Trent knew how to keep a secret.

Faith blocked the letter from her mind as she walked out her front door. She stopped thinking about her mother, Jeremy, Emma, Zeke—anyone who might cloud her mind. She was armed to the teeth. There was a kitchen knife inside the duffel bag, hidden below the cash. Zeke's Walther was stuck down the front of her pants. She was wearing an ankle holster with one of Amanda's backup S&Ws pressed firmly against her skin. The metal chafed. It felt obvious and bulky in a way that made her have to concentrate so she didn't limp.

Faith walked past the Mini. She refused to drive her car to her mother's house. It was too much like every other normal day when she loaded up Emma and her things and drove the block and a half to her mother's home. Faith had been stubborn her entire life and she wasn't going to stop that now. She wanted to at least do one thing today on her own terms.

She took a left at the bottom of her driveway, then a right toward her mother's house. She scanned the long stretch of street. Cars were pulled into carports and garages. No one was out on their front porch, though that was hardly unusual. This

410

was a back porch neighborhood. For the most part, people minded their own business.

At least they did now.

There was a parked mail delivery truck on her right. The carrier got out as Faith passed. Faith didn't recognize the woman—an older, hippie-looking type with a salt-and-pepper Crystal Gayle ponytail down her back. The hair swung as she walked to Mr. Cable's mailbox and shoved in a bunch of lingerie catalogues.

Faith shifted the duffel to her other hand as she took a left onto her mother's street. The canvas bag and the cash inside it were heavy, almost fifteen pounds all together. The money was in six bricks, each approximately four inches high. They had settled on $580,000, all in hundred-dollar bills, mostly because that was the amount of cash Amanda could sign out of evidence. It seemed like a credible amount of money if Evelyn had been mixed up in the corruption that had taken down her squad.

But she hadn't been involved in the corruption. Faith had never doubted her mother's innocence, so the confirmation from Amanda had not brought her much peace. Part of Faith must have sensed there was more to the story. There were other things her mother had been mixed up in that were equally as damning, yet Faith, ever the spoiled child, had squeezed her eyes shut for so long that part of her couldn't believe the truth anymore.

Evelyn had called this kind of denial 'voluntary blindness.' Normally, she was describing a particular type of idiot—a mother who insisted her son deserved another chance even though he'd been twice convicted of rape. A man who kept

411

insisting that prostitution was a victimless crime. Cops who thought it was their right to take dirty money. Daughters who were so wrapped up in their own problems that they didn't bother to look around and see that other people were suffering, too.

Faith felt a breeze in her hair as she reached her mother's driveway. There was a black van on the street, directly in front of the mailbox. The cab was empty, at least as far as she could tell. There were no windows in the back. Bullet holes pierced the metal on one side. The tag was nondescript. There was a faded Obama/Biden sticker on the chrome bumper.

She lifted up the yellow crime scene tape blocking off the driveway. Evelyn's Impala was still parked under the carport. Faith had played hopscotch in this driveway. She had taught Jeremy how to throw a basketball at the rusty old hoop Bill Mitchell had bolted to the eaves. She had dropped off Emma here almost every day for the last few months, giving her mother and daughter a kiss on the cheek before driving off to work.

Faith tightened her grip around the duffel as she walked into the carport. She was sweating, and the cool breeze in the covered area brought a chill. She looked around. The shed door was still open. It was hard to believe that only two days had passed since Faith had first seen Emma locked in the small building.

She turned toward the house. The door to the kitchen had been kicked open. It hung at an angle from the hinges. She saw the bloody handprint her mother had left, the space where her ring finger should've pressed against the wood. Faith held her

412

breath as she pushed open the door, expecting to be shot in the face. She even closed her eyes. Nothing came. Just the empty space of the kitchen, and blood everywhere.

When she'd entered the house two days ago, Faith had been so focused on finding her mother that she hadn't really processed what she was seeing. Now, she understood the violent battle that had taken place. She'd worked her share of crime scenes. She knew what a struggle looked like. Even with the body long removed from the laundry room, Faith could still recall the placement, what he'd been wearing, the way his hand fanned out against the floor.

Will had told her the kid's name, but she couldn't remember it. She couldn't remember any of them—not the man she had shot in the bedroom or the man she had killed in Mrs. Johnson's backyard.

After what they had done, they didn't deserve for her to know their names.

Faith turned her attention back to the kitchen. The pass-through was empty. She could see straight down the hallway. It was the middle of the afternoon, but the house appeared to be in dusk. The bedroom doors were closed. The blinds covering the large windows on either side of the front door were drawn. The only unfiltered light came from the bathroom window. The shade was pulled up. Faith walked past the dining room and into the front foyer. She stood with the hallway on her right and the kitchen on her left. The living room was in front of her. She should take out her gun, but she didn't think they were going to shoot her. At least not yet.

413

The room was dim. The curtains had been pulled closed, but they were more sheer than opaque. A gentle breeze stirred the material where the glass door had been broken. The room was still turned upside down. Faith couldn't recall what it had looked like before, though she'd lived here eighteen years of her life. The packed bookshelves that lined the left-hand wall. The framed family photos. The console stereo with the scratchy speakers. The overstuffed couch. The wingback chair her father sat in while he read. Evelyn was sitting there now. Her left hand was wrapped in a blood-soaked towel. Her right was so swollen it could've belonged to a mannequin. Two broom handles were duct-taped around her leg, keeping it straight out in front of her. Her white blouse was stained with blood. Her hair was matted to the side of her head. A piece of duct tape covered her mouth. Her eyes widened when she saw Faith.

'Mama,' Faith whispered. The word echoed in her brain, conjuring all the memories Faith had from the last thirty-four years. She had loved her mother. She had fought with her. Screamed at her. Lied to her. Cried in her arms. Run from her. Returned to her. And now, there was this.

The young man from the grocery store was on the other side of the room, leaning against the bookcases. His vantage point was ideal, the top of a triangle. Evelyn was down and to his left. Faith was fifteen feet away from her mother, forming the second base angle. He was in shadow, but the gun in his hand was easy to see. The barrel of a Tec-9 was pointed in Evelyn's direction. The fifty-round magazine jutted out at least twelve inches from the bottom. More clips hung out of his jacket pocket.

Faith dropped the duffel bag onto the floor. Her hand wanted to go to the Walther. She wanted to shoot the entire clip into his chest. She wouldn't aim for the head. She wanted to see his eyes, hear his screams, as the bullets ripped him apart.

'I know what you're thinking.' He smiled, his platinum tooth catching a bit of what light was in the room. ' "Can I pull my gun before he pulls the trigger?" '

She told him, 'No.' Faith was a quick draw, but the Tec-9 was already pointed at her mother's head. The math was against her.

'Get her gun.'

She felt the cold metal of a muzzle pressed to her head. Someone was behind her. Another man. He wrenched the Walther from the waist of her jeans, then grabbed the duffel bag. The zip ripped open. His laughter was like a child's on Christmas morning. 'Shit, man, look at all this green!' He bounced on the balls of his feet as he walked toward his friend. 'Goddamn, bro! We're rich!' He threw the Walther into the bag. He had his Glock tucked in the back of his pants. 'Goddamn!' he repeated, showing the bag to Evelyn. 'See this, bitch? How you like that? We got it anyway.'

Faith kept her eyes on the kid from the grocery store. He wasn't happy like his partner, but that was to be expected. This was never about the money. Will had called it hours ago.

The man asked Faith, 'How much is in there?'

She told him, 'A little over half a million.'

He gave a low whistle. 'You hear that, Ev? That's a lot of money you stole.'

'Damn right.' The partner fanned out a stack of bills. 'You coulda stopped all this two days ago, bitch. I guess they call you Almeja for a reason.'

Faith couldn't look at her mother. 'Take it,' she told the man. 'That was the deal. Take the money and leave.'

His friend was ready to do just that. He dropped the bag beside Evelyn's chair and picked up a roll of duct tape from the floor. 'Yo, man, let's go straight up to Buckhead. I'm'a get me a Jag and—'

Two shots rang out in rapid succession. The duct tape dropped to the floor. It rolled under the chair where Evelyn sat, then the boy's body collapsed in a heap beside her. The back of his head looked like someone had taken a hammer to it. Blood gushed onto the floor, pooling around the legs of the chair, her mother's feet.

The young man said, 'He talked too much. Don't you think?'

Faith's heart was pounding so loudly she could barely hear her own voice. The concealed revolver in her ankle holster felt hot, like it was burning her skin. 'Do you really think you're going to make it out of here alive?'

He kept the Tec-9 aimed at her mother's head. 'What makes you think I want to get out of here?'

Faith allowed herself to look at her mother. Sweat dripped from Evelyn's face. The edge of the duct tape was pulling away from her cheek. They hadn't bound her. The broken leg ensured she wasn't going anywhere. Still, she was sitting up straight in the chair. Shoulders back. Hands clasped in her lap. Her mother never slumped. She never gave away anything—except for now. There was fear in her eyes. Not fear of the man with the gun, but fear of what her daughter would be told.

'I know,' Faith told her mother. 'It's all right. I

416

already know.'

The man turned the gun to the side, squinting his eye as he aimed down on her mother. 'What do you know, bitch?'

'You,' Faith told him. 'I know who you are.'

CHAPTER NINETEEN

Will had his eye pressed to the rifle scope when the Tec-9 went off. He saw the flashes first, two bright strobes. A millisecond later, he registered the sound. He flinched away; he couldn't help it. When he looked back in the scope, he saw Faith. She was still standing in the front entrance hall, facing the family room. Her body swayed. He waited, counting the seconds, making sure she didn't fall.

She didn't.

'What the hell happened?'

Roz Levy was on the other side of the Corvair. He looked under the car and found himself staring at the business end of a bright nickel Colt Python. Will didn't know how she managed to keep the thing steady. The gun's barrel was at least six inches long. The .357 magnum load could produce hydrostatic shock, meaning the impact from a chest wound was great enough to cause brain hemorrhaging.

He tried to keep his voice calm. 'Could you please point that somewhere else?'

She drew back the gun and uncocked the hammer. 'Motherfuck,' she mumbled, pushing herself up. 'Here comes Mandy.'

Will saw Amanda running through the backyard.

417

Her shoes were off. She had her walkie-talkie in one hand and her Glock in the other.

'Faith's okay,' he told her. 'She's still in the house. I don't know who—'

'Move,' Amanda ordered, darting past the Corvair and into Roz Levy's house.

Will didn't follow orders. Instead, he used the scope to check Evelyn's hallway again. Faith was still standing there. She had her hands out in front of her, palms down, as if she was trying to reason with somebody. Had the flashes been warning shots or kill shots? The drive-by shooter favored two hits, one right after the other. If they'd killed Evelyn, Faith wouldn't be standing there with her hands out. Will knew in his gut that she'd either be on the floor or on top of the killers if anything happened to her mother.

'Will!' Amanda snarled.

He kept the rifle close to his body as he ran past the car and into the house. The two women were standing in what must've been a screened porch at one time but was now a laundry room. Before he could close the door, Roz Levy started yelling at Amanda.

'Give me back that!' the old woman demanded.

Amanda had the Python. 'You could've killed all of us.' She opened the chamber and ejected the load of .38 Specials onto the dryer. 'I should arrest you right now.'

'I'd like to see you try.'

Roz Levy wasn't the only one who was pissed. Will felt his throat clench around the effort to keep from yelling. 'You said this would be an easy exchange. You said they'd take the money and give Evelyn—'

418

'Shut up, Will.' Amanda spun the empty cylinder back into the revolver and tossed it onto the washer.

She must've taken Will's silence as following orders, but the truth was that he was so furious that he didn't trust himself to speak. Arguing wouldn't change the fact that Faith was stuck in that house without a clear exit plan. There was nothing they could do now except wait for SWAT to show up and pretend this was a hostage negotiation instead of a suicide mission.

Unless Will went in himself. He gripped his rifle. He should go in there. He should do exactly what Faith had done two days before and bust down the door and start shooting.

Amanda's hand clamped around his wrist. 'Don't you dare leave this room,' she warned him. 'I'll shoot you myself if I have to.'

Will's teeth started to ache from grinding together. He pulled away from her, banging into a metal lawn chair in the middle of the room. He couldn't help but take in his surroundings. A high-speed camera was mounted on a tripod, pointing out the window in the door. Roz Levy had covered the glass with black construction paper, leaving a small hole for the lens to peer through. A shotgun was beside the door. No wonder she hadn't allowed Will into the house. She didn't want him obstructing her view.

Will looked into the camera viewfinder. The lens was sharper than his scope. He could see sweat dripping down the side of Faith's face. She was still talking. She was trying to reason with the shooter.

One shooter. One man left standing.

Two bad guys had gone into that house. Both were dressed in black jackets and hats. One had been shot. Will was certain of that, at least. He had watched both kids forcing Evelyn across the lawn and into the house. The one in back had done all of the heavy lifting. He was expendable, just like Ricardo, just like Hironobu Kwon, just like every other man who'd tried to get his hands on Evelyn Mitchell's money.

But it had never been about the money. Chuck Finn wasn't pulling the strings. There was no wizard behind the curtain. Here was the head of Roger Ling's snake: an angry kid with blue eyes and a Tec-9 and some kind of grudge he was intent on carrying out.

Will spoke through clenched teeth. 'It's just him now. This is what he wanted all along.'

'He'll never spend a dime of that money.'

He struggled to keep his voice down. 'He doesn't care about the money.'

'Then what does he care about?' She grabbed his shoulder and jerked him away from the camera. 'Come on, genius. Tell me what he wants.'

Mrs. Levy mumbled, 'You know what he wants.' She was loading the cartridges back into her revolver.

'Zip it, Roz. I've had enough of you for one day.' Amanda glared at Will. 'Enlighten me, Dr. Trent. I'm all ears.'

'He wants to kill her. He wants to kill both of them.' Will finally dropped the biggest I-told-you-so of his life. 'And if you had deigned for once to listen to me, none of this would be happening.'

Anger flared in Amanda's eyes, but she told him, 'Go on. Get it all out.'

420

In the end, it was her acquiescence that sent him over the edge. 'I told you we should slow this down. I told you we should figure out what they really wanted before we sent Faith in there with a target on her back.' He closed the space between them, backing her against the washer. 'You were so hell-bent on proving your dick is bigger than mine that you didn't stop to think that I might be right about something.' Will leaned in close enough to feel her breath on his face. 'Any blood spilled is on your hands, Amanda. *You* did this to Faith. You did this to all of us.'

Amanda turned her head away from him. She didn't answer Will, but he could see the truth in her eyes. She knew that he was right.

Her silent acceptance was no consolation, but Will backed off anyway. He had been looming over her like a bully, clutching his rifle so hard that his hands were shaking. Shame crowded out his anger. He made his grip loosen, his jaw relax.

'Ha,' Mrs. Levy laughed. 'You gonna take that tone from him, Wag?' She had re-loaded the Python. She snapped the cylinder home, telling Will, 'That's what we used to call her—Wag, because she shut up and wagged her tail like a dog every time a man was around.'

Will was shocked by her words, mostly because he couldn't imagine anything that could be further from the truth.

Mrs. Levy hefted the Python in her hands. She told Amanda, 'Talk about swinging your dick around. You could've stopped this twenty years ago if you'd'a had the balls to force Ev to—'

Amanda hissed, 'Spare me your sanctimonious bullshit, Roz. If it wasn't for me standing between

421

you and your cookie recipe, you'd be on death row right now.'

'I warned you when it happened. You don't mix pigeons and bluebirds.'

'You don't know what the hell you're talking about. You never have.' Amanda barked more orders into the walkie-talkie. Her voice shook, which worried Will as much as anything that had happened in the last ten minutes. 'Take out that black van. I want all four tires down. Clear out this block as quickly as you can. Call in APD to gumshoe it and give me an ETA on SWAT within the next five minutes or don't bother showing up for work tomorrow.'

Will put his eye back to the camera. Faith was still talking. At least, her mouth was moving. Her arms were crossed over her chest. Will found his mind working through Roz Levy's mildly racist choice of words: pigeons and bluebirds. Mrs. Levy was full of old adages, like the one she'd told him two days ago: A woman can run faster with her skirt up than a man can with his pants down. It was a strange thing to say about a pregnant fourteen-year-old girl who'd had a baby by the age of fifteen.

Will asked the old woman, 'Why didn't you take that Python over to Evelyn's when you heard the shots the other day?'

She looked down at the gun. There was a bit of petulance in her tone. 'Ev told me not to come over no matter what.'

Will hadn't pegged her as an order-follower, but maybe her bark was worse than her bite. Poisoning was a coward's choice, cold-blooded murder without the inconvenience of getting your hands dirty. He tried to push her toward the truth. 'But

422

you heard gunshots.'

'I assumed Evelyn was taking care of some old business.' She jabbed her thumb Amanda's way. 'Notice she didn't call *her* for help.'

Amanda rested her chin on the walkie-talkie. She was watching Will like she was waiting for a pot to boil. She was always ten steps ahead of him. She knew where his brain was going even before he did.

She told Mrs. Levy, 'I knew Evelyn was seeing Hector again. She told me months ago.'

'Like hell she did. You were as shocked to see that picture as I was when I took it.'

'Does it matter, Roz? After all this time, does it really matter?'

The old woman seemed to think that it did. 'It's not my fault she was willing to gamble away her life for ten seconds of pleasure.'

Amanda laughed, incredulous. 'Ten seconds? No wonder you murdered your husband. Is that all the old bastard could give you—ten seconds?' Her tone was cutting, rueful, the same one she'd used on the phone half an hour ago.

There are other things a man can gamble with besides money.

She was talking about Will and Sara. She was talking about the inherent risks that came with love.

Will turned back to the camera. Faith was still talking. Had Roz Levy set up the camera today, or had it been there all along? The view into the house was clear. What would she have seen two days ago? Evelyn making sandwiches. Hector Ortiz carrying in groceries. They were comfortable around each other. They had a history. A history

423

that Evelyn was trying to hide from her family.

Pigeons and bluebirds.

Will looked up from the camera. 'He's Evelyn's son.'

Both women stopped talking.

Will said, 'Hector's the father, right? That's the mistake Evelyn made twenty years ago. She had a son by Hector Ortiz. Was the bank account used to help support him?'

Amanda sighed. 'I told you, the account doesn't matter.'

Roz made a disgusted sound. 'Well, I'm not going to keep it a secret anymore.' She gleefully told Will, 'She couldn't very well raise a brown baby, could she? I always said just switch it with Faith's. That girl was wild. No one would've been surprised to hear she was running around with some wetback.' She cackled at Will's stunned expression. 'Fast-forward twenty years and she did it anyway.'

'Nineteen years,' Amanda corrected. 'Jeremy's nineteen.' She looked around the room, finally realizing what Roz Levy had been up to. 'Christ,' she mumbled. 'We should've charged you for a front-row seat.'

Will asked, 'What happened?'

Amanda pressed her eye to the camera. 'Evelyn gave the baby to a girl we worked with. Sandra Espisito. She was married to another cop. They couldn't have children of their own.'

'Can we get them here? Maybe they could talk to him.'

She shook her head. 'Paul was shot in the line of duty ten years ago. Sandra died last year. Leukemia. She needed a bone marrow transplant.

424

She had to explain to her son why he couldn't be a donor.' She turned back to Will. 'He looked into his father's side of the family first. I suppose Sandra thought it might be easier. Hector invited him to a get-together. That's how he met Ricardo. That's how he got mixed up in Los Texicanos. He started using drugs. Pot at first, then heroin, then there was no looking back. Evelyn and Hector had him in and out of rehab.'

Will felt a burning in his gut. 'Healing Winds?'

She nodded her head. 'This last time, at least.'

'He met Chuck Finn there.'

'I don't know the details, but I imagine so.'

If Will had known this earlier, there was no way he would've let Faith go into that house alone. He would've tied her up. He would've shoved Amanda inside Mrs. Levy's trunk. He would've called in SWAT from every police force in the country.

Amanda said, 'Go ahead and get it out. I deserve it.'

Will had already wasted enough time yelling at her. 'What does the back of the house look like?'

She couldn't process the question. 'What?'

'The back of the house. Faith is standing in the foyer. She's looking into the family room. The whole back wall is windows and a sliding glass door. You said the curtains were pulled closed. They're thin cotton. Can you see anything like a shadow or movement?'

'No. It's too bright outside and the lights are off inside.'

'When is SWAT supposed to be here?'

'What are you thinking?'

'We need to get the helicopter.'

For once, she didn't ask questions. She got on

425

the walkie-talkie and patched directly into the SWAT commander.

Will pressed his eye to the camera as Amanda negotiated the request. Faith was still standing in the foyer. She wasn't talking anymore. 'Is there some reason you didn't tell me that Evelyn had a love child with Hector Ortiz?'

'Because it would kill Faith,' Amanda told him, seemingly unaware of the irony. Her next words were more directed toward Roz. 'And Evelyn didn't want anyone to know, because it's nobody's damn business.'

Will took out his cell phone.

'What are you doing?'

'I'm calling Faith.'

CHAPTER TWENTY

Faith's cell phone vibrated in her pocket. She didn't move. She just stared at her mother. Tears were streaming down Evelyn's face.

'It's all right,' Faith told her. 'It doesn't matter.'

'Doesn't matter?' the man echoed. 'Thanks a lot, sis.'

Faith flinched at the word. How blind she'd been. How selfish. It all made so much sense now. The extended leave her mother had taken from work. Her father's sudden business trips and angry silences. Evelyn's expanding waistline when she'd never been overweight before or since. The vacation she had taken with Amanda the month before Jeremy was born. Faith had been furious when, after nearly eight months of shared imprisonment, Evelyn had announced that she was going to drive to the beach for a week of fun with Aunt Mandy. Faith had felt betrayed. She had felt abandoned. And now, she felt so stupid.

Remember our time together before Jeremy—

That's what Evelyn had said in the video. She was giving Faith a clue, not strolling down memory lane. *Remember that time. Try to recall what was really going on—not just with you, but with me.*

Back then, Faith had been so wrapped up in herself that all she cared about was her own misery, her own shattered life, her own lost opportunities. Looking back now, she saw the obvious signs. Evelyn wouldn't go outside during the daytime. She wouldn't answer the door. She woke at the crack of dawn to shop at a grocery store on the other side of town. The phone rang plenty of times, but Evelyn refused to answer it. She isolated herself. She cut herself off from the world. She slept on the couch instead of in her marital bed. Except for Amanda, she talked to no one, saw no one, reached out to no one. And all the while, she had given Faith the one thing every child secretly longs for: every ounce of her attention.

And then everything had changed when Evelyn returned from her vacation with Amanda. She called it 'my time away,' like she'd gone down to the springs to take the cure. She was different, happier, as if a burden had been lifted from her shoulders. Faith had seethed with jealousy to find her mother so altered, so seemingly carefree. Before the trip, they had luxuriated in their shared misery, and Faith could not understand how her mother could so easily let it go.

Faith was weeks from delivering Jeremy, but Evelyn's life went back to normal—or as normal as could be expected with a sulky, spoiled, extremely pregnant teenager in the house. She started going back to their regular grocery store. She had lost a few pounds during her time away, and she set about taking off the rest with strict diet and exercise. She forced Faith to take long walks after lunch and eventually started calling old friends, her tone of voice indicating that she'd survived the worst of it and, now that the end was near, was ready to jump back into the fray. Her pillow was no longer on the couch, but back on the bed she shared with her husband. She let the city know she'd be returning after Jeremy was born. She had her hair cut in a new, short style. In general, she started acting like her old self. Or at least a new version of her old self.

There had been cracks in the happy façade, something Faith only now realized.

For the first few weeks of Jeremy's life, Evelyn cried every time she held him. Faith could remember finding her mother sobbing in the rocking chair, holding Jeremy so close that she was afraid the baby couldn't breathe. As with everything, Faith was jealous of the bond between them. She had sought ways to punish her mother, keeping Jeremy away from her. Staying out late with him. Taking him to the mall or the movies or any number of places a baby didn't belong—just to be spiteful. Just to be mean.

And all the while Evelyn had been aching not just for a child, but for *her* child. This angry, soulless young man who now pointed a gun at her head.

Faith felt the phone stop ringing. Almost immediately, it started back again. She told her mother, 'I'm so sorry I wasn't there for you.'

Evelyn shook her head. It didn't matter. But it did.

'I'm so sorry, Mama.'

Evelyn glanced down, then back at Faith. She was sitting on the edge of the chair, her injured leg straight out in front of her. The dead man lay on the floor less than two feet away. The Glock was still stuck in the back of his pants. It might as well be miles away. Evelyn could hardly jump up and grab the gun. Still, she could've reached up and taken off the tape covering her mouth. The adhesive was already detaching. The corners of the silver tape were folding back. Why was she pretending to be silenced? Why was she being so passive?

Faith stared at her mother. What did she want her to do? What *could* she do?

A heavy *thunk* got their attention. They both looked at the man.

One by one, he pushed the remaining books off the shelves. 'What was it like growing up here?'

Faith was silent. She wasn't going to have this conversation.

'Mommy and Daddy sittin' around the hearth.' He kicked the Bible on the floor. Pages fluttered as it flew across the room. 'Musta been real nice coming home every day to milk and cookies.' He kept the gun at his side as he walked toward Evelyn. Halfway there, he turned back, pacing in a tight line. His street slang slipped again. 'Sandra had to work every day. She didn't have time to come home and make sure I was doing my homework.'

Neither had Evelyn. Bill worked from home. It was her father who'd made sure they had snacks and did their book reports.

'You kept all his shit in your closet. What's up with that?'

He meant Jeremy. Faith still didn't answer. Evelyn had made her keep everything because she had known that one day, Faith would cherish it more than anything else save for Emma's things.

She looked at her mother. 'I'm so sorry.'

Evelyn glanced back down at the dead man again, the Glock. Faith didn't know what her mother wanted her to do. He was at least fifteen feet away.

'I asked you a question.' He'd stopped pacing. He stood in the middle of the floor, directly across from Faith. The Tec-9 was pointed straight at Evelyn's head. 'Answer me.'

She wasn't going to tell him the truth, so she gave him the last clue that had clicked it all into place. 'You changed out the lock of hair.'

His smile turned her blood cold. Faith had realized this morning that the strand of Jeremy's hair hadn't darkened with time. The baby blue bow holding the lock of hair together was different from the one that held Jeremy's. The edges were crisp, not frayed, where Faith had rubbed them like a talisman the last few months of her pregnancy with Emma.

The silverware. The pens. The snow globes. Sara was right. It was something a kid would do for attention. When Faith first met the man in the bathroom, she had been so concerned with remembering his description that she hadn't processed what she was seeing. He was Jeremy's age. He was around Faith's height. He had chewed his lip the way Jeremy did. He had Zeke's bully bluster. And he had Evelyn's blue eyes.

The same almond shape. The same deep blue with specks of green.

Faith said, 'Your mother obviously loved you. She kept a lock of your hair.'

'Which mother?' he asked, and Faith was startled by the question.

Had Evelyn kept a lock of his hair for all of these years? Faith had an image of her mother at the hospital, holding her baby for what she knew would be the last time. Was it Amanda who had thought to find a pair of scissors? Had she helped Evelyn clip a piece of hair and tie it in a blue bow? Had Evelyn kept it with her for the last twenty years, taking it out every now and then to feel the soft, baby-fine strands between her fingers?

Of course she had.

You didn't give up a child and not think about him every day, every moment, for the rest of your life. It wasn't possible.

He asked, 'Don't you even want to know my name?'

Faith's knees were shaking. She wanted to sit down, but she knew that she couldn't move. She was standing in the front foyer. The kitchen door was on her left. The front door was behind her. The hall was to her right. At the end of the hall was the bathroom. Beyond that bathroom was Will and his Colt AR-15A2 and his excellent shot, if she could just get this bastard to make a move toward her.

He turned the gun on its side, gangster-style, as

431

he lined up the sights. 'Ask me my name.'

'What's your name?'

'What's your name, *little brother*?'

She tasted bile on her tongue. 'What's your name, little brother?'

'Caleb,' he said. 'Caleb. Ezekiel. Faith. I guess Mommy likes her Bible names.'

She did, which was why Jeremy's middle name was Abraham and Faith's first name was Hannah. Why had Faith chosen Emma's name because it was pretty instead of honoring her mother's tradition? Evelyn had suggested Elizabeth or Esther or Abigail, and Faith had been stubborn just because she didn't know any other way.

'This is where he grew up, too, right?' Caleb waved the gun, indicating the house. 'Your precious Jeremy?'

Faith hated the sound of her child's name in his mouth. She wanted to punch it back down his throat with her fist.

'Watched TV. Read some books. Played some games.' The bottom cabinet of the bookcase was open. He kept one eye on Faith as he pulled out the board games and tossed them on the floor. 'Monopoly. Clue. Life.' He laughed. 'Sorry!'

'What do you want from us?'

'Damn, you sound just like her.' He turned back to Evelyn. 'Ain't that what you said to me, Mommy? 'What do you want from me, Caleb?' Like you can pay me off.' He stared back at Faith. 'She offered me money. What do you think about that? Ten thousand bucks to go away.'

Faith didn't believe him.

'All she cared about was protecting you and your spoiled bitch kid.' The platinum tooth glimmered in the low light. 'You got two kids now, right? Mommy can't keep her little brown baby, but you got no problem keeping yours.'

'It's different now,' she told him. Evelyn's condition may have been a secret, but Faith had brought down enough shame on her family to last a lifetime. Her father had lost longtime clients. Her brother had been forced into exile. What would they have made of Evelyn Mitchell raising a child who was obviously not her husband's? There had been no good choice. Faith could not begin to imagine how her mother had suffered. 'You have no idea what it was like back then.'

'Two for two. Mom said the same thing.' He pointed to her pocket. 'Are you going to get that?'

Her phone had started vibrating again. 'Do you want me to?'

'SOP,' he said. Standard operating procedure. 'They wanna know my demands.'

'What are your demands?'

'Answer the phone and we'll find out.'

She rubbed her hand on her leg to wipe off the sweat, then pulled out the phone. 'Hello?'

Will said, 'Faith, this guy is—'

'I know who he is.' She stared at Caleb, hoping he could see every ounce of hate she had for him. 'He has demands.' She held out the phone to Caleb, praying that he would come get it.

He stood rooted to the floor. 'I want milk and cookies.' He paused as if giving it some more thought. 'I want my mom to be there every day when I get home from school. I want one day to go by where my ass isn't dragged to mass at the crack of dawn and my knees aren't sore from having to pray every night.' His hand swept in an arc toward

433

the bookshelf. 'I want my mom to read books to me about happy goats and moons. You did that with ol' Jaybird, right?'

Faith could barely speak. 'Don't say his name.'

'You took little Jay to the park and to Six Flags and to Disney World and to the beach.'

He must have memorized every picture in Jeremy's keepsake box. How much time had he spent in her home? How many hours had he spent pawing through Jeremy's things? 'Stop saying my son's name.'

'Or what?' He laughed. 'Tell 'em that's what I want. I want y'all to take me to Disney World.'

Faith's arm was shaking from holding out the phone. 'What do you want me to tell him?'

He snorted in disgust. 'Hell, I don't need nothin' right now. I got my family around me. My mom and my big sister. What else do I need?' He went back to the bookcase and leaned against the shelves. 'Life is good.'

Faith cleared her throat. She put the phone back to her ear. 'He has no demands.'

Will asked, 'Are you okay?'

'I—'

'Speakerphone,' Caleb said.

Faith looked down at the phone so she could find the right button. She told Will, 'He can hear you.'

He hesitated. 'Is your mom comfortable? Can she sit down?'

He was asking for clues. 'She's in Dad's chair, but I'm worried about her.' Faith took a deep breath. She kept her eyes on her mother's. 'I might need insulin if this drags on.' Caleb had been in Faith's refrigerator. He would know she was

434

diabetic. 'My blood sugar was at eighteen hundred this morning. Mom only has enough for fifteen hundred. I had my last dose at noon. I'm going to need the next one by ten at the latest or my blood sugar will start swinging back and forth.'

'All right,' he agreed, and she prayed that he really understood the message and wasn't just giving a quick answer.

She said, 'Your phone—' Her mind wasn't quick enough. 'Do we call you on your phone if we need something? Your cell phone?'

'Yes,' he paused. 'We can have your insulin there in five minutes. Just let us know. Let me know.'

Caleb's eyes narrowed. She was talking too much, and neither Will nor Faith was good at this.

'Be careful.' Faith didn't have to pretend to be scared. Her voice shook without any effort on her part. 'He's already killed his partner. He has a—'

'End it,' Caleb said.

Faith tried to find the button.

'End it!' he yelled.

The phone slipped out of her hand. Faith scrambled to get it off the floor. She remembered the revolver on her ankle. The S&W felt cold under her fingers.

'No!' her mother screamed. Her mouth had opened so wide that the tape finally pulled loose. Caleb had the gun jammed into her ribs. His free hand pressed against her broken leg.

'No!' Evelyn screeched. Faith had never heard another human being make that kind of noise. That it was coming from her mother was like a hand reaching straight into her chest and wrenching out her heart.

'Stop!' Faith begged, standing up, holding out

her hands. 'Please, stop! Please, just—please!'

Caleb released the pressure, but he kept his hand hovering over the broken leg. 'Kick the gun over here. Slow, or I might kill the bitch anyway.'

'It's okay.' She knelt down. A tremor rushed through her entire body like a seizure. 'I'm doing what you said. I'm doing exactly what you said.' She lifted her pant leg, then pinched the gun between her thumb and forefinger. 'Don't hurt her anymore. Look.'

'Easy,' he warned.

She slid the gun across the floor at an angle, praying that Caleb would go back to where he'd been standing. He let the gun sail by, staying at Evelyn's side instead.

He said, 'Try something like that again, bitch.'

'I won't,' Faith told him. 'I promise.'

He rested the Tec-9 on the back of the chair, angling the muzzle down toward Evelyn's head. The tape was dangling from her mouth. He ripped it away.

She gulped in air. The breath wheezed in and out of her broken nose.

He warned her, 'Don't get too used to breathing that clean air.'

'Let her go.' Evelyn's voice was raw. 'You don't want her. She had no idea. She was just a child.'

'I was a child, too.'

Evelyn coughed out a spray of blood. 'Just let her go, Caleb. It's me you want to punish.'

'Did you even think about me?' He kept the gun to her head as he knelt down beside her. 'All them times with her bastard little baby, did you even think about me?'

'I never stopped thinking about you. Not a day

went by without—'

'Bullshit.' He stood back up.

'Sandra and Paul loved you like their own flesh and blood. They worshipped you.'

He looked away from her. 'They lied to me.'

'All they ever wanted was for you to be happy.'

'Do I look happy now?' He indicated the dead man on the floor. 'All my friends are gone now. Ricky, Hiro, Dave. All of them. I'm the last one standing.' He seemed to be forgetting his part in the carnage. 'My fake father is dead. My fake mother is dead.'

Evelyn said, 'I know you cried at her funeral. I know you loved Paul and—'

He smacked the back of her head with his open palm. Faith moved without thinking. He waved the gun in her direction and she froze.

She looked back at her mother. Evelyn's head had dropped down. Blood dripped from her mouth. 'I never forgot about you, Caleb. You know that somewhere in your heart.'

He slapped her harder this time.

'Stop,' Faith begged. She didn't know if she was talking to her mother or to Caleb. 'Please just stop.'

Evelyn whispered, 'I always loved you, Caleb.'

He raised the rifle and slammed the butt against the side of her head. The impact knocked over the chair. Evelyn fell hard to the floor. She screamed in pain as her leg twisted around. The broom handle splint broke in two. Bone stuck out of her thigh.

'Mama!' Faith started for her.

There was a pinging sound. Wood kicked up from the floor.

437

Faith froze. She couldn't tell if she'd been shot. All she could see was her mother on the floor, Caleb standing above her with his fist clenched. He kicked Evelyn. Hard.

'Please stop,' Faith pleaded. 'I promise—'

'Shut up.' He looked up at the ceiling. At first, Faith didn't recognize the sound. It was a helicopter. The blades chopped through the air, shaking her eardrums.

Caleb had the Tec-9 pointed at Faith now. He had to raise his voice to be heard. 'That was a warning shot,' he told her. 'Next one goes right between your eyes.'

She looked down at the floor. There was a hole in the wood. She took a step back, swallowed the cry that wanted to come out of her throat. The chopping sound receded as the helicopter pulled up. Faith could barely speak. 'Please don't hurt her. You can do anything to me, but please . . .'

'Oh, I'm gonna hurt you soon enough, sister girl. I'm gonna hurt you real bad.' He held up his arms as if he was on stage. 'That's what this is all about, yo. I'm gonna show your precious baby boy what it's like to grow up without his mama.' He kept the gun on Faith. 'You were good yesterday running after him in the street. A little closer and I'd'a had him dead on the ground.'

Vomit came into her mouth.

He pushed Evelyn with his sneaker. 'Ask her why she gave me up.'

Faith didn't trust her mouth to open.

'Ask her why she gave me up,' Caleb repeated. He raised his foot, ready to kick her mother's shattered leg.

'Okay!' Faith yelled. 'Why did you give him up?'

438

Caleb said, 'Why did you give him up, *Mom*?'

'Why did you give him up, Mom?'

Evelyn didn't move. Her eyes were closed. Just as the panic started to well up inside Faith, her mother's mouth opened. 'I didn't have a choice.'

'Yo, ain't that what you've been saying to me for the last year, Mom? Everybody's got choices?'

'It was a different time.' Her good eye opened. The lashes stuck together. She stared at Faith. 'I'm so sorry, baby.'

Faith shook her head. 'You have nothing to apologize for.'

'Ain't this nice. A little mother-daughter reunion here.' He shoved the chair so hard against the wall that the back leg broke. 'She was ashamed of me, that's why.' He paced over to the bookcase and back. 'She couldn't explain some little brown baby squirting outta her. Not like you, right? Different times.' He started pacing again. 'And you think your daddy was so good growing up. Tell her what he said, Mom. Tell her what he made you do.'

Evelyn lay on her side, eyes closed, arms out in front of her. The shallow in-and-out of her chest was the only thing that indicated she was still alive.

'Your good ol' daddy told her it was me or him. What do you think about that? Mr. Galveston Insurance Agent of the Year for six years running and he told your mama that she couldn't keep her baby boy, because if she did, she'd never see her other kids again.'

Faith struggled not to show that he'd finally managed to hit the mark. She had adored her father, worshipped him like only a spoiled daddy's girl can, but as an adult, she could easily see Bill Mitchell giving her mother this ultimatum.

439

Caleb had moved back to his original spot near the bookcase. The gun was down at his side, but she knew he could swing it up at any moment. His back was to the sliding glass doors. Evelyn was to his left. Faith was at a diagonal, about twelve feet away from him and waiting for all hell to break loose.

She prayed Will had understood her message. The room was a clock. Faith was at eighteen hundred, or six o'clock. Evelyn was at fifteen hundred, three o'clock. Caleb was swinging back and forth between ten and twelve.

Faith had offered at least twenty times over the last month to take Will's cell phone off military time. He kept refusing because he was stubborn and full of an odd mixture of shame and pride where his disability was concerned. He was also watching her through the bathroom window right now. He had told her to give him a sign. She ran her fingers through her hair, pulling her thumb and index finger into an okay sign.

Faith looked down at her mother lying on the floor. Evelyn was staring at her with her one good eye. Had she seen Faith give Will the signal? Was she capable of understanding what was going to happen? Her breaths were labored. Her lips were blistered. She had obviously been choked. Dark bruises circled her neck. There was a cut on the side of her head. Blood seeped from an angry gash in her cheek. Faith felt a rush of love wash through her, straight to where her mother lay. It was like a light shining out from her body. How many times had Faith gone to this woman for help? How many times had she cried on her shoulder?

So many times that Faith had lost count.

Evelyn raised her hand. Her fingers trembled. She covered her face. Faith turned around. A blinding bright light came through the front windows. It pierced the flimsy blinds, shining a spotlight inside the house.

Faith ducked down. Maybe muscle memory recalled some training exercise from years past. Maybe it was human nature to make yourself as small as possible when you sensed something bad was about to happen.

Nothing happened in the immediate. Seconds went by. Faith found herself counting, '. . . two . . . three . . . four . . .'

She looked up at Caleb.

Glass shattered. He jerked as if someone had punched him in the shoulder. His expression was a mixture of shock and pain. Faith pushed herself off the floor. She lunged toward Caleb. He pointed the gun at her face. She looked straight into the threaded muzzle, the dark eye of the snubbed barrel, staring back. Rage took hold, burning inside of her, urging her forward. She wanted to kill this man. She wanted to rip open his throat with her teeth. She wanted to cut his heart out of his chest. She wanted to watch the pain in his eyes as she did everything to him that he had done to her mother, her family, their lives.

But she would never get the chance.

The side of Caleb's head exploded. His arms jerked up. Bullets fired from the Tec-9 brought down a rain of white chalk from the ceiling. Muscle memory. Two pops, close together, one after the other.

Slowly, he collapsed to the ground. The only thing Faith could hear was the sound of his body slamming into the floor. First his hip, then his shoulder, then his head popping against the hard wood. His eyes stayed open. Dark blue. So familiar. So lifeless.

So long.

Faith looked at her mother. Evelyn had managed to prop herself up against the wall. She still held the Glock in her right hand. The muzzle started to tilt down. The weight was too much. She dropped her arm. The gun clattered to the floor.

'Mama . . .' Faith could barely stand. She half walked, half crawled to her mother. She didn't know where to touch her, which part of her body wasn't bruised or broken.

'Come here,' Evelyn whispered. She pulled Faith into her arms. She stroked her back. Faith couldn't help it. She started to weep like a child. 'It's all right, baby.' Evelyn pressed her lips to the top of Faith's head. 'Everything's going to be all right.'

THURSDAY

CHAPTER TWENTY-ONE

Will tucked his hands into his pockets as he walked down the hallway to Evelyn Mitchell's hospital room. He was almost giddy with exhaustion. His vision was so sharp that the world was his Blu-ray. There was a high-pitched whine in his ear. He could feel every pore in his skin. This was why he never drank coffee. Will felt wired enough to power a small city. He had spent the last three nights with Sara. His feet barely touched the ground.

He stopped outside Evelyn's room, wondering if he should've brought flowers. Will had cash in his wallet. He turned around, heading back toward the elevators. He could at least get her a balloon from the gift shop. Everybody liked balloons.

'Hey.' Faith pushed open her mother's door. 'Where are you going?'

'Does your mom like balloons?'

'I'm sure she did when she was seven.'

Will smiled. The last time he'd seen Faith, she was crying in her mother's arms. She looked a little better now, but not by much. 'How's she doing?'

'Okay. Last night was slightly better than the one before, but the pain is still bad.'

Will could only imagine. Evelyn had been rushed to Grady with a full police escort. She'd been in surgery over sixteen hours. They'd put enough metal in her leg to fill a deluxe erector set.

He asked, 'What about you?'

'It's a lot to take in.' Faith shook her head, as if she still couldn't make sense of it. 'I always wanted another brother, but that was only because I thought he might beat up Zeke.'

'Seems like you can take care of yourself.'

'It's a lot more work than you'd think.' She leaned her shoulder against the wall. 'It must've been so hard for her. What she went through. I can't imagine giving up one of my children. I'd just as soon rip out my heart.'

Will looked over her shoulder at the empty hallway.

'I'm sorry. I wasn't thinking about—'

'It's okay,' he told her. 'You know, a surprising number of orphans end up in the penal system.' He gave her some of the better examples. 'Albert DeSalvo. Ted Bundy. Joel Rifkin. Son of Sam.'

'I think Aileen Wuornos was given up by her parents, too.'

'I'll let the others know. It's good to have a woman on the list.'

She laughed, but obviously her heart wasn't into it. Will looked over her shoulder again. There was a large nurse with a bouquet of flowers walking down the hall.

Faith said, 'I was sure that we weren't going to make it out of that house.'

There was something in her voice that told him she still wasn't past what had happened to her family. Maybe she never would be. Some things never left you, no matter how hard you tried.

Will said, 'We should really get better codes in case this happens again.'

'I was terrified you wouldn't understand. Thank God we had all those arguments about changing your phone off military time.'

'Actually, I didn't understand.' He grinned at her

446

shocked expression. Will had kept his cell on speakerphone while he talked to Faith. Roz Levy had rendered her opinion as soon as the call ended, telling them the room was a clock and that she'd be more than happy to run over there with her Python and take out the punk standing at noon.

Will told Faith, 'I'd like to think that I would've figured it out eventually.'

'You realize that a blood sugar of eighteen hundred would probably mean I was either dead or in an irreversible coma?'

'Sure, I knew that.'

'Jesus Christ,' she whispered. 'So much for our well-oiled machine.'

He felt the need to tell her, 'The helicopter was all me. The infrared camera told us where you were, confirmed that his partner was dead.' She didn't seem impressed, so Will added, 'And the lights were my idea.' They'd lined up two squad cars and blasted their xenon lights at the front windows. Caleb's shadow against the curtains had given them something to aim for.

'Well, thanks anyway for shooting him.' She could obviously read his expression. 'Oh, Will, it wasn't you?'

He let out a long breath. 'Amanda promised me she'd give me one of my testicles back if I let her take the shot.'

'I hope you got that in writing. She didn't exactly hit a bull's-eye.'

'She blames my rifle. Something about me being left-handed.'

The grip was universal, but Faith didn't argue. 'Well, I'm glad you were there. It made me feel

447

safer.'

He smiled, though he was fairly certain all of this could've happened without his presence. Amanda was resourceful, and Will had basically hidden behind a wall while Faith risked her life.

She said, 'I'm glad you're with Sara.'

He fought the silly grin that wanted to come. 'I'm just hanging in there until she decides she can do better.'

'I wish I thought you were joking.'

So did Will. He didn't understand Sara. He didn't know what made her tick or why she was with him. And yet, she was. And not just that—she seemed to be happy about it. Sara had been smiling so much this morning that she could barely purse her lips to kiss him goodbye. Will had thought maybe some toilet paper was stuck to his face where he'd cut himself shaving, but she'd told him that she was smiling because he made her happy.

He didn't know what to do with that. It didn't make sense.

Faith knew how to stop the grin on his face. 'What about Angie?'

He shrugged, as if Angie hadn't left so many messages on his home and cell phone that both voicemail boxes had run out of space. Each message got nastier and nastier. Each threat more severe. Will had listened to every message. He couldn't help himself. He could still see Angie with that gun in her mouth. He could still feel his heart rattle at the thought of pushing open his bathroom door and finding her bleeding out in his bathtub.

Thankfully, Faith didn't dwell for long on the negative. 'Have you told Sara you're terrified of chimpanzees?'

'It hasn't really come up.'

'It will eventually. That's what happens in relationships. Everything comes up whether you like it or not.'

Will nodded, hoping his quick acquiescence would shut her up. He wasn't that lucky.

'Look.' She put on her mom voice, the one she used when he wasn't standing up straight or wore the wrong tie. 'The only way you're going to screw this up is if you keep worrying about screwing it up.'

Will would rather be stuck in Mrs. Levy's trunk again than have this conversation. 'It's Betty I'm worried about.'

'Really.'

'She's become quite attached.' That much was true. The dog had refused to leave Sara's apartment this morning.

'Just promise me that you'll wait at least a month before you tell her that you're in love with her.'

He let out a stream of breath, longing for the isolation of the Corvair. 'Did you know that Bayer used to own the trademark for heroin?'

She shook her head at the subterfuge. 'The aspirin company?'

'They lost the trademark after World War I. It's in the Treaty of Versailles.'

'You learn something new every day.'

'Sears used to sell preloaded syringes of heroin in their catalogue. A buck fifty for two.'

She put her hand on his arm. 'Thank you, Will.'

He patted the back of her hand once, then again, because just once was probably not enough.

449

'It's Roz Levy you should thank. She's the one who figured it out.'

'She's not quite the sweet little old lady, is she?'

There was an understatement. The old biddy had made sport of watching Evelyn's worst nightmare play out. 'She's a bit of a devil.'

'Did she give you her 'pigeons and bluebirds' lecture?' Faith turned around when she heard talking. The door to her mother's room opened. Jeremy came out, followed by a tall man with a military haircut and a square jaw that instantly brought to mind the word *jarhead*. He held Emma on one of his broad shoulders. The baby looked like a sack of frozen peas hanging off a skyscraper. Her body gave a slight jerk as she hiccupped.

'This should be fun.' Faith pushed away from the wall with a groan. 'Will, this is my brother Zeke. Zeke, this is—'

'I know who this douche is.'

Will extended his hand. 'I've heard a lot about you.'

Emma hiccupped. Zeke glowered. He didn't shake Will's hand.

Will tried for light conversation. 'I'm glad that your mother's okay.'

He kept glowering. Emma hiccupped again. Will felt bad for the man. As the owner of a Chihuahua, he knew the difficulties of acting tough while holding something impossibly tiny in your hand.

Jeremy saved them from their staring contest. 'Hey, Will. Thanks for coming.'

Will shook his hand. He was a scrawny-looking kid, but he had a strong grip. 'I hear your grandma's doing better.'

'She's tough.' He draped his arm around Faith's

shoulders. 'Just like my mom.'

Emma hiccupped.

'Let's go, Uncle Zeke.' Jeremy grabbed him by the elbow. 'I told Grandma we'd move my bed downstairs so Mom can take care of her when she gets out of the hospital.'

Zeke took his time breaking eye contact. Emma's continued hiccups probably had something to do with his decision to follow his nephew down the hall.

'Sorry,' Faith apologized. 'He can be a bit of an asshole. I don't know how it happened, but Emma loves him.'

Probably because she couldn't understand a word he said.

Faith asked, 'Do you want to go ahead and talk to Mom?'

'I was just here to check on you.'

'She's already asked for you a couple of times. I think she wants to talk about it.'

'She can't talk about it with you?'

'I've got the gist. There's no reason for me to know the gory details.' She forced a smile onto her face. 'Amanda told her that she promised you an hour.'

'I didn't think that'd actually happen.'

'They've been best friends for forty years. They keep each other's promises.' She patted his arm again and started to leave. 'Thanks for coming.'

'Wait.' Will reached into his jacket pocket and pulled out the envelope that had come in the mail this morning. 'I've never gotten a letter before. I mean, other than bills.'

She studied the sealed envelope. 'You didn't open it.'

451

Will didn't need to. She would never know how much it meant to him that she'd known that he could read the letter. 'Do you want me to open it?'

'Hell no.' She snatched it out of his hand. 'It's bad enough Zeke and Jeremy saw those videos I made. I had no idea I was such an ugly crier.'

Will couldn't disagree.

'Anyway.' She looked down at her watch. 'I need to take my insulin and eat something. I'll be in the cafeteria if you need me.'

Will watched Faith walk down the hallway. She stopped in front of the elevator and looked back at him. While he was watching, she tore the letter in two, then tore it again. Will saluted her, then pushed open the door to Evelyn's room. Almost every surface was covered with flowers of all kinds. Will felt his nose start to itch from the heavy perfume smell.

Evelyn Mitchell turned her head toward him. She was lying in bed. Her broken leg was elevated, Frankenstein bolts jutting out of a hard cast. Her hand rested on a foam wedge. Gauze was packed where her ring finger should've been. Tubes ran in and out of her body. The gash on her cheek was held together with white butterfly tape. She looked smaller than he remembered, but then, what she had been through was the sort of thing that could reduce a person.

Her lips were chapped and raw. She held her jaw still, talking with as little movement as possible. Her voice was stronger than he'd imagined it would be. 'Agent Trent.'

'Captain Mitchell.'

She showed him the trigger for the morphine pump. 'I've held off on this because I wanted to

452

talk to you.'

'You don't have to. I don't want to cause you any more pain.'

'Then please sit down. It hurts my neck to look up at you.'

There was already a chair pulled up beside her bed. Will sat down. 'I'm glad that you're well.'

Her lips barely moved. 'Well is a bit down the road. Let's just say I'm hanging in there.'

'Beats the alternative.'

She said, 'Mandy told me about your part in all of this.' Will assumed that had been a very short conversation. 'Thank you for looking out for my daughter.'

'I think you get more credit for that than I do.'

Her eyes watered. He wasn't sure whether it was from pain or the thought of losing Faith.

And then he remembered that she had lost another child, too. 'I'm sorry for your loss.'

She swallowed with obvious difficulty. The skin on her neck was nearly black with bruises. Evelyn Mitchell had been forced twice now to choose between her family with Bill Mitchell and the son she'd had with Hector Ortiz. Both times, she had made the same decision. Though Caleb had made it pretty easy for her the last time.

She said, 'He was a very troubled young man. I didn't know how to make it better. He was so angry.'

'You don't have to talk about it.'

A gravelly chuckle came from her throat. 'No one wants me to talk about him. I think they'd rather he just disappear.' She indicated the cup of water on the table. 'Could you—'

Will picked up the cup and angled the straw so

453

that she could drink. She couldn't lift her head. Gently, Will reached around and supported her.

She drank for almost a full minute before releasing the straw. 'Thank you.'

Will sat back down. He stared at the bouquet of flowers on the table across from him. There was a business card attached to the white bow. He recognized the logo from the Atlanta Police Department.

Evelyn said, 'Hector was a CI.' Confidential informant. 'He snitched on his cousin. They were in this gang, and it had started as something small, a reason to break into cars and snatch purses so they could play video games, and then it got really mean really fast.'

'Los Texicanos.'

She nodded slowly. 'Hector wanted out. He kept talking and I kept listening because it was good for my career.' She waved her good hand in the air. 'And then one thing led to another.' Her eyes closed. 'I was married to an insurance salesman. He was a very kind man and a very good father, but . . .' Breath stuttered through her lips as she sighed. 'You know how it is when you're out there in the street chasing down bad guys and your heart is pounding and you feel like you've got the whole world bucking between your legs, and then you go home and—what?—cook dinner? Iron shirts and give the kids a bath?'

'Were you in love with Hector?'

'No.' She was firm in her answer. 'Never. And the strange thing is, I didn't realize how much I was in love with Bill until I had hurt him so badly that I was going to lose him.'

'But he stayed with you.'

454

'On his terms,' she told him. 'I was out of the negotiations by then. He met with Hector. They came to a gentleman's agreement.'

'The bank account.'

She turned her gaze toward the ceiling. Slowly, her eyes closed. He thought she had fallen asleep until she started talking again. 'Sandra and Paul had a lot of debt from helping her family back home. They couldn't afford a child, even if they could've had one of their own. Part of the money in the account was from Hector. Part of it was from me. Ten percent of every paycheck I got went to Caleb. It was like tithing, only not for the church—but still for penance.' The corner of her mouth went up slightly in something like a smile. 'Though I suppose that Sandra gave a lot of that money to the church every week. They were very religious. Catholic, but that didn't bother me like it bothered Bill. I thought they would give him a strong moral foundation.' The sound of laughter came from her mouth. 'So much for that.'

'Caleb found out about you when Sandra got sick?'

She looked at Will. 'I got a call from her. She sounded like she was warning me, which didn't make sense at the time, so I ignored it. The first time I saw him as a grown man was at her funeral.' She shook her head at the memory. 'God, he looked just like Zeke at that age. More handsome, if you want to know the truth. More angry, which was the problem.' Her head kept moving side to side. 'I didn't see how angry he was until it was too late. I had no idea.'

'Did you talk to Caleb at the funeral?'

'I tried to start a conversation, but he just

walked away. A few weeks later I was cleaning the house and I noticed things were out of place. My office had been searched. He did a very good job. I wouldn't have noticed if not for the fact that I was looking for a particular thing.' She explained, 'I kept a lock of his baby hair hidden somewhere the children didn't know about. I went to look for it, and it was gone. I should've known then. I should've realized how obsessed he was with me. How much he hated me.'

Evelyn stopped to catch her breath. Will could see that she was tired. But still, she continued. 'I called Hector to meet. We'd been in touch since Sandra got sick. There wasn't much time to catch up. We'd go to a Starbucks down by the airport so nobody would see us. It was the same as before—all that hiding. All that sneaking around so that my family wouldn't find out.' She closed her eyes again. 'Caleb was constantly in trouble. I tried everything with him—even offered to give him money so that he could go to college. Faith's struggling to help Jeremy with his tuition, and here I was offering this boy a full ride. He just laughed in my face.' Her tone turned sharp, angry. 'The next day, I got a call from an old friend in narcotics. They'd picked up Caleb with some serious weight on him. I had to get Mandy to pull some strings. She didn't want to. She said he'd been given too many chances already. But I begged her.'

'Heroin?'

'Coke,' she corrected. 'Heroin would've been beyond my reach, but the coke we could work with. They knocked it down because we agreed to send him to rehab.'

'You sent him to Healing Winds.'

'Hector lives a few miles from there. His cousin's boy had been at the facility, Ricardo. And Chuck was there. Poor Chuck.' She stopped, swallowing to clear her throat. 'He called me at the beginning of this year to make amends. He's been sober for eight months now. I knew that he was doing some counseling work at Healing Winds, and I thought Caleb would be safe there.'

'Chuck shared his story with them.'

'Apparently, that's one of the steps. He told them about the money. And of course, even though Chuck assured them that I had nothing to do with it, they didn't believe him.'

'It was Chuck in the hospital that day. He was the cop who asked Sara whether or not the kid was going to make it.'

She nodded. 'He saw what happened to me on the news and came down to see if he could help. He didn't stop to realize that with his record, no one would want his help. I've asked Mandy to try to smooth things over with his parole officer. It was really me who got him into trouble. My guys have always stood up for me, even when it wasn't in their best interest.'

'Do you think Caleb thought you were on the take like the rest of them?'

She was obviously surprised by the question. 'No, Agent Trent. I really don't think he did. He had this preconceived notion of me as cold and uncaring, the mother who never loved him. He said that the only thing he'd inherited from me was my black heart.'

Will remembered the song that had been playing when Faith pulled up to her mother's

457

house. ' "Back in Black." '

'It was his theme song. He kept insisting I listen to the words, though who the hell knows what all that screeching is?'

'It's about taking revenge on the people who've given up on you.'

'Ah.' She seemed relieved to finally understand. 'He played it over and over again on my kitchen radio. And then Faith came and the music stopped. I was terrified. I don't think I've ever held my breath for that long. But they didn't want Faith. Not Caleb's crew, at any rate. Benny Choo told them that he would handle everything. He kept Ricardo back with him. The H inside him was much too valuable, but he told the other boys to take me and leave, so they did.'

Will wanted to be sure about the sequence. 'Caleb was there at the same time as Faith?'

'He looked at her out the window.' Evelyn's voice trembled. 'I have never been so frightened in my life. Not before that, anyway.'

Will was more than familiar with that kind of fear. 'What happened before Faith came? You were making sandwiches, right?'

'I knew Faith would be late. Those sessions usually run long. There's always some jackass in the first row who wants to show off.' She was silent for a moment, collecting her thoughts. 'Hector came to get me at the grocery store. He knew my routines. That's the sort of man he was. He paid attention when you told him something.' She was silent a moment, perhaps in honor of her former lover. 'He'd gone to visit Caleb at rehab and been told that he'd checked himself out. They don't lock them down. Caleb just walked out. We shouldn't've

458

been surprised. I had already made some calls and figured out that Ricardo was getting himself mixed up in things that were not going to be good for any of them.'

'Heroin.'

She let out a slow breath. 'Hector and I put it together as I drove him back to the house. We knew that Ricardo was working at Julia's shop, just like we knew that nothing good was going to come out of any of these boys getting together. *Folie à plusieurs.*'

Will had heard the phrase before. It referred to a psychological syndrome where a group of seemingly normal people developed a shared psychosis when they were together. The Manson Family. The Branch Davidians. There was always an unstable leader at the center of the sickness. Roger Ling had called it the head of the snake. A man like Roger Ling should know.

Evelyn said, 'Part of me wanted Faith to come home early. I wanted her to meet Hector, so I would be forced into explaining.'

'Did Caleb kill Hector?'

'I think it must've been him. It was sneaky, and cowardly. I heard the gun—you don't forget the sound a silencer makes once you've heard it before—and I looked out into the carport. The trunk was closed and there was no one there. I didn't think twice. Maybe I had thought this was going to happen all along. I scooped up Emma and took her into the shed. I came back with my gun and there was a man in the laundry room. I shot him before he could open his mouth. And then I turned around and there was Caleb.'

'You struggled with him?'

'I couldn't shoot him. He was unarmed. He was my son. But I got the better of him.' She looked down at her wounded hand. 'I don't think he was expecting me to be so aggressively opposed to his trying to cut off my finger.'

'He cut it off right then?' Will had assumed it was part of a later negotiation.

'One of the other boys sat on my back while Caleb cut it off. He used the bread knife. He sawed it back and forth like you'd do with a tree. I think he enjoyed hearing me scream.'

'How did you get the knife away from him?'

'I don't really know. It's one of those things that happens without your thinking about it. Actually, I don't remember much of what came next, but I do recall that other boy falling on top of me, and the feel of that knife going into his stomach.' She exhaled sharply. 'I ran into the carport to get Emma and get the hell out of there. And then I heard Caleb screaming. "Mama, Mama."' She paused for another moment. 'He sounded like he was hurt. I don't know what made me go back inside. It was instinctual, like with the knife, but that was self-preservation, and this was self-destruction.' She obviously still struggled with the memory. 'I was aware of it—how wrong it was. I remember thinking quite clearly as I ran past my car and back into the house that this was one of the stupidest things I would ever do in my life. And I was right. But I couldn't stop myself. I heard him crying for me, and I just ran back inside.'

She paused again for breath. Will could see that the angle of the sun had changed so that it was shining into her eyes. He got up and tilted down the blinds.

She breathed out an exhausted-sounding 'Thank you.'

'Do you want to rest?'

'I want to finish this, and then I never want to talk about it again.'

That sounded exactly like the kind of thing Faith would say. Will knew better than to argue. He sat down in the chair, waiting for her to continue.

Evelyn didn't start back immediately. For a full minute, she just lay there, her chest rising and falling as she breathed.

Finally, she said, 'For about three years after he was born, around once a month, I'd tell Bill and the kids I had to go do paperwork at the office. Usually it was a Sunday while they were at church, because it was easier.' She coughed. Her voice was getting raspier. 'But I'd really go to the park up the street, and I would sit on that bench by myself, or if it was raining, I would sit in my car, and I would just cry and cry. Not even Mandy knew about it. I've shared everything in my life with her, but not this.' She gave Will a meaningful look. 'You don't know how hard it was for her with Kenny. She couldn't give him children, and he wanted a family. His own blood. He was very insistent about that. Telling her about how I longed for Caleb would've been cruel.'

Will felt a little squeamish hearing something so personal about his boss. He tried to get Evelyn back to the day she'd been abducted. 'Caleb tricked you to get you back into the house. That's why you didn't take Emma and leave?'

She was silent long enough to let him know that she was aware he was changing the subject. 'You can't fool someone who doesn't want to be fooled.'

461

Will wasn't so sure about that, but he nodded anyway.

'I ran into the kitchen. There was Benny Choo. Of course it was Benny Choo. Carnage everywhere. He was in his element. We had a bit of a struggle, which he won, mostly because he had help. He wanted the money. Everybody wanted the money. The place was filled with angry men demanding money.'

'Except Caleb,' Will guessed.

'Except Caleb,' she confirmed. 'He just sat on the couch eating sandwich meat right out of the bag, watching them run around and tear apart my house. I think he loved it. I think it was the most fun he had ever had in his life—watching me sitting there, scared to death, while his friends ran around like chickens with their heads cut off looking for something that he knew wasn't there.'

'What about the *A* on the bottom of the chair?'

She gave a stuttered laugh. 'That was an arrow. I assumed that the crime scene techs would find it. I wanted them to know that the main culprit was sitting on the couch. Caleb must've left hair, fiber, fingerprints.'

Will wondered if Ahbidi Mittal's team would've figured out the message. Will had certainly botched the job.

She asked, 'Tell me, did they really dig up my backyard?'

Will realized she meant Caleb's crew, not Ahbidi Mittal's. 'You told them the money was there?'

She chuckled, probably thinking about the boys running around in the dark with shovels. 'I thought it seemed plausible, inasmuch as it's happened in the movies.'

Will didn't confess that he'd seen too many of those movies himself.

Abruptly, Evelyn's demeanor changed. She looked back at the ceiling. The tiles were stained brown. It wasn't much of a view. Will recognized an avoidance technique when he saw one.

She whispered, 'I keep struggling with the fact that I killed my son.'

'He was going to kill you. And Faith. He killed countless more people.'

She kept staring at the tiles. 'Mandy told me not to talk to you about the shooting.'

Will knew that Caleb Espisito's death was being reviewed by the police, but he assumed Evelyn would be cleared in a few days, just as Faith had been. 'It was self-defense.'

She let out a slow breath. 'I think he wanted me to make a choice between the two of them. Between him and Faith.'

Will didn't confirm that he shared this opinion.

'He could forgive his father. Hector had a nice life, but he never married and he never had another child. But when Caleb saw what *I* had—what I had struggled to build back with Bill and the children—he resented the hell out of it. He hated me so much.' Her eyes glistened with tears. 'I remember one of the last things I told him before all of this happened was that holding on to that kind of grudge was like drinking poison and waiting for the other person to die.'

Will guessed this was the kind of advice mothers gave their sons. Unfortunately, he'd had to learn that lesson the hard way. 'Do you remember anything about where they kept you?'

'It was a warehouse. Abandoned, I'm sure. I yelled enough to wake the dead.'

'How many men were there?'

'At the house? I think eight. There were only three at the warehouse, counting Caleb. Juan and David were their names. They tried not to use them, but they weren't very sophisticated, if you get my meaning.'

Juan Castillo had been shot outside of Julia Ling's warehouse. David Herrera had been shot in cold blood right in front of Evelyn and Faith. Benny Choo, Hironobu Kwon, Hector Ortiz, Ricardo Ortiz. In all, eight people were dead now because of one man's twenty-year grudge.

Evelyn must have been thinking the same thing. Her voice took on a desperate tone. 'Do you think I could've stopped him?'

Short of killing Caleb before it happened, Will didn't see how. 'Hate like that doesn't burn out.'

She didn't seem comforted. 'Bill thought what happened with Faith was my fault. He said that because I was with Hector, I took my eye off my children. Maybe he was right.'

'Faith is pretty determined to do her own thing.'

'You think she takes after me.' She waved away Will's protest. 'No, she is *exactly* like me. God help her.'

'There are worse things.'

'Hm.' Evelyn's eyes closed again. Will stared at her face. Her features were almost obscured by the swelling. She was about Amanda's age, the same kind of cop, but not the same kind of woman. Will hadn't spent a lot of his life feeling envious of other people's parents. It was a waste of time to think about what could've been. But talking to

464

Evelyn Mitchell, knowing the sacrifices she had made for all of her children, Will couldn't help but feel a little jealous.

He stood, thinking he should let her sleep, but Evelyn's eyes opened. She pointed to the pitcher of water. Will helped her drink from the straw. She wasn't as thirsty this time, but Will saw her hand clench around the morphine trigger.

'Thank you.' She put her head back on the pillow. She pressed the trigger again.

Will didn't take his seat. 'Can I get you anything else before I leave?'

She either didn't hear the question or chose to ignore it. 'I know Mandy is hard on you, but it's because she loves you.'

Will felt his eyebrows shoot up. The morphine had started working fast.

'She's so proud of you, Will. She brags about you all the time. How smart you are. How strong. You're like a son to her. In more ways than you know.'

He felt the need to glance over his shoulder in case Amanda was laughing from the doorway.

Evelyn said, 'She *should* be proud of you. You're a good man. And I wouldn't want my daughter partnered with anyone else. I was so happy when you two got together. I only wish it had turned into something more.'

He checked the door one more time. No Amanda. When he turned back around, Evelyn was staring at him.

She asked, 'May I be honest with you?'

He nodded, though Will wondered if that meant she hadn't been honest so far.

'I know you've had a difficult life. I know how

465

hard you've worked to turn yourself into the right kind of person. And I know you deserve happiness. And it's not going to come from your wife.'

As usual, Will's first impulse was to take up for Angie. 'She's been through a lot.'

'You deserve so much better.'

He felt the need to tell her, 'I've got some demons of my own.'

'But yours are the good demons, the kind that make you stronger for having them.' She tried to smile. ' "If I got rid of my demons, I'd lose my angels." '

He took a wild guess. 'Hemingway?'

'Tennessee Williams.'

The door opened. Amanda tapped her watch. 'Time's up.' She waved for him to leave.

Will looked at the clock on his cell phone. She'd given him exactly an hour. 'How did you even know I was here?'

'Walk and talk.' She clapped her hands together. 'Our girl needs her rest.'

Will touched Evelyn's elbow because that was the only place that wasn't bandaged or hooked up to something. 'Thank you, Captain Mitchell.'

'Take care of yourself, Agent Trent.'

Amanda gave Will a shove as he left the room. He almost knocked down a nurse in the hallway.

Amanda said, 'You tired her out.'

'She wanted to talk.'

'She's been through a lot.'

'Are there going to be any problems on her shooting Caleb Espisito?'

Amanda shook her head. 'The only person who should be worried is Roz Levy. If it was left to me, I'd have her up on obstruction charges.'

Will didn't disagree, but Mrs. Levy had perfected her old lady act. No jury in the world would ever convict her.

'I'll get the old hag eventually,' Amanda promised. 'She's like a stick—always stirring up shit.'

'Right.' Will tried to wrap this up. Sara had gotten off work five minutes ago. This morning, he'd suggested they have lunch together, but he wasn't sure she would remember. He told Amanda, 'I'll see you tomorrow.' He started walking toward the elevator. To his dismay, Amanda followed him.

She asked, 'What did Evelyn tell you?'

He lengthened his strides, trying to lose her, or at least make her have to work for it. 'The truth, I hope.'

'I'm sure it was buried in there somewhere.'

Will hated that she could so easily sow doubt in his mind. Evelyn Mitchell was Amanda's best friend, but the two women were nothing alike. Evelyn didn't play games. She didn't take pleasure in humiliating people. 'I think she told me what I needed to know.' He punched the down button on the elevator. He couldn't resist. 'She said that you were proud of me.'

Amanda laughed. 'Well, that doesn't sound like me at all.'

'No.' A thought occurred to Will. Maybe Evelyn had been dancing around the truth after all. Had she secretly given him a clue? Will felt a wave of nausea come over him.

You're like a son to her. In more ways than you know.

He turned to Amanda, preparing himself for the

467

worst day of his life. 'Are you going to tell me that you're really my mother?'

Her laugh echoed down the hallway. She braced her hand against the wall so she wouldn't fall over.

'All right.' He punched the button for the elevator again. And again. And then a third time. 'I get it. Very funny.'

She wiped tears from her eyes. 'Oh, Will, do you really think a child of mine would turn out to be a man like you?'

'You know what?' He bent down so that he could look her in the eye. 'I'm going to take that as a compliment, and you can't stop me.'

'Don't be ridiculous.'

He walked toward the emergency stairwell. 'Thank you, Amanda, for saying such a nice thing to me.'

'Come back here.'

He pushed open the door. 'I will treasure it forever.'

'Don't you dare walk away from me.'

Will did just that, taking the steps two at a time, safe in the knowledge that her little feet could not keep up with him.

CHAPTER TWENTY-TWO

Sara took off her reading glasses and rubbed her eyes. She had been sitting at the table in the doctors' lounge for at least two hours. The patient's chart on the tablet in front of her was starting to blur. She had slept a total of six hours in the last four days. Her level of exhaustion was reminiscent of her residency, when she'd slept on a cot in the broom closet behind the nurses' station. The cot was still there. Grady had undergone a billion-dollar renovation since the last time Sara worked in the emergency department, but no hospital had ever wasted money on making residents' lives easier.

Nan, the student nurse, was on the couch again. She had a half-empty box of cookies on one side of her and a bag of potato chips on the other. Her thumbs were barely visible as they furiously tapped on her iPhone. She giggled every few minutes as, presumably, a new email came in. Sara wondered if it was possible that the girl was getting younger before her eyes. Her only consolation was that in a few years, the junk food Nan loved so much would start to matter.

'What's up?' Nan asked, dropping the phone. 'You cool?'

'I'm cool.' Sara was oddly relieved that the girl was talking to her again. Nan had been pouting since she'd realized that Sara was not going to share the juicy details of her part in the hospital shooting.

The girl stood, brushing crumbs off her scrubs. 'You want lunch? I think Krakauer was gonna order from the Hut.'

'Thanks for asking, but I've got plans.' Sara looked at her watch. Will was supposed to take her to lunch. It would be their first date, which said a lot about the way Sara's life was going lately considering Will was the reason she wasn't getting any sleep.

'Later.' Nan didn't so much push open the door as throw her body against it.

469

Sara took a moment to enjoy the peace and quiet in the lounge. She reached into her pocket and pulled out a folded sheet of paper. She'd accidentally left her glasses in her car this morning and had to hike back up the stairs in the parking deck to fetch them. That was when she'd found the note stuck under her windshield wiper. Oddly enough, it wasn't the first time someone had left the word *cunt* on Sara's car. She supposed she should be grateful that this time it wasn't keyed into the paint.

Sara didn't have to consult a handwriting expert to know that the message was from Angie Trent. There had been another note left on Sara's car yesterday morning, though this time the greeting had been waiting for her when she left her apartment. Angie was getting better. This second note packed more punch than the more innocuous 'Whore' from the previous day.

Sara wadded up the paper and threw it toward the trashcan. Of course she missed. She got up to retrieve the note. Instead of tossing it into the trash where it belonged, she unfolded the paper again and stared at the word. It was certainly nasty, but Sara could not help but think it was deserved. In the heat of the moment, she never let herself think about the wedding ring around Will's finger. The cold light of day was another matter. He was a married man. Even without that legal designation, there was still a bond between him and Angie. They were both connected in a way that Sara would never understand.

And it was very clear that Angie was not going to bow out gracefully. The only question was how long it would take before the woman managed to

470

drag Sara down into the gutter with her.

There was a knock at the door.

Sara made sure the note was in the trash before opening the door. Will was there. He had his hands in his pockets. Though they had been together in every way possible, the first ten minutes between them were always awkward. It was as if he was perpetually waiting for Sara to make the first move, to give him some sort of sign that she hadn't yet tired of him.

He asked, 'Is this a bad time?'

She opened the door wide. 'Not at all.'

He glanced around the room. 'Am I allowed back here?'

'I think we can make an exception.'

He stood in the middle of the room. His hands stayed in his pockets.

Sara asked, 'How's Evelyn doing?'

'She's good. At least, I think she is.' He took his hands out of his pockets, but only to start twisting the wedding band on his finger. 'Faith's going to take some time off work to take care of her. I think it'll be good for both of them to have some time together. Or really bad. You never know.'

Sara couldn't help it. She looked at the wadded-up note in the trashcan. Why was he still wearing his wedding ring? Probably for the same reason Angie kept leaving notes on Sara's car.

Will asked, 'What is it?'

She indicated the table. 'Can we sit down?'

He waited until she was seated, then took the chair across from her. He said, 'This doesn't sound good.'

'No,' she agreed.

He tapped his fingers on the table. 'I think I

471

know what you're going to say.'

She said it anyway. 'I like you, Will. I really, really like you.'

'But?'

She touched his hand, resting her finger on his wedding ring.

'Yeah,' he said. No explanation. No excuse. No offer to take off the ring and throw it to the wind. Or at the very least, stick it in one of his damn pockets.

Sara forced herself to continue. 'I know that Angie is a big part of your life. I respect that. I respect what she means to you.'

She waited for a response, but none seemed to be coming. Instead, Will took her hand. His thumb traced along the lines in her palm. Sara couldn't stop the reaction her body felt from his touch. She looked down at their hands together. She let her finger slip under the cuff of his shirt. The ridge of the scar felt rough against her skin. She thought about all of the things she did not know about him—the torture he had endured. The pain he'd brought on himself. And all of it had happened with Angie right by his side.

'I can't compete with her,' Sara admitted. 'And I can't be with you if I'm worried about you wanting to be with her.'

He cleared his throat. 'I don't want to be with her.' She waited for him to say that he wanted to be with Sara. But he didn't.

She tried again. 'I can't be second place. I can't know that no matter how much I might need you, you'll always go running to Angie first.'

Again, she waited for him to say something—anything—that would convince her that she was wrong. Seconds ticked by. It felt like an eternity.

When he finally spoke, his voice was so quiet that she could barely hear him. 'She cried wolf a lot.' He licked his lips. 'When we were little, I mean.' He glanced up to make sure Sara was listening, then looked back down at their hands. 'There was this one time when we were placed together. It was a foster home. More like a factory farm. They were doing it for the money. At least the wife was. The husband was doing it for the teenage girls.'

Sara felt her throat tighten. She struggled against the impulse to feel sorry for Angie.

'So, like I said, Angie cried wolf a lot. When she accused the guy of molesting her, the caseworker didn't believe her. Didn't even open a file. Didn't listen to me when I said she wasn't lying this time.' His shoulders went up in a shrug. 'I would hear her at night sometimes. Screaming when he hurt her. He hurt her a lot. None of the other kids cared. I guess they were happy it wasn't happening to them. But for me . . .' His words trailed off. He watched his thumb move along the back of her fingers. 'I knew that they'd have to open an investigation if one of us got hurt. Or hurt ourselves.' He tightened his grip around her hand. 'So, I told Angie, this is what I'm going to do. And I did it. I took a razor blade out of the medicine cabinet and I cut myself. I knew it couldn't be a half measure. You've seen it.' He gave a strained laugh. 'It's not a half measure.'

'No,' she agreed. It was hard to understand how he'd managed not to pass out from the pain.

'So,' Will said. 'That got us out of that home and they shut it down and the people running it weren't allowed to foster kids anymore.' He looked up, blinking a few times to clear his eyes. 'You know, one of the things Angie said to me the other night was that I would never do that for you—never cut myself like that—and I think she's right.' There was a sadness in his smile. 'Not because I don't care about you, but because you would never put me in that kind of situation. You would never ask me to make that choice.'

Sara looked into his eyes. The sun streaming in through the windows turned his eyelashes white. She could not imagine what he'd been through, the level of desperation that had driven him to take that razor in hand.

'I should let you get on with your day.' He leaned over and kissed her hand, letting his lips linger for a few seconds. When he straightened up, something about him had changed. His voice was firmer, more determined. 'You have to know that if you ever need me, I'll be there. No matter what else happens. I'll be there.'

There was something final in what he said, as if everything was settled. He almost seemed relieved.

'Will—'

'It's all right.' He gave one of his awkward laughs. 'I guess you're immune to my astounding charm.'

Sara felt a lump in her throat. She couldn't believe that he was giving in so easily. She wanted him to fight for this. She wanted him to pound his fist on the table and tell her there was no way this was over, that he wasn't going to give her up that easily.

But he didn't. He just slid his hand out of hers and stood up. 'Thank you. I know that sounds stupid.' He glanced at her, then at the door. 'Just—thank you.'

She heard his footsteps cross the floor, the noise from the hallway as the door swung open. Sara pressed her fingers to her eyes, trying to stop the tears. She couldn't get past his tone of resignation, his easy acquiescence to what he clearly felt was inevitable. She had no idea what his story about Angie was meant to accomplish. Was Sara supposed to feel sorry for the woman? Was she supposed to find it romantic that Will was ready to kill himself in order to rescue her?

She realized now that Will was more like Jeffrey than she'd wanted to admit. Maybe Sara had a thing for firemen, not cops. Both men had shown a propensity for running straight into burning buildings. In the last week alone, Will had been shot at by gangsters, threatened by a psychopath, browbeaten by at least three women, emasculated in front of strangers, crammed into the trunk of a car for hours on end, and willingly volunteered himself to go into a situation where he knew there was a high probability that he would be killed. He was so damn intent on rescuing everyone else in the world that Will didn't realize what he really needed was rescuing from himself. Everyone took advantage of him. Everyone exploited his good graces, his decency, his kindness. No one thought to ask Will what *he* needed.

His whole life had been spent in the shadows, the stoic kid sitting in the back of the classroom, afraid to open his mouth for fear of being found out. Angie kept him in the dark because it served her selfish needs. Sara had quickly realized her first time with Will that he'd never been with a woman who really knew how to love him. No wonder he had capitulated so easily when she'd told him it was over. Will had taken it as a given that nothing good in his life would ever last. That was why he had sounded so relieved. His toes had been dangling over the edge. He was too afraid to take the leap because he'd never really fallen.

Sara felt her mouth open in surprise. She was just as guilty as the rest of them. She had been so desperate for Will to fight for her that it had never occurred to her that Will was waiting for Sara to fight for him.

She was through the door and running down the hallway before logic could intervene. As usual, the ER was packed. Nurses ran with bags of IVs. Gurneys flew past. Sara sprinted to the elevator. She stabbed the down button a dozen times, silently begging the doors to open. The stairs exited at the back of the hospital. Parking was in the front. Will would be home by the time she ran around the building. Sara looked at her watch, wondering how much time she had wasted feeling sorry for herself. Will was probably halfway to the decks by now. Three structures. Six stories of cars. More if he'd used one of the decks for the university. She should wait in the street. Sara tried to map the roads in her head. Bell. Armstrong. Maybe he had parked at the Grady Detention Center.

The doors finally opened. George, the security guard, was standing there with his arm resting on his gun. Will was beside him.

George asked, 'Everything okay, Doc?'

Sara could only nod.

Will stepped off the elevator, a sheepish look on

476

his face. 'I forgot that Betty's at your place.' He gave that familiar, awkward smile. 'At the risk of sounding like a country music singer, you can take my heart, but I can't let you take my dog.'

Sara was bumped by an EMT passing behind her. She braced her palms against Will's chest to keep from falling. He just stood there with his hands in his pockets, smiling down at her with a curious look on his face. Who had ever taken up for this man? Not his family, who'd abandoned him to state care. Not the foster parents who'd thought he was expendable. Not the doctors who'd experimented on his busted lip. Not the teachers and social workers who'd taken his dyslexia for stupidity. And especially not Angie, who had so easily gambled with his life. His precious life.

'Sara?' Will looked concerned. 'Are you okay?'

She slid her hands up to his shoulders. Sara could feel the familiar hard muscle beneath his shirt, the heat from his skin. She had kissed his eyelids this morning. He had delicate lashes, blond and soft. She had teased him, kissing his eyebrows, his nose, his chin, letting her hair drape across his face and chest. How many hours had Sara spent over the last year wondering how the scar above his mouth would feel against her lips? How many nights had she dreamt about waking up in his arms?

So many hours. So many nights.

Sara stood on her toes to look him in the eye. 'Do you want to be with me?'

'Yes.'

She relished the sound of his certainty. 'I want to be with you, too.'

Will shook his head. He looked like he was

waiting for the punch line to a very bad joke. 'I don't understand.'

'It worked.'

'What worked?'

'Your astounding charm.'

His eyes narrowed. 'What charm?'

'I changed my mind.'

He still didn't seem to believe her.

'Kiss me,' she told him. 'I changed my mind.'

ACKNOWLEDGMENTS

As always, tremendous thanks go to Victoria Sanders, my agent, and my editors Kate Elton and Kate Miciak. Angela Cheng Caplan should be in here somewhere, too. I would also like to thank everyone at my RH for their continued support. Adam Humphrey, I appreciate your letting me kill you. And beat you. And humiliate you. And all the other things Claire takes for granted. Speaking of Claire Round, thanks for not letting some strapping Ozzie carry you away from us. Same for you, Rob Waddington. None of us could live happily ever after without you. Susan Sandon, you're the bluebird to my pigeon, the cardinal to my jay, the wind beneath my wings.

I'd like to give Georgina Hawtrey-Woore her own line for being the patron saint of authors. Your patience, professionalism and perseverance have supplied the solid foundation upon which my writing life has been built, and I cannot thank you enough for your continued support.

Thanks to the incomparable Vernon Jordan for regaling me with tales of 1970s Atlanta. You, sir, are a legend. David Harper, this is at least your tenth year of helping me make Sara look like a doctor. As always, I am enormously grateful for your help and apologize for any errors, which were committed in service of story. Special Agent John Heinen, the same goes for you. Any gun mistakes are my own. I have many people to thank at the Georgia Bureau of Investigation, including Pete Stuart, Wayne Smith, John Bankhead, and

Director Vernon Keenan. Y'all are so generous with your time, and so passionate about what you do, that it's a pleasure to be in your company. Speaker David Ralston, I appreciate your tremendous help.

Daddies don't get much page time in this book, but I'd like to thank mine for being such a wonderful father. I'd write a story about you, but no one would believe how good you are. And speaking of goodness, DA—as always, you are my heart.

To my readers, please note that this is a work of fiction. Though I have been an Atlanta resident for more than half my life, I am also a writer, and have changed streets, building design and neighborhoods to suit my dastardly needs. (Come on, Sherwood Forest, you know you deserve it!)